BROKEN

A Truth or Lies World Collection IV

ELLA MILES

TRUTH OR LIES WORLD
COLLECTION SERIES ORDER

ENZO & KAI'S STORY

Taken (Collection I)
Stolen (Collection II)

ZEKE & SIREN'S STORY

Sinful (Collection III)
Broken (Collection IV)

LANGSTON & LIESEL'S STORY

Vicious (Collection V)
Endless (Collection VI)

TANGLED PROMISE

PROLOGUE
ZEKE

romises are meant to be broken.

Not to me—I don't break promises.

Ever.

I keep my word.

I'm loyal, honest, and keep my promises—no matter what. It's all I have: my vows, my truth, my devotion. I may be a criminal in most people's eyes. I've watched hundreds of men take their last breaths at my hands, slitting their throats, or firing a bullet between their eyes.

I've tortured men. I've stolen, cheated, murdered.

But my one redeeming quality is that I don't break my promises. When I make a vow to someone, I keep it. I'm loyal. Enzo Black, my boss and best friend, has never had to question my loyalties; I've always given him everything. Langston, Liesel, and Kai, all of my friends, never had to wonder if they should trust me or not. They just did because I never gave them a reason not to.

They are my family. I don't get more loyal than with family. They aren't my blood, but it doesn't matter. Each of them would take a bullet for me, and I would for them.

I'm good at making sacrifices. I've stayed away from them for so long, trying to protect them. But one mistake changed everything.

One moment of weakness brought my friends back into my world. One choice changed the future of my family.

I've never been one to regret things, but I regret this. I regret it. I'm not going to be able to keep all of my promises.

I've made three crucial promises in my life.

Three.

All made in love. The woman I loved as a best friend, the woman I loved as a sister, and the woman I loved as everything.

My best friend.

My sister.

And my everything.

Three promises to three strong, beautiful, powerful women.

I thought I could keep them all. I thought I had good reasons to keep all of my promises.

I never thought I'd have to choose. There was no way to know these three women would cross paths. No way to know these women would not just intersect, but their fates would become tangled with one another. No way to know the danger I put them all in by making a promise to each of them.

I can't choose between the three most important women in my life. Even if I could put one above the other, it's going to kill me to break my promises. I can only choose one. I can only keep one woman in my life forever.

When I choose whose promise to keep, that woman is the only one who will stay in my life. The others will hate me. Or end up dead.

Save one.

Destroy the rest.

An impossible choice, but a choice I'm stuck with.

This is why I don't let women into my life. This is why I want simple, uncomplicated days. This is why I'm better as the muscle, the brute, the security force in a team of people. I can protect anyone when it's just me and my muscle and my gun.

But no amount of muscle, weapons, or trickery is going to get me out of this situation.

I'm fucked.

Three pairs of eyes stare back at me, deep into my soul, begging to be the one I choose—the promise I keep.

Choose.

Choose which of these incredible women gets to live. Choose which die.

I could no sooner choose a favorite testicle.

My heart is shattered. My heart is broken in three. No matter who I choose, I'm only keeping one tiny part of my heart. That's not enough to sustain me. It's not enough to give to the woman I save.

Choose.

Break two of my promises.

Choose the woman who remains in my life. Choose the woman who lives.

CHAPTER 1
SIREN

ne Week Ago

"Do you love him?" Bishop, the man who owns me, asks.

Owns—he can think he owns me all he wants, but no man owns me.

Bishop's eyes pierce mine as I stand barefoot, in jeans and T-shirt, in his kitchen. If anyone walked in on us, they would think we are just having a domestic conversation—not that he thinks of me as his prisoner and I think of him as scum that I'm about to wipe from this earth.

"Who?" I ask as I stare out the window to the garden out back that is too beautiful to be owned by a man like him.

"Doesn't matter who, you know who he is, do you love him?"

I pull out a knife from the stack on the counter and throw it at him. It hits the cabinet behind him.

He doesn't flinch. This man has experienced pain. He knows when I'm aiming to kill or just threatening. He's a lot like me in that way.

"Just because you own me, doesn't mean I'll answer your questions," I say.

7

"I don't own you," he says.

"Oh, really? Then what was the contract you signed with Hugo? What about the chains, the dungeon I sleep in, the other women?"

"Those are all physical. Sure, for now, I own your body. But that's not what I want."

I frown. "What do you want?"

"To own you. Someday, I'll truly own you. When you go to sleep at night, and I'm there. When you fuck your man, and I'm there. When you close your eyes, and I'm there. That's when I'll own you. When you can think of nothing else but me. When you can think of nothing but my words ringing in your ear. When you only see me in the darkness. When you do exactly as I say, that's when you are mine."

I shake my head. "You'll be waiting a long time."

"Why? Because you are already owned by another man?" He smirks.

"Julian Reed, perhaps?"

My eyes widen. *How does he know about Julian?*

"Or perhaps your lover? Are you owned by him?"

"I'm owned by no man."

He shakes his head. "I thought you couldn't lie."

"I can't."

"That sounds an awful lot like a lie, Siren."

"It's not," I say, my throat tightening. I grab another knife and fling it, this time brushing the edge of his ear, causing the tiniest bit of blood.

Bishop still doesn't move. The pain is nothing.

"You know, Siren, I've been in love before."

Why is he telling me this?

I still, waiting for the trap he's setting. With men like Bishop, there is always a trap waiting to be sprung.

"Love is the ultimate prize. It's what everyone wants. Some claim they want money, fame, power. It's all lies. All any person wants is to love and be loved."

Who knew the man is a sap?

"What happened to the woman you loved?" I ask. *Did she die?* I hate Bishop, but I don't want anyone to die because of their association with him. She probably didn't even love him. *How could a woman love a man like Bishop?*

"She stopped loving me," he says with pain in his eyes. His blue eyes have become clouds of gray and black. If he had any tears to shed, he would, but I can tell he's long past tears. It wouldn't matter that I'm here as his slave. He would cry. He would mourn his loss in front of me without shame. He just has nothing left to get out. No emotions left except for an empty, hollow shell.

His eyes glaze over for a minute as he thinks about the woman he loves. And then he snaps back to me.

"Do you love him?" he asks again.

I suck in a breath. *Does it matter if I do? What is it going to hurt telling this man?* He's a kindred spirit. He knows what loving someone who doesn't love you back does to a person. He can be my enemy and still understand how I feel.

"Yes," I breathe, and it's the truest word I've ever spoken. *Yes, I love Zeke.* I will always love Zeke until my dying breath, which, if Bishop has his way, will be sooner than later.

Bishop nods, already knowing it to be true.

"Then save him," he says.

I frown, not understanding. "I already did."

He shakes his head. "No, all you did was bring him to the fire. Right now, he's standing on the edge, just breathing in fumes. One tiny push will launch him into the heart of the flames, and once he's there, there is no going back. He'll be engulfed."

I have no idea what Bishop is talking about.

"He's not in any danger. I made sure of that."

Bishop grits his teeth. "He's loved by you—a siren. There is nothing more dangerous than being loved by you."

♡

Present Day

. . .

Bishop's words ring in my ear. *There is nothing more dangerous than being loved by you.*

The words that followed are burned into my brain forever.

You're owned.

By a dangerous, ruthless, broken man.

Bishop is a man who has loved and lost. There is nothing more dangerous than a man who has lost everything. A man who has nothing to live for except to numb his pain—except for maybe a woman who has lost everything. That woman may be the most dangerous of all.

I stand in the entry of Zeke's house. Staring at the door that I forced Zeke out of with one word—Lucy.

He loves her. He doesn't love me.

He loves the mysterious woman at the ball. He doesn't love me.

Even if he does—he had to leave. He can't be with me. Bishop's words are true. If Zeke stays, he'll die, because of me.

Zeke had to leave, and I need to fix everything before he comes back. Zeke will come back. He always keeps his promises, even to evil men like Julian Reed.

Right now, I can't think about any of that. Right now, I can't even breathe.

I sob.

Tears fall hard and fast in streams over my red cheeks. If tears could burn, these would.

I feel myself shaking. My legs tremble, barely holding me up. My arms shake, and my heart breaks having just watched Zeke walk away from me. Watched him choose another woman. Watched him leave because I told him to.

He didn't fight. He hardly questioned why. He just left.

It's for the best.

Tell that to my broken heart.

My heart thumps slowly, then quickly, two thumps, then one, then three in quick succession. It no longer knows how to beat. Something so simple, something my body never had to think about, has become complicated. It can't beat anymore. It's too hard.

I wouldn't be surprised if I keel over dead. Slowly, I fall to my knees as my legs collapse.

I can't breathe, my chest constricts around my lungs, purposefully trying to suffocate me to stop the pain. My throat tightens, and air can barely make its way through the tears pouring down my cheeks over my nose and mouth.

My body wants to die. *Maybe I'll have a heart attack? Maybe this will be the end?* Dying alone of heartbreak.

My heart skips a beat, as if to say not today. *Today, I don't die. Everything I'm doing is for love.*

I'm strong.

I'm a fighter.

I won't give up.

Not like this.

Just because I can't be with the one I love doesn't mean my love ends. It doesn't mean my life is no longer worth living. I may never love again as I love Zeke, but I can love him from afar. I can protect him by keeping him away from me.

Someday, if I'm lucky, maybe I'll be able to love someone, and they can love me back without fear of danger. Maybe I won't be a siren anymore. Maybe I won't be dangerous to every person I love.

Maybe I'll go back to just being Aria Torres. *Do I want to be Aria, when Zeke calls me Siren? When I've always been Siren to him? When the name I hear falling from Zeke's lips is always Siren?*

I hear footsteps coming up the drive.

Zeke?

My tears dry up immediately. My heart beats regularly again, if not faster than usual. I stand, my legs stronger than they've ever been.

He came back.

He's not gone.

If he came back, that means he loves me. He doesn't care about our fucked up past. He doesn't care about the risk. Our love can conquer all. *Right?*

I hold my breath, knowing that I'm dreaming a little too much if I really think that is going to happen. I listen more carefully. The footsteps are too light to be Zeke. *He's not coming back, stupid heart, why don't you listen to me?* You're the one who got us into this mess. I was just fine on my own until you got involved. I didn't need to love.

The door opens—Nora.

"What are you doing here?" I ask.

She sighs. "Just a feeling that my best friend needed me."

I frown. "You're a terrible liar."

Nora walks over to me and holds open her arms.

I just shake my head. I can't be hugged by her. Not because of the lie I told Zeke. Bishop didn't ruin touch for me. Bishop ruined love for me.

I can't be touched because if she hugs me, I'll fall apart again.

"What are you doing here?" I ask, again.

Nora drops her arms. "I'm here to get you drunk."

"How did you know I needed you?"

I follow Nora into Zeke's kitchen, where she is already pouring us both drinks. "I can't say."

"Zeke?"

Nora blinks rapidly. *Yes—Zeke texted her.* I don't know whether to feel touched or angry or emotional or what. Zeke didn't care enough to fight, to stay, to figure out why I pushed him away. But he cared enough to call Nora and tell her to come, that I needed her.

"I don't need a babysitter," I say.

Nora laughs. "Good, because I'm a terrible babysitter. Can you imagine me with kids? Eww, all that slobber and poopy diapers, no thank you."

*Kids...*I imagine little babies walking around, babies with long dark hair, a sturdy frame, and Zeke's rare smile. My heart clenches. Even if Zeke came back, I could never have kids with him. There is no way to bring kids into this world. It would be a death sentence for all of us.

"Oh, beautiful. I'm so sorry," Nora says, and this time, she doesn't ask permission. She hugs me, pulling me tight to her chest. I let her.

I'm expecting to fall apart in her arms. Instead, I feel stronger, absorbing some of Nora's strength through the hug.

Strength I immediately need as there is another knock at the door. *Zeke!*

Zeke wouldn't knock. This is his own home. But that fact doesn't stop my heart from pitter-pattering, hoping it's him.

Nora looks at me as she continues to hold me in her arms.

She sighs at the expression on my face.

"It's not him," she says before even going to the door.

"I know," I whisper back. But I don't know. I'm full of hope for even a one percent chance that Zeke is behind that door.

Please, please, please.

As much as I want Zeke to stay, I need him gone to protect him. *Unless...*

Nope, he has to go. That's what's safest.

Nora walks me to the door, most likely because she doesn't think I can stand on my own. She's right; I can't. Or at least, I don't want to.

I hate that a man controls my emotions. That I'm this hurt by a man. I'm strong and independent, just like Nora. And yet, it still crushes me knowing that might have been the last time I ever spoke with Zeke in person. He could go to Lucy and then back to his old life and never return. It would be up to me to keep Julian and the rest of the danger from coming after him.

Nora opens the door with a murderous glare, prepared to destroy whoever is on the other side for interrupting her taking care of me.

Julian.

Fuck.

He grins at me. "Have a moment to talk, Aria?"

"No, she doesn't have a moment. She's been through hell these last few days. Something you don't give a shit about. You should have tried to rescue her or stop it from happening!" Nora yells at him.

Julian's eyes flitter to me as he takes in my broken appearance for the first time. Other than making sure I can still hold a gun and seduce men for him, he doesn't care.

"I did," Julian says, shocking us both.

"No, Zeke rescued me," I say.

"And I helped him. How do you think Zeke found out where Hugo was?" Julian asked.

At the mention of Hugo, my stomach coils. The first man I loved, my husband for years, the man who sold me. Now he's dead, and I'm torn because Hugo was also a man I loved. He was a broken man who needed help. As much as he deserved to die for what he did, it still hurts.

Zeke killed Hugo. He never told me, but I know he was the one who pulled the trigger, not Julian, Zeke. And I'm thankful for it.

"It doesn't redeem you for everything else you've done, you bastard. Get out! Aria needs to heal," Nora starts pushing Julian off the front step.

"Wait," I say.

Nora's head swivels to mine.

Julian breathes.

"You really helped Zeke?" I ask.

Julian pulls down his shirt, revealing a bullet hole in his shoulder. "The asshole shot me for helping him."

The beginning of a smile pulls at the corner of my mouth. It's not a real smile. A real smile will take ages. I don't even know if I can smile, but it warms me to know that Zeke shot Julian.

"Come in," I say.

Nora frowns but steps back so Julian can enter. We all walk to the living room. Nora and I sit on the couch, and Julian rests in a chair next to us.

Julian and I both stare at Nora—telling her to leave.

She crosses her arms over her chest. "'I'm not leaving. I'm involved in this world now. I may not have skills like Aria or be able to shoot a gun, but I do know she's my best friend, and my role is to keep her sane and protect her. I'm staying."

I raise my eyebrow at Julian, waiting for him to challenge her. He doesn't. No man does.

And then the other corner of my mouth lifts. I can heal. I can get past this. I can smile again. Maybe not today or next month, but sooner than I think.

I feel the stab of my heart, reminding me that even when I smile again, it won't take away my pain. Nothing will.

"What do you want, Julian?" Nora asks, clearly impatient.

"I wanted to check on Aria. And Zeke—"

"He's gone," I say.

"Oh? And where did he go to? That wasn't part of our arrangement. Zeke is supposed to stay here until our deal is over," Julian says.

I shake my head. "You don't care about Zeke. Not really. You want me. You want your power. Your money. You don't need Zeke."

Julian shakes his head. "You have a week to get him back on this island and ready to complete his third task."

"Not going to happen. I want to renegotiate."

Julian laughs. "You have nothing left to negotiate with." He stands. "One week, Aria. Remember our deal."

Like I could forget.

"I'll get him back," I say, telling another lie. I have no intention of getting Zeke back here. If I was finally able to drive him away, then good. He'll be safe. I'll steer Julian's attention elsewhere, no matter the cost to me. I just want Zeke safe.

Julian nods and leaves. He still doesn't know I'm capable of lying. The longer I keep that fact a secret, the better. It means I have a power I've never had before.

When the door shuts, Nora turns to me. "What was that about?"

I shake my head and then curl up on the couch. "Just the same old bullshit. Julian thinks he can make me do whatever he wants."

"But your deal is over, right? Hugo is dead. He has no power over you anymore."

I nod. *Another lie.* Julian holds all the power, and he knows it.

Nora strokes my hair. "Come on, let's get you into bed."

"I'm not sleeping in Zeke's bed. We should go to your place."

"Nope, we are sleeping in Zeke's big ass bed." Nora helps me up, and I don't fight her. I'm exhausted from keeping track of all the dangerous men in my life.

Nora helps me strip off my clothes and slip into one of Zeke's T-shirts and sweatpants.

"Are you purposefully trying to torture me?" I ask through tears as I breathe in his scent.

Nora strokes my hair. "No, I'm helping you."

She pushes me into the bed. I have no idea how she's helping me. This seems like the opposite of moving on.

I close my eyes, feeling the pull of darkness. Zeke is gone. He didn't come back. He's gone. The pain is deep. It makes me toss, turn, and writhe.

Bishop...his eyes, his voice, his words—they push out the pain. Bishop owns me now. I don't know if I'm thankful he took away my pain or scared that the most dangerous man yet owns my dreams.

CHAPTER 2
ZEKE

I step into the darkness of my bedroom.

The room is completely black, not even the light from the moonlight shines in through the slits on the blinds.

As long as I don't make a sound, no one will know I'm here if that's what I want. I haven't made up my mind. I don't know what to do with Siren. I don't know how to get her to trust me. To share the truth with me. To stop keeping her damn secrets and trying to protect me. I'm a grown-ass man with plenty of deadly skills and am completely capable of protecting myself.

Siren hurts me while trying to protect me. All it does is make our relationship more complicated. Somehow, I still end up staying. Trying to figure out the truth. Trying to find a way I can love her. Loving her and earning her love in return could be the greatest thing I've ever experienced.

So here I am, standing in the shadows of my own bedroom as I watch Siren and Nora sleep in my bed.

Nora has her arm draped over Siren's waist. Siren doesn't move. For a woman who claims she can't be touched, she doesn't seem to have a problem with Nora holding her. *Maybe it's just my touch she has a problem with?*

And for a woman who says she hates me because she thinks I sold women, when I didn't, she doesn't seem to have a big enough problem with me to not sleep in my bed.

I step closer to Siren's side to really see her.

I suck in a breath at the sight. Even in the darkness, I can see the wet spot on the front of her shirt. Her cheeks and eyes are swollen and red. She's been crying. It doesn't take a genius to know she's been crying over me.

Because she thinks I'm a monster who sold women? Or because I left?

Only she can answer that.

Siren moves, and I freeze. I'm not sure I'm ready to face her right now. I just "left" today. I don't know if just a few hours is long enough for me to figure her out. To decide what I want to do. What move to make next.

Siren isn't going to wake up, though. She's thrashing; she's murmuring; she's shaking. She's lost in a nightmare. One that Bishop most likely caused. I don't know who Bishop is, but I'm going to destroy him. I'm going to make him pay in so many more ways than the money he made me pay. I'm going to make him suffer with everything he has.

Nora, on the other hand, wakes up and looks at me with disappointment in her eyes.

"Don't look at me like that," I whisper.

She raises an eyebrow. "Look at you like what? Like I'm annoyed you are playing games with Siren. You didn't really leave, and you're having me play spy. You see that Siren is in pain and aren't immediately wrapping your arms around her. You should be lucky all I'm doing is looking at you like this."

I swallow down the guilt. This is nothing compared to what Siren has done. *Right?* I'm just doing this to learn the truth—to protect Siren.

"Don't," Nora says.

My eyes bore into hers. "Is she alright?"

Nora strokes Siren's cheek, tucking her hair behind her ear. "What do you think?"

"I think we are both so fucked up. There is no way we can ever be together."

Nora shakes her head. "Then you don't deserve her. Siren needs a fighter. She's had to fight her entire life. If you aren't willing to fight through the walls she puts up to protect both of you, then leave for real. And don't come back. We can deal with Julian and make sure he doesn't come after you and your friends. But if you love her, then stay and fight."

Nora's right, but staying scares the shit out of me. Not because I'm afraid of a fight. I've been jonesing for a good fight. I'm scared of having real feelings for Siren. She didn't believe me before when I told her I loved her. Or she didn't care. Or she hates me because she thinks I sold women. I can't tell with her anymore. And if I tell her my feelings again, and get rejected again, I don't know if I'll be able to handle it.

It doesn't matter if you say them, you already feel them. You love her.

Nora's face lightens as she realizes my truth. "Follow your heart, Zeke." She strokes Siren's hair one more time and kisses her on the cheek, something I'm dying to do. "Be careful with her. Whatever Bishop did, it might have been her breaking point. She needs you to heal her. To show her love is worth it. She's been burned too many times." Nora stands.

"And what if I've been burned too?"

Nora touches my shoulder. "Then you let her heal you too."

Nora isn't careful as she walks out of the bedroom, shutting the door a little too loudly, almost like she wants Siren to wake up and find me here. *But what do I want?*

Siren is tossing more now, the pull of whatever Bishop did to her stronger. She's fighting it. Trying to push the dreams out of her head. Suddenly, she stills as if she's given up.

No! Fight dammit! I need you to fight! Stop giving up on us.

I step closer, trying to decide what to do. *Wake her or disappear?* That's my choice. I can learn more about her if I disappear and follow her actions as I did today. I can learn what she doesn't want me to know.

Or I can wake her, earn her trust, and get her to tell me the truth. I can remind her I lov—

"Zeke," she cries out. Her eyes are still closed. She's still in the nightmare, but she's fighting now.

Choose. Now.

"Zeke," she breathes out again, and my body makes my choice for her. I cradle her in my arms.

"I've got you, baby, I've got you. You're safe. It's just a dream," I say soothingly into her ear as I hold her against my chest and stroke her face. I want her to wake up from the nightmare, but I don't want it to be traumatic if I can avoid it.

Her eyes flutter open, and she smiles up at me. It's the clearest moment I've had with her. This is what I want. To make her smile. A real, genuine smile only I can put on her face. I bring her comfort and protect her. I keep her safe, and I make her come alive. That's why she's smiling. That's what I want to keep doing—making her smile, making her happy. My heart warms, watching her smile, and I can't help my own grin from spreading across the depths of my cheeks.

The moment lasts only a second. For one second, we are both happy with each other. We forget the truths. We forget the lies. The secrets. The betrayals. We forget all of it. And in this moment we just are. We love without speaking because I'm here, holding her. My touch is like fire to her, choosing her over protecting another, and she's letting me, despite thinking I'm a monster.

But moments are never meant to last.

In one blink, everything floods back into her brain, and she jumps back in the bed out of my arms.

I don't move; I stay seated on the edge of the bed.

"Zeke?" she asks cautiously, like I could be anyone else.

"It's me."

Her eyes widen as she looks around the room, trying to make sense of what's happening.

"What are you doing here?" she asks.

"What do you think?" I say, neither of us willing to say the words. Neither of us ready to say the obvious reason that I'm here—because I love her. No matter what. No matter if she hates me. No matter if Lucy is in danger. I love Siren. And I won't run away from my feelings.

"What about Lucy?" she asks.

"Don't worry about Lucy. Worry about yourself," I say with sin in my eyes and a wolfish grin. I know exactly how the rest of our night is going to go, and I can't fucking wait to push her to her limits.

CHAPTER 3
SIREN

All the feelings flood over me at seeing Zeke.

Excitement.

Fear.

Lust.

Love.

The fear is strong; it's real. I'm scared for what it means that Zeke is here instead of chasing after Lucy. I'm scared for what it means to Zeke that I failed in keeping him safe. I'm most scared for what it means for my heart. I can't handle another heartbreak.

But the love at seeing Zeke again...that love is stronger than all of the other feelings combined. I have to do everything to fight it, to not to fling myself at Zeke. To keep from hugging, kissing, and fucking.

"You came back," I say, carefully, my mind still in the terrible nightmare I was having before Zeke brought me out of it.

"I never left," Zeke answers.

You could have fooled me. It sure felt like you left, at least to me.

"What does that mean?"

"It means I've been here. I didn't go after Lucy myself; I sent someone to check on her. I chose to stay."

23

He chose to stay. He chose to lie. He chose to spy on me. To try and figure out the truth of what I wasn't saying.

I'm fuming, but I'm also in awe. Zeke learned a lot from my manipulative ways.

What truths did he learn? Was Nora in on it? Did he bug the house? Did he hear Julian and I's conversation?

It doesn't matter because he's here.

He may not have said he's here because he loves me like he did before, but he chose me, he's here. I don't have to keep fighting alone.

Yes, you do, Bishop's voice haunts me.

I squeeze my eyes shut, trying to block him out.

"What did he do to you?" Zeke asks, his voice pained.

He drops his head in defeat when I don't answer. I'll keep the truth until my dying breath. The truth would destroy Zeke. Abso-fucking-lutely destroy him.

It destroyed me. I will never be the same. I will never believe the good in people again. I will never trust. I shouldn't even trust Zeke or Nora, but my heart belonged to both of them long before Bishop. Those connections were hard for him to sever, but he did. He destroyed my hope for any future relationships. He destroyed my ability to fully trust—even Zeke.

"Let's play our game, Siren."

Yes.

No.

I can't.

"Okay," is what comes out of my mouth.

I don't have to ask what game—our sin or truth game.

"This time will be a little different, though," Zeke says, standing over me, a looming, determined wall of muscle. He ties his hair back, and I swallow hard to keep the drool in my mouth.

"How so?"

"We won't just play one round. We will play as many as it takes."

"It takes to do what?"

"To break you."

"Why would you want to break me?" I ask, pain burning around my heart. He didn't come back to save me; he came back to hurt me.

"Because the only way to heal you is to break you completely. Remove the hold Bishop has on you."

How does he know?

Zeke's eyes look at me with everything—pain, fear, love. He knows this is the only way to help me truly. It pains him to hurt me, even in the name of healing me.

I nod, silently agreeing. I will do anything to get rid of the torture I feel. To be free of Bishop. To think clearly instead of what Bishop wants me to think.

"You don't get to ask me any questions. You don't get to commit any sins."

I frown, not liking this at all.

"What do I get out of this?"

"Besides healing?" he asks, thinking that's good enough.

"You can't heal me. What do I get when you fail?"

"My truth. The one truth you've been dying to know. Not because Julian wants answers, but because you do." Zeke is stone as he speaks to me. He's serious. He's resolved.

Lucy. He'll tell me about Lucy. *Do I want to know the truth about her? Do I want to know who she is? Do I want to know what she means to him? Do I want to hear about his past, or current, love for her?*

Yes.

I need to know.

I'll do anything to know. If he still loves her, maybe it will stop me from needing him, from risking everything for him.

I don't have to verbally tell Zeke my answer. He already knows.

Zeke stands still, but his eyes circle the room, the wheels turning in his head as he tries to determine how he is going to break me —heal me.

He can't. I know what Bishop has done to me, Zeke doesn't.

Zeke thinks I can't stand to be touched by Zeke—it's not the truth. Zeke isn't safe around me; he needs to go away. I already failed at that, and my heart is too weak to try again.

"Can't stand to be touched by me?" Zeke asks.

I nod my lie. I can stand it. I want it. But it hurts, it fucking hurts.

No one else's touch hurts as much as his. No one else's touch feels as good either.

Zeke narrows his eyes. *Can he tell I'm lying?*

He nods, though. *So I guess not.*

Zeke cracks his neck and hands, preparing for what he's about to do. He's trying to intimidate me, but nothing intimidates me more than his love. The possibility that he really loves me scares the shit out of me. He admitted to loving me before, but it wasn't enough. His 'I love you' wasn't strong enough for me to believe because he left. His love scares me. Everything else is just physical pain. Or psychological. Not emotional. The emotions are what I can't handle.

"Do you think I sold the women? Truth or sin," Zeke asks.

I open my mouth to answer, but Zeke cuts me off. "Tell me the truth Siren, if you choose truth. If you lie, there will be consequences."

"Death, that was our original agreement. Are you going to kill me, Zeke?" I taunt, knowing he won't.

His eyes darken, his face turns gray. "No, but I won't tell you my truth."

I stare him down. He knows, or at least, he suspects I've lied to him before. I need Zeke's truth. I can't risk it now, but I also can't risk him knowing the truth.

Zeke is going to push me with each question to choose sin. He's going to push me to my limits; he's going to make me want to answer him to get him to stop.

Bring it on.

"Sin," I say. He can't know the truth—that I don't think he sold the women into sexual slavery.

Zeke silently walks toward me. I'm still sitting at the top of the bed on the pillows, leaning back against the headboard.

I watch as he pulls a knife from his pocket and extends it.

I suck in a breath. *Is he really going to start with pain?* He thinks that is how he's going to break me. *Does he realize the kind of pain I've been through?* He's going to need to bring me to the edge of death to have a shot at breaking me. I've been there before, and that didn't even do it.

Pity lives in my eyes for what I'm sure is going to be a feeble attempt at hurting me. Zeke can't hurt me. Not really.

He doesn't speak. He grabs the hem of my shirt, pulls it away from my body, careful not to touch me, and slices the knife through the material up to my neck.

"Stand," he commands.

I take a deep breath and do as he says. The shirt falls from my body, leaving my upper body exposed.

Instead of sliding my sweatpants down my body like a normal person, Zeke inserts the knife in my waistband, pulls the material from my body, and thrusts the knife down, shredding my pants until they fall to the floor. Until I'm naked and exposed in front of him.

"That's all you got?" I ask, goading him a little.

His heated stare is his response. It chills me until I visibly shiver.

God, I want his hands on me. His lips. I want him to undress. I want to feel him inside me. I want—

"Next question," Zeke says, pointing toward the bed.

I sit back down, wordlessly.

"Do you think I'm a monster?"

No.

Again, I can't answer.

"Sin," I say.

Zeke walks to his closet and returns with silk ties.

"I didn't realize you owned any ties," I say.

"There's a lot you don't know about me, Siren. Just like there is a lot I don't know about you. But I'm about to find out a whole lot."

He holds out the tie. "Wrists."

I hold out my wrists together, obeying him, making his job easier. He carefully ties my wrists together, being so gentle and calm. Not once does he touch me, even when I squirm a little, hoping that it will force his fingers to brush against my skin.

When my wrists are tied together, he jerks them over my head until I fall back on the center of his bed. Then he ties me to the headboard.

He gathers two more ties and secures each around one of my ankles, spreading my legs wide as he ties them to the bedposts.

Nothing about how he ties me ensures that I stay put. He's just putting me in a position where he seemingly has more control, more power. Where I can't touch him, and he won't touch me.

Fuck, what did I get myself into?

My body is already heated from his longing gazes. My skin is tingling with desire from being so close to Zeke but not getting the reward of connection. My nipples are already puckered for him. I could blame it on being cold in the room, but it's because of Zeke. There is no doubt the wetness leaking between my legs is because of my desire for the man.

He's done nothing.

He's barely spoken.

He hasn't touched me.

He hasn't stripped for me.

He hasn't whispered any dirty thoughts.

He's done nothing to turn me on, except that intense glare. That flicker of desire in his eyes. The control of his body. The control over me. He's got all the power. And he plans on using it against me.

He grabs another tie, and I know exactly what he's doing—shutting me off from him. Ensuring I can't see him. I can't beg him for things with my eyes. The only way this stops is with the truth, and the truth involves breaking me.

Just before the blindfold goes over my eyes, I give Zeke one last glance.

Please, please break me. You have to. You have no idea the cost of failure...

CHAPTER 4
ZEKE

I have to do this right. I have to break her. Siren's eyes told me everything. There is more at stake than just saving us. Something deeper I have to find my way to. *But what?*

I tighten the blindfold around her eyes, doing everything I can to not touch her. It's part of my plan—good thing I have the calmest, steadiest hands.

I step back with my work done. Siren is tied up naked in my bed. Every man's dream, except it's my nightmare. I don't get to fuck her. I don't get to taste her or touch her. I have to break her.

It's killing me. I have a lot of willpower, a lot of self-control, but this is taking everything I have not to touch her, kiss her, fuck her.

I clear my throat, along with the dirty thoughts of what I could do to her in this position. I try to ignore the way her nipples peak and seem to be pointed at me no matter where I move in the room. I try to ignore her soft, throaty moans before I've even touched her. I try to ignore the wetness dripping between her thighs onto my bedspread.

Focus.

"Did you know Julian is worth billions?" I ask another question I know she won't answer. I need to ask as many questions as I can, each question more tempting to answer as I torture her body. I don't plan on breaking her with pain or torture. I plan on breaking her with the one thing neither of us has ever experienced before—love.

Love is the most powerful thing between us. It's driven us both to do things out of character. To hurt one another. It's the only way to heal us.

I watch as Siren takes shallow breaths, not able to take a full breath as she lays naked before my eyes. Her body is on high alert, trying to decide her best move to get what she wants. The problem is I don't know what she wants, and neither does she. She's a confused mess. Her desires to want me, to love me, have been pushed aside for so long in an attempt to protect herself and me.

For once, I want her to stop thinking about how to save us because the more time I've spent with her, the more I realize the best way to save us both is to give in to our emotions. To try fighting together instead of keeping each other in the shadows and fighting apart.

"Siren? Tell me the truth or let me sin," I say, growing impatient with her. I'm usually strong and in control, but I only have so much patience now. Every second I have to stare at her naked body and not touch her is another second that I have to use all of my rapidly dwindling self-control.

"Sin," she says calmly. She's worked up. I know the feeling, because my cock aches in my pants. My heart is racing. My breathing is calm only because I need her to think I'm calm and unaffected. If Siren only knew what was going on inside my body—the war I'm fighting with myself.

When she says the word, I make my move. I don't have everything planned out. I don't know how many rounds this is going to take. All night if I had to guess. Siren is a stubborn, strong woman who won't allow herself to break.

What if I break first? I think as I walk calmly to the kitchen, not letting my footsteps make a sound. I'm sure Siren is straining her ears trying to figure out what I'm doing—the waiting is part of the torture.

Being out of the same room as her reduces my ache, but only minimally. The only way to get rid of my ache is to fuck her. And I doubt that is happening.

I stare down at my erection. *Sorry, buddy, you're just going to be in pain for a while.* My heart thumps, reminding me it hurts too. *Poor heart, poor cock, poor me.*

No, I'm not a victim. I'm a fighter. And I know what I want. I don't care if this takes all night, all week, or all month. I'm going to break Siren. I'm going to rid her of whatever Bishop did. Whatever Julian did. Only when there is nothing left of her can we rebuild. Only then do we have a chance at starting over together, as it always should have been.

I grab a cup and fill it with water. I chug the glass, trying to keep my cool and get the images of Siren naked out of my head. But as soon as I push them out, the thoughts of what torture Bishop must have inflicted on her overwhelm me.

Fuck.

I'm not strong enough to heal her.

Yes, you are. I see Kai Miller in my head. A woman I once helped. A woman who soon became one of my best friends. A woman I would protect with my life. A woman who embodies strength.

You can help her, just like you helped me. And when she's healed, she will give you all the strength you need to fight.

I can do this.

I fill the cup with ice and take my time walking back to the bedroom.

Siren is right where I left her, even though she could escape the ties if she wanted to. She wants me to heal her. She wants this to work as much as I do.

She doesn't speak when I enter. Her lips are pursed like she's been focusing on her breathing. Her body stills even though I see a hint of redness around her wrists telling me she most likely pulled at the ties before getting a grip on herself again.

I set the glass down on the table with a thump and watch as Siren jumps. She didn't know I was here until just now.

I smile. I like how reactive she is to me. Even without me touching her, she responds.

This is going to be fun. Or it's going to be the death of me.

Carefully, I reach into the glass and pull an ice cube out so she can't hear what I'm doing. Her head turns toward me, sensing where I am.

I put the ice cube between my lips as I climb onto the bed, careful not to touch her despite how desperate I am. Siren said she couldn't be touched. I've watched her be touched by Nora without her reacting, so she either lied or she just can't stand my touch. Either way, by the end of the night, she's going to be begging for my skin on hers.

"Zeke," she whispers, knowing I'm over her.

I give her my answer, with an ice cube to her nipple.

She gasps in delectable delight. Her nipple hardens beneath the ice cube as I move it gingerly over her nipple, teasing it. Her body arches, and I have to pull back to keep from touching with her anything but the ice cube. I push the ice cube over her other nipple, taunting it.

She expects it this time, but her body still reacts. Her skin pinks. Her nipples sharpen. Her fucking moans shoot straight to my cock. I thought it was hard before, but I've never been this hard in my life.

Her nipples taunt me, and I lose control for just a moment. I nearly bite and taste her, just before I regain my composure. It's enough for me to forget about the ice cube. It slowly slides down her stomach. She arches and writhes. I follow the cube with a heavy gaze and watch as it stops just over her clit.

I grin as I watch her toes curl.

"Zeke," she gasps again. This time my name sounds like a prayer. The begging has already started. Maybe this won't take all night like I first thought. Maybe it will be over in a matter of minutes, because Siren can't stand not to fuck me just like I can't stand not to fuck her.

I oblige both of our desires. I take the cube in my mouth again and rub it over her clit in small circles.

Her hands grab at the headboard, her toes cling to the sheets, and her hips buck into me, begging for more.

I can smell her sweet scent as I turn her on. It draws me in, making it even more difficult for me not to touch her. When the ice cube once again slips from my mouth, I come face to face with her clit. I'm tempted. *So fucking tempted.*

But my arms remind me of what I'm doing this for. I push myself backward off the bed so quickly that I stumble onto my ass on the floor.

Jesus, that was close.

"Zeke," her voice is needy and scared. She knows this can work. I can break her. And that scares her. For some ridiculous reason, she thinks pushing me away is the only way to protect me. *Not going to happen. Not again.* I'm going to get her back. Or more accurately, make her truly mine. And then I'm never letting go.

Goddammit, though, she needs to stop saying my name, or I'm going to lose it. How can one word affect me so much?

I shake it off and try to think of my next question. I need to keep this moving before I do something stupid.

"Do you still love me?" I ask.

She sucks in a breath at the same time I do. I realize I want the truth. I don't want the sin. I need a break from this. I need one moment to collect myself because I may have more muscles than any other man I know, but I'm weak when it comes to her.

Somehow, our eyes meet beneath the poorly tied blindfold over her eyes. She sees me clamoring to my feet. She sees me weak. For a moment, I think she's going to answer. I see her want to. I see her form the words. I see her come so close.

"Sin."

CHAPTER 5
SIREN

*J*esus, *did I want to answer his question honestly.* Yes, I still love you, you ogre.

Yes, I've always loved you.

Yes, I'll always love you because you're my damn match. You push me. You see me, really see me. You see past the bullshit. You see past the manipulation. You detected the first lie I ever told you. You knew I needed help.

You knew.

And now here Zeke is already breaking.

But the thing is, I know how strong Zeke is. I know he's stronger than this moment. In three seconds, he's going to realize it too, and that scares me. Once he realizes finishing this game is the only chance we have at being together, then any chance I have at protecting him will be gone.

I should end this. I should start telling truths. It could save him, but I'm tired of saving him and not having him.

Right now, I'm a little bit selfish. I want it all. The man of my dreams and saving him, even if it puts both of our lives in more risk. Maybe he really can get the thoughts out of my head. Maybe he really can free me of Bishop and Julian.

Being my own person would make it easier to keep us all safe, right?

I don't know. Maybe it's just my selfishness talking, but I want to believe that. I want to believe that being with Zeke is better than fighting for him on my own.

We lock eyes under the crack of my blindfold. *This is your only chance. Fight for me, for us, or lose me forever. Either way, I'm protecting you with my life.*

Honestly, I have no idea which way will ensure your protection, Zeke. But of course, I love you.

He sees my unspoken words, and like I suspected, I no longer see the fear or sense the uncertainty. He's ready to break me. There is no going back. He's going to succeed. My heart is happy, but my mind is freaking out, convinced I shouldn't let him break me. My mind screams that it's the wrong move.

But my heart is tired of listening to my brain. My heart wants to feel good for once.

Heart or brain? Which is right? Please, for once, let it be my heart.

I hiss as I feel hot wax hit my chest. It's such a stark contrast from the coolness of the ice that, at first, it completely shocks my system.

Eventually, just like the ice, the heat turns me on. It makes me wish Zeke was the one touching me, especially with my heightened senses —I want more.

But then my brain does what it does, trying to protect us all. I'm quickly brought back to Bishop.

Any man can pour wax on your body. He isn't special. He's not worth saving. Bishop's voice rings in my head.

"Don't let him win," Zeke says, sensing the battle brewing inside me.

I gasp as more wax hits my stomach.

"Don't let me win either," he continues.

Wax hits my nipple, and I moan at the pleasure. "What do you want, Siren? Not Julian, not Bishop, not me—you? What do you want? What does that voice in your heart say?"

That it wants you. That together, we are stronger. But I've fucked up so fucking much. Zeke can't trust me. I don't even trust me.

No one trusts you. So listen to me, Bishop's voice says.

Zeke sighs and scrapes the wax off my stomach with some plastic tool.

"Have you ever lied to me with your words?" Zeke asks next, his voice stronger, more determined.

Yes.

"Sin," I whisper.

I hear a growl and then the familiar press of a knife against my heart. He holds it in place but doesn't pierce my skin.

"I'm not afraid of you," I say.

"And why is that?"

"You won't hurt me."

And then I feel a slice. It's not deep, but it's enough to get my attention.

"I can. I will. In any relationship, whether it be friends, family, or lovers, you always end up hurting the other person even when you don't want to. You can't be afraid of me hurting you or you hurting me. We've hurt each other plenty, and we still want each other."

I can handle the pain. What about you, Zeke? You haven't been handling it well so far.

He slices me again, against my stomach just over the mark Hugo made. It hurts, knowing he did the same thing Hugo did. It causes my eyes to water, especially when he doesn't immediately bandage and heal me. He doesn't immediately apologize.

Suddenly, I feel his breath against my ear. "I fucked up. I'm sorry. I never want to harm you. If I could promise I would never hurt you, I would promise it. But it's a promise I've learned I can never keep, because I'm human. I'm not a god. But I will do everything I can to make it up to you."

He removes my blindfold. Then he lifts his own shirt and slices across his beautiful abs in the same way he did mine.

"Never again," he promises. "Never again will I hurt you with a knife. That I can promise, but I can't promise I won't hurt you in other ways."

I nod.

It's not enough.

"Do you want me to touch you?" he asks.

We are both panting. Both desperate to fill our ache, our desire. That's not what I need, though. I know what I need to be rid of Bishop. It won't happen, because no man can love a siren like me, not after what I did.

"Sin," I say stronger than ever.

He blinks away hope, like he thought he was close. He walks over to the nightstand and pulls out a vibrator. The buzzing sound makes my toes curl before he even touches me with it. But it's not what I want.

"No," I say.

"It's not up to you; you chose sin."

He presses it against my clit. I'm so sensitive that I expect to come immediately. I expect the release I don't want.

My body is stronger than I realize. It doesn't want a release from a rubber object, either. It wants Zeke.

Zeke rubs the vibrator against my body. Every nerve is firing. I'm moaning like a maniac. My body moves, unable to decide on leaning into the vibrator or away from it.

My head is a mess, unable to decide what to do. My body is a conflicted bundle of nerves. But my heart, it's strong. Stronger than ever. It won't budge. It won't let me come. It won't let Bishop in. Not even Zeke.

Zeke made everything clear. He healed me by pushing out everything else. All the doubt. The confusion. The control.

I finally feel powerful. I feel like I can take on the world. I know exactly what I want and how to get it.

After a few minutes of me not coming, Zeke stops. He turns the vibrator off and lets it fall to the floor.

Zeke is exhausted. He's weary. He bites his lip to keep from screaming in frustration, most likely. He doesn't know the victory that just happened in my own body.

"Do you want me to fuck you?" he asks, his voice defeated.

I grin, liking his choice of question. Because this time, I'm going to answer. This time, I'm done choosing sin. I'm done saving Zeke while denying us both what we really want. There is no point in saving Zeke if I don't let us both live. If I don't trust him. If I don't love him.

"No, I don't want to fuck you, Zeke."

His eyes widen in shock.

"I want something else from you. Something I'm not sure you're willing to give. Something I don't deserve because I've been scared. I've been fighting it, trying to protect you. Not because it was the best way to protect you, but because I was scared. I'm done being scared, Zeke."

He grins. "Finally."

CHAPTER 6
ZEKE

I don't know what happened. I don't even know if I should believe she broke and healed. But I choose to because we need a fresh start. We need this. We need each other. I'm afraid we are both the missing pieces. Without the other, there will be no more healing.

"I love you, Siren. I love you, Aria. I love you. I'm still learning who you are. I'm still learning how to trust and earn your trust. I don't even know what loving you means. But I love you. I fell, and now I'm ready to deal with any consequences of loving you," I say.

Siren closes her eyes, and for a moment, I think I did the wrong thing. Maybe it was wrong to tell her I'm in love with her. *Did I just undo any healing progress?*

A single second later, her eyes open like fire. The next second, she's free of her bindings. Then she's coming at me like a dragon, full of fire, rage, and strength. The beautiful, magical kind of dragon you don't think exists, but then you see it with your own eyes and don't have a choice but to believe.

Siren doesn't need me. She doesn't need a man in her life, but damn, do I need her.

She stops short of me, inches from my face, neither of us touching.

"I love you too, Zeke Kane. That's how I should have responded when you told me you loved me before."

My heart breaks. *Who knew that hearing 'I love you' can damage a heart as much as her walking away from me?*

She places her hand on my aching heart. Her touch heals me.

"I'm sorry for lying. I'm sorry for so many things. I thought I was doing the right thing. I thought I was protecting us both. I'm sorry for not trusting you. I'm so sorry," she says, her eyelashes fluttering, but not in the manipulative way I've seen her behave around other men. Her eyes are fluttering because she loves me. Just like her hand is on my heart because she loves me.

I hold her hand to my chest. "I can touch you?"

"Yes, it never hurt." She winces, scared to tell me the truth. "Well, it did because I was scared. I was scared of what Bishop did to me, and I thought it was better that you got as far away from my fucked up head as possible."

"What did he do to you?" I ask, needing to know.

She blinks, her eyes blank. "This is going to sound weird, but I honestly don't know. I did, but when I pushed Bishop out of my head, it's like my memories disappeared."

I study her eyes. It's the truth. I want to know what happened, but maybe it's better this way. The pain is permanently gone from her memory.

She looks up at me with a tinge of fear.

"I love you, focus on that," I say.

She bites her lip. "Prove it."

That's all I need. We've both been torturing ourselves for hours. I plan on making love to her and fucking her at the same time.

She yanks my pants off, and our bodies collide in more ways than one. Our lips, our hands, our stomachs lock. Our blood mixes together against each other's stomachs. My cock settles between her legs instantly.

"Don't make me wait, Zeke." Her voice is soft and needy.

I lift one of her legs and slide home.

She swallows hard at the connection that's always been between us, but now we accept as right, not wrong. We have a lot to figure out—a lot of trust issues and truths that need to be said. But for now, this is enough.

"Fuck me," she says.

"Love me," I respond as I thrust into her hard, pushing her back onto the bed. Her legs widen for me and wrap around my waist, pulling me deeper inside her, where I've always belonged.

"I hate you for making me wait for this. For torturing me and not letting me feel you inside me," she says over my lips as we taste, gnaw, and bite at each other.

"You think you had it rough? I had to stare at the most beautiful naked woman in my bed and not touch her."

She giggles. "You get to touch me now."

"Forever," I say with seriousness in my eyes.

We both stop moving as I say the word forever. It's such a big word. In some ways, it's a bigger word than love. Love can change, grow, or disappear, but forever never ends.

I don't want to take the word back. I mean it. I want forever with Siren. I can't imagine another woman in my life—only her. Our life together may still be short. People like us don't live forever. We'd be lucky to hit forty. We won't have the fairytale: the kids, the house, and the PTA meetings. We won't have a steady job or normal income or friends we meet up with on the weekends.

We could have our forever, though. We could stop the lying, the deceit, the secrets. We could promise each other to put each other first. To love each other first.

Siren's lips fall open as her eyes search mine for the truth of how I feel. To see if I'm full of crap. To see if I'm manipulating her into loving me so I can destroy her like she's destroyed me.

I let her in, past the bullshit and lies. I let her see me—the man beneath the armor I always wear.

"I'm your anchor, Siren. And you're mine. There is a reason we keep coming back together, even through the lies. We need each other. We've been going about this all wrong. We've been loners for so long. Together though—together—we would be unstoppable."

Her eyes water.

Shit, I didn't mean to make her cry. I'm so sick of hurting her. I pull out a little, but she grabs at my chest, reaches up to the base of my ponytail, and yanks me to her, my cock slamming deep inside her.

We both growl at the pleasure—pleasure we both need more of. *Why did I decide now was the time to talk?*

Because we are both vulnerable, and it has to happen.

Slowly, Siren reaches up and kisses me tenderly on the lips. It's different than her other kisses. There are no fireworks, but it doesn't mean it isn't the best damn kiss of my life. This kiss is full of promise, tenderness, and love. This kiss vows we are in this together—no matter what, we will work together as a team.

The unity gives way to a massive eruption. We can't hold back anymore, not after controlling ourselves for so long. We still have so much to discuss. So much hurt to work through. But that doesn't matter anymore. We love each other, and love can get us through anything.

I drive inside her, needing her to know how badly I need her. Her nails dig into my back, telling me she wants this as much as I do.

Her hands sneak up to my hair, and she rips the scrunchie from my hair.

I half-laugh, half-growl. "You really don't like the scrunchie, do you?"

Her eyes fall back as if she's thinking about something else. "I'm undecided about the scrunchie." She slips it onto her wrist, in the same way I saw my friend Kai wear my old scrunchie earlier. "But I know I love my beast-man."

"I thought I was your anchor?"

I thrust longer, forcing her to arch her back to take me in deeper.

"You are. But in the bedroom, you're my beast."

I grin. Then I make good on my nickname. I turn into a beast. I grab her hips, angling her up so I thrust deeper inside her. My teeth clamp onto her nipples, nibbling on the soft points, and I can feel her cascade of wetness wash over my cock as I do.

"Fuck, Zeke," Siren purrs.

How can missionary feel so good? I'm usually an ass man and prefer taking women from behind. But with Siren, it's all good. Everything. Being face to face with her, eye to eye, lip to lip, chest to chest, and cock to pussy, is my new favorite.

The face Siren makes is full of frustration, desperation, and need. I got her so worked up before and so close to orgasm, but then denied her. Her body is having a hard time letting go. Even though the sex is out of this world, she's still in her head.

"I got you, baby," I say with every emotion I feel.

"Just shut up and kiss me," she says, trying to pull my lips back to hers as I thrust again, changing the angle, and I watch with amusement as her eyes go big at the deeper penetration.

I do kiss her. I sweep my tongue inside her mouth, and her tongue battles mine right back. It's not going to be enough to get her over the edge. I know what will, though.

I slow down my thrusts to painstakingly slow, and then I brush her hair behind her ear, making sure to touch every sensitive spot on her neck as I do.

"Zeke, please," she begs me to speed up again. To make her come.

I am, beautiful. I am.

My lips hover over her ear, breathing hard, hot fire down her neck as I pull my cock out, so only the tip still rests inside her. She squirms, trying to get me back inside.

"I promise I'll love you forever, Siren."

And then I slam inside her as a gasp escapes her throat.

Her body lets go, no longer holding back. I promised her with my words; now it's time to promise her with my body. I pump into her once, twice, and then I feel it, her orgasm clenching down, pulsing around me.

"Love—Zeke," she screams. Her words not a complete sentence like mine were, but she gets her point across.

Her words alone would have made me come but combined with the thrusting, her walls pulsing around me, and the beautiful naked woman beneath me, I explode in my own orgasm.

I wish I could say I did the gentlemanly thing and cleaned us both off. But instead, I collapse on top of her, not even having the strength to pull out of her.

But I don't miss her whispers before I fall asleep.

"Forever."

Forever—a promise and a curse. A promise we both vow to keep.

I have no idea if either us are going to be able to keep our word.

CHAPTER 7
SIREN

orever.

There have been plenty of moments that completely changed my life. Decisions I made. People I met. Answers I gave.

But I suspect nothing will have as big of an impact as that single word—forever.

It's what I've wanted my entire life. To be loved by a man forever. And to love him in return forever.

Loving him isn't the problem, I realize.

Forever, is.

There is too much we both still don't know. Loyalties we have to people from our pasts. Truths we have yet to spill. I want to tell him everything. *But if I do, will he still love me?*

Probably not.

But I'll tell him everything he wants to know. EVERYTHING. I'm not going to sit for an hour and spill my guts. For one, it will take much longer than an hour to tell him everything. But if he asks, I'll tell him the truth—no more games.

Zeke will tell me his truth in return. I'm just not sure I want his whole truth yet.

We made so many promises. Promises I wish we could keep. Promises of love, of trust, of forever.

Promises that should be easy to keep. But we are human. We're flawed. The dangers we face are worse than most.

Last night, the promises came easily. *But how will Zeke feel in the morning? In the daylight, when we aren't fucking, and it's just us? Will he still want to be with me? Still want to be with the siren who has hurt him more than loved him?*

The morning light shines in my eyes, and I roll over, ready to face whatever Zeke wants. I'm hoping he's up for a round of morning sex, even though my aching, sore pussy thinks we should rest for a few days first.

The bed's empty.

What the hell?

I grab the sheets to cover my body as I sit up and search the room for Zeke. The room's empty. I listen for the sound of the shower running in the bathroom—nothing.

Shit. Was last night all a dream? I remember Nora in my bed. *Did I want Zeke in my bed so badly that I imagined everything I desperately needed? For him to love me, heal me, fuck me?*

No, no, no, no...

This can't be happening.

It had to be real.

My heart bursts. My tears fall. My face crumples in my hands as I realize it was all a dream.

I hear footsteps. Nora's most likely.

I wipe the tears, trying to hide my pain from her. I'll feel so embarrassed if she knows I had a dream last night so vivid I thought it really happened.

The door opens and...

Zeke.

He's standing in the doorway, looking hot as ever. He's shaved his face, and he has a new scrunchie tying his hair up.

Wait!

I look down at my wrist and see a red scrunchie wrapped around it. I move my legs and feel the familiar ache from a hot round of sex. I take in the softness of Zeke's eyes, and then he mischievously winks at me.

Last night wasn't a dream. It was real.

I sigh into the sheets, my heartbeat returning to normal levels.

"You okay?" he asks, no doubt noticing the redness around my eyes and dried tears on my cheeks.

I smile. "Never been better."

He looks at me suspiciously. "Siren."

"Yes?"

"We promised, no lying."

I bite my lip. "I'm not lying. I've never been better. Now five minutes ago, I was in hell thinking last night was all a dream, but then I realized it was real."

He exhales. Apparently, thinking I was already lying to him hurt him worse than I realized.

We are both so fragile right now. Both been through so much pain. We have to be careful with each other if we are both going to survive.

But then I see what's in Zeke's hands—a suitcase.

"Where are you going?" I ask.

"To see Lucy," he answers.

Anger shoots through me so fast. He was in my bed last night, promising me love and forever. This morning, he goes running off to the first love of his life.

"Siren, do you have something else you would like to ask before you murder me?" Zeke says lightly, amused by my reaction.

That's when I spot a second suitcase. I don't pack much of anything when we've traveled before, but apparently, Zeke thinks I'm going to need clothes to travel to the ends of the earth where I've ensured Lucy is safe.

"Are you going alone?"

"No, you're coming with me."

I smile. "I am, am I? You haven't even asked."

"That's because I already know the answer."

I shake my head. "We are going to be the death of each other, aren't we?"

"Probably." He grins, and it's adorable.

I remember why he's going to see Lucy. I lied to him and told him she wasn't safe. I said she needs him. Lucy, I'm sure, isn't exactly safe. At least not by most people's standards, but she's as safe as she can be for the moment.

My anger washes away and quickly gets filled with regret. I lied to him to push him away, and now it's backfiring on me. I have to try out the new thing we promised each other. Telling the truth.

I'm terrified, that with one sentence, I'm going to destroy the promises we agreed to. That I'm going to hurt him again. That he's going to stop loving me. Everything I did, I did to protect him, save him. It's hard to explain unless you have all the facts. It could take years to explain to Zeke all the facts.

"Zeke?" I say.

"Yes?"

I let out a whoosh of a breath. There is no going back now. Just tell him.

"Lucy isn't in any new danger. At least not any more than she was."

Zeke blinks.

"I lied earlier to get you to go away because I thought it was safer for you not to be with me," I continue.

He just stands like he's waiting for a bomb to drop, but I just dropped it. I have nothing else to say.

"Zeke?"

"Yea?"

"I need you to talk to me, with words."

"Okay."

"Okay? That's not words. Plural. I lied to you. I hurt you again. I'm sorry."

"Okay."

I sigh, frustrated. "Again, that's not really telling me how you feel."

"I already knew you lied. At least, I had a good hunch. It's why I'm here and not chasing after Lucy."

I wince. *Okay, that hurt.* The only reason he stayed was because he knew I lied, not because he chose me over Lucy.

"You're upset," he says.

I nod. "A little."

"Why?"

"Nevermind." I climb out of bed, but Zeke races over, boxing me in from leaving the room. I'm naked. He's dressed. I'm vulnerable. He has his armor up. It isn't fair.

"Tell me the truth."

"I'm just hurt and jealous of your relationship with Lucy."

Zeke smiles like an idiot.

"Why are you smiling?"

"Because you're cute."

"How am I cute? I lied to you. You should be mad at me."

"I am."

"You sure don't look it."

He grins brighter. "I've already forgiven you for lying. That was a tiny lie for a good reason, compared to the other shit. Right now, I'm more amused that you are jealous of Lucy."

I fold my arms over my chest, which pushes my boobs up. He stares at them, smiling bigger. *Asshole.*

"Stop staring at my breasts."

"Why? I like your breasts and your breasts like the attention."

"Not right now, they don't. I'm mad."

He folds his arms, mimicking me. "Why are you mad?"

"Because you are being ridiculous. You should be mad, not wanting to fuck my boobs."

"Can't I be both?"

"No."

He rolls his eyes with lightness in his eyes.

"Stop trying to undress me with your eyes."

He smirks. "You're already undressed, baby. I don't have to imagine."

"I'm not your baby."

"Fine, what do you want me to call you?"

"Not baby."

"Okay, I'd really like to fuck you, not baby."

I sigh at his playfulness this morning. "You're exhausting."

He takes my hand and spins me to him, so my back is to his front.

He kisses my cheek. "And you're grumpy in the morning. How did I not know that?"

"Seriously? You aren't mad?"

He lets go. "I'm mad. But I love you more. I want this to work. Sure, I could explode. We could fight. And then have awesome makeup sex. Or we can just get right to the sex and skip over the mad part."

"I can't skip it."

He shakes his head. "You can. You just don't want to."

He runs his hands down the side of my body, and I shiver.

"Lucy isn't a threat to you."

I bite my lip. "She sure feels like one."

"That's because you don't know the truth yet."

"Then tell me."

"I'd rather show you."

"Show me?"

"That's why we are going to Lucy. Not to check on her, but to keep my promise to you. To show you who she is to me."

I exhale the anger.

"I love you, Siren. I trust you. I don't want to hide my past from you. As much as I love your jealous side, I'd prefer you not kill my old friends just because you're jealous. So I'm going to fix it. Okay?"

"Okay."

"Now, I'm going to fuck you, and then we are going to get on Nora's plane, and she's going to take us to Lucy."

I shouldn't want to fuck again, not after our fuck session last night. But I'm already wet and turned on. There is no way I'm getting on a long plane ride without fucking Zeke first.

"Fuck me, Zeke."

He grins. "My pleasure, forever."

"Forever?"

"Yea, your new nickname. I think it works. I'll fuck you into next week, forever."

I smile. It's silly and cheesy and romantic. And exactly what I want.

CHAPTER 8
ZEKE

"So...um..." I rub my neck nervously in the back of the airplane that Nora is flying us in.

Siren sits next to me with her eyes closed. "Spit it out, Zeke."

I'm trying. I really am, but I've never been in this position before. It's a little embarrassing. She will understand and be completely fine with my new situation. At least, I think she will be. I just don't exactly know what her position is either.

We may be screwed. I don't know how to fix this situation.

"Um..." I start again, but I can't say the words. I'm the type of man who handles things. If there is a problem, I don't say the problem until I've already found a solution. But I don't have a solution.

Siren rests her hand on my thigh, and she isn't helping the situation. Even when she strokes my leg in a comforting manner, all she's doing is turning me on.

I hold her hand, getting her to stop.

She looks at me, wide-eyed. "This is serious, isn't it? Whatever you're about to say?"

I nod.

She sits up, holding my hand tighter, and looking at me.

"Um..." *Goddammit, why is this so hard for me?*

"What is it?"

"Idon'thaveanymoney," my words come out in a rush all together, so there is no way for her to decipher what I just said.

She cocks her head to the side in confusion. "Can you try that again? I didn't catch a word of it."

"Yea, and speak louder, so Aria doesn't have to re-tell the story to me later," Nora shouts from the cockpit.

Siren laughs at my mortified expression.

"You're going to tell her?"

"Well, I don't know what I am or am not going to tell her yet, since you haven't actually told *me*. But yes, usually, I tell my best friend everything."

"I'm not your best friend?"

She smiles. "Am I yours?"

Yes, no. I don't know.

She shrugs. "She's my best friend. Just like you have other friends. What we have is so much more than friendship. It's better."

I nod, this conversation is so not helping my manhood.

"Tell me."

I stare at the cockpit where Nora sits. She'll find out eventually, so I might as well get this over with.

"I'm broke!" I quickly yell at the top of my lungs.

She frowns. "What do you mean? You had plenty of money last I checked. Millions, in fact, and an amazing credit score."

"You looked up my credit score?"

"Of course." She doesn't look the least bit guilty.

I shake my head. "Well, look again. It's all gone."

"Did you get robbed?"

"Not exactly."

She looks at me blankly, not understanding.

"Bishop demanded I pay him everything I had to get you back."

Her eyes are wide as I look away in embarrassment. Not because I gave up everything to get her back. I would do that time and time again, but because I have nothing to offer her. No money. No future.

Her hand touches my cheek in a comforting manner. "You think I care about your checkbook?"

My eyes meet hers and say it all. I'm the man; I'm supposed to provide for you; take care of you. I can't do that if I don't have any money.

She strokes my cheek, her eyes searching mine for why I feel this way. I'm usually secure. I know exactly who I am. But with Siren, I want to be better than who I usually am. I want to be stronger, more powerful, more manly. I want to be everything she deserves.

Her eyes soften, and I swear I see a tear in the corner of her eye. She sniffles, and the tear is gone.

"You're incredible, do you know that?" she says.

"I'm incredible because I'm broke?"

"No, you're incredible because you did what it took to get me back. You gave up everything to get me back. You valued me more than you valued money that you worked your ass off, and most likely risked your life, to earn. That's incredible."

She touches me against my cheek, and the spark hits me like a ball of fire. It hits me in the heart, and if I wasn't already hers, I would be now.

"The money was nothing compared to you. It was an easy decision."

"And it's an easy decision to love you even if you are poor and going to be poor forever, because let's face it, you don't have any skills that are going to earn you money again," she rolls her eyes, and every word is soaked in sarcasm.

I smile and then stretch my arms over my head before reclining the chair back.

"You know what? I think I'm going to enjoy this sugar momma life. You make all the money while I just look pretty and wait for you to fuck me," I say.

She hits me playfully on the chest. "Uh, uh. You are going to get a job, mister. I don't care if it's just serving fries at McDonald's, I'm not going to do all the work."

"Really? Even if me not working means I'll have more energy for this?"

I whisper into her hair over her ear. I'm sure Nora could hear us if she really wanted to. I can see her out of the corner of my eye, making out half her body. Nora seems focused on flying the plane, and I'm focused on convincing Siren that I'm in this forever and getting in her pants.

My hand slips beneath the band of her jeans, and then I'm cupping her sex, providing just enough heat and pressure to drive her wild, but not enough to leave her satisfied.

"Zeke, what are you doing?" she hisses, but her voice doesn't sound angry. It sounds turned on, with a drop of need.

I tuck her hair behind her ear and brush my tongue over her earlobe. "I'm showing you how good it would be to be together forever. Whether we are both working or not. Whether we are poor or rich. Whether we are free or always on the run. It could always be like this..."

I unbutton the button on her jeans, then roll down the zipper.

Siren puts her hand over mine as she eyes Nora in the front of the plane.

"Zeke, we can't. Not here," she says.

I'm not planning on fucking her in the back of the plane. But I do want to hear her moan, pant, lose control. I do want to know that I can turn her on anywhere anytime. I want to know that I'm the only man in her life who can make her feel this intense amount of pleasure.

I dip my finger beneath her panties. "I can stop."

She curses as I touch her sweet spot, already wet, already buzzing with need.

"Yes," she manages to get out.

I stop, but I don't remove my hand. She's going to have to tell me to remove my hand.

She blinks like she can't believe I actually listened to her, that I actually stopped.

She bites her lip, debating with herself.

"Nora, how much longer until we land in Miami?"

"Thirty minutes. I need to focus on landing, so don't expect me to chat much until we land," Nora shouts back.

Siren's eyes lighten in mischievous desire, her cheeks pink, and her tongue licks her bottom lip.

"Don't stop," she whispers, knowing Nora won't be paying us any attention. Not that I care if Nora hears Siren's screams, or notices that my hand is in her best friend's pants.

I lean forward, taking her bottom lip in mine at the same time my fingers start moving in her pants again.

Her eyes roll back in her head, and a soft cry bellows from her throat.

"You're going to want to bite down on something," I say, nibbling on her ear, then kissing my way down her throat as I dip two fingers inside her.

"I can be quiet," she says so softly I can barely hear her, proving her point.

I smirk and then rub my thumb over her clit. She squeals.

She clamps her hands over her mouth. She wasn't that loud, but she got my point. If she doesn't want Nora to hear her, she needs to bite down on something.

"Fine," she says, grabbing my face and pulling my lips to her. She chooses my bottom lip.

It's sexy and painful, and I love it when her teeth sink into my flesh. I growl. She raises her eyebrows as if to say I better be quiet or she won't be rewarding me later for what I'm about to do to her.

I laugh quietly, but then she nips at my lip again until I taste blood. We are eye to eye, mouth to mouth, finger to pussy. And I can't think of a better position I've ever been in.

I feel heat cover my lip as she groans into it, trying to keep herself as silent as possible while my fingers work. In and out of her slick entrance. Over her tight clit.

Siren trembles in my arms, her eyes are wide, her teeth sink further into my lip until I'm sure she's creating a hole in my lip. I don't care about my pain, or soon-to-be disfigured lip. It's all worth it to know how I'm driving her wild, how crazy I'm making her.

She grabs my shirt, gripping it like she's trying to hold onto a bucking bull for eight seconds. She can't decide between letting me finish, knowing the consequence will be her screaming my name, or telling me to stop and denying herself an orgasm.

I see the moment she no longer has a say. She's already hanging onto the edge of her orgasm, and even if I stopped everything, she'd still come. *It would be less intense, but what fun is that?*

I want her to scream my name. I want Nora to know, along with the people on the other end of Nora's headset. I want the world to know how I make Siren come, and I'm the only man who gets the pleasure.

Siren tries to bite down on my lip; she tries to hold it in. It's a good effort, but not one I'm going to let her win.

I squeeze her clit, intensifying everything. She gasps at the same time she screams. Then I feel her coming around my fingers. Her body shatters, her eyes roll back, and her teeth sink down back into my lip when she realizes she's supposed to be biting down on my lip, not screaming my name.

It takes her a full minute to recover enough to release my lip from her clutches. Another minute to let go of my shirt. Another minute until her breathing returns to semi-normal instead of marathon levels.

She closes her eyes and runs her hand through her hair, taking a deep breath. And then she looks at me with a bright, bashful smile.

"That was—there are no words," she says.

I put my hands behind my head, leaning back. "Good, because if I was going to lose my bottom lip, I wanted it to be worth it."

"What?" she screeches, sitting up and staring at my lip. She grabs my cheeks and turns me toward her. Her shoulders slump back into a relaxed state when she realizes I was kidding.

It doesn't stop her from playing nurse. She finds a Kleenex to clean off the blood on my lip and grabs an ice cube, wrapping it in a paper towel to hold against it.

"I'm sorry for hurting your lip," she says.

"I'm not, and you're not really sorry, either."

She grins. "I'm not. I just thought it was the right thing to say."

I shake my head. "The right thing to say is the truth, Siren. You won't hurt my feelings if you are being honest."

She nods. "I like being honest with you."

"Good, because I like everything with you."

"Five minutes till landing," Nora shouts. "Seatbelts."

Siren buttons her jeans, and we both put our seatbelts on. Nora turns her head and gives me a wink. There is no doubt she saw, or definitely heard, what we were doing.

I won't tell Siren, though. That's something the two friends can talk about if they want. I'll stay out of it. But I don't regret making Siren come. The glow of her skin and the weight off her shoulders every time I get her to relax is worth it.

"I didn't want to ask you earlier, but now that you are relaxed, what did you tell Julian? Or does he think we are both on the run?" I ask, not sure what answer I'm hoping she gives me.

I want Julian out of our lives. But I want us safe. I want to play our cards right when it comes to Julian. He has all the power, the money, and who knows what allies on his side. As much as I want to say that we are both running from him, it's not a smart move. I don't think Siren would do anything reckless without discussing it with me first.

She takes a deep breath. "I told Julian you ran."

I nod. It makes sense to make me the bad guy in this.

"I told him I was going after you. That I'd follow you and see if you led us to Enzo Black first before I got you."

She swallows, apparently not liking what she has to say next. "I told him I'd bring you back."

I nod and then stare straight ahead as we land. Siren has to keep her promise to Julian. We need him to think that she's still loyal to him, whatever promises she has made, whatever men she's determined to keep safe. She has to keep her promise to Julian, just like I have to keep all the promises I've made.

We have to go back. We have to find a way to defeat Julian before my five rounds with him are up. I've completed two rounds. I have three left. My time for figuring out how to destroy him is limited.

Lucy has one missing piece of the puzzle. One clue as to why Julian is after Enzo Black. Although, I'm not sure if Lucy is going to agree to help me or not.

Siren stashed Lucy in Lithuania for goodness sakes. It's not exactly a fun tourist place where Lucy could enjoy her life. She's going to be pissed that I got her involved in this life again when I promised her I wouldn't.

But I promised Lucy I'd keep her safe above everything else. The same promise I made to Enzo to keep Kai safe. The same promise I made to myself to keep Siren safe.

My list of people I need to protect keeps growing, getting longer every day. It doesn't bother me, though. That's who I am. I protect. And someday, I'm going to die protecting someone I love.

I glance over at Siren, the woman I promised forever to. I just hope, for her sake, that day comes a long, long time from now.

CHAPTER 9
SIREN

Flying to Lithuania took forever. Days, not hours. Especially when you fly to Lithuania by way of Antarctica.

Okay, so we didn't really fly to Antarctica first, but we might as well have. To keep Lucy safe and away from Julian, we needed to keep them from tracking us. We took every precaution. We flew under aliases. We boarded a train when we got to England and then flew out of France. We took buses. We chartered small planes under other identities.

We could have still been followed, but we did everything we could to prevent that from happening. And even with all of our precautions, Lucy will likely need to be moved again.

Zeke takes my hand as we step outside the airport in Lithuania. It's freezing cold. Both of us bought a coat, but it does nothing to prevent the chill of the wind from pulsing through us. There is a reason I prefer the tropical climate of St. Kitts to this.

Both Zeke and I are on edge, but for completely different reasons. We haven't talked about Lucy at all. About what seeing her means for her, and for us. But it's been on the forefront of our minds. When we traveled, when we fucked, when we slept in cramped motel rooms we paid for in cash so Julian couldn't find us.

Lucy was always on our minds.

Zeke, I'm sure, is thinking about ways to keep her safe. Us arriving is an oxymoron. Zeke and I are the most skilled people to protect her, but we are risking her life by being here. Julian only cares about Lucy because we do.

I want to know who Lucy is, and I'm scared she means more to Zeke than I do. I'm fucking terrified.

When I moved Lucy from Seattle, I did it from afar. I met with the team in person, ensuring they were prepared for the job. And then I spent my time traveling in the opposite direction of Lithuania, hoping Julian would follow me instead of her. I respected Zeke, and decided it was best not to meet Lucy in person until he wanted me to.

Zeke squeezes my hand as if to tell me everything is going to be okay. I try to believe him, but I can't. Not without meeting Lucy in person. Not without seeing their relationship. Not without the truth.

This is the first stop on a long list of painful truths we both have to share with the other. But it's a part of loving each other. If we can survive each other's truths, we can survive together forever.

"So this Lucy girl..." Nora starts.

Both Zeke and I glare at Nora for ruining our moment of silence. Neither of us has talked about Lucy. But of course, leave it to Nora to force the issue.

"What about her?" Zeke asks.

"Who is she exactly? I mean, I've flown around the world twice, ridden on a rocky train, and thrown up in disgusting buses. I slept in the grossest motels for this woman. I think I deserve to know who she is," Nora says, with her hands on her hips.

"You didn't have to come," I say, shooting her look to drop it.

"And miss out on all these hot Lithuanian guys? I don't think so," she says.

I frown. "We aren't here to get you laid."

"I know, but it sure would help if I have to listen to you two fuck. God, I almost sprung for a nicer hotel last night just so I could get some sleep. Motel walls are paper thin."

I roll my eyes.

Nora looks to Zeke. "So, who is Lucy?"

Zeke stills as if it is going to hurt to tell us who Lucy is.

"Is she an ex? A best friend? A sister? Your baby mama? What?"

"Yes," he says, and then hails a cab.

He lets go of my hand, grabs our suitcases, and starts lifting them into the back of the cab. I stand frozen, partially from the frigid cold, and partially from the shock of how Zeke just answered Nora.

Yes.

One fucking word. *Did he mean yes to all of them? Or yes to some of them?*

Lucy is an ex-girlfriend, a best friend, his sister, and his baby mama?

I don't know which hurts worse. My hands clench over my stomach.

The last one. The last one fucking hurts.

Lucy had his baby. *Zeke is a father?*

It's something I will never do. I will never bring a baby into this world. Not until it's safe. I'll never be a mother.

I glance over at Nora, who has the same reaction as I do. A rarity, Nora always has words.

Finally, Nora walks over to me. She puts her hands on my shoulder. "It's going to be okay."

I realize in the moment why Nora felt like she had to come. Not because of the adventure or hot guys, but because she instinctively knew I needed her here. I would need my best friend to face Lucy and Zeke's relationship.

I lean my head onto Nora's shoulder. "Thank you," I whisper, holding back my fear and tears.

She strokes my hair. "No matter what happens, we will always have each other."

I nod, even though it's not exactly true. There are plenty of things I can think about that Nora can't be there for me. I only allowed her to come because this trip isn't that dangerous; at least it's only dangerous for my heart.

When I'm faced with real danger, Nora won't be by my side. I won't let her. I won't let her be dragged down into my fate. My world. My life. Someday, I'll push her out.

We climb into the back of the cab, all three of us. Nora sits in the middle. Zeke doesn't object. He looks out the window. Nora pulls out her phone and uses Google Translate to communicate with the cab driver.

"What is Lucy's address?" she asks Zeke.

I'm the one who answers. After all, I'm the reason Lucy is here instead of France or Italy, somewhere more comfortable where I'm sure Zeke would have tried to hide her. But it wouldn't have been as safe.

She gives the cab driver Lucy's address, and then we sit in silence as the cab moves us through the city.

Finally, he stops in front of an old house that looks like it should be condemned. I wince when I see it. Whoever Lucy is to Zeke, she didn't deserve to have to live in these conditions. I was just trying to keep her safe; I wasn't trying to ruin her life. Although, I have a feeling it's going to be hard for Lucy to understand.

Nora pays the driver, and we all step out. Zeke gets the bags, and we all stand in front of the house. A strong wind would probably knock it over.

Nora and I both stare at Zeke, waiting for him to take charge and walk to the door first, but he doesn't. He just stands, holding our bags.

"Zeke," I say quietly, hoping it's enough to break whatever spell he's under.

It doesn't.

I look at Nora, not sure what to do.

"Does she have any security guards?" Nora asks.

"Yes, but I already texted them and told them we were coming," I answer.

"So if I go knock on her door, they aren't going to shoot me?" Nora asks.

I shake my head.

Nora steps forward. I grab her hand, getting her to stop. "You don't have to..."

"I know. But you'd do the same for me," Nora answers.

I let go of her hand as she walks to Lucy's front door confidently. Not like she's about to destroy my relationship with the man I love.

Nora knocks.

I stand quietly.

Zeke continues to hold our bags.

No answer.

Nora rings the doorbell.

One second.

Two.

Three.

A million.

And then the door opens. A woman steps out. She doesn't look like I expected. I thought she'd look like an angel complete with wings and a halo. I thought I would never live up to her beauty.

And I won't, but just because we are so different.

My olive skin is beautiful, but not comparable to her light.

My long dark hair is the opposite of her blonde with blue highlights.

My skin is scared with knives; hers is marked with tattoos.

But we do share something in common—pain and love for Zeke. It's clear her life here hasn't been easy, but when she spots Zeke, everything about her body language changes. When she looks at Zeke, it's like everything she cares about returns to her.

"Zeke," Lucy breathes out, as if she's seen a ghost.

And then she is running past Nora like she didn't even know she exists.

My eyes land on Zeke, to see if he's still frozen or not. He's definitely not still frozen. He drops the bags and is running toward her. They both have a smile, but there is also something more intense behind their gazes. Something that they both recognize. Something I'm not privy to.

I watch as they move closer to each other. Five feet of distance becomes three, then one.

They both halt less than a foot apart. Close enough they could lean forward and kiss each other.

They don't kiss. They don't touch. They just stare at each other, trying to gauge what the other is thinking, and breathing each other in like two dogs trying to determine if they've met each other before.

And then...SLAP.

Lucy slaps Zeke across the cheek.

He huffs at the sudden hit but doesn't seem surprised. When his face turns back, they both smile and laugh. Then they start on some ridiculous handshake they've obviously shared for years. The kind school kids have with each other. They've known each other for a long time.

"Don't ever ship me off to a country this cold and poor ever again," Lucy says.

And then it happens. The moment I've feared. Zeke lifts Lucy up off the ground and spins her around like she's his favorite person on the planet. She giggles, and then she grabs his cheeks and kisses him right on the lips.

I can't watch. I turn my head. She kissed him. He didn't stop her. He didn't turn away. He let her kiss him.

I meet Nora's gaze, which is soft and passionate but not angry. *Did she not see them kiss?* She should be ready to kill Zeke on my behalf right now.

"Lucy, let me introduce you to my friends," Zeke says.

Friends? Really, I'm just his friend?

I give Nora an eye roll. She gives me a 'play nice' look back. We are both walk toward Lucy and Zeke with fake smiles on our faces.

Zeke's smile is completely genuine and stretches wider than I've ever seen it. Whoever Lucy is to him, one thing is for sure: she makes him happy.

"Lucy Greene, this is Nora Taylor. She's an excellent pilot and the sassiest woman I know," Zeke says, walking Lucy over to Nora.

Nora smiles genuinely at Lucy, as she shakes her hand.

Geez, is everyone falling for this woman?

"And this is Aria Torres," Zeke says. I get no other introduction. No smart remark. Nothing to tell Lucy who I am to him.

I'm just his friend.

I hold out my hand. "I'm the reason you are in rural Lithuania in winter instead of relaxing on a beach somewhere."

She takes my hand, gripping it tightly, all while keeping her smile firmly on her face so Zeke has no idea we've just become enemies.

"Pleasure to finally meet you, Aria. I've thought about you a lot these last few weeks," Lucy says.

"I'm sure you have." *Just like I've thought a lot about you.*

I still have no idea how Lucy fits into all of this. Except I do…I just don't want to admit it. I don't want to know Lucy is Zeke's real love of his life. I'm just a fun distraction.

"We should go inside, it's freezing out here," Lucy says.

We all smile at her, as Zeke keeps his hand at her waist, while Lucy leads us inside.

I can do this. I can do this. Lucy has been through a lot. Don't be a bitch. Zeke is just being nice to his friend and ex-lover and whatever else she is to him.

I look around carefully once inside. Her two guards are sitting in the living room watching TV.

Jayden and Dylan.

I nod at them, silently thanking them for keeping the bitch alive. Although right now, I wish they would have done a worse job.

That is until I see Zeke's eyes lighting up at some joke Lucy told him. His giggles are high-pitched, the opposite of masculine. But it's so damn sexy, how free he is right now. He's not worried about Julian, or Bishop, or even my deceit. With Lucy, he can just be himself.

I won't stand in the way of that. If Lucy is the woman for him, then so be it. I'm sure he acts this way around his friend Enzo Black. Seeing Zeke like this makes it even more clear that I need to get him back to his regular life and stop hogging him all to myself.

"What are we watching?" Nora asks, plopping down on the couch between the two brawny men.

The men stare at her. "Football," Jayden says, looking at her suspiciously like she's a spy or something.

"Excellent! I love the English team," Nora says, snatching a beer from Jayden's hand and drinking it.

Jayden blinks rapidly like he can't believe this woman, but then he smiles. Just the tiniest bit. I doubt this tough man ever smiles. Nora got him to smile in two seconds flat.

I wrap my arms across my body as I stare at Zeke and Lucy locked in a conversation about the good old days.

Lucy looks at me and flashes me a look of ownership, staking her flag on Zeke.

Fine, he's yours. You win. I just want him happy.

I try to say all of that back. I'm afraid I'm not used to this acting nice thing, and it comes out as a threat.

Lucy smirks and then tangles her hand in Zeke's hair at the base of his neck, twisting his mane around her finger just like she thinks she has Zeke twisted around her finger.

Fuck. I can't do this. I know Zeke wanted to bring me here to tell me the truth about who Lucy is to him, but I can't stand to find out she's the love of his life or was. Or is his baby mama.

"We need to talk, privately," Zeke says, his eyes cutting to mine for the smallest of seconds, letting me know I'm not invited to this private meeting.

"Of course, babe," Lucy says, taking his hand and purposefully interlocking their fingers.

Don't look. Don't watch. But I can't tear my eyes away from them as Lucy drags Zeke down the hallway to a bedroom—*her bedroom.*

I feel like I'm about to cry, but I also want to storm down the hallway and break the door down to demand answers. If Zeke doesn't want to be with me, if this whole time he's been playing games, then I deserve to know the truth. Instead, I'm left in the dark.

"Come here, babe," Nora says, using the same nickname Lucy used for Zeke.

"Don't call me 'babe' ever again," I say as I walk over to Nora, who is holding her hands out like she wants me to sit on her lap. So I do.

"Move over, boys, give us room," Nora says as she cradles me in her lap.

Instead of moving away, though, the two men move closer. Dylan puts my feet in his lap as he rubs my legs gently. Jayden strokes my hair.

My eyes widen. "Guys, what are you doing? This isn't in the job description. You are supposed to protect Lucy, not me."

Dylan shrugs. "You hired us to protect Lucy. And Lucy is not the one who's hurting right now. She has her protection. But you, you need us."

I glance up at Nora, who I know is the real reason these two men are comforting me. Nora wants them to, and they both want in Nora's pants. If they play their cards right, they will both end up in her bed tonight, probably at the same time.

"Thanks," I say, loving a moment of attention.

"Always, babe," Nora says with a smirk.

I'm going to kill you, I whisper back.

CHAPTER 10
ZEKE

"**W**hat the hell was that?" I ask as soon as I close the door carefully behind me, ensuring Siren doesn't realize I'm pissed as fuck at Lucy.

Lucy sits on the edge of her bed, crossing her legs so her skirt rises up dangerously high on her thigh.

"Don't play games with me, Lucy. I know you better than anyone."

She tsks. "No, you used to know me better than anyone when we were kids, teenagers, not now. Now, you don't know me at all."

"I know you aren't a heartless bitch. I know you were trying to goad Siren into thinking our relationship is still something it isn't with that kiss."

"Siren?" Lucy raises her eyebrows.

"I mean, Aria." I run my hand through my hair, still not understanding why I introduced Siren as Aria to Lucy. The only possibility is that I want to keep Siren to myself.

"Siren is some nickname? I'm guessing she really fucked you up if that is what you call her," Lucy says, her voice soft.

I don't answer. I don't need to explain to Lucy what Siren means to me. What we've been through. What we will go through. Lucy isn't privy to every piece of my life anymore.

She sighs then pats the bed next to her. "Sit."

I do.

We both sit in comfortable silence. Like it's been days since we've seen each other instead of years.

"You doing okay?" I ask.

"As well as I can be," Lucy answers.

"Can you really believe it's been ten years?"

Lucy snorts. "Yes, you look like an old man. I think I even see a gray hair." She plucks at my hair, and I fight her off.

"I don't have any gray hairs."

"And you've really let yourself go. Geez, where is the scrawny boy I used to know?" She punches the muscles in my arms.

"I've never been small."

"Nope, you weren't."

"And what happened to the sweet, high school cheerleader? Now you have tattoos and blue streaks in your hair?"

She shrugs.

"It fits you," I say.

"Thanks, it does, doesn't it?"

I nod.

She lets out a loud breath. "What am I doing here, Zeke? I get a call from Aria, Siren, whoever she is, saying I have to go. To pack one bag and head to the airport. Bodyguards would take me to safety. What the hell? And why the hell weren't you the one who called me?"

"I failed," I say, letting the weight of my words hit me.

I look at Lucy. "I failed. I'm so sorry."

She frowns. "I guessed that."

"A man named Julian Reed is looking for you. I don't think he realizes who you are or what you have yet. But I owe him a debt, and so does Siren. He threatened you to keep me in check, not because he knows who you are."

Lucy's eyes go big. "I guess it was bound to catch up with me eventually. I just hoped it would happen when I was in my eighties and had lived a long and happy life."

"I'm not going to let anything happen to you, Lucy."

She shakes her head. "You can't promise me that."

"I promised I would protect your secret. And I've kept my word all this time."

She stands up, pacing, as if she's just now realizing the danger she's in.

I stand up and grab her shoulders, looking into her eyes. "I promise. I won't let Julian or any other man hurt you. They won't find out your secret; I won't let them."

She doesn't blink, so neither do I. We are locked in a staring contest, both trying to let the other know how badly we need these promises to be true.

"Why are you here, Zeke?" she asks, her voice so quiet I'm not even sure she said anything.

"What?"

"You heard me. Why are you here? You aren't here because you want to promise to continue to protect me like you always have. Why are you here?"

I drop my arms, preparing to cover my jewels before Lucy knees me in the balls. "Siren. I'm here because I need you to talk to Siren."

Lucy laughs. "I should have known it was for pussy."

"Siren isn't pussy. She's..."

"She's what? Your girlfriend, fiancée, wife? Don't kid yourself, Zeke. Whatever she is, this is all she'll ever be. She'll never be your serious girlfriend, and definitely never your wife."

"Why not? I could be a great husband."

Lucy shakes her head. "You could be, if you changed everything about your life. You can't be a good husband, not when you would give your life to protect your boss and his friends. You can't be a bodyguard and a husband. You can only be one or the other. You can't protect others while vowing to put your wife first. You have to choose. And you already know you will choose as you always have: a life of protecting others."

"What if I'm tired of protecting others?" I ask.

She looks at me with sadness. "I shouldn't have made it seem like you have a choice. You don't. It's in your DNA. If put in a situation where you had to choose between saving yourself so you could return home to your wife and kids or protecting Enzo Black, it wouldn't even be a choice. You would save Enzo every time, even if it meant certain death. That's who you are. You can fight it, but in the end, it's your destiny."

She touches my cheek like that is somehow going to take away some of my pain. "It's why I had to let you go."

Our eyes meet. It's only a partial truth. The real reason she let me go is much more complicated. But I don't call her out on it.

"Will you talk to Siren?" I ask, ignoring the intensity of our conversation. I don't believe Lucy's words are true. There has to be a way I can be a good husband someday while still protecting my boss and my friends. There has to be. I just haven't figured it out yet. In the meantime, I need Siren to trust me. Lucy is the biggest area of distrust.

I can tell Siren about my past, but it would mean more coming from Lucy.

"She doesn't trust me," Lucy says.

I raise my eyebrows. "I wonder why."

Lucy shrugs like how she behaved earlier was completely innocent instead of marking her territory on me. A territory Lucy no longer gets claim to.

"It's really good to see you again, Luce. I never thought I'd get the privilege."

"I feel the same," she smiles.

I walk to the door. "She doesn't trust me either, and it hurts." I open the door, knowing just how to play Lucy to get her to help me. I just put the final nail in.

"Okay," Lucy says.

I smile, not looking back.

"I'll do it," Lucy says.

I turn to give her a curt nod and then head out to the living room to deal with Siren and Nora. I have a feeling I'm about to walk into a lion's den. Both women are going to be pissed, and rightly so.

I needed to talk to Lucy first to get her on my side again and to reprimand her for the kiss like I'm hers. Now that that's handled, I have to deal with the consequences. I just hope I barely fractured Siren's heart instead of stabbing it.

But when I see Siren curled up on the couch, snoring in Nora's arms, two large men stroking her, and Nora's glare up at me, I know I've really fucked up. A simple apology won't work.

CHAPTER 11
SIREN

I keep my eyes closed to hold in the tears and pain. The longer I keep my eyes closed, the longer I can pretend Zeke is still mine. I can pretend that we still have a relationship. That he didn't bring me here to destroy me by showing me how much he still loves Lucy.

I can pretend all of this isn't real.

But I can't stay this way forever. I'm not a coward. If Zeke doesn't love me, doesn't want me, it's time to face that.

Nora scratches my back as if to agree—it's time.

So like a flipped light switch, I open my eyes.

The living room is small. The room only has a couch and a TV sitting on a box, not even a TV stand, not another chair.

There are four of us on the couch. Dylan, Jayden, Nora, and I. But none of them is who I see when I open my eyes.

I see Zeke Kane leaning against the doorframe staring at me with regret in his eyes.

Well, too bad. You should have thought about how it would feel before you let that bitch kiss and touch you. *Of course, I'd be pissed.*

His eyes search mine for forgiveness. I can forgive. I've done plenty of bad shit. But not here, not like this, not in front of everyone. My pride is too hurt.

I sit up, half sitting on Nora's lap and half on Dylan's.

Zeke's jaw ticks as he sees where Dylan's hand is rubbing on my back, dipping low, almost touching my ass on each downward stroke. He's jealous, just like I was. That has to be a good sign.

"I'll make you coffee," Zeke says, staring at me.

Coffee. In the past, he's been able to make things better by bringing me coffee. I could use some caffeine. My body is sore and groggy after my little nap. I stare at the TV. The soccer game is still tied one to one. I didn't sleep for that long; I'm just tired. I guess watching the man you love fall back in love with his ex will do that to you.

Zeke walks into the tiny kitchen. There's just a coffee pot, microwave, and single cabinet.

He starts fidgeting with the coffee maker, cursing up a storm when he can't get the thing to turn on.

Jayden snickers, obviously aware of how to fix it. But now he's on team Nora, which includes team Siren. So he won't be helping him.

"It's broken," Lucy says, now leaning against the doorframe where Zeke was a moment ago.

"I'll go get you some coffee then," Zeke says, ready to run out into the freezing cold to get me coffee. To do anything to keep me from giving him dirty looks like I'm currently flashing him.

"No," Lucy says.

The room stills, like a chilly sheet of ice just covered us all, forcing us to freeze. That's the effect Lucy has on a room.

"It's really not a problem. I'll be gone ten minutes," Zeke says.

Lucy shakes her head. "You don't know where the good coffee shop is."

"Okay, so tell me," Zeke answers.

"Siren and I can go get it. We need to chat anyway," Lucy says, staring me down, daring me to say no. And it's Siren now, not Aria. Zeke must have slipped up and told her what he calls me.

I look at Nora, begging her to come with me.

"Nope, I'm not coming. This is a nail-biter. I don't want to miss the end of the game," Nora says.

I frown at her. *Some friend she is.*

I stand up, deciding it's best if Lucy and I just go alone. There's a good chance only one of us will be returning, and if I was a betting person, I'd bet on me.

Zeke senses it. "Maybe I should go, too."

Lucy grins. "Nope, girl talk. It would bore you." Then she flashes Zeke a look, clearly confident that she can take me.

I smirk. So cocky. She has no idea what I'm capable of.

"At least take Dylan or Jayden with you," Zeke says.

Lucy laughs. "I think they'd both rather stay and protect Nora. You might want to hire me new bodyguards because I'm pretty sure they will follow Nora when you leave."

"Hey, you can't blame us for falling for the hot, sassy woman. Like Siren would let us go anyway," Dylan says.

"Still, I'd feel better if one of them does their damn jobs and goes with you," Zeke says.

Lucy rests her hand on Zeke's chest, while flashing me a grin and a look from the corner of her eye. She knows exactly what she's doing.

"Siren is more than capable of protecting me. I bet she knows how to use a gun better than either of my guards do," Lucy says.

She's right. I do.

I raise my eyebrows and cross my arms, waiting for Zeke to give me permission to take Lucy out on my own. Lucy looks like a strong woman, but from what I can see, she's never held a gun in her life.

"Fine," Zeke says with a pout.

"Good boy," Lucy says before walking to the tiny closet to grab her coat. She's still wearing a damn skirt even though it's a million below. She slips on some fury boots—like that's going to help her.

"Don't hurt her," Zeke says, grabbing my arm as I go to grab my coat.

I roll my eyes to wash off the sting of pain from him thinking I'd hurt her. And he didn't threaten Lucy not to hurt me.

"Don't worry, I'll bring her back in one piece. I wouldn't dare threaten your precious Lucy." I pull my arm free, grab my coat, and rush outside before even putting it on. As soon as the wind and snow hit me, I realize that was a mistake.

I FOLLOW LUCY INTO THE SUPPOSED BEST COFFEE SHOP IN TOWN. The smell that hits me when I first step inside instantly curls my stomach. There is no way I'm going to be able to drink anything from a place that smells like this.

"It smells retched in here," I say, scrunching my nose.

"Yep, welcome to Lithuania. If you wanted good coffee, you should have left me in Seattle."

I wince. I didn't even think when I was sending her here about the lack of good coffee. Coffee probably meant a lot to her working in the industry in Seattle. I was just trying to keep her safe, but good luck convincing Lucy of that fact.

There are exactly three tables in the coffee shop. They're all made of mix-matched furniture, with giant holes in the upholstery and bugs crawling around the feet. Lucy doesn't seem surprised or bothered at all as she walks up to the counter, greets the man in Lithuanian, and then orders a drink. Her pronunciation is a little choppy, but for only being here a few weeks, she's picked up the language well.

She turns to me, daring me to ask for her help with ordering. She doesn't know my past, though. She doesn't know that I've spoken English, Spanish, and French since I was born. I traveled with my parents when I was young on missionary trips. Language is as easy as breathing to me. Even if I don't know a language very well, I pick it up fast by just listening to others. It's the one thing I feel like I'm a fast learner at.

"Labas," I greet the man behind the counter.

"Labas," he huffs back.

I place my order in Lithuanian. "I'd like a coffee, black. Actually, some sweetener would be nice," deciding that whatever disgusting coffee he's about to serve me is going to need something to sweeten it up in order to drink it.

Lucy looks at me with raised eyebrows. "You grew up here? Is that why you sent me here?"

I shake my head.

She frowns and then rolls her eyes as she realizes I'm just good with foreign languages. "It was a good call on the sweetener. You won't be able to drink the sludge without it."

We both wait at the counter for our coffees and then take a seat at the table by the window, which I instantly realize is a bad choice as the window isn't very insulated. We both have to leave our coats on to stay warm.

I wince when I taste the coffee.

"You don't get to complain about the coffee. You are the one who dumped me in this hell hole," Lucy says full of fire.

"How about a thank you for saving your life?" I snap back.

"I wasn't really in that much danger. If I was, Zeke would have run to my side immediately. So forgive me for not thanking you for ruining my perfect life and sending me here to this frigid hell."

"I was just trying to protect you. But if you'd rather die, be my guest."

Lucy shakes her head. "Zeke hasn't even told you why you're protecting me, has he?"

I tap my fingers on the outside of the coffee cup, trying to keep my hands warm, while also trying to decide how to answer.

"No, he hasn't," I answer truthfully. Lying still sucks too much energy out of me.

Lucy studies me closely. "You really can't lie?"

"I haven't been able to lie for years. I've only recently learned how to, but it's very rare that I can. And I've only ever been able to lie to—"

"Zeke," Lucy finishes for me.

I nod.

"Do you love him?" she asks.

"Do you?"

"I asked you first. Whether I love him or not is irrelevant," she says.

"Why?"

She shakes her head.

"Why are we talking?" I ask, avoiding answering her question.

"Zeke thought we should."

"Why?"

"Because he wants you to know the truth, and he doesn't think you'll believe the truth coming from him."

I nod, realizing that as much as I hate Lucy, I do trust her to tell me the truth. Even the parts that Zeke might have tried to sugarcoat for me.

"Then tell me what you brought me here to tell me. Then I can figure out how to get you some better coffee."

Lucy chuckles. "You promise? Even after what I'm going to tell you?"

"Yes, I promise to get you better coffee, no matter what you tell me."

"I'm sorry," Lucy starts.

I frown, and my eyes squint, trying to understand how her story is starting by apologizing to me.

She laughs at my reaction. "I meant the story starts with an apology."

I grip my coffee cup harder. Lucy is going to be the death of me. I can feel it.

Lucy's eyes roll back as she remembers how she and Zeke met. "'I'm sorry'—those were the first words Zeke ever said to me. He apologized for stepping on my foot. Even at five years old, he was large compared to me. It hurt, but then I saw the sweetness in his eyes, and the pain melted away."

This hurts. The sweet childhood memories. What I would have given to have a best friend like Zeke growing up.

"Zeke wrapped his large arm around my scrawny shoulders, and he told me that he would protect me. That was the promise that changed everything. If I would have known what he was going to have to protect me from over the years, maybe I wouldn't have let him make that promise."

I bite my lip, begging Lucy to continue. I need to hear what he means to her. Or, more importantly, what she means to him. It's more than a childhood friendship and a silly promise—so much more.

"For a long time, we were friends. I was his shadow, and he was my man of steel. He protected me from bullies, from older girls, even from my parents."

I nod, understanding how close you can feel to someone who protects you. It's why I felt so connected to Hugo for so long.

"We were best friends. And then we became like step-siblings. When I had no food, Zeke would feed me. When I had nowhere to stay, I would sleep in his bed. He protected me. But I wasn't part of his world. I wasn't part of his friend group. As we got older, he would stop hanging out with me publicly. He would only protect me with threats to the others in my class, but never with his physical protection. He said that was to protect me too. He wouldn't allow me to get messed up in the dangerous life of working for Enzo Black. I was better than that. I was destined for greater things. That's what he always told me."

Lucy takes a sip of her coffee, unaffected by the bitter grounds that I can see floating in her cup.

Please tell me this is where their story stops. They were friends who later became like siblings. I can live with that. But Lucy keeps talking.

"Senior year, everything changed. Zeke was one of the big men on campus. He never played sports. He didn't want to risk getting hurt. That would have taken him away from protecting his precious Enzo Black. But he didn't need sports to be popular. He didn't need a letterman jacket for the women to swoon and throw themselves at him.

"He dated most of our class, except me. I thought it was because he thought of me as a sister, not a girlfriend. But one drunken night when I crawled into his bed, feelings were spilled. I love you's exchanged. We didn't fuck that night. Just kissed. We both wanted to be completely sober when we crossed that final step. But it was a magical night. One of the best nights of my life..."

Fuck. No, I can't keep listening. Why would Zeke do this to me? Why would he bring me here to hurt me like this? I can't handle hearing how much they loved each other. How much they meant to each other. I can't handle hearing she was the love of his life, and I'm just getting in the way now.

Lucy stops talking as she notices my reaction. She's a strong woman who knows exactly what she's doing. She knows how to slice through my heart as easily as Zeke does, and she would have no problem inflicting the first wound.

She doesn't comfort me. She doesn't rush the story she wants to tell to explain that they were all wrong for each other. That their story ended in pain and hatred. She doesn't reassure me in any way. She just watches me like I'm an experiment she's running. If she says certain words, she wants to see if I'll react the way she expects.

I don't want to show weakness in front of this woman. I never show weakness. But I can't hide my tightened chest, my burning face, and flush hot skin. I shed my coat and fan myself with my hand, trying to take deep breaths.

One, two, three.

Finally, I'm calm enough to listen to the rest of her story. "I want to hear the rest." My voice is pathetic and weak. The complete opposite of who I am. I guess I'm weak for Zeke.

"The best night came the following night, when Zeke got us a hotel room overlooking the ocean and fucked my brains out."

Yep, those words hurt. I already guessed that they'd fucked, but hearing her say it, hearing her say they were in love, that she was Zeke's first love—there is nothing that could prepare me for this.

I down the cup of coffee, just to have something else for my senses to focus on. The bitterness, the sharp taste of the sludge, the erosiveness of the coffee on my teeth and throat.

Lucy smiles with her eyes—*the bitch*.

"Can you handle more?"

"Yes," I hiss back, reminding myself that caring for a man I love is not weakness. It's strength. I love Zeke Kane. I love him, and there is nothing Lucy can say that will change that. I just don't know if Zeke will love me back when this conversation is over.

"We fucked like bunnies for months. In Zeke's bed, his car, the janitor's closet at school, the beach—"

"I get it; you fucked a lot."

"It was the best spring and summer of my life. I finally found someone who understood me, who loved me, who cared about me."

Zeke is a good man. I don't know how this story ends. I don't know how they dissolve their relationship, or if today is the day they pick it back up. But I know that Zeke is a good man, a great man, in a relationship. He's a giver, a protector, always worrying about the person he's with.

"And then...it happened," Lucy says.

I close my eyes, preparing my heart. "What happened?" I ask, opening my eyes, needing to see the truth.

"I got pregnant," Lucy says.

Turns out, Lucy doesn't need a knife. She doesn't need a gun to shatter my heart. Just three little words.

She got pregnant.

She had Zeke's baby.

It's incredible that Zeke has a child. Something that is part of him. Something I can never give him. My world is too dangerous to bring a child into, but what I wouldn't give to have the option. To be able to have a family with Zeke.

Lucy watches me, my every movement. The torture, the pain, the heartbreak. Not only can I not win, but I shouldn't if there is a child involved. I shouldn't interfere if they love each other. I should give them a chance to be a family.

Damn.

I want to be selfish, truly selfish. I want to take Zeke and run. I want to prove to Lucy that he loves me more than her. That I win.

But I can never win.

"More?" she asks.

I suck in a breath and then nod. I'm not sure I can handle more. I don't want to hear about the happy birth of their baby. I don't want to hear about what tore Zeke away, and why he's back.

But I don't have a choice. I have to know.

"I lost it..."

I was staring down at the table, feeling completely sorry for myself, until I hear Lucy speak. I don't have to look at her to know her eyes are filled with tears, her throat has tightened, and pain has spread through her body.

When I finally look at her, I see it all on her face. The pain I felt earlier was nothing compared to the torment I see on Lucy's face now.

I take her hand instinctively, forgetting all about myself, just needing to comfort a woman who has lost something it's clear she desperately wanted.

Lucy lets me take her hand. For a moment, we sit in her pain. There are no words that can bring her comfort. Nothing can ease the pain she felt all those years ago.

"I'm so sorry," I finally say.

"Thank you," she says.

I squeeze her hand but don't let go. Whatever else she has to tell me, she needs to know I'm on her side. I won't let my own pain and cattiness hurt her any more than she's already been hurt.

"When I lost the baby, I wasn't sure if I was relieved or broken. Zeke would have made a great father. He would have protected that baby with his life. But we were still babies ourselves, barely nineteen. Zeke had a career ahead of him with Enzo's company. And I...well, I realized as much as I loved Zeke, he wasn't mine."

Her words heal me. *Zeke isn't Lucy's. But is he truly mine?*

"We both took the news hard, not sure really how to feel. We both felt like we lost a bit of ourselves. Slowly, the fucking reduced until we were no longer fucking. The calls stopped. The texting became only the bare minimum. Until we no longer knew what each other was doing. Until we didn't really know each other anymore. Until we both became each other's secrets.

"Sure, we would smile when we saw each other. The hugs Zeke gave me were some of the best. But we were never the same. The loss made us realize that."

I nod.

But that doesn't mean they stopped loving each other. It doesn't mean that now that they are older, and have lived a part, they won't want to start a relationship up again.

"More?" she asks.

Fuck, there's more. I can't handle more. My heart is hurting for Lucy, for Zeke, for myself.

I need to hear whatever else she has to say. I look her in the eye, telling her to finish, but that I can't handle much more.

"I thought Zeke was out of my life for good. I thought he was only going to be the odd stranger that if we ever ran into each other at the supermarket, we'd laugh and say how we should catch up. I didn't think we'd be a big part of each other's lives ever again."

Shit.

"I needed a protector. I was in trouble. And I knew only Zeke could help me. And he did. He protected me. He saved me. He promised me. And he's kept my secret for years."

I stiffen. "What secret?"

"I can't tell you my secret. But Zeke can."

"What's taking them so long?" I ask, pacing to the front door again to peer out the peephole and hoping to see Siren and Lucy walking up the front steps. But just like the last dozen times, I don't see either of them.

"I'm sure they have a lot to talk about," Nora says.

I glare at her.

"You don't get to be pissy. You could have told Siren yourself the truth about Lucy. You chose not to. Now you have to deal with the consequences."

"Which are?"

"Only one of them is coming back alive," Nora says with a straight face.

I growl. "This is not the time for jokes."

She laughs. "They'll be fine."

I raise my eyebrows.

"Okay, so they probably won't be. But the worst that will happen is a catfight with nail scratches. They aren't going to really hurt each other."

I rub my neck. It's not just what they'll do to each other that worries me. I'm worried about Julian or Bishop coming after them. I'm worried about other untold danger, enemies hurting them. I shouldn't have let them go by themselves. I should have demanded I or one of the useless bodyguards go with them. Instead, they're drinking beer and watching a soccer game on their asses.

I feel Nora rubbing my back, her hands unable to reach my shoulders while I'm standing and her being so much smaller me.

"What are you doing?" I ask.

"Rubbing your back," Nora answers.

"Why?"

"Because you seem tense, and I'm trying to see what all the fuss is about. Lucy and Siren are right; you have great muscles, Zeke. What exercises do you do to get your back muscles to look like that?"

"I strangle people who annoy me with my bare hands," I answer.

Nora smiles but stops. "Fine, I was just trying to help. I'm going to order a pizza; I'm starving."

I stare at her wide-eyed. "I don't think it works that way here. We aren't in New York City or something. You can't just order a pizza to be delivered."

Nora sighs. "Fine, then I'm going to get food."

"No, you sure as hell aren't. It's not safe."

"Then, I'll bring one of the guys."

"You mean Beavis and Butthead? They are both drunk off their asses. They couldn't fight a fly right now and win," I say.

"Hey! Don't judge. You don't know us at all," Dylan says.

I run my hand through my hair, trying to keep calm. I really need to punch someone. Dylan will do. I don't understand why Siren hired them. It's like she was purposefully ensuring that Lucy wasn't safe, which pisses me off. Siren can hate Lucy, but she damn better respect that I care about Lucy and want her safe.

I throw a punch at Dylan without thinking.

"What the hell, man?" Jayden asks.

I throw a second with full intention of breaking his nose, but Dylan is prepared. He dodges me, the alcohol apparently not slowing him down.

"Easy man, we don't want to fight you," Dylan says.

"Well, too bad. If you'd done your damn job, then maybe I wouldn't have to fight you," I say back.

I take out Jayden's legs, and then finally land a punch to Dylan's face.

But I only angered a sleeping giant in both men. They fight back, hard. Harder than I expected for the two lazy drunks.

"Stop it before I hurt you," Dylan says.

I laugh. "You can't hurt me."

Just to prove a point, I let him punch me. I don't move. I'm a rock. A sheet of stone. A piece of solid steel.

Dylan blinks in surprise. "What's your problem?"

"My problem is you are supposed to be protecting Lucy, and instead, you are drunk watching a soccer game," I huff, shoving Dylan against the wall.

"Uh, Zeke. I don't know what they've been drinking, but it sure isn't alcohol. I've been drinking the same stuff, and I should be drunk right now, but instead, I'm sober," Nora says.

I stare at Jayden and then reach for the bottle to read it more carefully. It's non-alcoholic. I was wrong.

And then Dylan lands a punch that actually hurts. Not physically, but because I let my emotions cloud my judgments.

"And as for protecting Lucy, we've been watching her on our phones. We have a man she doesn't know about who works at her favorite coffee shop. We spent the first week fighting her every time she went out to take us with, so we thought it'd be better to give her the illusion of independence when we are really watching her," Dylan says, thrusting his phone at me. "They are driving back, see?"

I do see. Both Lucy and Siren seem fine. Although, the redness and puffiness around both of their eyes scare me.

I fall back onto the couch. "I'm sorry."

Jayden shakes his head. "We understand, man. Lucy is special. And we've known Aria for a long time. She's one incredible woman."

I nod, trying to get my shit together and stop attacking everyone.

"I'm going to get you all some ice," Nora says.

"We're fine, ma'am. We are used to taking a hit," Dylan says.

Nora frowns. "I'm getting the ice. I don't want to look at a bruised nose and eye for however long we are here. And this way, I get to play nurse." She winks at Jayden before heading to the kitchen.

"Don't worry, boss. We won't let Nora affect our ability to do our jobs," Jayden says.

I nod, giving them the benefit of the doubt. Although, they don't know Nora like I do. If she wants to fuck them, she will, and she won't let them worrying about their job stand in her way.

"Give me your phone," I say to Dylan, needing to watch to ensure Siren and Lucy are okay the whole way here.

I sit on the couch and watch them drive in silence. I watch them park in front of the house. I resist the urge to run out the door and escort them inside.

"We brought dinner," Lucy says, as both women carry a bag into the room.

I stand up and take the bags from them, trying to read each of their faces, trying to see where they stand with me. But both of them hide their emotions well. I try to brush my fingers against Siren's, but she pulls away.

That's all I need to know. She's pissed.

Not that I blame her. I want time to talk alone, but there isn't anywhere in this house except the main bedroom to talk. And I feel weird taking Siren into the bedroom when it's Lucy's bedroom.

"Soup?" Nora asks.

"Borscht," Jayden responds. "Borscht is about the only thing we can get around here. It's why we are all so lean. It's the beet diet, guaranteed to make you lose weight."

Nora laughs. So does Lucy.

Siren is lost in thought.

"Hey, can we talk?" I ask Siren, needing a moment alone with her. Just a minute to connect. A second even. I'll take anything she gives me.

"We should eat. Don't want the soup getting even colder," Siren responds with a tight grin.

Nora meets my gaze and gives me an encouraging smile. Even Lucy notices Siren shutting me out, but Lucy gives me no clue as to how Siren feels about me.

We all get a bowl of soup, and then the three women sit on the couch, while the men eat the soup standing or on the floor as the TV gets changed to a rugby game.

"All we get are sports and news. What I wouldn't give to watch a good rom-com, a drama, a comedy—anything," Lucy says.

"You poor girl," Nora says, touching her arm. "I don't think I'd survive."

Lucy eyes Nora's Prada shoes, Balenciaga jeans, and Gucci shirt. "You wouldn't."

Both women laugh. Siren is lost in her bowl of soup. I want to go to her. Screw our audience. But Lucy catches my gaze and shakes her head, telling me to give her time.

So I do. It kills me, but I do.

The minutes tick by like hours. Hours like days. Finally, Lucy yawns, followed by Nora.

"Time for bed," Lucy announces.

Everyone mumbles their agreement.

Lucy stands and frowns. "Sorry, but I'm not giving up my bed. I have to live here a lot longer than one night, or however long you are planning on staying."

"Of course, you should get the bed," Nora says. "There doesn't happen to be a Park Hyatt or Four Seasons around here, does there?"

Lucy snorts.

The guys chuckle.

Nora sighs. "That's what I thought."

"There are two air mattresses the guys have been sleeping on and then, of course, the couch. There are blankets and pillows in the hall closet, but that's all I can offer you," Lucy says with a frown. She looks at me, asking if I want to share her bed like old times.

I glance over at Siren. It would make the sleeping arrangements easier for me and Lucy or me and Siren to share the queen in the only bedroom. But Lucy isn't offering her bed to me and Siren. I'll end up in bigger trouble if I sleep in the same bed as Lucy, even though nothing would happen.

I shake my head.

Lucy nods then disappears down the hallway.

"Aria and I can share the couch," Nora offers.

That leaves the two blowups.

"I'll sleep on the floor," I say.

Both men nod, and everyone gets to work making up the beds as best as they can with what we have. It feels like what I assume a frat house looks like after a night of partying. Everyone just finds what they can to use as a pillow, a blanket, a bed. And then a few moments later, everyone is asleep. Well, almost everyone.

I'm awake.

And so is Siren.

"Siren?" I say from my spot on the floor, hoping she's awake. I'm hoping for more than that; I'm hoping she's willing to talk to me.

"I'm awake, Zeke," she answers after two beats.

She spoke.

"Can we talk?" I ask, my voice hesitant.

"Isn't that what we are doing now? Talking?"

I sigh. She's not going to make this easy.

"Did Lucy tell you the truth?" I ask.

A breath.

"Yes."

There is a lot of emotion in that yes. A lot of pain. A lot of fear. And, if I look closely, love. At least I hope there is still love.

"Good, you needed to hear Lucy's truth."

"What about yours?" Siren asks.

"I'll tell you anything you want to know."

"Did you love her when you were teenagers? When you were fucking? Were you in love with her?"

"Yes, I loved her." I swallow, hoping my words don't cause Siren any more suffering.

"Were you devastated when you lost..." she clears her throat. "When you lost the baby?"

I close my eyes, feeling that pain for the first time in years. *It hurt, but was I devastated?*

"No. It hurt, but I felt relief. I wasn't ready to be a father." I wait for what I assume is going to be her next question. *Am I ready to be a father now?* I don't know how to answer that.

"Are you still in love with her?" Siren asks the most important question instead.

I smile. This question, I know how to answer. But I'm not answering it from the floor where she can't see the truth in my eyes.

I stand up, looming over Siren, who has been staring up at a water damaged ceiling. She's picking at a thread on the blanket nervously.

She stops when she sees me.

"No, I'm not still in love with Lucy. I love her like a friend, a sister. I would protect her with my life. But I'm not in love with her."

Siren lets out a whoosh of a breath.

"I can't love her because my heart is already taken. I'm in love with you, Siren. I wasn't lying when I called you my forever. Even if we separated, even if you stopped loving me, my heart wouldn't stop. I'd love you forever. You're it for me."

A tear rolls down her cheek. Then I lift her off the couch, catching the tear with my lips as I cradle her in my arms.

"You're it for me, forever," I whisper into her hair, feeling whole again with her in my arms.

"You're my forever too. My anchor. My love."

We kiss. The kind of kiss needed to heal old wounds. But somehow the kiss opens more wounds than it closes. It opens the pain of letting Lucy slip from my life, at losing a baby, a future. The pain at knowing Lucy was in danger.

The kiss pulls me and Siren closer together while also pushing us apart. We are both desperate to be together. To stay together. To love each other forever. But the harder we fight for that, the more it feels like we are also slipping from each other. This thing between us can't last. Any time either of us has loved before, it didn't last. It ended.

I carry Siren to the hallway; it's as much privacy as we are going to get.

"Will you tell me about the secret? What are you protecting for Lucy?" Siren asks.

"Yes, I just can't here."

She nods. "I don't want you to here. I just want to know that you will. Right now, all I want is you."

CHAPTER 13
SIREN

Zeke still loves me. I could cry. Jump for joy. Do all the things that most people take for granted. He loves me, that's all that matters.

His past with Lucy doesn't matter any more than my past with Hugo matters. At one point, I loved Hugo. And at one point, Zeke loved Lucy.

But this thing between us is different. This thing kept us both awake all night. This thing has ended in us making out in a dark hallway like two horny teenagers trying not to wake their parents up. Except instead of parents, we are trying not to wake up Zeke's ex-lover, my best friend, and two bodyguards.

None of them even enter my mind when Zeke starts kissing down my neck with just the right about of pressure and just enough tongue to make my insides tingle.

"Zeke, we can't," I say, trying to hold onto my fleeting logic.

"We can't what?" Zeke says. "Do this?" He grabs my bottom lip with teeth as he pushes my shirt up my stomach until he finds my bare breasts. I'm not wearing a bra, which right now, I'm thankful for. It gives Zeke good access without having to get completely naked in case someone gets up in the middle of the night to pee or something.

Bathroom! We should move to the bathroom.

But then Zeke's head drops, and he's sucking, licking, tormenting my nipple, and I forget about my idea.

My shirt is up around my neck. So much for decency if someone comes into the hallway.

"Bathroom," I mumble, my head dazed, my eyes barely able to focus. Instead, they keep rolling back in my head as Zeke slides his tongue down my chest and over my stomach, dipping down into my pants before he stops.

His hand finds its way between the waistband of my pajamas and underwear, cupping my pussy, just resting his hand, letting me know what he could do, but not giving it to me yet.

He gives me a wicked grin. "I'm tired of bathrooms. Too small."

And then one finger slides inside me. I groan, my back arches against the wall as my nails dig into the nape of Zeke's neck.

"Don't scream, Siren. Not unless you want to wake everyone up and let them find you naked."

"I'm not naked—"

But then, I am. My shirt is gone; my pants and underwear hang around my ankles. I'm naked in the hallway, feet away from where four other people are sleeping.

Zeke raises an eyebrow as if to dare me to tell him to stop. Tell him this isn't happening. Tell him that I don't want this.

I can't. I want this. After my conversation with Lucy, after every painful thing she said, I can't not have Zeke. I need the connection. I need to know he still chooses me, no matter what else is going on.

"You have no idea how worried I was when you were gone," Zeke says, as if reading my thoughts.

He grabs my cheeks, holding my head as he stares down at me and kisses me tenderly on the lips.

"Yea? Worried I was going to hurt Lucy?"

He frowns, his eyes darkening into slits. "No, I was worried you would get hurt."

We kiss. Our lips and tongues meld together as his erection, still locked away in his pants, pushes at my stomach.

"I'm a tough girl, I don't get hurt easily," I say, lifting the hem up his shirt up and tossing it to the ground so I can I feel every rippling muscle of his against my skin.

"I know you can take care of yourself, but there are dangerous men out there," he says, taking my nipple in his mouth again.

I curse, probably too loudly, but it feels too good not to express exactly how I feel.

"Dangerous men are my specialty," I say.

Zeke bites down.

I yelp.

"I'm not just worried about you getting hurt by dangerous men. I didn't want Lucy to... I mean, I didn't want..."

He stops licking my nipples and looks me dead in the eyes. He was scared he was going to lose me. But that was the risk he was willing to take. He needed me to know the truth. He needed me to know how serious he is about us.

"Make love to me against the wall Zeke. Love me hard and fast like you're the only man in the world who could ever satisfy me. It's the truth. I want you; no other man will do. Just you."

He smiles. "Just you, forever."

And then we aren't calm anymore. I'm ripping off his pants as he lifts one of my legs up and thrusts into my aching pussy. I arch my back, accepting all of him, needing this more than I need air after my conversation with Lucy.

There are more conversations to have. More truths. More sins. But I have no doubt that through it all, there will be love.

This cements it. Here in this dirty, filthy hallway. In the darkness. Us both naked connecting in a way we've done dozens of times before. But lately, each time we fuck, it becomes more and more magical. More and more important.

This time is no different. I can see it in Zeke's eyes. I can feel it in the way he glides in and out of me. The intensity of our kisses. The carnalness of our groans. It's everywhere. It's inescapable.

And it's scary as fuck.

I won't be able to escape Zeke. Even if he hurts me, even if he stops loving me, he'll still be there. He'll keep haunting me. Living with me. The love we are forming won't just leave because I need it to. It won't vanish because we are over each other.

It will remain forever.

Somehow, each time we say the word, each time we promise forever, it gets a little less scary. A little less daunting. Forever is only scary when you haven't found the right person. With Zeke Kane, I've found more than the right person. I've found everything.

"Zeke," I dig my nails into his back, trying to hold onto him as much as I'm holding onto this moment. These few minutes where I feel right. Where I feel like we finally found the right person in the right moment at the right time. This moment feels like destiny.

"Forever," he whispers against my hair softly, before biting down hard drawing blood.

Forever.

We both come hard and fast, holding onto each other terrified that after this moment ends, everything will change. That the promises we made to each other will mean nothing. And that's a scary thought. If we can't keep this promise to each other, we are doomed.

We both take a deep breath and exhale, calmer now than if we had just spent the entire day meditating.

"Gross."

"Disgusting."

Zeke and I both freeze, staring at each other like we just got caught by our parents. Really we just got caught by Nora and Lucy.

"Get a room," Nora says, walking toward the bathroom. "Although, that ass...momma like."

I snarl. "Go to the bathroom and leave us alone."

Nora wiggles her eyebrows while staring at Zeke's bare ass. Zeke just laughs, watching my reaction to Nora.

"It is a good ass," he says with a wink.

My face reddens.

I see Lucy out of the corner of my eye, smirking at the two of us. "You do realize I heard you the entire time, right?"

I wince. "Thanks for letting us finish first," I say, my voice ringing higher and chipper than it should.

Lucy shakes her head, but she's smiling. "You owe me," she says.

I nod. *I do.*

But then she tilts her head, taking in Zeke's ass.

My pleasant mood disappears.

"It is a really a good ass," she sighs, turning away. "If you stay tomorrow night, you can have my room. But you are washing the sheets and getting me a new mattress afterward."

Lucy disappears into her bedroom. Nora takes her sweet time in the bathroom.

I look up into Zeke's eyes, and I no longer care. His eyes don't see Nora or Lucy. They don't even acknowledge we were just interrupted. His eyes only see me.

He tucks a strand of hair behind my ear and kisses my forehead. All of my anxiety vanishes.

"Are you jealous that they saw my ass?" he asks.

"They saw more than just your ass," I say.

"Yea, they saw how much I'm in love with you."

"Definitely."

Siren falls asleep in my arms as I lean against the base of the couch. Nora is fast asleep on the couch. Dylan and Jayden are fast asleep on the blow-ups. All three of them are snoring. I should be in hell, leaning against a broken couch on a cold floor, unable to sleep.

But I'm in heaven. Siren is snuggled against me, and she's mine. She's really mine. I feel it. I know it. This time, I won't lose her. This time, instead of fighting, we will work together. This time we will be able to get free of the monsters of our past.

And then what?

I don't have a clue. *Go back to working for Enzo Black, probably?* Even that isn't required for me to be happy.

This is all I require. Siren in my arms. Siren relying on me. Siren letting me protect her, love her.

Siren starts snoring as well. I bite back a laugh at how adorable she is.

I won't be able to sleep in this position. I can't stretch my legs fully out without hitting the wall. My head is too high and can't rest on the back of the couch. I don't care, though. I plan on watching Siren sleep all night. Or maybe I'll wake her up in an hour or two, and we can fuck in the hallway or bathroom again, before everyone wakes up. Yea, that sounds like a good plan. Nora and Lucy scolded us for doing it earlier, so there's nothing they haven't seen or heard from us. *What does it matter if we get caught again?*

But right now, Siren is peaceful. I wouldn't dare wake her up, not when she seems so content, so happy. Something so rare for her—to have a moment where she isn't worrying or having to protect others. She's just herself.

Tomorrow, we have a lot to figure out. I've shared Lucy with Siren. Siren knows everything. Well, almost everything. She knows the painful parts. The rest is more about me trusting her to continue to keep Lucy safe. I already trust her, even though Siren and Lucy will never be best friends. *How could they?* They were both in love with me at different points. It's natural for them to fight over me a little, even though Lucy and I have long since gone our separate ways.

We can't keep staying here. Siren and I being around Lucy is only putting her at risk. She can't stay here, though. She needs to move somewhere safe, and someplace she can tolerate better than this freezing country.

Once we move Lucy somewhere safe, the hard part begins. Figuring out a way to destroy Julian, Bishop, and any other men the two are connected to.

I hug Siren closer to my chest. Her lips part, and a tiny drop of drool drops on my chest.

God, I could get used to this.

I stroke her hair and kiss her forehead. I'll protect you. I promise I'll protect you no matter what.

We can destroy Julian, Bishop, and every other enemy we have, together. But we are only strong together.

I let my eyes fall closed for a moment. Of course, the only together moments I'm thinking about are Siren naked, her nipples puckered, her hips rolling meeting mine as my cock drives into her.

What I wouldn't give for a bed. *When's the last time Siren and I fucked in a bed? Not a bathroom, hallway, or alleyway?*

I want to go back to St. Kitts, back to Julian's property, just so we have a bed I can claim her in again. A bed that's mine. *No, a bed that's ours.*

I won't be able to sleep in a bed again without Siren by my side. Hopefully, naked and ready to ride my cock. And in the morning, getting woken up with her smart mouth, knowing if I fuck up, if I hurt her in any way, she'd have no problem using a knife or gun to set me straight again.

Siren is what I've been searching for all this time. An equal. A woman I can love and protect, but who doesn't need my protection. If I was with a woman who couldn't protect herself, I would spend my entire life worrying. I'd never be able to leave her alone.

I still worry about Siren but in a healthy sense. I worry about her because I love her. I'm not crippled with worry, though.

I can close my eyes and know she's safe. I can let her go and know she will come back to me. I can even let her face her own enemies alone, knowing if something happens, she can protect herself until I can get to her—not that I will ever allow that to happen again.

My eyes fly open from my unsettling thoughts. But I'm not the only one who is unsettled.

Siren is twitching in my arms. She's been deep in sleep for over an hour, but now she's restless. She moans and starts thrashing. She's having a nightmare.

"Siren, baby, I got you. You're safe," I whisper into her ear.

She doesn't stop.

Dammit.

"Siren," I say louder, holding her against my chest tightly, hoping my comfort will be enough to settle her back into a restful sleep.

"No," she groans, still asleep.

"Siren!" I yell, not caring about waking up the entire house. I can't keep watching her struggle in her nightmare.

But it's not enough. I shake her. I say her name over and over. I tap her cheek. I consider getting up and splashing water on her face, surely that would do the trick. But just before I'm about to get up to get the water, Siren's eyes fly open.

It takes her a minute to adjust to reality and get out of her dream. When she finally does, she says, "He's here."

I shake my head, not understanding. "You're safe. I'm here. Zeke's here."

Siren blinks up at me rapidly, but my presence doesn't seem to make her feel safer. In fact, she seems more concerned that I'm here. I'm not sure if it's because she thinks I'm the enemy, or if she doesn't want me to be in harm's way.

I don't have time to ask her. I don't get to ask what her nightmare was about, or what premonition she had about who is here. Suddenly, the familiar sound of gunfire thrusts me into action.

I push Siren down instinctively, protecting her with my body.

Dylan and Jayden jump up, their internal alarms going off as well at the sound we've all faced numerous times. They have guns in their hands and are firing back through the windows.

"We'll get Lucy," Dylan says, and they're both running toward Lucy.

Lucy will be safe, I repeat to myself. They are both good men, good guards. I just hope they are great shots as well.

Nora stirs on the couch.

"Get down!" I shout at her.

She ducks, just as a bullet flies over her head, barely missing her.

Fuck, that was close.

I reach for my gun and start shooting back through the windows, but I can't see who is shooting at us, not without getting closer to the windows, closer to the danger.

The first task is to get everyone to safety, the second task is to get rid of the threat, and the final task is finding out who is attacking us.

"Go to the bedroom, both of you," I shout to Nora and Siren. "I've got this."

Nora scrambles off the couch.

"And keep your head down, crawl if you have to," I shout, firing again, hoping it provides enough protection for Nora to make it to the bedroom. There is only one small window in that room. It will be safer than the front of the house.

There has to be more than a dozen men firing at us, something I've dealt with hundreds of times. I can take them down, but it will take some time. In the meantime, Lucy, Nora, and Siren aren't safe in this house.

I feel Siren moving behind me. *Please, obey my orders for once.*

She moves out from behind me. "I'll cover you, go back and protect Nora," I say, hoping that reminding her to protect her friend will be enough to get her out of harm's way.

"I'm not falling for that," Siren says, her gun out and firing through the window on the other side of the house. She's wearing pajama pants and a tank top. No bra. Her hair is disheveled. She's barefoot. She couldn't be less protected, but she looks fierce as fuck.

I can't argue with her about wearing more protective clothing. I'm wearing my boxers, and that's it.

"This will be over much faster if we both fight. I'll take the left side of the house, you take the right," she orders.

Dammit, I curse under my breath as she runs off toward the left side of the house. She crouches low as she moves, her gun raised and firing when she gets a chance. A bullet flies in, and she moves easily out of the way before it has a chance to hit her.

Siren is strong. That's one of the many reasons I love her. She can protect herself. *Go do what you do best, destroy these motherfuckers.*

I glide effortlessly through the string of bullets to the right window. My eyes cut through the broken glass, peering out at my enemies. There are two men by a tree.

I wait for the bullets to spray in, and then I fire back, hitting the two men square in the chest. *Pop. Pop.*

I wait. More bullets are fired, but I can't see where they're coming from.

I roll under the window to get a better angle. Spotting two more men, both are dead with two more shots.

Most people don't understand why I do what I do. *Yes, I love protecting people.* I feel good knowing that I protect my friends, my family. But that isn't the only reason I do this. It's been a long time since I've been in a gunfight.

There is nothing like the high. Nothing like the adrenaline pulsing through my body as I take on my enemy, not knowing if I'm going to live or die. Although, I already know the outcome, and that's my secret. I may not act like a cocky asshole in every area of my life, but when it comes to doing my job, I'm as cocky as it gets. I know I'm going to kill them all. Mercilessly, and without a second thought.

I'm going to win. I'm going to walk out of here without a scratch. It's the only way to do this job. If you don't already know you are going to win, then you won't be able to step out into battle. You won't be able to risk everything.

The bullets slow. Only one left on my side. I don't know how Siren is doing. We shouldn't kill them all. If we do, we have no one to torture. No one to tell us who they are working for and why they are here. We can find out other ways, but there is nothing easier than torturing someone. Very few people can handle the pain. All it takes is a broken finger, a knife to the stomach, a twist of the neck to make people talk.

I take a deep breath. Keeping people alive can be the hardest part of the job. Disabling them, but keeping them alive so I can torture them. I have to hit them in just the right spot. Avoid major arteries or organs so they don't bleed out and die before I get to them. I don't want them to think they are actually dying. A dying man can be at peace more than a living man. A dying man stops feeling pain. A dying man lets go; he doesn't surrender.

Unless he's a pussy. Unless he's scared of death. Very few men in this world are, though.

I see the last man behind a car. It's not an easy shot from this angle. His head is in clear view, but a head shot almost always ends in death or paralysis. I need him alive.

I aim for his shoulder, knowing one slip and I'd hit his heart. Game over.

I take a deep breath, readying myself for the shot, keeping my body calm and relaxed.

And then...*pop*.

I look to my left. I didn't fire the shot, Siren did.

I blink rapidly.

"You would have hit his heart. You were too tight, not relaxed. We needed him alive," she says.

I look at the man, who has fallen to the ground gripping his bleeding hand. The gun has fallen out of it. She hit him right in the hand.

"Come on," she says, jumping out the window, breaking the remaining glass as she does. I follow after her, watching as she calmly walks toward the man. He reaches for his gun, but she fires at his other hand, stopping him from ever being able to hold anything again.

Siren is fucking incredible as she walks with all the confidence in the world. That cockiness you need in a gunfight, that knowledge to trust your instincts—Siren has that in spades.

I speed my steps up, so I reach the man at the same time she does.

"Who do you work for?" I ask in my husky, take no prisoners, no bullshit voice. Siren could have asked him, but my voice is deeper, more powerful sounding than hers.

She folds her arms, not the least bit upset that I spoke first. She knows I'm more likely to get him to talk than she is.

The man starts crying, holding both of his hands against his chest. *Fuck, I hate the cryers.*

Siren rolls her eyes and looks at me. We both know that if we were in his position, we'd die with dignity. We wouldn't mention our boss's name, and we wouldn't be crying like a coward.

I raise an eyebrow at Siren, excited to play bad cop, good cop with her. *I'll hurt him; you comfort him.* Siren just huffs and kneels in front of him, gripping his neck tightly in her hand.

I smirk. *Yea, like Siren could ever be the good cop.* She's just a fierce as I am. Somehow when she speaks, her voice comes out like honey. "Tell us who your boss is, and I'll kill you instead of Zeke. Trust me, you want me to be the one who kills you. I'm the better shot. I'll kill you cleanly. Zeke over here, he's pissed. You ruined a perfect night for him. The kind where you have perfect sex and have a half-naked woman drapes over you all night, with the promise of a good morning fuck. You feel me? You ruined that for my man here. He's not going to let you die an easy, quick death. So, again, who do you work for?"

He shudders and weeps at Siren's words. She releases him, obviously disgusted by his weakness. She looks at me, allowing me a turn.

I don't want to torture men in front of Siren. I don't want her to be afraid of me, but I don't really have a choice. We need answers. We need to know who is coming after us.

I shoot Siren a warning look to look away if she's at all squeamish about blood and pain. She's seen her fair share, but this is different. This is me torturing a helpless man to get information. She's seen me hurt Hugo, but we want answers fast. There are two ways to do that. Both end in a lot of blood and screams.

She nods.

And then I do it. I pull a knife from my pocket. "Last chance," I threaten low and commanding, my voice so calm, it scares most men when I get in this mode.

"I can't," his voice trembles. He can't because his boss would kill him. Whoever his boss is, he isn't as bad as I am. Not when someone threatens people that I love. This man just threatened two women I love, Siren's best friend, and two loyal guards. This man is about to see how vile I can truly get.

I hold the knife to his eye, summoning everything into my action: my anger, my fear, my love. I jab the knife into his eye. His screams are high and retched. The kind that tell me this is as bad as it gets. No physical pain can be worse. Although, I can think of a lot of worse things. A whole fucking lot.

I look over at Siren, who is watching me carefully. Worse than a knife to the eye is losing a woman you love because you had to torture a man viciously to keep her safe.

Finally, I pull the eyeball free from his socket. Blood goes everywhere, along with puss, and god knows what oozing from the socket. Most people would vomit at the sight, but it's one of my favorite tricks. It's easy to do and is almost a hundred percent effective. And I prefer it to the other option that is usually a hundred percent effective —castration.

"Who do you work for?" I ask, dancing the knife across his cheek toward the other eye, threatening completely remove his sight.

The man is sobbing now. He cringes away at the knife on his face. He's pissed his pants.

Oh, Jesus. Maybe I should have gone with something easier. I may have just scared him into not being able to talk. The tongue can also be an effective torture device.

"Bi—," the man finally cries out but then collapses.

Siren and I exchange glances, not entirely sure what he was about to say, but guessing he meant Bishop.

Siren leans down to check his pulse. "He's gone."

"Do you think he meant Bishop?"

She nods.

Fuck.

I take a deep breath and look at Siren, afraid she's never going to be able to get over what I just did to that man.

She laughs at my expression.

"What?" I ask.

"You're scared," she says matter of factly.

I nod.

"You think me watching you cut out a man's eye makes me think less of you? Makes me think of you as an evil man?"

I nod again. *That about covers it.*

She shakes her head with a smile. "I usually find seduction works well to get a man to talk when I have the time. I get more information that way."

"I'll keep that in mind, although, most men don't find me very attractive."

She laughs and then throws her arms around my neck. She raises up on her tiptoes, so our lips are almost pressed together. "And I can't be mad at you for something I've done before. Although, your technique might be better. You've probably had more practice. I usually just go for the balls."

"Is it wrong to say that's so fucking hot?"

She shakes her head and brushes her lips over mine. "No, it just means we are perfect for each other."

We kiss, the kind of hungry, desperate kiss, reassuring each other that we are okay. We are unhurt. Somehow, we are even more in love.

"Zeke," I hear Lucy's desperate voice from behind me, instantly chilling any heat between Siren and me.

"I think Dylan...I think he's dead," Lucy says.

Dammit. I didn't know the man for more than twenty-four hours, but he seemed like a good man. He didn't deserve to die like this.

Siren grabs my hand, and we race inside, both hoping Lucy's wrong. Hoping he isn't dead, and we weren't making out while a good man was dying.

CHAPTER 15
SIREN

"Fuck!" Zeke yells as he does chest compressions on Dylan.

I count with him and then give Dylan breaths in between Zeke's compressions. We both know Dylan is dead, but we've seen people come back from the dead before, so we don't stop. Not when we both feel guilty. He's dead because of us. We weren't fast enough.

It's one of the many reasons why Zeke and I have never fallen in love before. It puts our job at risk. We can't do as good of a job when we are thinking of each other, instead of the people we should be protecting.

So we keep trying. Zeke hammers into Dylan's chest. I try everything to breathe life into his lungs. And we both ignore Nora and Lucy's sobs as they hold each other in the corner.

"He's dead," Jayden says, standing over us, trying to get us to stop.

Jayden puts a hand on my shoulder, knowing Zeke is too focused. Zeke doesn't lose men. I'm the one who is going to need to convince Zeke to stop.

I sit back on my heels with tears in my eyes. Dylan was a good man, a good worker. He was always someone I could call when I needed someone for a job. It kills me to feel responsible for his death.

"Shit," I curse, wiping my mouth and gripping my hair at the scalp.

"It's time. We have to go, or we will have more death on our hands," Jayden says, looking at a terrified Nora and Lucy.

I nod. *I can do this.*

"Zeke, we have to go," I say, gently touching his shoulder.

"Not yet, I can bring him back," Zeke says, pumping over him.

"Zeke, we have others to protect," I say.

Zeke frowns. "I can't. I don't let men die. I don't—"

"Zeke," I demand. "We have to go, now." My voice is firm and loud.

Zeke looks up at me, his face full of pain matching my own. But I don't let my pain out. Zeke can't see my pain. He needs to see the machine. He needs to see that we have to keep going. We have more people to protect. We failed, but we can't fail again.

I hold out my hand. Zeke takes it reluctantly.

I look to Jayden. "Car?"

He nods. "Follow me."

Jayden leads us into the bedroom, pushes the bed out of the way, and lifts a hatch to an underground tunnel.

Zeke and I eliminated the immediate threat. But if Bishop is smart, he'll have more men coming. Or he'll be tracking us. So it's safer to disappear down a tunnel then head back out to the main street.

Jayden hops down.

"Go," I say to Lucy and Nora.

Both eye the gun I've picked up carefully. "I won't let anything happen to either of you," I promise them.

They nod, and then follow Jayden down. I pick up Zeke's gun and hand it to him.

"Let's make good on my promise," I tell him.

He nods, back in protection mode. We both follow, ready to shoot anyone who follows us, but no one does.

We clomp through a dirty tunnel, exit through a hidden door at the end, and hop into the parked van just outside.

"Where to?" Jayden asks.

"The small private airfield. I'll arrange a plane, but..." Zeke starts.

He can't pay for it.

"But I don't have the money. I'm going to have to borrow more from you, Nora," Zeke finally says. He spent all of his money saving me.

"Take my money," Lucy says.

"Luce, I couldn't," Zeke says.

"You're using it to save my life. Take my money—all of it. As much as you need," Lucy says.

I bite my lip to keep from saying something bitchy. "Lucy, I don't want to sound like a bitch, but a private plane and fuel could cost hundreds of thousands of dollars on such short notice."

Lucy smirks. "I'm worth a hundred million. I think I can afford it."

My mouth drops. *What?*

Nora's eyes go wide, the shock of seeing a man die fading as Lucy admits her net worth.

"How?" Nora asks.

I glance at Zeke, but he doesn't seem surprised in the least. He reaches behind him to where Lucy is sitting next to Nora in the van.

"Thank you," he squeezes her hand. "I'll pay you back."

She shakes her head, squeezing his hand back. "No, pay me back by protecting us."

"I promise," he says. Then Zeke is on the phone making last-minute arrangements to get us an airplane. Lucy starts barking bank account numbers at him.

I notice Nora in the corner, shaking. "I can't fly."

I frown, seeing how nervous she is. "Yes, you can."

She shakes. "I can't. I'm having a panic attack."

I grab her hand. "Then we will do it together." I don't have a clue how to fly a plane, but I have no doubt Nora can do this. She just needs a little encouragement. She's a kickass, strong woman.

Zeke stares down at me, with worry in his eyes as he finishes the call. "You're bleeding."

I look down to my ribcage, where blood is trickling out of my tank top. Then I see Zeke's arm.

"So are you."

He frowns. We don't have time to deal with our wounds now; neither one is life-threatening. I tell him with my eyes we are both fine, we just need to get on the plane and then we can take care of each other's wounds.

He nods reluctantly. He stares down, and for a second, I think he's going to take his boxers off to try and tie around my wound to put pressure on it.

I laugh and shake my head. That's not going to happen, but it warms my heart what he's willing to do to make sure I'm okay. That I'm safe.

Jayden drives us to the tarmac where a plane sits.

"I can't fly that," Nora says as we pull up.

I turn around and take her hand again. "Yes, you can. I'll be there with you the whole way to keep you calm. You've flown hundreds of times; you got this. Just take your time. We already took out the bad guys. Any others coming won't be here for a while." I tell her the truth, mostly. At least I don't think we are being followed or will need to make a quick getaway. For now, my job is to keep Nora calm and collected. Get her on the plane, into the cockpit, and then her instincts will take over.

Nora shakes her head. "No. I mean, I can't fly that plane as in I don't know how. That's a different type of plane requiring a different type of license. It's bigger than any plane I usually fly. It's different. I don't have the training to fly this plane."

I spot Zeke stiffen out of the corner of my eye. We may not be followed right now, but we shouldn't fly commercial. We will be tracked. And Zeke wasn't able to hire a pilot on such short notice.

We could try to find a different pilot, my raised eyebrows tell him.

His eyes scream the urgency of our situation.

I nod. *We need to leave now.*

"What do you need to be able to fly this plane?" I ask, staring at Nora.

"Um...I'm not sure."

"Let's get you into the cockpit and see what you think," I say.

Nora exhales a sharp breath. "This definitely isn't legal."

I smirk. Nora never breaks the rules. She never has to. Her money, good looks, and status always allow her to get away with anything.

Zeke throws the door open to frigid air, still only in his boxers.

"I'll call to see how long it would take to get a pilot here, but if she can fly this thing, it would be better," Zeke says.

I agree. It would involve fewer questions and be less likely we would be followed.

I grab Nora's hand and pull her out of the van with me.

Jayden and Lucy follow, with Jayden holding Lucy tightly and scanning for any attackers. I'm beginning to think she has a bigger part in all of this than I understand. If she is worth as much money as she says she is, it had to come from somewhere. Even if she was an executive at some coffee company, she wouldn't be worth a hundred million.

But I don't have time to ask more questions about Lucy or ask Zeke what the secret was that he never had time to tell me. We have a plane to fly.

I drag Nora into the cockpit, knowing Zeke and Jayden will handle everything else.

My eyes fly wide, and my mouth falls open as I stare at the panel in front of me.

"Holy shit," I say, blinking rapidly and hoping I'm not seeing what I'm seeing. I understand now why Nora said she couldn't fly it. I've sat in cockpits numerous times in Nora's plane. It's like the difference between driving a cardboard car and a Ferrari. It's not even comparable.

There are hundreds of buttons and switches on this jet, compared to the dozen on her propeller plane.

Nora hops into the seat, trying to appear confident.

"I need you to sit in that seat and do exactly as I tell you," Nora says.

I nod, sitting down calmly. *Maybe she has this.*

Nora stares wide-eyed at the buttons, not touching any of them.

"If you can't, it's okay. We will find someone else," I say. I'd rather take my chances in a gunfight than be thousands of feet in the air and not be able to land.

"Um..." Zeke says suddenly from behind us. "How is it going?"

"Not that well," I say.

He looks at me with concern. "Then, I'm going to need you to bandage that up and grab your gun."

"Why?"

"Because Jayden spotted a car coming at us quick, less than a mile out," Zeke answers.

They are here—Bishop's men.

I pat Nora on the shoulder. "Get in the back and hide. We will take out these men and find another pilot or way out of here."

"No, I'm not hiding. Not again. I'll be here, figuring out how to fly this thing," Nora says.

I want to argue with her, but instead, I nod, gritting my teeth. I want to demand she move to the back of the plane where it's safer, but I don't know if we are going to be able to take out the men this time. Who knows how many are coming.

If Nora can get us off the ground, we will worry about landing later.

CHAPTER 16
ZEKE

"S iren!" I holler into the cockpit as I load our guns with ammunition, staring out the door at the car barreling toward us, filled with angry men seeking revenge for their fallen co-workers. They will face the same fate, though.

"You want a shirt to put on?" Jayden asks me, loading his own weapons calmly like the professional he is, not like a man who just lost his friend and is about to go into battle again.

"Why? You going to let me borrow yours?" I ask.

Jayden smiles. "Not a chance in hell. You'd stretch it out."

I grin. "I would. I don't think we have any shirts handy anyway."

"Don't put on a shirt or pants. I think the wild Tarzan look works for you. You're much scarier without a shirt," Siren says with a wink.

We are all being playful, trying to keep things light, even though we know the seriousness we are about to face.

I stare at the blood covering Siren's shirt. "Any luck with finding a first aid kit?" I ask Lucy in the back of the plane.

She frowns. "Not yet."

I sigh and walk over to Siren. I kneel in front of her, and she grins like I'm about to propose instead of ruin her clothes. I grab her pant leg and rip it in half around the knee. And then I stand and wrap the fabric around her chest, tying it off, so it covers the wound in her side and hopefully reduces the bleeding.

It won't help if her adrenaline starts pumping fast, and we have to move or run, but it's better than nothing.

"Thanks," Siren says with heat in her eyes.

"That wasn't meant to be sexy," I whisper against her lips, my hand dipping behind her head, holding it in place as my thumb brushes over her bottom lip.

"Taking care of me is incredibly sexy," she says back, licking her lip.

I bite my lip as I feel my cock get hard. "There is nothing more enjoyable than going into a fight with a hard-on. Thank you for that."

"At least it will be entertaining," she says.

"Guys," Jayden says.

We both drop our smiles and pick up our guns. We're all crouched inside the plane, peering out the single door as the van drives onto the tarmac, followed by three more cars.

We have the high point and will be able to shoot down at them, but we are sitting ducks. We can't move unless Nora figures out how to get us off the ground. And if they have a bomb, we're screwed.

"Ready for round two?" I ask.

"Yes," Siren and Jayden say at the same time.

"Good, let's finish this," I say, even though I suspect whoever these people are, it's only the beginning.

The car parks, and we all aim. But only a single man steps out, his arms raised in surrender.

"Hold fire," I say to Siren and Jayden.

They continue to aim their guns at the man, but neither of them shoot.

"Give us Lucy, and we will go," the man says.

"No way in hell," I yell back.

The man shakes his head. "This isn't your fight. Give us Lucy. We won't harm her. You know that. Give us Lucy, and you are free to go."

Shit.

I spot Lucy in the back of the plane, inching forward, like she's willing to turn herself over to save us.

"I made a promise, and I plan on keeping that promise," I scold Lucy.

I ignore Siren's stare and need to understand the final piece of Lucy's and my relationship. I turn my attention back to the negotiator.

"No. But I'm giving you one chance to surrender—one chance to turn around and leave. If you stay and fight, you are all dead. Just ask your friends scattered about in our front lawn."

He sneers. "I'll ask your dead friend."

I shoot. So do Siren and Jayden. I'm not one to start a fight. I usually wait for the enemy to attack first. When I kill them, I can tell myself it was all in self-defense. But this time, it's not just about protection. It's about revenge.

We fire, taking down man after man as soon as they step out of the car. We are going to win easily.

But then I see more cars coming—dozens. I see one with a man standing out the sunroof with a rocket launcher on his shoulder.

"Shit. Nora, how is it coming up there?" I ask, listening to the engines purr to life. At least she got them started.

"It's coming!" Nora says.

I turn to Siren, and we exchange worried expressions. In this field, you always have a plan A through Z. You almost never get to stick to plan A. We need more plans. If they fire a rocket at us, we are all screwed.

"They won't," Siren says.

I frown. "Why not?"

"They want Lucy. We would all be dead if they fired that at us," she answers.

She's right.

They want Lucy. *But would they rather have her dead than us escape with her?* Once again, I glance at Lucy. I reassure her with my eyes that I'm going to protect her, no matter what.

"Fuck," Siren curses as a bullet grazes her cheek. She rolls back, hiding behind the metal frame of the plane.

"Siren?"

"I'm fine," she says.

Fine—fuck, I hate that word. And I hate that I was paying attention to Lucy instead of protecting Siren.

It's then that I realize I'm not going to be able to save everyone, definitely not everyone I made promises to.

I fire more shots, trying to focus on winning the battle.

"What's plan B?" Jayden asks, firing next to me.

I have a plan B, but Siren isn't going to like it.

"No," Siren says beside me, reading my mind. I could charge forward as a diversion while they all slipped out the back and hopefully steal one of the nearby cars.

"What's plan C?" Jayden asks as we continue to fire, but for every man we take down, more show up.

"I become the diversion instead," Siren says.

"Nope," I say, not even considering it.

"Well, I guess I might as well offer myself up as a diversion then," Jayden says.

"No, we aren't going to sacrifice anyone in order for the others to escape," I say.

"Plan E, then?" Jayden asks.

"Plan E is we fly the hell out of here," Nora shouts, and the plane lurches forward.

"Holy shit," Siren curses, looking me in the eye. She's not sure if she's happy or scared to death we are moving. If we are moving, it means Nora is going to attempt to fly this thing. That only ends two ways—us flying away safely, or us crashing to our deaths. There is no middle ground.

I grab her hand, and we lock fingers as we continue to shoot as the plane moves to the runway. One of the cars follows, but it's a futile attempt.

"Lock that door and put your seatbelts on," Nora yells, her voice full of determination.

"Can she really fly this thing? It's huge!" Jayden asks.

"Do you have a plan F?" I ask.

He stares out the window at all the cars of men waiting for us to turn around or crash so they can kill us.

"Nope," he answers.

"Then we are going with plan E," I say.

"God, help us all," Jayden says, making his way to the back where Lucy is. I hear him mumble to her about the back is actually the safest spot on an airplane and how to brace if we crash.

I look at Siren, still gripping her hand. I kiss the back of it tenderly. Neither of us speak. Neither tells the other we love the other. Neither of us gives a heartfelt speech about how we feel in case these are our last moments on this earth. Neither of us has to. For once, we've said the important things. We've shared our feelings. Holding each other's hand with our heads leaning close is all this moment needs.

"Hold on," Nora says, her voice calmer.

The engines roar, the plane speeds up, and we are thundering down the runway. We stop shooting, and I quickly close the door, barely avoiding more incoming bullets.

I turn, looking at Siren, wanting her face to be the last thing I see before I die if this is to be my time.

"We've survived hundreds of gunfights, we've won against countless enemies, you survived a drowning, I survived a crazy madman. We are not going to die in a plane crash, you idiot," she says with more confidence than she should have.

"Sometimes, it's the little things that kill you. It's not often the most dangerous thing that kills you. It's moments like this you let your guard down and aren't prepared to battle death."

"We aren't going to die," Siren says, laughing at my jumping leg.

"We might."

"You'd think that even if we were flying a regular plane. You hate Nora's flying."

"I do."

"We aren't going to crash."

"How do you know?"

"Because we are already in the air, you idiot."

I look past her for the first time, out the window. We are in the air. *Holy fucking cow! We are in the air. We're flying!*

"Woo, hoo! Take that, bad guys!" Nora shouts.

We all applaud her, and Siren jumps up and runs to Nora in the captain's chair.

"You did that! You were incredible! I'm so fucking proud of you," Siren squeezes her tightly.

"Okay, okay," Nora says, pushing Siren off her. "I still have to fly this plane and then land, which isn't going to be an easy task."

"But one you are going to handle amazingly, because you are a fucking badass motherfucker," Siren shouts, squeezing her friend again.

Nora laughs. "Yes, I'll be prepared for landing by the time we get where we are going. Which by the way, where are we going?"

I stand up and lean into the doorway of the cockpit. "As far as this plane will take us."

"Somewhere warm would be nice," Lucy shouts. "Especially, if you are planning on leaving me there again."

"I second that. Somewhere warm," Jayden says.

"How far can we go?" I ask Nora.

Nora takes a second to read the computer screen and fuel gages. "We are flying southeast. We could go all the way to New Zealand with a short fuel stop."

"New Zealand work for you?" I ask Lucy, already knowing the answer.

"Hell, yes! I've always wanted to go to New Zealand. Finally, somewhere I can get on board with," Lucy says.

I laugh.

We all laugh.

Siren grabs my cheeks and plants a kiss firmly on my lips. I lift her up, dragging her back to her seat.

"What are you doing?" Siren asks, as I lean her chair back.

"Taking care of you," I say. "First-aid kit?" I ask Lucy.

She tosses it forward. I catch it in the air and set it on the floor in front of me, as I turn toward Siren.

"Did we find any clothing on board?" I ask as Siren's eyes rake down my body.

"Nope, not yet," Jayden answers.

I stare at Siren with intensity in my eyes. "You are going to have to behave then."

She bites her lip. "And what if I don't want to behave?"

"Then, I'll punish you."

Her lips curl up.

Fuck, I really need to try a different tactic.

"Let me see," I say, looking at the wound on her side.

She moves her hands away from her core. I carefully untie the makeshift bandage and then lift her shirt.

She winces slightly; the ribs can be sensitive. It looks like she broke a couple, and there is a large gash on her side.

"I just broke a couple of ribs. I'll survive. It isn't the first time I've broken them," she says, trying to comfort me.

I fucking hate seeing her in pain, even pain I know she can handle.

"Yea, well, I know how badly it hurts. I first broke my ribs when I was seven in a wrestling match with my friends Enzo and Langston. It hurt to breathe, to think, to move."

"I broke mine when I was five," she says.

I frown, not liking the sound of this. *Did her parents abuse her? Did someone else? How else does a five-year-old girl break her ribs?*

"I thought I could fly, so I climbed to the highest branch I could find and jumped," she laughs at my shocked reaction.

"Are you serious?"

"Yes, it hurt like hell. Way worse than this. We didn't have medical insurance, so I just toughed it out. I stayed in bed a lot and ate lots of ice cream. I survived when I was five; I think I'll survive now."

"I know, but if I could take your pain away, I would. I'd take it all myself," I say, pulling some antiseptic out and gauze. The wound isn't deep enough to need stitches.

"I wouldn't let you," Siren says, taking the antiseptic from me and dabbing some on a few cuts on my chest she's been eyeing. They're more superficial than her wounds.

I take my time placing the gauze across her ribs, giving me more time to examine her reaction when I touch her wound. She barely reacts, though, knowing I'm trying to prove she's in more pain than she's letting on.

Then I look to her cheek. Another cut marks her beautiful skin. I dab antiseptic on it and move to get a bandaid, but Siren grabs my wrist, stopping me.

"Let it breathe," she says, her voice dropping to a serious tone. I realize she's telling me to let her breathe. Don't stifle her; we will never last if I do.

I nod and stop babying her. I close the first aid kit, shivering under her gaze.

"Stop looking at me like that," I say.

"Like what?"

"Like you want me to fuck you. As much as I'm desperate to, I'm tired of fucking you in a bathroom. Even though this plane is huge, there aren't any other rooms on the plane. I'd rather not give Lucy and Jayden a show."

She smirks. "Fine, then we should talk."

I frown. "About what?"

She swallows, fluttering those beautiful lashes at me. Suddenly I wish I had taken her to the cramped bathroom and fucked her no matter how exhausted we both are.

"Lucy," we both say together.

I nod for her to ask her question, intending to answer her.

"Why are those men after Lucy? Why is Bishop after her?" Siren asks.

I open my eyes to answer her, when I feel Lucy's gaze on me. I turn and meet Lucy's gaze. Lucy is fine with me telling her secret. But when I look at Lucy, I realize I'm not fine with it.

I made a promise to Lucy—to keep her secret. I can trust Siren, she would protect the secret, but the secret is dangerous. We have enough enemies. I won't add any more to Siren's list.

"I can't tell you," I say.

Siren blinks rapidly. "You're shitting me, right?"

"No."

Siren waits, looking at me with trepidation, like I might change my mind. I won't. Not about this. I protect. I protect everyone. That's what I do.

Siren stands. "I thought we were done hiding things from each other. I thought we were done with the lying. I thought we love each other. I thought we were sharing everything. I guess I was wrong."

Siren walks into the cockpit, slamming the door. I wince, my heart heavy. I look back at Lucy, and I know I made the right decision. I have to keep the people I love and the people I protect separate.

CHAPTER 17
SIREN

My anger flows through me all thirty hours it takes us to get to New Zealand. I stay in the cockpit the entire time, only ducking out to pee and grab food for Nora and me.

I let the anger pull me into a deep sleep in the seat next to Nora, expecting to dream about how much I hate Zeke for letting me love him. For teasing me with the idea that we could have more, and then taking it all away. We can't have more; this is all we can have.

Sins.

And lies.

No truths.

That's who we are. We commit sin after sin. We murder, steal, torture. Then we lie and lie and lie to each other, hiding who we truly are. I'm not even sure I know who Zeke really is. *What kind of man is he?*

My brain drifts off, and I force Zeke out of my head. I can't think about him. I need sleep. Peaceful, quiet sleep. As soon as I push Zeke out, I leave room for another man to enter...

"See, I told you he would betray you," Bishop says.

"He didn't betray me. He's just not telling me the truth."
He laughs. "Same difference."
"What do you want?"
"The same thing I've always wanted—you."

I wake up in a sweat, staring at blue sky and gray tarmac in front of me.

We landed.

I look over at Nora. "Sorry. I considered waking you, but I thought it might be better you were asleep while I tried to land this thing."

I nod, looking down at my pajama pants and tank top. I'm covered in blood, sweat, and fear.

The images of Bishop haunt me, the words he never spoke to me linger—I let him in again. Zeke didn't heal me. He didn't get rid of Bishop, he just pushed him to the outskirts of my mind. As long as I was thinking about Zeke, Bishop was gone.

Zeke's still my anchor. I'm still in love with him. He is the only man who can save me from Bishop. And yet, I can't shake the feeling that Zeke is also the one man I need to stay away from in order to keep Bishop from succeeding.

"Are you okay?" Nora asks me.

I smile. "Shouldn't I be asking you that? You just flew a plane you had no training to fly. You took off while men were shooting at us. You are one badass woman, you know that, Nora Taylor?"

She blushes. "I'll add it to my resumé. But you are the one who had the man you love lie to you again."

"He didn't lie."

She raises an eyebrow and crosses her arms.

"Okay, close enough."

She takes my hands. "I may be a badass, but only because I learned from the best. You, Aria Siren Torres, are one badass woman. Don't let him have all the power."

I nod. "Let's go."

We walk out of the cockpit, but everyone has already left.

"Lucy hired a limo to pick us up. She said she was tired of riding in shitty cars. If she was going to die soon, then she wanted to enjoy her life and money," Nora says.

Of course, she did.

I walk down the stairs and climb into the back of the limo where Lucy, Jayden, and Zeke are all waiting. Lucy must have had clothes delivered, because Zeke now has on jeans and a clean shirt.

"There are clothes in the bag for you, Siren," Lucy says.

"What? Are you tired of the high schooler in a horror film look?" I ask.

Lucy just smiles, like she's won. She didn't have to tell Zeke to not spill her secrets to me. He did it on his own.

Does he love her more than me? Maybe. Maybe not. It doesn't matter, because he doesn't trust me enough with the truth.

I dig through the bag and pull out a designer sweatshirt and pull it on, getting it covered in blood and sweat.

Lucy winces.

Even Nora cringes as the expensive fabric becomes saturated.

Zeke's lip twitches, but I don't look at him. *Nope.* Not until he starts talking. I'm holding a silent protest when it comes to him. He won't talk to me, so I won't talk to him.

"Where are we going?" Nora asks.

"The house I bought," Lucy smiles.

"More like a mansion," Jayden says.

"Isn't that inconspicuous? Don't you want to hide somewhere less obvious?" Nora asks.

"Yes, she should," I say.

I feel Zeke's stern glare on me, pleading with me to be nice. I'm tired of being nice. I'll go back to being a bitch. I'm good at it. Nice is overrated anyway. You still end up with the same hurt no matter what.

"The house is secluded, near the ocean. I'd rather have an awesome view and die young, than live the rest of days in a shithole," Lucy answers.

"Plus, she hired a huge security team," Jayden says like it's a good thing.

I want to glance at Zeke so badly. We both know bigger isn't always better. You want a highly *skilled* team. That's all that matters. You need a team that will sacrifice everything for you—a smart person in charge, who can jump quickly between plans and is loyal above everything else.

I have no idea who Lucy hired. Just because she can throw her money around doesn't mean she's being smart about it. If she didn't let them know how important it was to not tell a soul who they were working for, then hiring them is more dangerous than not hiring anyone.

But I'm done helping Lucy. Not without lots of answers first. I'm done.

The limo pulls up in front of a mansion on the beach, just like Lucy said. *Yep, definitely not inconspicuous.* Everyone on the damn island knows we are here now.

We all file out. I make sure to exit after Nora and ignore Zeke completely. As soon as we step out, we are greeted by a large staff asking us if we have bags and if we are hungry.

I glance at Nora since I can't look at Zeke. This is going to end badly for Lucy.

But I catch Zeke drop his head out of the corner of my eye. He feels the same, and it kills him to not be able to protect his friend.

"Lucy, let's talk a minute," I say, not asking, but telling her. I grab her arm and yank her into the house, up the stairs, to what I assume is the master bedroom. If not, it is one hell of a spectacular room.

"What are you doing?" I ask, releasing her arm.

"Living."

"No, you are risking everything. Why?"

Lucy walks to the window and looks out at the ocean. "Because I'm dying. And I'm tired of dying without really living."

"What are you talking about?"

She turns toward me, with a tight smile. "I'm dying, Siren. I have breast cancer. Stage four."

Shit. I want to apologize for every bad thing I've ever said to her. "I'm so sorry."

"Don't. I don't want your sympathy."

I walk to the window where she's standing. "I'm not going to pretend to understand. But I'm here if you need me."

She nods. "I don't need you. I don't need anyone."

"That's not true. Everyone needs someone, especially if—"

"I'm dying. No, I don't need anyone."

"But, Zeke..."

"He would do everything and anything. He would move mountains trying to find doctors to save me. He would sacrifice everything to be with me. I don't want that."

"There has to be someone you want by your side," I say.

"There was, but I broke up with her."

"Her?"

"Yes, I'm bisexual. I fell in love with a woman after Zeke. Maybe no man could ever compare to Zeke, so I never even tried to love a man again. I don't know. No, that isn't true. I just love who I love. And I love Palmer. But I can't be with her in the end. I won't let anyone watch me die."

"Lucy, that's not fair. Does she know?"

"Yes, and she was more than happy to be let off the hook to take care of me," Lucy says.

I take her hand as the tears fall from both of our eyes.

Fuck.

Life isn't fair.

Love isn't fair.

Lucy loved two people in her life. But neither love was enough to last, not even to the end of her short life.

"I can be here, if you want."

Lucy shakes her head. "No, I don't want that. I want my solitude. But I want to die, here, alone. Not suffering. Not letting anyone else see my pain. I want to be pampered and spend my money how I want. I want to live the rest of my days in paradise."

"Whatever you want. I understand," I say.

She nods.

"Can I ask you one thing?" I ask.

"You can ask me whatever you want. It doesn't mean I'll answer."

I smile at that. "Do you still love Zeke?"

Lucy's bottom lip quivers, and she looks down to the beach where Zeke is standing, pensively looking out at the ocean. The ocean is where he belongs. I've never seen him on the ocean when he was whole and not hurt or trying to stay alive, but I know the ocean still calls to him.

"Yes, how could I not love him?"

I suck in a breath. *Love is so not fair.*

"But he loves you more," Lucy continues. "I won't take him away from you. Even when I'm dying. I don't want to take him from you."

"It doesn't matter who he loves more. He protects everyone he loves. And he loves you. His love for you is different than his love for me. Just like his love for Enzo and his family is different. It makes no difference the level of his love. He protects us all the same." I squeeze her hand in reassurance that if she wants Zeke's help, she's got it. No matter what.

Zeke's good at protecting. He just compartmentalizes all of us, keeping us separate. It makes it easier for him to protect us. He never has to choose who deserves to be saved. He just saves us.

"You should tell him. He deserves to know the truth," I say.

"You deserve the truth, too," Lucy says.

I suck in a breath. "Maybe, but he has to be the one to tell me the truth. I want the truth, but only if he's willing to give it. I don't want to hear you tell his truth."

"I know. I wasn't suggesting I tell you what Zeke won't. Just know that he will. He'll open up to you someday, because you're wrong. He doesn't treat us all the same. One day, he'll have to choose. And he'll choose you."

"What do you want me to do?" I ask.

"Tell Zeke you think I'll be safe here. I didn't hire idiots. I had Jayden hire the team—a team he said you would approve of."

"Okay."

"Convince Zeke to leave. To fight like he always does."

"What will you do?"

"I'll live and keep fighting until my dying breath. Whether it be cancer or a bullet that kills me, it makes no difference."

I nod. "I'll honor your wishes for as long as I can. But if Zeke asks, if he suspects you're sick, I won't lie for you. I'll tell him the truth."

She squeezes my hand. "I'm counting on it."

We both stand, looking out at the ocean with tears in our eyes. *Who knew that we would be like this?* Not friends, but more. We share a connection. We share a love. I don't know how we could get any closer to each other.

The vibration of my phone breaks the beautiful moment.

I walk into the hallway to take the call, letting Lucy have her moment of solitude.

"Yes?" I answer, already knowing who's calling me.

"I want him back here. I have a task for him," Julian says.

I hang up, not answering him. *Shit, shit, shit.*

I slump to the floor as I cry. For Lucy. For Zeke. For me.

Love really isn't fair.

CHAPTER 18
ZEKE

I'm sitting on a wicker chair on one of the six balconies this house has. *Six!* It's ridiculous. It's huge, beautiful, and so Lucy. But that doesn't mean that I understand why she's risking her life to live in this beautiful house. She should hide out for a few weeks and then buy something like this when it's safe.

Nora sits in a wicker chair to my left. Siren sits across from me, not looking at me.

Nora is the first to break the silence. "I called this meeting to discuss our next plans. Siren would like you to know she's interviewed all of the security team and staff, and she thinks this is the best place for Lucy."

"Bullshit," I say, looking at Siren. She doesn't look up at me.

"Siren would also like you to know that Lucy is giving you her bank account to spend as you see fit."

"I'm not taking Lucy's money. I'll tell her that myself," I grumble.

Nora sighs. "Siren would also like you to know that Julian called. He wants her to bring you back."

"What else does Siren want me to know? Does she want to suck my dick? Ready to spread her pretty legs for me? Or is she planning on slitting my throat in my sleep? Tell me, Nora, since you speak for Siren."

Nora frowns. Siren doesn't react.

"Siren would like to discuss how to handle Julian. She thinks it's a good idea to go back. To see what he's up to, and devise a plan to kill him. You have too many enemies right now. It's time to eliminate one."

I growl. "I'm not talking to you through Nora, Siren. That's not what's fucking happening. If you want to talk to me, you talk to me. Understand?"

Siren doesn't react. She doesn't look at me. She doesn't speak.

"I get it. You're pissed I won't tell you the truth. Well, I'm pissed you won't tell me what's up with Lucy. We both know this is the worst place for her to be. Bishop and his men will find her in a heartbeat, and then everything we've been through, losing Dylan, will be for nothing."

Nothing. I get fucking nothing out of her.

"I'll arrange flights back to St. Kitts," Nora says. "Should we fly commercial or private again? I don't mind flying, but I need some rest first."

"Nora, can you give Siren and me a minute alone? As for flights, don't worry about them. We aren't going anywhere until Siren talks to me. She's stubborn, so it could be years before I crack her." I stand up and feel Nora's eyes on me. But Nora's eyes aren't whose I care about. I lean forward and whisper in Siren's ear. "I'm counting on it taking at least a couple hours. Three to be exact. Three hours to break you into talking to me. And I'm going to love every second of it."

Nora leaves, and I grab Siren's hand. She tries to pull away, acting like her hand just touched a hot stove she can't get away from fast enough. Not like it's me, who her body craves to touch, with every part of her being.

I yank her up and sit down on her chair, forcing her down onto my lap. Her hands start fighting against me like I knew they would. There is no passion behind her fighting; she isn't really trying to get me to stop holding her. She just wants to be left alone to stoop and be angry.

Not happening.

"I can't tell you Lucy's secret," I start, hoping she will at least hear my words, and they will spark a fire in her body.

I feel her body heat up, and her core twitch as she sits on my lap, dying to fight me. To hurt me. To show me how much I hurt her by not telling her.

There's my girl. Fight me. Show me you care.

"I can't tell you Lucy's secret because it will put you in danger. If Bishop and his men found out you knew Lucy's secret, they would be after you the same way they're after her. They'll try to torture you to get you to spill the information."

I grab her chin, turning her head to look at me, to see how much I care.

"I'm not hiding the truth from you because I don't trust you. I'm not hiding the truth because I think you will use it to hurt Lucy. I'm not telling you the truth to protect you."

She pushes my hands away, still not putting much energy into the motion.

"I'm sorry, Siren. So fucking sorry," I say, my words filled with all the conflict I feel.

She turns her head, but I snap it back.

"I'm sorry," I say again with everything I have in me. Finally, I see it. I see her break just a little. The hard shell she put up now has a crack in it. I plan on pushing my way through until she lets me all the way in and doesn't let me back out again—ever.

She slaps me.

It stings, but more because it's a surprise move than an actual shock to my face. The redness will leave in less than a minute, the pain I won't feel after a second. It's just not Siren's style. She's not a slapper; she's a puncher.

She doesn't want to fight. She wants to hide away. That's the only way she thinks she can keep her heart safe from me.

After watching a man die, a man who was too young, I'm tired of waiting. I'm tired of not fighting for what I want. And I want Siren —forever.

"I'm sorry," I say again. Then my lips capture hers, tasting their soft deliciousness.

She pulls back and gives my chest a hard shove. She stands, but I grab her wrist, jerking her back to me.

This time, she punches me in the jaw.

I let go of her hand as I see stars for a second, but I can't wipe the smile off my face. She's pissed. That's a good sign. It means I'm winning. It means I'm getting under her skin. It means she still cares.

I move my jaw side to side, trying to loosen the pain, and then I chase after her. She's only made it into the kitchen when I reach her.

"Siren!" I yell, my voice is gravelly and deep. My voice hits her deep and lands right between her legs. I'm not just saying I'm sorry. I'm saying I love you. I want to make it up to you. Let me love you.

She gives me a stern warning to stay away with her tightened eyes and a clenched jaw.

I smile at her reaction. It's exactly what I want. If I can't get her to admit that she still loves me, then I want her to hate me. Her hating me is the same as her loving me. The only difference is that when she hates me, it's only because she's trying to protect herself. She's trying to push me away to protect us both.

Not going to happen. Not again.

I walk over to her. To my surprise, she doesn't run. I figured I'd have to chase her across half the property. But then I see why she's not running. Lucy is standing in the kitchen, fixing herself a peanut butter sandwich.

"Lucy," my voice is a warning.

"Yes?" Lucy answers. One sassy word used to be able to put me on my knees when it came to this woman. I would do whatever she wanted. Not anymore.

I love Lucy, yes. But not like I love Siren. Not anywhere near what I feel for her. Right now, this isn't about Lucy. This is all about Siren.

I walk over to Siren, who is standing next to Lucy. The two women exchange glances, and the look runs deep, to a level of understanding that only women who have been best friends for years typically share. Something happened between the two of them. Something brought them closer, possibly even closer than I am to Lucy.

I don't care about that right now. I only care about Siren. I round the island they are standing at, and box Siren in with my hands. I don't touch her, but it's clear that I'm about to.

She growls. It's the first sound she's made. It's not a word, but it's the first step to her telling me off. I'll take it.

"Lucy, could you give Siren and I some privacy?"

Lucy laughs. "This is my house. You can't order me out of my own kitchen. If you want privacy, go to a bedroom."

"Oh, we will. But not yet," I say, my voice full of threats.

Lucy takes her time finishing the sandwich, which is just fine with me. It gives me more time to watch Siren sweat. More time for her anger to stew. More time for her to get riled up and ready to fight back.

Finally, Lucy walks over to me, holding the last bite of sandwich in one hand.

"Don't hurt her." She slaps me hard across the face.

"What the hell was that for?" I ask.

Lucy looks from me to Siren. "You fucked up. You deserved to be slapped, although I'm sure Siren can more than make you pay for what you did to her. That's for hurting my friend. Don't do it again."

Then Lucy walks away.

Yea, these two definitely got close, and I don't understand how. I mean, I love them both. I would love them both to be able to be in my life, but the fact that they've become friends so quickly is suspicious.

I eye Siren, but I only get one shot at getting her to talk to me. As much as I'm curious about what brought on their friendship, I care more about getting Siren to talk about us.

"I'm sorry," I say the words again that I know will cut deepest.

Siren shakes her head, trying to keep from being affected. With us, it's impossible not to feel everything the other is feeling.

I grab her hips, pulling her to me. Her hands go on top of mine, her nails dig into them, making it as hard as possible for me to hold onto her body. I don't care about the pain. I care about her. I would hold her close to me, feeling our hips pressed together, even if there were a thousand knives being driven into me at the same time.

"Fight me, Siren. Tell me how wrong I was. Tell me what I did was wrong. Tell me how you hate me for hurting you," I say, taunting her.

She just digs her nails in deeper into my hands, until I suspect she's drawing blood.

I tilt my head, leaning down. "Kiss me."

She shakes her head.

"You know you want to. Kiss me."

She growls.

I grin, moving my lips over hers.

She bites her lip, trying to keep it from me.

"I'm so sorry, Siren. I hate hurting you." I slide my hands up her body, while her hands try to push me down. I kiss her, but she doesn't push me away immediately. She doesn't kiss me back, either. She simply lets me explore her mouth. She lets me massage her tongue with my own. She lets me moan into her mouth.

Quickly, she grabs my balls and tightens her grip so tight I'm afraid she's going to rip them off.

Her eyes raise, challenging me to touch her again and have her rip my balls off.

"Tell me to stop, and I'll stop. Your body is telling me to bend you over the counter right now and fuck you."

She narrows her eyes, calling bullshit.

I smirk, careful not to move because she does have my balls in her fist. As much as I love her down there, I'd prefer her to be more level headed when she's touching me.

"I guarantee if I dipped my hand beneath your panties right now, they'd be wet." I glance down. "Your nipples are peaked on your beautiful breasts."

Her eyes drop, noticing what I can see so clearly beneath her white shirt. "Your lips are plump, pink, and wet, begging me to kiss you. You can hate me. You can be mad at me. Talk to me. Get it all out. Then we can have the best makeup sex of our lives."

She shakes her head.

"No? You don't want to kiss me?"

She releases me, her fire dimming. She's telling me to leave her alone. She doesn't want to talk. Not about us. Only about whatever plan she has to take down Julian.

But I don't give a shit about Julian right now. Not when she's hurting. Not when I'm failing her.

"Fine, you don't want me to kiss you, then I'll leave. I'll make sure Lucy is safe, and then I'll disappear out of your life forever."

I release her, and take a step back, calling her bluff.

I look up the stairs to where Lucy went. *Can I really leave Siren? No.*

But Siren can't handle me leaving either.

I take a step toward the stairs, and she flings herself at me. Her arms go around my neck, her lips press against mine, and my erection presses hard into her crotch.

The kiss knocks me back, to the opposite side of the kitchen into the counter behind me. I should have taken her to the bedroom. I really miss fucking her in a bed. But I don't think either of us can make it up to the bedroom right now.

Her kisses are hungry and aggressive; she uses her teeth as much as her tongue with every kiss. I give her the sharp points of my teeth right back.

We go bite for bite, nibble for nibble. Drawing the taste of blood on each other's lips.

Our teeth aren't the only thing drawing blood. Our nails claw into each other's backs.

I grab her shirt, ripping it from her body.

She does the same to mine, our shirts flung to the floor and ripped to shreds.

"Don't ever wear a bra again," I say, staring down at her gorgeous breasts.

She responds by biting down on my earlobe.

I push Siren back until her ass is shoved into the counter.

She smirks, goading me on.

"Oh no, my love, I'm about to give you so much more," I say.

I grab her jeans, unbuttoning and unzipping, yanking them down her body. My hand disappears beneath her panties a second later, and just as I knew they would be, they are soaked.

"You can pretend you don't want me all you want, but your body will never lie to me."

There is a storm brewing in her eyes as she grips the counter while my fingers circle her clit. She lets me. She lets herself feel how good it feels.

It doesn't matter that we are in the middle of a kitchen that more than a dozen people could walk into at any moment. Siren may not be talking, but she's groaning loudly enough to send a warning to everyone to stay the fuck away.

As if a timer goes off in her head, Siren only lets herself enjoy the moment for a minute. Then she's grabbing my jeans, shoving them over my hips, and searching for what she needs beneath my boxers. She grabs me roughly, taking all of me in her hand with desperation in her eyes.

We both tease and taunt each other with our hands; our mouths go to work devouring each other. It's not enough, not nearly enough. I need all of her. I need to be inside her. And she needs me there. We both need each other.

I bend her over the counter, her ass in the air, my cock pressing between her legs at her slick entrance. Her body is so damn ready for me. If only her mind and heart would get there just as fast. I push, but she pushes back.

"Enough," she says, turning and pushing me from her body.

We are both standing bare naked in the kitchen in front of each other. Panting, wet, and smelling like the sex we never finished. Both bleeding from our lips and back. Both bruised from where our hands touched each other too hard.

I want to fuck her. Make love to her. But I got her to speak. And her words are what I needed more.

I'm quiet, begging her to talk.

"You hurt me, Zeke. I'm tired of being hurt. You aren't the only one hiding a secret. I'm hiding secrets too. And I hate it!" Her voice breaks, her bottom lip trembles, and a tear drips from the corner of her eye.

"I'm tired of hiding every truth. Even if I'm doing it to protect you. I'm tired of carrying that burden alone. I'm so tired, Zeke."

Dammit.

"I love you isn't enough. Choosing me over everyone isn't enough. We will always have to hide the truth. Hurt each other. Go it alone in order to protect each other." Siren takes a step toward me. Each step is strengthening her as she finds her voice. Her words. Her truth.

"What are we doing together, Zeke? Loving each other isn't enough. We will never settle down. We will never get married. We will never have kids."

My heart clenches. *Damn, do I want all those things with her.* I want to get down on one knee right now and propose with the biggest ring I can find. But how can two people be married when all they do is lie and hide the truth? Even if we could find a way, I don't have a dime to buy even the smallest of rings.

"It's a sin to keep the truth from you, a man I wish was my husband. And yet, I have to keep committing the sin over and over. And you have to do the same."

She grips her stomach. "Jesus, what I wouldn't give to have your baby inside me. To be growing a life you and I started. But we can never even discuss the topic because of the lives we chose."

I stare at her bare beautiful stomach, trying to imagine how incredible it would be to see her round and plump, my baby inside her. I can't think of anything better. *But how could we bring a baby into this world of danger?* I can barely keep Siren safe. *How could I keep a baby safe?*

"Our love story will end tragically. We should just end it now. End it before it really starts. End it before we hurt each other more than we already have," she says.

I hold her tear-stricken cheeks in my hands, rubbing the tears with my thumbs. Finally, I find my voice to help her understand what's inside of me.

"I don't know how our story ends. I don't know if I can propose marriage. I don't know about filling a house with babies. But I do know this—our love story will be the most powerful and epic of all time. We make sacrifices for the other no one else has to make for love. We are willing to give it all up—the chance to be married, have kids, live happily ever. We are willing to go through all the pain to love each other, however short it is. It all tells me that we love each other more than two people have ever loved each other. It tells me that our love story is going to be epic."

How could I ever give up this man?

This man would give up everything for me. This man is torn up inside at having to keep truths from me, but willing to carry that burden forever, because he loves me, and he can't stand to hurt me.

Most people wouldn't understand our love. Most wouldn't understand how what we are doing is love. But, I don't give a fuck about other people. This is our love story, dammit, even if we have to hide everything from each other—every truth, every lie, every sin. We will do it for love. We will fight for love. We will fight for someday in the future to be able to spill every truth we've ever learned.

"Sin," I say.

"What?"

"Sin. I can't tell you the truth. And neither can you. I think it's time to commit a sin."

"Oh, yea?" His brow raises.

"Yea."

He grabs me and throws me over his shoulder. He carries me up the stairs, heading into the first bedroom he can find.

We fall onto the bed together, naked, his cock settling between my thighs, and our mouths pressing against each other in broken kisses.

I feel his tip push at my entrance.

"Zeke," I say, pushing his lips back. My voice is soft and full of emotion.

"Yes?" he asks, his voice strained, trying to keep it together before he can take me in this bed.

"I haven't taken the pill. I left it in Lithuania," I say.

"Fuck," he curses. He looks around the room, begging to find a condom somewhere. He crawls up my body and reaches into the nightstand drawers, throwing each drawer open and slamming it shut in frustration when he doesn't find what he's looking for.

He takes a deep breath and then moves back onto his forearms, resting around my head as his cock still sits waiting impatiently at my entrance.

"Do you trust me?" he asks calmly.

I don't know what he's asking. *Do I trust him to take care of a baby if he gets me pregnant? Do I trust that he won't come inside me? What?*

"God, does it even matter? I just need you," I say, grabbing his hair and yanking his lips back down on my body.

He slides in as I greedily kiss his lips like I haven't kissed him in months.

In and out Zeke slides. Our bodies already so familiar with each other that we know exactly what the other wants. Desires. Needs.

I shift my hips as his hand glides under my ass, holding me up so he can drive deeper inside me.

My lips open wider, begging his tongue to come in deeper.

I need more.

Deeper.

Harder.

All of him.

He can't get deep enough inside me either.

"I can't promise you a traditional marriage," Zeke says, thrusting.

"I can't promise you the large diamond ring you deserve."

He pulls out, then pushes all the way in, filling me completely just like his words.

"I can't promise you, babies."

He kisses me as his body pushes me deeper, harder, longer.

"But I can promise you forever. I can promise to love you, to protect you with everything I have. Over everyone else in my life. You're first. You're it. You're everything. And I'll do everything in my power to make the ring, the wedding, the babies come true if that's what you want. I want everything for you, everything."

I don't want him to put me first. I don't want him to ever have to choose me over someone else he loves. Hopefully, it will never come to that. If it does, I won't let him keep that promise.

For now, it's what I need to hear.

"I promise you the same," I say.

"I love you."

"I love you, too."

All the built-up anger, frustration, and pain takes over at the same time that all the love, happiness, and joy hit me. It makes for one explosive orgasm.

Zeke pulls out and his cum coats my stomach. He collapses on top of me, not giving a damn that he's smearing his cum all over both of our bodies. We can't part yet. We need to stay connected.

Connected—it's how we fall asleep.

"Do you have it yet?" Bishop asks.

"Have what?"

He growls. "Lucy's weapon."

"What? Lucy's what?"

"Zeke knows. You need to get it from him, before someone else does."

I wake up in a sweat. From the nightmare or the big brute of a man on top of me.

I can't control my breathing. My tears. My voice.

Zeke wakes up instantly. He rolls off of me but pulls me close as he grabs a gun, assuming I'm worked up because there is a threat in the room. There is none.

When he realizes we're physically safe, he drops the gun and looks at me. He cups my face in his hand.

"Baby, I got you. It was just a nightmare. I got you; you're safe."

Safe.

There is no such thing as safe in my world.

Zeke rocks me in his arms, like I'm a child waking up needing to be coaxed back to sleep.

After several minutes pass, he asks, "Bishop?"

I don't answer. He already knows. I hate that he failed. That he didn't take the nightmares away. That I'm still in this pain. Still terrorized by a man whose actions I can't even remember.

"I'm scared," I say instead.

"Me too."

"We have too many enemies. We can't keep fighting from three different angles. It's too much."

Zeke nods. "Who do we go after first?"

"Julian Reed."

Zeke takes a deep breath and kisses my temple. "I agree."

"We need more people on our side. We're not—"

"We are plenty strong enough. But I agree, it's time to bring more people to our side."

"How? Who?"

"Let me worry about that. For now, we need to go face Julian. And we need to draw Bishop away from Lucy."

We are going to take down Julian Reed. I never thought the day would come. I never thought I'd be free. I'm still not sure it can be done, or if it's the right move.

I don't know who Julian is working with, where he got his money, or how many enemies we are going to make by taking him down. But I'm tired of living in fear. We are going to do this—together. Our love is strong enough to take down any enemy. Even the devil.

CHAPTER 20
ZEKE

We drive from the airport straight to Julian's. We have a plan. And a plan after that one and another plan after that one. We won't stop until he's dead. Not this time.

Julian Reed has too much power. Too much money. We have to eliminate him.

I stop my truck in front of Julian's house. We both climb out silently, and then I take Siren's hand as we walk into the house without knocking.

We are tired of pretending we don't care about each other. Tired of pretending that Siren is loyal to Julian. She isn't. I don't care what Julian is holding over her; we are about to end it.

"Remember, we have one shot. We have to do this now. We can't —" Siren says.

I turn to her, kissing her on the lips. "I know. We won't fail."

I won't fail. I will do whatever it takes to free her of Julian. And then I'll keep fighting until all of our enemies are dead. Until she is safe.

Of all our enemies, I don't know which man scares me the most.

Julian scares me because she's worked for him for so long. He's wealthy. And he's hiding too much shit.

Bishop scares me because somehow he got into her head and fucked it up. We both still don't know what he did and didn't do to her.

We walk into Julian's office. Siren texted him earlier today, so he should be expecting us. We find the whole house empty, except for a crackling conference speaker on Julian's desk. Julian's voice greets us as we enter his office.

"Oh, look at that. How sweet? Walking in here like you are on the same side. Like she's yours," Julian says. He must be watching us from the cameras on the ceiling.

"It's over, Julian. I'm not yours anymore. I never was. You're not even here to face me, you coward," Siren says.

"Hmm, I'm sure you believe that, Aria, but you've figured out how to lie now, so I'm not sure."

"I can't lie," she says.

Julian laughs. "You just did. Even if I were there in person, you wouldn't kill me," Julian says.

"You have no idea what I'm capable of, Julian," I threaten.

"I know how to stop Bishop from being in her head," he says.

Fuck...

"As I was saying, we are on round three of our little game. Keep playing, and I'll tell you how to rid Siren of Bishop. Truth or sin?"

"Sin," I say wearily.

"Get me a yacht."

I frown.

"Not just any yacht. The best," Julian says.

Fuck, he means an Enzo Black yacht. One of the yachts belonging to my best friend and former boss.

I pound my fist on the desk next to the speaker. "And when I bring you your damn yacht, you will tell me how to stop the voices in her head."

"When you finish all five rounds, I'll tell you."

"No, after this round."

"When you finish all five rounds, I'll tell you."

Goddammit.

I grab Siren's arm and pull her out of the room, desperate to finish this. Desperate to save her from all of our enemies. Desperate to ring Julian's neck with my bare hands. Desperate to keep the love I just found.

CHAPTER 21
SIREN

I punch Zeke in the shoulder, but it barely moves him as we step outside of Julian's house.

"Ow, what was that for?" Zeke grumbles, rubbing his bicep like I just shot him there.

I roll my eyes. "You know exactly what that was for. You didn't even fight. You didn't even try. That was our chance! Our chance to take down Julian Reed forever," my lip trembles as I speak, and my voice drops out.

I blink rapidly as my brain becomes overtaken by men. So many damn men in my head.

Kill him, Bishop says.

You will never get free, Julian says.

You're mine, Zeke says.

"Stop!" I yell, squeezing my head, trying to get the fucking voices to stop.

"Siren, baby, take a deep breath. I got you."

I hear Zeke's words, but I don't register them. I'm lost to the fog that is my brain. The voices are going to haunt me forever. Long after the men are gone, the voices are still going to be with me. Threatening me. Telling me what to do. Trying to control me.

I fall to my knees, shaking viciously. "Get out of my head!"

Zeke holds me, for a long time. We just sit on the driveway in front of Zeke's truck. It isn't safe here. We shouldn't stay at Julian's for a second longer than we need to. But neither of us care.

I need Zeke to hold me. I need to feel safe. I need to feel protected, even if I'm not. Bishop fucked with my head. His voice was one too many. It was bad enough to hear them when I was dreaming, but now I hear them everywhere I go.

Finally, I stop shaking, and Zeke lifts me up and puts me in the truck. Then he climbs into the driver's seat and drives us away.

"This is why I made the deal. You can't live like this. You need help. We need help. Doctors aren't going to be enough to save you," Zeke says.

I frown. Hating that he's right, but he is. He's fucking right. Whatever Bishop did to me goes beyond normal medicine.

"I'm going crazy," I say.

Zeke takes my hand in his large palm and kisses the back of my hand. "You're not crazy. But I don't want you alone. Not anymore. Promise me?"

I nod.

I shake my head, like that will somehow clear my thoughts of the voices. *Just start talking, think about something else, that will help.*

"Where are we going?" I ask.

"To the airport. And then, Miami."

"Miami?"

Zeke nods slowly.

"Are we going to meet..." I can't finish the sentence; I'm in too much shock.

"Yes, I'm taking you to meet my family," Zeke says, referring to his former boss, his friends, his life before I saved him.

I suck in a breath. I've wanted nothing more for months now, ever since I saved Zeke, and Julian put me to task to learn who Enzo Black is. I've wanted nothing more since I fell in love with Zeke and wanted to learn and know everyone he loves. Zeke has already met everyone in my life. It's pathetic, but I only have one true friend. A dead ex-husband. Dead parents. And a sociopath trying to control my life.

Zeke may have also come from the underground, criminal world, but he had friends, family, a life he loved. I don't know much about Zeke. I don't know what kind of house he would choose to live in. I don't know his favorite foods or movies. I don't know if he prefers pop or rap or hip-hop music. Or if he's a secret country music lover. I don't know anything about his life before. Not really. I know he's good with a gun. I know he protects his people with his life. But I don't know what he loved outside of people.

"Hey," Zeke says softly, his finger slipping under my chin to look up at him.

"You have nothing to worry about. They are going to love you," Zeke says.

I pick at my nails. "I'm worried about Julian or Bishop or someone following. I hate that I'm the reason you have enemies. And we're bringing our enemies to them."

Zeke nods. "I know. I feel like I failed. But we are out of options. We both agree we need help. This is how we get it. These are the best people I know. They are strong and smart. We will win. Trust me."

Zeke looks out the windshield again. "Nora can't come with. I don't want more people involved than need to be."

"I agree. If she knows about your friends, then Julian could torture her. I don't want that."

"Good."

I exhale an exhausted breath. "Maybe I shouldn't come either."

Zeke's eyes go to me like a moth to a flame, not caring about the road in front of him. "Why?"

"Because I've fucked up. I've hurt you. You shouldn't trust me."

"Are you going to betray my friends to Julian?"

"Only if I have to in order to save your life," I answer honestly. The only way I would ever betray his friends would be to save him.

He looks at me with disappointment in his gorgeous dark eyes. He runs his hand through his hair, full of desperation. "You can't do that, Siren. You have to protect them. Put them ahead of me."

"I can't. That's why I should stay."

Zeke considers for a second. "I can't leave you."

"Why?"

"Because Julian or Bishop will come. They will kidnap you. They will..." Zeke looks at me, and I see the moisture in his eyes, I see his knuckles turn white as he grips the steering wheel, I see the vein in his neck bulge, and I see his face redden.

"Promise me you will consider all the options before you ever hurt my friends. Everything you can think of if you have to choose between them and me. Promise me you will try, as if they were your own friends."

I take his hand gently in my hand and stroke his arm, trying to calm him down. "Of course, Zeke. If I ever have to choose, I'll protect them with my life. But if it comes to saving you or protecting someone else, I will always choose you. I love you."

"I love you too," he says. We drive the rest of the way to the airport in silence. We fly in silence. The silence gives me too much time to think.

A voice in my head says, *"He never said he'd choose you over everyone else. If it comes down to you and them, he'll pick them."*

For once, that voice wasn't Julian's or Bishop's or Zeke's. That voice was mine.

♡

I HAVE BUTTERFLIES IN MY STOMACH. ENORMOUS, GIANT WINGED butterflies that have migrated from my stomach to my chest and throat. I can't ever remember being so nervous before. I don't get nervous.

I'm unshakable. I'm strong. I fight back. But right now, I'm anxious, nervous, all the stress-inducing words.

We're riding in the back of a cab headed to meet Zeke's family. Not his blood family—those people deserted him years ago. Just like me, he's an orphan. But unlike me, he has more than one person in the world who cares about him.

The cab makes a stop in front of a popular pier lined with boat after boat. Most are huge yachts. *Holy shit*, I think, staring up at the giant things. I've been around boats. I've borrowed plenty of Julian's living on the island. But I've never seen anything as impressive as this.

"Ready?" Zeke asks.

I nod, knowing I won't be able to speak, so I don't even try.

We both climb out after I pay for the cab. Lucy put money into Zeke's account after a long fight between the two of them, but he won't spend it unless it's an emergency. Although, he winces when he watches me pay, hating that he's making me spend my money.

"I'll get a job. I'll wait tables, tend bar, something—"

"Zeke, I have a million dollars in my bank account. I can afford to pay for a cab ride. I understand why you don't want to spend Lucy's money. And no, you aren't working as a waiter. We are going to take out our enemies, and then you can return to whatever life you want. Whatever you did to earn your millions before."

"You mean killing people?"

Now I wince. I sigh. We have a lot to talk about.

Right now, neither of us can think about our future. All we can think about is today. All we can do is focus on survival. Once we survive, then we can figure out our shit. Then we can pay for all the sins we have both committed and decide if that is still the life we want.

Zeke takes my hand silently.

We walk down the pier, past boat after boat, yacht after yacht. He turns left then right, zigging through the maze of boats, apparently knowing exactly where we are going.

"Did you call Mr. Black to let him know we are coming?" I ask, my voice catching in my throat.

Zeke stops abruptly. "Did you just call Enzo Mr. Black?"

"Um...yea?"

Zeke laughs and then kisses my forehead sweetly. "Stop being nervous. You have nothing to be nervous about. And don't call Enzo Mr. Black. He's family."

Family. These people are part of Zeke's family. Unlike me. *What am I?*

His lover?

His girlfriend?

His almost fiancée?

The woman who betrayed him?

We've never put a label on it. Suddenly, my heart is fluttering, my world is spinning, and I have no idea how to make it stop.

We keep walking, until finally, Zeke stops. I feel his pulse in his hand. I look up. He's biting his bottom lip and running his other hand through his hair. It never occurred to me that Zeke would be nervous.

Other than a possible brief encounter before, he hasn't seen them in months. I don't know if he's scared they will be angry at him for making them believe he was dead all this time or what.

But I squeeze his hand, doing my best to reassure him.

And then Zeke jumps onto the yacht. He motions with his head for me to follow. There is a ramp a few feet down, but fuck that.

I jump over just as Zeke did. The exhilaration of jumping tampers the anxiety in my chest.

Zeke winks at me with a smile, and my heart melts. *How did I get a guy like him to fall for me?* I would experience everything dark in my life again just to have a moment where he loves me.

"Stingray," Zeke says the word like a prayer. Like he doesn't believe his own eyes, if this moment is real. The tears in his eyes are real.

I follow Zeke's gaze, not having a clue who stingray is. I gasp when I see her.

The woman I saw before in the ballroom. She's here, and she's just as beautiful as before. She's in dark jeans and a gray shirt that forms over her flat stomach and breasts. Her hair is almost jet-black, shiny, and straight. She has it tied back in a red bandana. The most captivating thing about her is her eyes. They are a piercing green-blue color, like the ocean. She belongs to the ocean.

Zeke quickly lets go of my hand, like he's completely forgotten I was here. The two run to each other.

I've seen Zeke's reunion with a long-lost love before. I saw him greet Lucy and that was painful. But it was nothing compared to this reunion.

This reunion is giving me all the feels. Jealousy at seeing Zeke wrap his arms around this woman in a hug tighter than any he's ever given me. Rage at his cute nickname for her, while me, he still calls Siren to remind himself of what I've done to him. Pain at seeing the tears flow down the woman's cheeks as she holds onto his neck like she can't bear to ever let him go. And love—so much damn love as they hold each other like lovers who just survived a war.

Unlike when I watched Lucy interact with Zeke for the first time, this is different. With Lucy, it was like two lovers and friends catching up, but with Zeke and this woman, it's like they are both part of the same soul that has been split between two bodies and is finally reconnected again.

I've never seen anything so beautiful. I've never seen such love between two people before that doesn't feel anything like romance. They aren't kissing. Their hands aren't moving up and down each other's bodies, trying to cop a feel. All they want is the hug—the closeness. The connection they've both been missing for so damn long.

Zeke pulls back so he can look into her eyes. "I'm so sorry," he says through his tears.

"You have nothing to be sorry for," she says through her own tears.

"For letting you think I was dead. For only telling you that I was alive and not letting you tell anyone else. For not running to you that night in the ballroom. I was too scared of bringing danger into your life again, but I'm afraid I did just that."

The woman holds his hand. I stare at the connection. Not romantic, not like what Zeke and I have. But something just as strong. Surprisingly, I don't feel jealousy over the connection, although I don't understand why.

A voice behind me startles me. "I don't understand it either. Sometimes I think his connection to her is stronger than mine, and I'm married to her. I've died for her. But I don't feel jealous when I see them together. All I feel is love."

I stare at him, realizing he must be Enzo Black. The woman is his wife.

I nod. "Love is more than just romance. It just is."

"I would never deny her love by any man, least of all him," Enzo says.

Our voices carry, getting their attention. This reunion just got bigger.

CHAPTER 22
KAI

Zeke's alive.

He's here.

My heart is whole.

I didn't realize until I had him back in my arms again how much I was hurting, how broken I truly was.

I knew Zeke was alive.

I'd even seen it with my own eyes.

But this...this is what I needed.

I needed him back.

In my life, permanently.

I don't care what enemies are following him. I don't care why he left us for over a year. *He's back.*

And no matter what, I'm not letting him go again.

I love him. I'm not in love with him. I have a perfectly incredible husband. But Zeke is part of my soul. When he called me stingray, the nickname that everyone who knows me has adapted because of him, I lost myself. At the same time, I found myself. I became whole.

I will do everything in my power to keep my heart full. I don't let people I love go. Zeke's here. I'm ready to fight for him.

I spot the woman behind him. A woman who I hope loves him as much, if not more, than I do. Zeke deserves that kind of love. And I won't let him settle for anything less.

Zeke's alive.

I have no fucking idea how.

How the hell did he survive getting shot and falling into the middle of the fucking ocean?

Not a clue.

But he's here.

Standing on my boat.

Hugging my beautiful wife, who has so many tears in her eyes. Tears she cries for him and only him. A love between them I will never understand.

I let them have their moment. But that moment seems to last forever.

Then I see I'm not the only one watching the exchange. A woman stands a few feet in front of me, staring with heartache in her eyes.

This woman loves Zeke. I'm not sure if she understands their connection isn't a romantic one. If it was, Zeke really would be dead. But when I approach and see this woman's tears up close, I realize she can see what their connection really is, the same as me.

So I speak, reassuring her that she's right, while I try to make sense of what I'm seeing. *I didn't stay up too late last night with the twins, did I?* This is really happening, Zeke is really here.

Then my wife, Kai, spots me. She winks at me.

"Bastard," I curse under my breath.

The woman looks up at me questioningly, but I don't answer her.

My wife knew. Kai knew Zeke was alive this whole damn time. She's known and kept the secret to herself. I'm going to kill them both.

But first, I want a damn hug from one of my best friends who I thought was dead for over a year.

I clear my throat. "Get a room."

Zeke turns. "Jesus fucking christ."

I don't know who moves toward who, but I'm in his arms, being lifted up in the air. I'm a big man, but I have nothing on Zeke. Zeke is a monster of muscles. I'm just ripped.

Zeke is one of the only men I could fight one and one without weapons and probably lose to. I'm man enough to admit it, though.

"You're alive," I whisper, as I find I'm choked up.

"Clearly," Zeke tries to joke with me, but it doesn't work. I'm bawling worse than my twins.

Zeke puts me down, and I pull him into a normal hug, full of tears and pain and open wounds.

"You bastard," I finally say, hitting him hard on the back. "If you're alive, you're supposed to let a man know. Not make me think you're dead for over a year."

"I did let someone know," Zeke winks at Kai, and grips her hand again.

I sigh, knowing I won't be getting any alone time with my wife for days while these two catch up like chatty women. But I'm smiling. It's been a long time since I've seen Kai smile like this—truly letting her smile reach her eyes. Now that Zeke is back, she will be smiling a lot more.

All of our tears finally stop, enough for Zeke to realize he's been an idiot and hasn't introduced us to the woman he brought with him.

Zeke smiles brightly, though, like he didn't just fuck up. He's a guy and doesn't see that he's hurt the girl a little bit by taking so long to introduce us to her. But his damn smile is infectious, and even the woman is smiling as she walks over to us.

"That was some reunion," she says, wiping her eyes with a nervous grin.

I study the woman closer now, trying to make an initial assessment before Zeke or her say anything.

The woman is beautiful in a mysterious, take no bullshit kind of way. She reminds me of Kai in that sense. She's thin, tall, and her muscles are visible beneath her shirt. Her hair is lighter than Kai's, but just as long.

Zeke reaches out, grabbing her hand so he can pull her to him. Then I see it—the gun at her back.

I raise my brows at Zeke, asking about the gun. *Did he teach her like he taught Kai?*

He smirks, declaring that question ridiculous.

Interesting.

This woman is a fighter. She grew up in this world. She might be more like me than my wife, after all.

"Let me make some introductions," Zeke starts. "This is Kai Miller, also known as Stingray. She's—"

"Actually, it's Kai Black," I interrupt. "But continue."

Zeke grabs Kai's hand, finding the ring and the scrunchie she often wears to remember him.

"Sorry, this is Kai Black," Zeke says, not surprised at all that we are married. "Kai is one of my best friends in the whole world. Kai, this is..." Zeke hesitates for a second, looking down at the woman.

The woman just snickers. "Really? You're going to look to me to give you the answer?"

Zeke laughs at her snarky words. I like her already. Although, I have no idea why he hesitated when saying her name. Maybe he doesn't know how to introduce her to us. They haven't had *the talk* yet.

"Kai, this is Siren Aria Torres. But I just call her Siren. Siren is my girlfriend by title, but so much more belongs to her. She's the love of my life, my everything, my forever. She's the only woman I can ever imagine as my wife, mother of my kids, etcetera, etcetera. She's everything I ever wanted. And I'm completely embarrassing her right now, but I don't care," Zeke leans down and kisses a blushing Siren on the cheek.

Siren holds out her hand to Kai.

Kai takes it and pulls her into a hug. It instantly feels like they just became sisters.

Zeke and I look away, giving the two a private moment.

"I'm so glad he found you. I was afraid I was going to be the love of his life forever, and that just won't do," Kai says.

"I'm glad he has you. Trust me, he's needed you. I'm not always the best thing for him," Siren answers.

Kai chuckles. "I'm not either. But Zeke's life would be boring if he had perfect women in his life."

Dammit, I have a tear in my eye again. I wipe it quickly.

"Now that the hard introduction is out of the way, Siren, this is Enzo Black. My best friend since birth, boss, and all-around reason I am the man I am," Zeke says.

I hug Siren. It feels like the right thing to do even though I'm not much of a hugger.

"It's so nice to meet Zeke's family," Siren says.

"It's nice to meet the woman he loves," I answer.

She nods in agreement. Zeke pulls her to him, wrapping his arms around her chest protectively. It's such a weird thing to see. I've known Zeke all my life, but I've never seen him in a serious relationship. Sure, he's brought women around, but not very often, and never in a relationship kind of way.

If he ever had a girlfriend, he never told me. I don't know what he's been up to this last year, but he's happy. He's in love. And that makes me happy.

"Where is Langston? Liesel?" Zeke asks, looking for them both.

Kai and I both frown, exchanging glances.

"We have a lot to talk about," Kai says.

Zeke nods. "Us too."

Zeke thinks a moment. "Can we take the yacht out for a few hours? I think that would be the safest way to talk."

We all nod in agreement. As much as I'm glad that Zeke is back, I'm going to kick his ass for bringing danger to my doorstep.

CHAPTER 24
ZEKE

I don't feel like I'm ever going to stop crying or smiling. Or laughing or hugging. Or jumping for fucking joy.

This day seemed like it would never come. I thought I'd never see my friends, my family in every sense of the word, again. When I was floating in the water, about to drown, I thought that was it. I thought my life was over. I thought I was dead.

Even when Siren saved me, I thought I'd never survive to see them. And then I did survive, but I thought I would never get rid of the danger in order to go to them. But I have no choice, not anymore.

I grip Siren's hand. I'm too afraid of what Bishop did to her. He fucked with her head. I don't know what his endgame is. *How far did he go? How much control does he have?*

I have to save her. I can't live without her. And I know now, seeing Kai and Enzo again, that they are strong enough to fight. Of course, they welcomed any woman I love in with open arms. Siren is now part of the family, and they will do anything and everything to protect her.

"Come on, let's get this boat somewhere safe," Enzo says, patting me on the shoulder like he still can't believe I'm here.

I can't believe it either.

"You do remember how to do your job, right? Because I expect you to get back to work ASAP," Enzo teases.

"Absolutely," I say. *God, would I love to be back in this world.* As much as I want that right now, I can't stay. I just need their help. I'll minimize the risk to them as much as I can.

"Hey now, who's the real boss around here?" Kai's eyes light up.

I laugh, knowing full well these two can fight all they want about who is in charge. In the company or in their relationship, they are complete equals. That's why the relationship and company work so well.

Siren's eyes light up watching them. She's mesmerized when she sees Enzo pinch Kai's ass, then dip her before she pinches him right back, and they skip off to float us away from land.

"I like them. Why again haven't you introduced us before?" Siren asks.

I grin. "Help me with the ropes."

We both undo the ropes keeping us tied to the dock, and then I lift up the ramp. I guide Siren to the front of the yacht, put her in front of me, and glide my hands down to her hips, holding her back against my front as we move away from the Miami shoreline and out into the ocean.

"Welcome to my world," I whisper in her ear.

"It's heaven," she says back.

"I know. I could live on a yacht forever. I basically did when I worked for Enzo."

"I never want to leave," Siren says, and I'm not sure if she means the yacht or my arms as she pulls me around her waist.

I rest my head on her shoulder. *I never want to leave either.*

"Hey, lovebirds. I made Italian food and got out the good wine. You in?" Enzo shouts, leaning against the doorway that leads inside to what I know is the kitchen area.

"Can we eat out here?" Siren asks, looking hopeful as the sun sets.

"Where else would we eat?" Enzo smiles back.

"This is one of the most incredible boats I've ever been on," Siren says. Enzo heads back inside to start bringing out the food and wine.

It's just us, no cooks, or other employees on board. That's what's safest.

Siren runs her hands over the railing, amazed at the incredible piece of machinery.

I laugh. "It's pretty impressive, isn't it?"

I wiggle my eyebrows when she looks at me, and I glance down to my growing erection.

She just rolls her eyes at me.

"No sex jokes," Enzo says sternly as he carries out two large platters of food.

"Yea, because we aren't ever crass on this boat," Kai says, carrying wine glasses and a bottle of wine under her arm. She leans over to Siren. "It's nice having another woman on the boat. I usually hang out with a dozen men. I've tried to hire more women, but I've found that most women don't want to be away from their families for months at end if we have to be out at sea."

Siren smiles. "Here, let me help you." Siren takes the wine glasses from Kai and sets them on the table. We all take a seat, while Kai pours us glasses. Enzo dishes out the pasta meal he made.

"So catch me up. Where is everyone?" I ask, taking a big bite of the pasta.

Kai and Enzo exchange a look, but Kai is the one who starts talking first. "Beckett is out on a mission. The man you met before."

Enzo stops shoveling food in his mouth and stares back and forth between us. "Wait...Beckett knew you were alive?"

I nod.

Kai nods.

Even Siren nods.

"That fucking cunt," Enzo says. "Why didn't he tell me?"

"Because I told him not to," Kai says, at the same time I do.

We smile at each other. It feels so good to be here.

"How long have you known?" Enzo asks, staring at Kai.

"Zeke sent me a letter," Kai says.

Enzo shakes his head in frustration. "And you couldn't tell me?"

Kai looks at him in warning. "I'm sorry, but he was trying to protect us all. Do you blame him for trying to keep us safe?" She raises a brow at him.

"No." Enzo turns toward me. "Thanks for keeping the danger away as long as you could."

"In the spirit of full disclosure, I also saw him when I was in Paris a few weeks ago."

"What? Why didn't you tell me then?" Enzo asks.

Kai and I exchange glances, and I attempt to explain. "We didn't even talk. We just saw each other from across the room. We were there on separate missions. It wasn't the right time, and I still thought I could protect you from all of this."

Kai tears up. "You have no idea how hard it was for me to not come squeeze you and bring me home with you. No idea."

Dammit, and now we are all crying again. Even Siren and Enzo are dabbing at their eyes.

"What changed?" Enzo asks softly.

My eyes cut to Siren, who has stiffened next to me.

Enzo's eyes follow, and he knows why—Siren. Siren happened.

"Where are Langston and Liesel? Fighting somewhere or fucking?" I ask, laughing at our old running joke about the two of them.

Enzo picks up his wine glass, avoiding answering.

Kai drops her fork.

The clink of the fork on the plate is the only sound for a second.

"Liesel wanted some space. We actually don't know where she is at the moment. Last time we heard from her she was in Hawaii," Kai says.

"And Langston took off. He couldn't stand that Liesel didn't want to be with him, so he's been getting over her on safaris and expeditions. He's hard to get a hold of, because he's always in some remote location," Enzo explains.

My mouth gapes at them. Enzo, Langston, and I were like the three musketeers. We did everything together. I was as close, if not closer, to Langston than I was Enzo.

And Liesel was always around. When I left, the tension between Langston and Liesel was high. I thought for sure the two would end up together.

"I'll make sure to contact Langston and let him know you are alive. He needs to know. I thought about telling him sooner, but he needed space, and I wanted to honor your wishes," Kai says.

I nod, but the awkward air continues. There was a lot I missed while I was gone. Just like there is a lot they have missed.

We all finish eating. Enzo clears our plates. And then we drink our wine while the sun sets.

"I guess it's my turn to explain everything," I say.

All eyes are on me, as I explain everything. How Siren saved me. The dangers we are both in from Julian and Bishop. The nightmares Siren has been having.

I wait for Enzo to get pissed at me for bringing the danger to their doorstep, but he doesn't.

"I think we are going to need more wine," he says, getting up and fetching another bottle. He returns and fills all our glasses.

"Zeke didn't tell you everything, though. I hurt him. I—" Siren starts.

"I told them everything that matters," I say, cutting her off. I don't want her to talk about how she hurt me. How she betrayed me. I can forgive her, but I'm not sure they will.

Siren frowns, but Kai just smiles behind her wine glass. Enzo looks completely bewildered by what is happening.

"I'm sorry, I failed you all. I brought danger to your doorstep, when I shouldn't have. But I didn't have a choice...I..." I can't bring myself to talk to them about Siren with her sitting next to me.

She wouldn't let me anyway. She'd get frustrated that the only reason we are sitting here, the only reason we are risking my friends' lives is because of her. "We shouldn't have come here, but—"

"Yes, you should have," Kai says, once again with tears in her eyes.

"You should have come here first thing. You should have told us as soon as you healed and got to that island alive, you asswipe," Enzo says, cursing at me to keep from crying again.

His phone buzzes, and he looks down with a smile staring at the screen.

"The twins are up," he says, exchanging a glance with Kai.

He stands up but studies my face waiting for it to hit me. It does three seconds later.

"Wait. What? Twins? Please tell me he's talking about babies and not some hot blondes he has stashed away in a prison on this boat."

Enzo winks at me, "I'll be right back."

Kai can't stop smiling at me, and I can't stop smiling at her. But I don't speak, and neither does she. We wait for Enzo to return before she explains what the hell is going on. I imagine it's the most incredible thing possible.

Siren is chewing on her bottom lip nervously.

I glance over and whisper to her. "You okay?"

She nods, not telling me what she's worried about. I study her a moment longer, ensuring she is still present and not locked in another nightmare. She's still with us.

A second later, my heart jumps up in my throat when I see the two most beautiful babies in the entire world. Although, I'm not sure they are actually babies. They look so grown already, but they are definitely Kai and Enzo's. They are a spitting image of the two of them.

Enzo walks over, holding the sleeping children. "Zeke, Siren, meet these rascals who have stolen our hearts. This is Ellie," he hands me the first child.

I'm holding Enzo and Kai's child. I don't think life gets any better than this. And just like that, I'm crying again.

"That's your Uncle Zeke, sweetheart. Don't tug on his hair even though he should cut it off," Enzo says.

"Don't you dare tell him to cut it off," Siren teases back.

I smile, brushing my hand over the little girl's hair. "You want to hold her?" I ask Siren, knowing Enzo wants to introduce me to his son as well, and I'm not sure I'm ready to hold two squirming kids at once.

Siren sits frozen for a moment, not answering. "Siren?"

After a beat, she extends her arms, and I give her the child. She holds her to her chest like a natural.

"And this bastard, is Finn," Enzo says.

"Language," Kai hisses, but smiles at me, as recognition hits my face.

"For Langston and me?"

Enzo nods and puts his son, who he named after me, in my hands. Finn is both my and Langston's middle name. More tears are fall. Langston should be here celebrating this moment with us. But that's not why I'm crying like a baby for the millionth time tonight.

I'm crying because I can't imagine a more perfect life. I don't know how they do it. Live in this world filled with danger and have the two most perfect angels in it with them. But they do. They are able to do both, and when I glance at Kai and Enzo, I know they are doing it without fear.

I glance over at Siren. She looks absolutely perfect, holding Ellie. I realize what I want. *This*—this is what I want. I want to be married to the woman I love, with as many kids as she wants, a job we both have a passion for, and good friends to share our lives with. *I want this.*

And I know who I want to share this life with, but I'm not sure Siren can be persuaded. I don't know if she wants to get married again. I don't know if she wants kids. I don't even know if she wants me.

But I have no doubt—this is what I want.

CHAPTER 25
SIREN

When I hold Ellie in my arms, I feel whole. I thought I was whole before, but I was wrong. This, holding a child you love, changes everything.

I thought I could be happy if I just had Zeke in my life. I thought our love was enough. I was wrong.

This is what I want—a family.

I want a marriage.

I want kids.

I want friends I consider family.

I want a life outside of killing, murdering, and stealing.

But I have no idea how to make that happen. None.

I can't see how Kai and Enzo make it work. They are obviously still involved in their criminal endeavors, but yet, they have two small kids. *Isn't that reckless? Isn't that asking for the kids to be stolen? To be kidnapped? To be hurt to get to their parents?*

If Julian knew about the kids, he would have used them instead of Zeke to get what he wanted. And I'm sure Bishop would do the same.

But damn does my heart open to the idea, the possibility, the temptation. I don't dare look over at Zeke while I'm holding Ellie. I don't want him to know what I'm thinking, what I'm wanting. We are so far away from being able to consider having kids that it hurts. I'm sure Kai and Enzo were responsible when they had kids. I'm sure they thought about everything. I'm sure they took every precaution.

I'm sure they didn't lie to each other. Betray each other. *Hurt each other.*

I'm sure they were always kind, loving, and honest.

I bounce Ellie on my lap. Think about something else. Think about the ocean. Think about the incredible yacht we are on. Think about how good the wine tastes.

But all I can do is look into the beautiful green eyes of this tiny girl. A girl who doesn't understand the dangers in her life she has because of her parents. A girl, who at such a young age, already has dreams and aspirations and goals. A girl who deserves the world. And if given the chance, will conquer it.

"Siren, you want to help me feed them and put them down?" Kai asks.

I nod, not realizing we've been playing with the kids for a couple of hours now. I've barely spoken a word, but I've felt Kai's eyes on me. I've felt her staring, but I have no idea what she's been thinking.

Kai takes Finn. I follow Kai into the yacht with Ellie in my arms. We head downstairs to a door. Kai enters a code and does a facial and fingerprint scan before the door opens. "You can never be too careful," Kai says bashfully as we walk into the children's nursery.

I smile. I would want at least that much to be able to sleep at night.

Kai hands me a prepared bottle, as I sit in one of the rockers feeding Ellie. She feeds Finn his bottle, her eyes still lingering on me.

"Tell me what you're thinking. I know this is all a lot, and you're not as easy to read as Zeke is," Kai says.

I rock, looking down at Ellie before I clear my head and look at Kai. "What do you think Zeke is thinking? You know him well."

Kai smiles. "I do, and it's clear what that man is thinking. He's head over heels in love with you."

I exhale a breath preparing for my next question. "And what do you think about me? About our relationship? I mean, I don't think I'm right for him. I've hurt him too many times."

Kai laughs. "You're perfect for him because you think you're wrong for him. That means you want the best for him. And trust me, if you think Enzo and I's relationship was perfect, it wasn't. We've done things to each other you can't even imagine doing to Zeke."

"I've shot him," I say.

Kai's lips curl up. "I've shot Enzo."

I frown. "He bought me on an auction block."

"Enzo tried to sell me."

I take a deep breath. "I tricked Zeke into thinking I was on his side, while the whole time I was working for his enemy. Oh, and I was married to a man while with Zeke, and I didn't tell him."

Kai is quiet for a moment. Finn finishes his bottle, and she starts burping him. Ellie is still carefully working on her own bottle.

"We all do things in this world to survive. Stupid, dumb, horrible things. It doesn't mean you don't belong together. If everyone in this dark world were judged by everything they did, none of us would ever be worthy of a relationship. Don't judge yourself. Don't judge him. Somehow, you have both fallen in love. I can see why. But don't for a second think you don't deserve each other."

I swallow. "How do you do it?"

Kai knows what I'm asking. "I love Enzo. And I wanted babies. It wasn't planned. In fact, when I found out, I was scared to death. My life was extremely complicated at the time. When I had them, I thought they were going to be a blessing and a curse. But once they were here, I've never once thought of them as a curse. I have responsibilities to this company. I have men and women who count on me; I can't just quit my job. But I'm a mother and a wife first.

"Yes, I've brought them into a dangerous world. But in some ways, I think they are safer than most children. What other kids have a biometric security system, a yacht armed with enough weapons to take down a fleet of battleships, and a hundred men who would fight to the death to protect them? They will know what danger is and how to judge people before they turn five. They will know everything. There is nothing I will be able to hide from them.

"And if Enzo or I die protecting them, they will never have to wonder if they were loved, they will know. I can't think of a better way to raise a child."

I look down at Ellie, who is so content in my arms drinking her bottle. Her eyes are closed, and I think she's fallen asleep. She seems happy and loved and protected—everything a child needs.

Kai places Finn in his crib. And I place Ellie in hers. They are perfect.

Kai takes my hand. "Don't be afraid of your future. I know it seems bleak and scary right now because of the dangers you face, but I promise, it will be worth it. Zeke is worth it."

Zeke is worth it.

No, he's not. He's dangerous. He's going to hurt you. He's hiding things from you. You have to stop him. Get him to tell you the truth.

You're mine, not his. Mine, Bishop says.

No, get out of my head!

I will. When you do what I want.

What do you want?

"Siren! Siren, wake up! I'm here, I'm here," Zeke says, pulling me to his chest. As soon as he does, I'm pulled back to the world. He's my anchor to the real world. When he's holding me, he pushes Bishop out.

"Never leave," I cry into Zeke's chest.

"Never," he growls back, holding me tighter.

We sit on the floor, and it takes me a minute to register the babies crying and that I'm still in the nursery.

It takes me a few minutes more to return my breathing to normal, to calm down and be able to stand up. Kai and Enzo each have a child in their arms rocking them, trying to get them to settle down.

"I'm so sorry," I say when I stand, staring at the restless, crying kids.

"Don't be, it's not your fault. The kids are fine. Already going back to sleep," Enzo says. He looks from me to Zeke, giving him permission to take me somewhere calmer.

"Actually," Zeke rubs his neck. "I need to talk to Kai a minute."

Kai nods.

He leans down to me. "If I start you a bath while I talk to her, will you be okay?"

I nod. "Yes." Although, I have no idea. I can't control my nightmares. I can't control who has control of my thoughts or voices in my head. I can't control anything anymore.

"Five minutes. I promise," Zeke says as he leads me to a bedroom and then into the bathroom.

"I can't believe there is a tub on a boat."

"Yea, Kai loves having a bath, so Enzo installed a bathtub in several of the bathrooms. And now that they have kids, it's necessary."

Zeke starts filling the tub with warm water. Then he kisses me tenderly before lifting my shirt up. He kisses my neck, over the curve of my breasts, and then down to my flat stomach.

"What are you doing?"

"Worshipping your body."

"I thought you were going to talk to Kai?"

"I am." Zeke kisses down my thigh as he strips off my jeans and panties. "But this way, I'll be thinking about you the whole time and hurry back."

I gasp when he kisses over my clit. His tongue stays in his mouth, but I feel just enough heat to turn me on and send chills up and down my body.

"Don't touch yourself while I'm gone," he says.

"Five minutes, and then all bets are off," I smirk as I climb into the tub.

He grins, watching me sink beneath the water. He kisses me on the forehead and is gone before either of us can change our minds. And then I'm alone.

"I can do this," I say out loud to myself. "One, two, three..." The only way I can force my mind on the moment is to count and focus on Zeke, so that's what I'll do until he returns.

CHAPTER 26
ZEKE

Leaving Siren alone kills me after she had another nightmare, but I need to talk to Kai. She needs to know all the facts to protect her family. And I need her help. I could ask Enzo, but Kai and I have a special connection. She will understand in a way that Enzo won't. Enzo will just want to protect his family, which I understand. But Kai has always considered me part of her family.

I find Kai leaning against the railing at the front of the boat, looking out at the dark sky.

I come up and stand next to her, not speaking. There is a shift in the air. A shift from the happiness we both felt before to a much more serious tone.

"When you were shot saving me, my heart broke. It was like nothing I've ever experienced before. Even thinking Enzo was dead didn't rattle me like losing you, Zeke. I can't explain our connection. It's different than any other in my life. It wrecked me. Maybe because you were the first person I ever truly loved that I lost. Maybe it's because you saved me by taking a bullet meant for me. Maybe we are really two halves of a soul."

"Stingray," I say, taking her hand.

Tears fall. Down her cheeks and mine.

"I'm not going to keep crying over you. I'm not going to feel guilty forever. I love you, Zeke. You know that. And when you died, a part of me died. I healed getting your letter that you were alive. I healed more seeing you alive in person at the ball. And seeing you now has done wonders to heal me. But you also hurt me by hiding. Promise me, never again?"

"Never again," I say.

She squeezes my hand.

"Now, tell me," she says.

I take a deep breath. "Siren has nightmares; she hears voices in her head, not voices...one man's voice—Bishop. He bought her. It's a long story that doesn't matter. But he had her, controlled her. We aren't even sure what he really did to her, but he fucked up her head. And now, at random times, she hears his voice. I've talked to doctors, but they say only time can heal her. That's not good enough. One man, Julian Reed, an enemy, says he can help her. But I don't know. I need help. I need to heal her. I'm scared for her. She can't keep living like this."

"We will do whatever we can to help you."

"Even give me a yacht?"

She laughs. "You can have all the yachts. Whatever you need."

"I'm not just here to talk about Siren."

"You're here to talk about Lucy and what you hid in my vault," Kai says, her lip twitching in anger.

"You're mad?"

"No, not really. I do wish you had told me. But that was before my time, so I understand why you didn't. Have you told Siren?"

My silence gives her her answer.

"You need to tell her the truth. I don't care about you hiding things from me, but if you love her, tell her the truth. About everything. Trust me."

"What does that mean?"

"Tell her everything you are feeling. Everything you want, as soon as you can. Don't wait. If you wait, it might be too late. There is only ever now in our world. Never a promise of tomorrow."

I nod, understanding. If I want to marry her, I need to tell her. Kids, tell her. A future, tell her.

"We will come up with a plan about the rest tomorrow, Zeke. I know you have a lot of enemies, but Bishop was on our radar before. And it sounds like Julian Reed is really after us, not you. We will fight them together. One by one. Just like we always do," Kai says.

"Thank you, but you need to know what I expect. I don't expect you or Enzo to put your life on the line, not when you have two young babies. Those babies will always come first. I will do everything I can to protect them above all else, I promise you," I say, looking her dead in the eye with the moonlight as my witness.

She frowns. "You can't promise me that. You have your own family to protect."

I've made promises to Lucy, to Siren, but this vow is just as important. I will keep my promises. To each of the women who are important in my life. I will protect them at all costs.

"I promise you, Kai. I'll keep you safe. I promise," I say again.

"You better," she says with a smile.

"I should get back to Siren."

"Go. Thankfully the rooms are soundproof. Have fun," she says with a wink.

Thank god for that.

I run back down the stairs, entering the code Kai gave me for the bedroom. Each room has top-level security. I can't think of a safer place than this yacht.

I walk through the bedroom and into the bathroom, where I find Siren, in the tub, touching herself.

"What. Did. I. Say?" I growl, my voice deep, dark, and scary even to myself.

Siren's hand freezes. Her eyes flutter up. Her eyelids are hooded. Her cheeks are shaded pink, and her lips are soft. Her legs are spread, and even though the soapy water blocks most of my view, my imagination and experience with her body fill in the rest.

"You going to join me?" Siren asks, her voice hopeful, not scared by my caveman-like voice earlier.

"I shouldn't."

"But you are," she smiles. She grabs my hand before I realize what she's doing, and yanks me down into the tub, clothes and all. I always forget that for such a tiny person, she has incredible physical strength. I've seen her do pushups. She has killer arms. I would love to workout with her and really understand the limits of her physical abilities. Although she's strong for such a tiny thing, her body is still small, and all muscles have limits.

I laugh, as water splashes out of the tub and soaks my clothes. "Did you miss me or something?"

"Or something. My hand wasn't doing as good of a job as your lips, tongue, or cock does."

"Oh, yea?" I ask, letting my finger fall between her naked thighs, teasing her entrance. I wish I could tell how wet she was, but her dark expression says it all—very wet.

I sit back on my feet and remove my wet shirt. She watches me with a thick intensity as she licks her lips and lets her hand fall back between her legs.

"No touching," I command.

She stops. "Then hurry. I need you."

Fuck, that voice. It does things to me. Drills deep into my core, telling me how much she wants me—no, needs me. If she only had a clue what that voice does to me. Her eyes fall to my crotch, where my erection is straining against my jeans, and I think she gets the idea.

I lean back and remove my shoes while she chews on her bottom lip, her breath speeding and cheeks flushing.

"You know I would have been faster if you hadn't had pulled me into the tub while I was still wearing clothes."

She moans. "Hurry."

I laugh and decide to take my time. I enjoy her watching me. And I enjoy having a perfect view of her body, while she has an obstructed one.

She arches her back and tosses her hair to one side in a fierce look. She leans close to me until our lips are inches from each other. "If you don't have your clothes off in the next five seconds and your cock slipping inside me a second after that, I'm going to come without you."

She falls back into the tub, her eyes full of her threat.

Damn.

I remove my pants and boxer briefs in record time, and then I'm pulling her on top of me, my cock resting at her entrance.

She grins.

"You know you shouldn't blackmail a man like that," I say.

"Mmm, I think I should, it seems to work," she shifts her hips and takes an inch of my cock inside her.

"You sure about that?" I slip a finger in her ass without warning as my cock drives inside her pussy.

Her nails dig into my shoulders as she moans, throwing her head back as the pleasure fills her body. "Ever had anyone inside this sweet ass?"

"No," she groans. "But now I want to."

I laugh. She's game for anything. I don't think she has sexual limits; she would try anything. Me slipping a finger in her ass barely even phases her.

Wheels turn in my head as I pump inside her with my cock and finger. "When we get out of the tub, this ass is all mine," I say into her ear before nibbling.

"God, why does that sound so incredible?"

"Because you love me and trust me to do anything in the world to your body."

"I do."

I glide her hips up and down over my cock, until both of us are in a delicious rhythm.

"We need to talk," I say suddenly.

She doesn't stop riding me. "Really? You want to talk now?"

"Yes," I breathe. Kai told me to tell her now. Not to wait. It feels like we should talk right the fuck now. I don't know why I feel so much urgency, but I do.

"We need to talk about our future. About marriage, and kids, and—"

Siren's head falls down, and she kisses me hard, her tongue pushing deep into my mouth, massaging my tongue and making me want to scream her name.

I forget about what I was going to say. Talking can wait. Kissing, fucking, and loving her cannot.

Our eyes lock open as she rides me and kisses me and makes me forget about everything but her until our orgasms rip through us like a hurricane. Like a bomb going off.

She freezes.

"What?"

"Do you hear that?" she stops writhing and kissing me.

"Hear what?" But as I speak, I hear it. There are bombs and bullets ringing off. A sound we both know too well.

I push Siren off me in a flash, and we both throw on ripped clothes and grab our guns before running out of the bedroom, headed straight for the babies' room. There was no communication. No need to discuss where we are going and that we would both put our lives on the line to protect them.

We aren't the only ones who are running to the babies. Kai and Enzo are running, half-dressed and flushed just like us. Both wielding guns in their hands. All of us wearing a look of fear on our faces. But I feel guilt more than fear. *What did we do? What were we thinking bringing danger to their perfect life?*

CHAPTER 27
SIREN

"Who's attacking?" Kai asks, looking at Zeke, then me.

Zeke frowns. "I'm not sure, but I'm about to find out."

"It's not Bishop," I say.

All eyes fall on me.

"I'd know. I'd feel him, trust me," I say.

"Okay, so that leaves Julian?" Kai asks.

I nod. I should know the most about Julian. I've worked for him for years, but I'm afraid I don't know him at all. "He's manipulative, but he has a lot of resources. If he attacks, it will be full force. But his goal is to manipulate and control."

Another round hits the yacht, and we all shudder at the sound as we stand outside the twin's bedroom. Enzo has the video camera pulled up on his phone. Somehow they are both sleeping silently inside.

"I've called for help, but the closest team is half an hour away," Enzo says.

Kai nods. For some reason, both men look to her to make a decision about how we are going to attack. She looks to her husband. "Stay with the kids. Protect them with your life. Don't let anyone into the room. No matter what. Promise me," she says firmly.

"But you should..." Enzo starts.

"You're a better fighter. They need you to protect them if we fail. Promise me, them first," Kai says.

"I promise," Enzo says with a frown. She gives him a quick kiss, and then he disappears into the room.

"The codes will no longer work. I can't even get into the room if I wanted to. It's bulletproof and bombproof. It would take sinking the ship to have a chance at getting access to the room," Kai says.

Zeke and I take a deep breath, knowing the babies are as safe as they can be.

"I don't think anyone knows you have kids," I say.

"Let's keep it that way," Kai answers.

"What's the plan?" Zeke asks, looking to Kai.

"We fight. Just like old times. We fight and hope we can outsmart a team of men who want to kill us. I'm going to head to the bridge to get this yacht moving as I'm the weakest fighter. You two do what you do best. Zeke, you are a master with a gun, and I have no doubt you are too Siren. Just cover us until I can get this yacht up to full speed. They won't be able to catch us then," Kai says.

We all nod as we head up the stairs.

I start heading to the right. Kai starts heading to the left to sneak up to the bridge.

Zeke stands in the middle, realizing he'll have to choose to go with Kai or me.

It should be an easy decision for him. I know who needs him more right now, but he stares at me like he can't bear to leave me.

I kiss him quickly. "Go, she needs your protection. If she doesn't get this yacht moving, we are all dead anyway."

He frowns, but I shove him toward Kai and head up the stairs before he has a chance to follow me.

My heart is racing harder than it ever has before, going into a mama bear protection mode over the two babies asleep downstairs oblivious to the dangers above. They aren't even my babies, but I feel the instinct. The intense desire to do whatever it takes to save them.

Kai and Enzo must feel double what I feel. I don't care how many men are out here trying to attack us; we will kill them all before they even realize there are babies asleep downstairs.

I see a shadow moving. They are on the yacht.

Fuck.

I aim my gun and shoot at the end of the shadow, knowing I'm only hitting an arm at best, but it will be enough to disarm the person. I hear the grunt, and then I dash in clear view to finish him before they get a shot off.

The man falls to the floor.

Three men behind him fire at me in the dark. I hate the darkness. I wish I could say that I'm used to fighting in the dark, but I'm not. I'm a good fighter, but I'm better in the daylight when I can manipulate with my words and body.

I shoot quickly, sneaking around to the front of the yacht. I let my eyes lift enough to see over the railing, but not enough to get shot in the head.

Holy shit.

I see at least twenty ships. *Twenty.*

We're doomed.

There is no fucking way we can take down twenty ships full of men trying to kill us. There are just four of us. We can't hold them off for the thirty minutes we need until the rest of Kai and Enzo's team gets here. There is nowhere for our yacht to escape.

I feel us moving. Kai must have gotten to the bridge, but we're barely creeping. There is no space for us to travel through.

Fuck.

I try to see who is in charge. *Julian or Bishop?*

Who do I want?

Julian.

Bishop scares the hell out of me.

But Julian has to die. We don't have a choice but to kill him, for so many reasons I'm still hiding from Zeke.

The boat stops completely a second later. I see more men on the boat. I kill them all one by one.

But then...

No!

I see a man holding a gun to Kai's head.

I see Zeke begging him to let her go. I see a dozen more guns aimed at Kai's head.

And then I see him—Julian Reed.

Of course, he's behind this.

You can end this, Bishop's voice says in my head.

I can, but not because Bishop wants me to. I want to.

I put my hands up and drop my gun, moving out of the shadows.

"Take me," I say, getting everyone's attention.

Zeke still has his gun pointed at Julian.

"Siren, what are you doing?" Zeke pleads me to stop, but he doesn't get a say. None of them do. If I can stop this, I will.

I turn to Julian. "Take me."

Julian grins. "Why my Aria, I'm glad you finally showed up. Thank you for leading me here."

"Liar. She didn't help you," Zeke shouts.

Kai tries to break free of the man who holds her.

Julian grins. "Fine, fine. You win. She didn't help me, but she was easy enough to track when I have a tracker in her body. She makes it easy to follow."

Fuck, when did he put a tracker in me? And where?

I feel violated in a whole new way.

"Let her go. You want me, not her," I say.

"No, I want you all," Julian says, moving to stand in front of Kai and study her.

"I have Kai. My associate, Bishop, has Lucy—" Julian says.

"No," Zeke and I both say at the same time.

Julian turns to me. *He wants me.*

"Me for them," I say, knowing he won't take the offer, but I need to try.

Julian grabs Kai's hair roughly, pulling her neck back so she's forced to look at him. She stands strong. I know she wants to say horrible things to him, but she won't. She's a mom. She has to survive for her babies. She won't piss him off.

"Nope. Care to try again?" Julian asks, looking at me with a darkness I've never seen.

"Me to get you to leave. Take all of your men and leave. Me for not killing Kai, Lucy, or anyone else on this boat," I say, stepping closer.

"Siren, don't," Zeke says.

I glare at him, pleading him to stop. I don't have a choice. I have to do this, and he can't stop me. The pain in his eyes tells me he doesn't have another plan. He agrees, but he can't tell me to go—good thing he doesn't have to. I would give my life for these two women any day of the week. And definitely to save those babies.

"Do we have a deal?"

"Yes," Julian says.

I step forward carefully, but Zeke grabs me at the last second. "Don't." I've never seen such pain. He's losing three women. All at once. He loves us all differently.

"I have to," I say slowly. "It will be okay. I'll protect them."

"I'm not worried about them. I know you'll protect them."

His eyes say he's worried about me.

"Come for us," I say, stepping out of Zeke's arms without a kiss, hug, or even an 'I love you.' If I did, I wouldn't be able to go. I walk over to Julian, trapped in his arms in an instant.

"It's nice to have you back where you belong, Aria," Julian says, kissing my hair, breathing me in, and dragging me toward his boat.

My eyes look at Zeke, who tries to chase after us. I shake my head. "Come for us. He wants to make a deal. It's all a game," I say, knowing Julian. *This is all a game to him.*

Then I say the thing that kills me. "Save them, not me. Promise."

Zeke doesn't promise. He doesn't say anything. He's just gone. I'm thrown into shackles, to be locked away with two other women Zeke loves. Women I promised I'd save no matter what.

I plan on keeping that promise.

CHAPTER 28
ZEKE

I lost.

I never lose.

We. Never. Lose.

Not like this. I've never lost a person I loved so much in this world. I was the one who was lost. I was the one who was killed. But them...they all survived. They all lived.

Today, that changed.

Julian has Kai and Siren.

And Bishop has Lucy.

I'm left heartbroken, with a hole in my heart the size of Texas. I failed—Lucy, Kai, Siren. I failed three women. I wasn't strong enough. I wasn't fast enough. I wasn't smart enough.

I let Julian Reed and Bishop outsmart me. I let them take people who were mine. They. Were. MINE.

Not anymore. Now, they are gone. Now, they are Julian and Bishop's. Now I have to fight to get them back, which is going to be harder than defending them in the first place. Now, I have to pray that nothing happens to them until I can get to them.

I have to leave right the fuck now. I can't give Julian more than a few minutes head start. I have to go. I have to save them.

Now.

But first, I have to do something just as difficult. I have to tell my best friend that I failed. I have to tell him that his wife is gone. That the mother of his children is gone. That this could be the end of the world as we know it.

He trusted me. And when it mattered, I couldn't protect them.

It feels a lot like last time. When I went into the ocean, I felt like a failure. Not because I was going to die, but because I wasn't sure that I had saved anyone. Although, this time, I know I failed everyone.

I walk down the stairs of the yacht, hearing a faint cry. Maybe it's my imagination. The rooms are soundproof, after all. The cry, fictional or real, breaks my heart all the same.

It's the cry of a baby who wants her mother.

I stand in front of the nursery door and knock. I'm not sure if Enzo can hear me or not.

"Is it safe?" he asks, through a speaker in the door.

"Yes," I answer back.

"What's the safeword?" Enzo asks.

"The what?"

"The safeword. Kai will tell you the word if it's really clear and safe. We didn't want someone to be able to be tortured into opening the door, so we came up with a safeword. Ask her what the word is. She'll have my balls if she finds out I opened the door without asking for the safeword first."

I grip my long locks in a fist, frustration, anger, and pain building and exploding through every pore in my body. I have to keep it together. I don't get to cry. I don't get to feel pain. Three women are depending on me. I have to save them. I have to protect them.

"Enzo, just open the door," I say.

"I can't. Where is Kai anyway?"

His voice is relaxed. He doesn't realize or even imagine that his wife could be gone.

No, she's not gone. Just missing—kidnapped. We can get her back.

"Enzo, please," my voice begs him to open the door. I can't explain to him what happened over an intercom. He needs to open the door.

Silence.

I think he's going to open the door, but he doesn't.

"Where is Kai? Where is stingray?"

Damn him for using the nickname I came up with for Kai. Damn him. The tears flow. The tears burn down my cheeks. I'm not going to survive this conversation.

"I failed. They're gone. All of them," I say, collapsing to my knees in front of the door like I'm asking for forgiveness, for mercy, but I deserve none. Especially not if Julian or Bishop lays a single finger on our girls.

Enzo doesn't respond. He doesn't answer at first. He waits.

Finally, the door opens. It shuts. It locks, keeping the twins safe inside.

"Get up," Enzo says, his voice low and deafening.

I stand, knowing what is coming, and I deserve it.

"Julian has Kai?" Enzo asks.

"Yes," I breathe, wishing I could take back the word. Saying it makes it true.

Enzo punches me. It's swift. It's efficient—a punishment for a crime. I failed him. I failed Kai, one woman I never thought I could fail. I deserve it.

I wait for a second punch. A third. A fourth.

But he doesn't punch me again.

I open my eyes. My face is spared more punches because he's a crying wreck on the floor in front of me.

"Did he take Siren too?" he asks. I sit next to him, leaning against the door with my own tears.

"Yes."

I expect another punch. Instead, he pulls me to him and hugs me. I hug him back. We sit like this for five long minutes. For five long minutes, we feel sorry for ourselves. We feel the pain, the fear. When our time is up, we abruptly stand up.

Enzo takes out his phone and makes a call.

I wait.

"Dammit, Langston, pick up your phone," Enzo yells into the phone. Then hangs up.

I frown. *Langston isn't coming.*

"You have to stay," I say, realizing our situation and hating it at the same time. It's why Enzo wanted Langston.

"Yes," Enzo breathes through his pain, cursing over and over again under his breath.

Enzo picks up his phone again. "I'll call Beckett. He can help you."

I nod. If Enzo trusts him, I trust him. Enzo makes the call.

"He'll meet you in St. Kitts in an hour."

I nod as my life flashes before my eyes.

I should have married Siren when I had the chance. I should have made her mine. I should have had babies and found us a deserted island away from all of this.

I should have killed Julian. I should have spent my time tracking Bishop and killing him, not trying to get closer to Siren by sharing my past with Lucy.

I should have told Siren every truth.

No—I shouldn't have. Not knowing the truth could save her.

"Zeke, you got this. Go get them back. Give them whatever they want. Money, power, everything. Do whatever it takes to get them back. Do you hear me?" Enzo says.

He grips my shoulders, staring at me with everything he has—all his pain on full display. I hear the babies crying, and his head turns. He left the monitor on. I see a man being torn in half—wanting to save his wife, but needing to protect his kids.

"Take whatever crew you need. Do whatever it takes, but bring them back," Enzo says.

"I will," I promise. I will. I have to. It's the one promise I will keep.

My head bobbles back and forth as the plane shifts in the air. My arms are tied behind my back; my ankles are tied up as well. My head is groggy after being drugged.

I could get out of the bindings in about five seconds. *But then what?* I'm thousands of feet up in the air. I can't fly a plane. I'm stuck until we land.

I look over at Kai, who is lying against the wall of the plane, still out of it from the injections they gave us. The drugs left my system hours ago, but her smaller frame takes longer to expel them from her system.

I watch her sleep. She looks peaceful, but a drug-filled sleep is anything but. It's deep, dark, and heavy. It pulls you under, playing with your mind until you can't think about anything other than wanting to escape. But you can't escape. The drugs have a hold of everything.

Kai's body twitches—she's coming out of it.

I pull my hand free of the bindings so I can stroke her back as she wakes up.

"Hey, I got you. Take a deep breath," I say, patting her back as Kai wakes up.

She sits up suddenly, rocketing from asleep to wide awake in seconds.

"What happened?" Kai asks.

I frown. "Julian Reed has us on a plane. He's kidnapping us and using us to get whatever is in your vault that belongs to Lucy, Zeke's old girlfriend."

Kai shakes her head, trying to clear her head. Then she nods in understanding. "I remember."

I bite my lip. Not remembering isn't good, but sometimes remembering can be even more torturous.

"Here, let me get those off you," I say, quietly, eyeing the closest guard who appears asleep in his chair a few rows in front of us. We're in the back of the plane, on the floor, hidden from view of most of the men.

I untie Kai's hands, and then we both untie our legs before leaning back against the wall. We enjoy feeling a little freer now that are hands and legs aren't tied up.

"Did Zeke tell you what's in the vault?" Kai whispers.

"No."

Kai frowns.

"Are you going to tell me?"

"I don't know. I want to protect you. And I don't know if you knowing is going to protect you or make you vulnerable."

I sigh.

"Ultimately, I need to honor what Zeke wanted, which was for you not to know. That's his way of protecting you."

I nod.

"Zeke will come. He'll fight. He'll rescue us," Kai says.

"So will Enzo."

"No, he has to stay with the twins. We made a promise to always put the twins first."

I swallow down the lump in my throat. If it comes down to it, Zeke better choose to save Kai, not me. I don't have little lives depending on me like Kai does. The world is better off if I'm dead. If I survive this, the wrath I'm going to bring down on this world has never been seen before.

"So, what's the plan?" Kai asks, her eyebrows raised.

"What? You mean you don't want to wait for Zeke or the guys to come save us?" I ask with a small smirk on my lips.

"Hell no."

"Have I mentioned how much I like you?" I ask.

She grins.

We take a few minutes to study our surroundings, to form a plan. There is a room at the front of the plane that I'm sure Julian is in. Then there are a few rows of guards in the seats near us. Then us at the back, given as much attention as cargo. They think we are tied up, drugged, helpless women. *They are wrong.*

"How confident are you with a gun or knife?" I ask Kai.

She takes a deep breath. "I'm better with a gun than a knife. Zeke helped teach me how to shoot. But I saw you on the yacht. You are way better at both than me."

I squeeze her hand. "If Zeke taught you how to shoot, then I trust your skills are above average."

"I'm so happy he found a woman like you."

"You mean a woman who gets kidnapped and brings him danger all the time? You sure he shouldn't have settled down with a nurse or teacher or something?"

Kai laughs quietly. "You're the woman for him."

"Thanks."

"Now, let's figure out a plan."

We formulate a plan, a plan that involves us attacking during landing.

We see land out the window quickly approaching. That's our cue.

I wink at Kai. *Sure, Zeke is a great partner to take down a plane with, but I suspect I'm going to enjoy working with Kai a lot.*

I creep forward on the plane, holding the rope used to tie up our arms and legs. They thought they could use it to bind us, but I'm about to use it to kill them all.

I reach the first man, a drunk playing games on his phone. *What an idiot to underestimate us.*

I throw the rope around his neck and pull hard, while Kai covers his mouth to keep him silent while he dies. The man struggles and succeeds in pushing Kai off him, but I hold tight. He makes a small gargled sound. I watch as one of the guards starts to turn around, but Kai already has a gun. She fires, hitting the man square in the head. Turning to the last guard, she shoots him square in the chest.

I blink rapidly. "I'd say you are better than above average. You can fight with me any damn day of the week."

I toss the rope to the floor, next to the body of the man I just strangled to death.

Kai's eyes widen. "Remind me not to get on your bad side." She looks down at the dead man.

I crack my neck as I walk up the aisle and grab one of the guard's gun.

That was the easy part. The hard part is going to be killing Julian, who most likely saw us kill his men on a security camera.

I move my hand to the doorknob.

"Come in, ladies. I've been expecting you," Julian says from inside before I open the door.

I frown at Kai, who looks worried. The lines around her eyes have deepened, and her jaw is tense.

We've come this far. We aren't just going to surrender. Not without a fight.

I open the door and step inside, my body blocking Julian's view of Kai.

But Kai doesn't want me to protect her. She steps inside the room right after me, and we both aim our gun at the man sitting at a table with a whiskey and a cigar.

He has five guards with guns aimed at us.

Julian looks at his watch. "I'm impressed. You took out three men while you were unarmed and still feeling the effects of drugs in under three minutes. Impressive."

I growl.

"Please, sit. You must be famished," Julian waves to the table in front of him where there is enough food to feed a dozen people.

"We aren't hungry. We're here for one reason."

"To kill me. Yes, I've heard that before. How many times have you or Zeke tried to kill me and failed?"

I frown. *Too many.*

"You forget why I know you won't kill me. You know the consequences if you are the one to kill me. And I'm not sure she is capable of killing me," Julian looks to Kai.

"I can kill you as easily as Siren can," Kai says.

Julian shakes his head.

"Try." He motions for his men to put their guns down. They do.

I glare at Julian, knowing this game too well.

Kai fires.

Julian ducks, and then fires back.

"No!" I scream, running to Kai.

"I'm fine, I'm fine," Kai says, her voice breathy from being shot in the arm.

"You didn't have to do that," I say.

Julian shrugs. "She shouldn't have missed."

I hold Kai as we collapse to the ground. I take off my shirt and tie it around her arm, ignoring the heated stare I'm getting from every man in the room. *Thank god I wore a bra.*

"What do you want, Julian? Why are we here?" I ask, knowing he'll answer. He always does.

"I want what's in the Black vault," Julian says, looking at Kai. She doesn't blink as she glares back with steely resolve.

"I need Lucy to be able to open it, once I have it," Julian says, looking off into the distance. *That's why he needs Kai and Lucy.*

"Why me?" I ask. He doesn't need me. He knows I know nothing about what's in the vault.

"Because I want you," Julian says. He's always wanted me. I don't have to ask what for. I'm done talking to him.

I hold Kai until we land in St. Kitts. I'm handcuffed, dragged off the plane, and loaded into a van next to Kai. The men are gentler with Kai.

"I'm fine, stop looking at me like that," Kai says.

"I'm sorry. We shouldn't have done that," I say.

"Yes, we should have. We got answers. We are one step closer to getting free," Kai says.

I nod. *She's right. We can do this. We can free ourselves.*

But when we are dragged to a dungeon on Julian's property, and I see Lucy in the cell—dirty, pale, and trembling—I'm scared.

It's all on me.

Kai is injured.

Lucy is dying.

I'm the only one strong enough to protect us. Kai can't because she has her kids to think about. Lucy can't; she can barely breathe, let alone hold a weapon.

It's all on me.

Zeke, hurry your ass up.

CHAPTER 30
ZEKE

I stare at the compound that is Julian's house, Beckett standing next to me.

"Wait. The plan is to just ring the doorbell?" Beckett asks. He's already heard the plan, but he thinks I'm crazy. Luckily, he's not in charge. Enzo and I are. And Enzo is good with my plan.

"Yes," Enzo and I say for the hundredth time. I say it in person, while Enzo says it from an undisclosed location where he's watching the twins and monitoring us through body cameras and earpiece radios.

Beckett sighs, running his one hand through his hair. He's a good man, but he's not Langston. Beckett cares about Kai; he's here for her. He and Enzo are brothers, so Enzo trusts Beckett with his life. Therefore, I do, but it's not the same.

We don't have enough time to wait for Langston to come back from off the grid. I'll deal with that asshole later.

"Let's go," I say, stepping forward. Beckett walks with me. The house is also surrounded by a dozen of Enzo's best men, ready to move in as soon as the civil negotiations end.

"Don't fuck up," Enzo says from the earpiece in my ear.

"Shut up, dipshit; you aren't helping," Beckett says, patting me on the back.

Neither of them is helping.

I ring the doorbell and wait.

Two seconds later, the door opens. It's opened by an armed guard, instead of one of Julian's house servants.

"Right this way," the man says, eyeing us both. He doesn't pat us down. He doesn't ask for our guns.

Somehow that feels worse. It means Julian is so sure we won't use them that he isn't even going to bother taking our guns from us.

We are led into a large room in the basement. Julian is waiting in the center of the room, and a dozen guards line the walls.

"Thank you for coming," Julian says. "Would you like a drink?"

"We aren't here to drink. Where are they?" I ask.

"I think we will all have a drink first." Julian snaps his fingers, and a man pours three drinks, setting them all at a circular table in the center of the room.

"Only three? Bishop isn't joining us?" I ask. Beckett and I reluctantly sit at the table.

"No, he had other business to attend to," Julian answers.

Fuck.

"Fuck," Enzo says in my head. "He's going after the vault, thinking we are all distracted with saving the girls. I have men protecting the vault, but my best men are there. It won't be enough."

Unless Kai already had the item they want moved. I wouldn't put her past her. She's smart. She knew the value of it. She knew the vault wouldn't hold it forever.

I ignore the bourbon poured for me. I reach into my pocket and slide the keys to the yacht across the table. "The yacht you requested."

Julian grins, staring at the keys. "I would say nice work, but that was the easiest task I've given you yet."

"Don't play games, the only reason you gave me that task was so you could track me and get the girls," I say.

Julian looks from me to Beckett. "Don't act like you really care about them. You would have brought more than a one-armed man with you to save them if you did."

Beckett and I both move to kill him, but Enzo shouts in our ear, "Don't fall for it. He just wants you to show your cards. Let him know how many people you brought with you. Don't fall for it."

I grab Beckett's arm, keeping him seated.

"Let's finish this truth or sins game. I'll tell you whatever you want. I'll answer your last two questions. Then we can be done with this," I say.

Julian takes a long puff on his cigar, blowing smoke in our faces.

"I don't need you to answer any questions. I have three women who are more than capable of answering questions," Julian says smugly.

A door opens behind him at his words, and I see them.

Lucy.

Kai.

Siren.

My heart beats faster and slower at the same time, seeing them all alive. I study each closely, though.

My heart stops looking at Lucy. I'm terrified for her.

Lucy looks horrible. She's whiter than a ghost, her bluish hair has faded, just like the life that has clearly seeped out of her. *What did he do to her? What torture did she suffer?* She's barely hanging onto life.

My heart skips a beat looking at Kai. I'm pissed.

Her arm is bleeding, and a shirt is tied around it, keeping the blood from spilling out. She looks strong, fierce, unbreakable. But beneath her armor, she's terrified she won't make it back to her family.

My heart races, looking at Siren.

Siren is the only one unhurt physically. She's standing in her jeans and sports bra, her hair tied back in one of my scrunchies. She looks like a warrior princess. I have no doubt her wheels are turning, figuring out how to kill every man who dares to touch her or her friends.

I let out a breath. *They are all still alive.* That's what I have to focus on.

"They're fine, chill," Julian says, sipping his drink while watching me.

"Lucy sure as hell isn't fine! Kai is bleeding! And Siren—"

"Siren is the only one you care about, and I haven't touched her," Julian says.

I growl. "I care about them all." I stand up, slamming my hands down on the table. I want to kick some ass, but I have to wait. I could take down every man in this room, but there are three women who could get seriously hurt if I'm not careful.

Beckett takes my arm and sits me back down.

"We will give you whatever you want. Do whatever you want. Just let them go," I say.

"I know, but you fascinate me, Zeke. You have since the moment I met you. Since you took Siren back even after she showed her loyalty was to me. I have what I need. You and I should part ways today. I don't need you to complete two more rounds of our game. But..." Julian takes a drink, pausing for dramatics.

"But Bishop isn't done with you. So I have to keep you around. I'll give you something in good faith."

"What do you mean?"

"You just completed a task. That earned you your choice of women, but only one."

I frown.

"Fine, then tell me the other two tasks now, and I can take all three with me."

"No, you get one. You get to save one. After I decide on your next task, you'll have a chance to save another. Although, I can't guarantee the state she will be in when I return her to you."

My hands ball into fists, and then I'm reaching for my gun. I just can't with this asshole anymore.

"You won't complete the final task I have planned for you, so the third woman—she'll be mine forever," Julian says.

I aim my gun at Julian's temple at the same time Beckett does.

"Give me all three, now," I say.

Then I notice the guns aimed at every woman's head. None of them tremble. None of them show weakness. All would die for me. And none of them would haunt me for eternity for letting them die.

"Choose. Which woman will you save? From torture, from suffering."

"You already hurt Lucy and Kai! I can't save them from all the pain."

"Lucy arrived in this state. Pretty sure she's sick and dying. You might want to save her, if you want her to live." Julian stands, walking over to Lucy, brushing his hand through her hair.

She doesn't fight him. That's not the Lucy I know. The Lucy I know, would have punched him. *How did I not see this before?* She's dying. I have to save her.

Julian walks over the Kai, who stands taller, not looking at me or him. If Kai looks at me, she knows I'll see the pain at not being with her kids. She knows I'll choose her. And she doesn't want me to.

"Are you going to choose this exotic creature? She must have a story and a history with you that I'm just itching to learn about. I would enjoy breaking her spirit."

"Don't touch me," Kai growls at him. He stops, loving her feisty reaction.

It makes me sick watching him touch her and imagining what he would do if I left her, if I couldn't save her. He would rape her, break her, maybe even kill her to get information from her.

"Don't worry, the bullet wound is just a surface scratch. You should teach her to aim to kill, though, so this doesn't happen again," Julian teases.

I frown, not wanting to know what happened to earn her that wound.

And then Julian moves to the woman I'm dreading looking at because I know what I'll find.

"Or will it be Siren, my Aria, here. She's everything you could want in a woman—strong, beautiful, can fire a gun better than most men. You're clearly in love with her. But is she in love with you? That's the question. Has she been tricking you this entire time? Is she still loyal to me? Would she be worth saving?"

Julian doesn't touch her. He knows he'll end up with a fat lip if he does. Siren has the most bindings on her—handcuffs around her wrists and ankles. Heavy chains constrain her while the others are just tied with rope. She broke free before in their presence. She can save herself. *But can I stand to leave her behind?*

"Choose one to save—one to leave with you. We can meet back

here in a week to discuss your fourth task. And if you complete it, that task will earn the freedom of one more woman."

A week is too long for him to have two of these women. I can't leave any of them here that long. But I can take one now. I can save one now without a fight. As soon as that person is free, then I can fight to save the other two.

Choose.

I can't choose. I love all of them.

"Zeke," Siren calls to me.

Don't look in her eyes. Don't...

But, of course, I do. She's already made the choice. She knows who I should save. And it's going to kill me to do it.

CHAPTER 31
SIREN

See, the bastard isn't even going to save you. He's going to choose to save someone else. He doesn't love you, Bishop's voice floods my head.

No, focus on Zeke. Let him be my anchor.

I push Bishop out. I won't let him back in. Not right now. Not when I need to help Zeke choose. I need to give him all my strength. *I can do this, I won't break.*

"Choose. Who will it be?" Julian asks, loving this moment—his sick, twisted game.

Julian and Bishop are just alike. They both like playing games, playing with people's minds. No wonder they work together.

I can't talk. Julian won't allow me, but I hold Zeke's gaze and tell him everything I can.

Lucy is dying. I should have told you, but she wouldn't let me. I've got her. I'll stay with her. I'll comfort her. She doesn't want to be saved.

Zeke looks at Lucy with a broken heart. Lucy nods and smiles at him, ready to die on her own terms.

Zeke swallows his pain and looks back at me.

Kai has two babies who depend on her. You know she's the choice. She's the only choice.

I'm strong enough to survive until you get back. Take Kai. Save her. Then come back to me. I won't let Julian or Bishop or any man touch me, I promise.

Zeke reaches into his pocket. Julian doesn't notice, he's too amused with the game he's devised to destroy the man I love.

Julian thinks he can destroy love.

He can, comes Bishop's voice. *Love doesn't exist.*

I grin.

Love does exist. Love can't be destroyed—not ever. Not a love like ours. Not a love like Enzo and Kai's. Not a love like Lucy's.

Zeke walks over to Lucy and whispers something in her ear. She smiles at him.

He walks over to Kai and looks her dead in the eye, a silent conversation passing between them. She shakes her head.

Then Zeke walks to me and presses something into the palm of my hand.

A ring.

I don't look down at it. I don't want Julian to see and take it away from me.

"Marry me?" Zeke whispers into my ear and steps back.

My heart flutters for an entirely different reason. For hope. For a future. For love.

I have something, someone to live for. I have someone who is going to love me forever. I'm not going to let Julian or Bishop take that from me.

"Yes," I breathe back with the biggest smile I've ever had on my face as I look at Zeke.

He grins back, his smile just as bright. For a second, I know that everything is going to be okay. Someday, we are going to live together. Someday, we might have kids and a beautiful house where we grow old together. *Someday...*

Julian looks at us. "So, I'm guessing you choose Siren?"

Zeke takes another second to look at me.

I nod my encouragement. *I've got this.*

Finally, Zeke looks at Julian, knowing he can't look at me when he speaks his decision. "I choose Kai."

CHAPTER 32
ZEKE

Siren said yes to marrying me. *She said yes!*

That's what I focus on as I lead Kai out of Julian's house. I focus on the small victory. I focus on the fact that it will only be minutes before getting to fight for Siren. *What can Julian do to her in minutes?*

Nothing.

But Lucy, god, Lucy...

Siren will protect her until I can get to her. Then I'll take her straight to a doctor.

As soon as we step out of the house, Kai punches me in the shoulder.

"Why did you save me?" Kai yells. She turns to Beckett. "And why did you let him?"

Beckett frowns, pulls out his phone, displaying a picture of the twins. "They are why we saved you—*them*. Don't you dare make us feel bad for choosing you."

"She's safe?" Enzo's voice breaks in my ear.

I pull out my earpiece and give it to Kai. "Talk to your husband. Then tell me we shouldn't have saved you."

Kai takes it. "Siren's strong. Stronger than me and more skilled. She'll be okay."

I nod. "I know she will. But Lucy..."

Kai rests her hand on my shoulder with a frown. "Even if you had chosen her, I don't think you could have saved her. Siren will be with her."

"I should be," I say.

"Then get your ass back in there and save her."

I look at Beckett. "Get Kai somewhere safe."

He nods. "Be careful. Julian's going to be prepared for you to attack. And we have no idea where Bishop is." Enzo said he never showed up at the vault.

I look at Kai, who just winks at me, telling me she moved the item they are all fighting for. I would trade it away in a second if it would free Siren and Lucy. But apparently, Julian and Bishop would rather play games.

Fine, I'll finish the game by killing them all.

I take the earpiece back from Kai. "Get ready to attack on my cue," speaking to the men surrounding the house, waiting to attack.

"Go get your girl," Kai says.

"I asked her to marry me," I say.

She laughs. "Of course, you did. Good, we can have a big double wedding when this is all over."

"I thought you were already married?"

"I am, but I want a big wedding where we can celebrate with all of our friends."

I grin. "Double wedding it is."

"Where am I taking Kai?" Beckett asks.

"Airport. You remember, Nora? She'll get you to Enzo," I say.

Beckett stills at her name, but nods. I'm not sure if he's happy or scared to be seeing Nora again.

I ignore him. Whatever drama is going on between the two of them can wait until later.

I check that all my guns are loaded. "Let's go," I say, giving my men the signal to move in.

With my size sixteen boot, I break down the front door. No one greets me this time. It's eerily silent.

I hear several of my men give all clears as they enter the house.

Hmm, strange. "Head to the basement, that's where I left them."

I open the basement door and head down the stairs first.

At the bottom of the stairs, nothing.

It's a ghost town.

Like moments ago didn't even happen. It was all a dream.

"Search everywhere," I command as men file down into the basement after me.

"Clear."

"Clear."

"Clear."

Each time a man says that, I become more afraid. *How the hell did they get out of here so fast?*

Where are they?

"Over here," one man says.

I run over to him.

"There is a tunnel," he starts.

"Fuck," I say.

"Through the tunnel, everyone," I say. *I'm coming Siren, just hold on.*

I jump into the dark tunnel first and start running, not waiting for my men to follow.

Suddenly, I hear the explosion.

I turn and run but get hit by a falling rock anyway. The tunnel is closed off as I stare up from where I am on the ground, pinned under a large boulder.

"Well, that couldn't have worked out better if I had planned it that way," a woman giggles. "Oh wait, I did plan that."

I stare into the darkness, trying to spot from whom the voice is coming, but I can't see anything but shadows in the dark.

"Who are you? What do you want?" I ask as I struggle to get free. I don't have my gun. It lays a few feet in front of me. I dropped it when the boulder hit me. The rest of my weapons are pinned under the boulder.

Fuck.

The woman leans down, out of the shadows, until I see her face.

"I'm your worst nightmare," she says.

In that moment, I realize I'm not going to be keeping my word. I'm not going to be able to keep my promise to Lucy or Siren. I'm not going to save them. They are on their own. It's going to be a struggle to even save myself. A struggle to even keep my promise to marry Siren someday.

CHAPTER 33
SIREN

We've been moved three times. Three different countries. Three different planes.

I hold Lucy to my chest as she coughs. I suspect it's pneumonia. Her body is weak; she can barely breathe. She has breast cancer, but right now, it's not the cancer that's going to kill her. It's the infection, the cold, the pain.

I hold the ring Zeke gave me in my hand, refusing to put it on. He should be the one who does that.

But I read the engraving over and over.

I promise...forever.

"He's not coming. He's going to break his promise," Lucy says.

I frown. "Zeke's coming."

Lucy shakes her head. "It's been three days."

"We've been moved all of those days. It takes a lot of effort to track people all over the world. He's coming."

"No, he's not. You have to save yourself, Siren. Save yourself."

"Stop. He's coming. And I'm here to protect you. You just focus on staying alive."

"I'm dying. There is no reason to save me. They can torture me, and I won't tell them about the weapon."

"Weapon?"

"Yea, my big secret. You should know."

"No, Zeke didn't want me to know." He thought it could save me. If I know, they can torture me. They can torture me now, and I won't be able to help them because I don't know the truth.

Lucy raises her eyebrows, reading my mind.

"My mom, she was a genius. A crazy, psychotic woman, but also a scientific genius."

Even if they torture this secret out of me later, I'm not stopping a dying woman's last words.

"She was always in the lab. Always studying. Determined. She was a horrible mother. Never around to watch out for me. But a genius in that lab."

Lucy takes a deep breath, her voice weak, her body trembling from the cold. I squeeze her closer to me, begging her to continue.

"One day, she discovered how to create the ultimate weapon. Guaranteed to kill any man..."

"What did she discover?" I ask, my voice weak.

"The cure."

I frown. That doesn't sound like a weapon.

"The cure for cancer."

"Lucy, that's a cure, not a weapon."

Lucy shakes her head. "No, she discovered how to help people live, but also how to infect people with a vicious form of cancer. A contagious cancer. One that can spread."

"But she discovered a cure. Why didn't you take it?"

Lucy looks up at me. "Because no one should live forever."

"But it wouldn't be forever. It would have given you a full-length life."

"Yes, but it would have destroyed everyone. I'm the only one who can open the container. The cure and the curse, the cancer that could be used as the ultimate weapon. This is my destiny. To die. To let the weapon die with me."

"Oh, Lucy. You're the bravest, strongest woman I know." I stroke her hair, holding her chilled body tighter in my arms.

She smiles. "I'm pretty badass, aren't I?" coughing her words.

Her suffering kills me.

"What can I do?"

"I want to see the stars one last time."

We are locked in an underground dungeon with bars and keys and locks.

"Okay, I can do that. Julian!" I shout.

It takes a minute, but it gets his attention via a guard.

And then he's standing at the door, watching me.

He smirks. "Yes?"

"Give us five minutes outside, alone."

"And why would I do that?"

"I'll give you what you want."

"Which is what?" Bishop enters the basement, crossing his arms.

Both of them in the same room scares the shit out of me.

"Lucy told me how to access the weapon. I'll tell you whatever you need to know. I'll even give you myself to own, just let us outside," I lie.

Lucy coughs.

"Who are you promising that to? We can't both control you," Bishop asks.

Julian rolls his eyes. "We are on the same side. Does it matter?"

Bishop leans forward. "Yes, it does."

"You two can decide who gets to control me later. Do we have a deal?"

The men exchange glances, then Bishop nods. Apparently, he's the one in charge, which terrifies me.

Julian and I already have an agreement, an understanding. He knows I won't break my promise, and I know he won't either. But Bishop, I have no idea.

Julian unlocks the door. "Five minutes. If you run..."

"She's dying. I won't leave her," I say angrily.

I lift Lucy up and carry her up the stairs. I don't know where we are, but it's somewhere warm, I realize when I stand outside. I make my way over to a patch of grass overlooking a small pond. I lay Lucy in my lap, looking at the water.

The sky is clear, the stars and moon shining down on us.

"Here we go, Lucy. The stars are beautiful, aren't they?"

She nods.

For a moment, we are just two women, who have been lucky enough to be loved and be in love, looking up at the sky.

"Can you do something for me?" Lucy asks.

"Anything," I say, trying to hold back my tears as I hold her.

"Tell Palmer I loved her. She was the love of my life. Not Zeke. She's mad I chose death over our love. Tell her I love her. It was always her. And if could, I would have lived forever for her."

I can't hold back the tears now. They stream down my cheeks.

"I promise," I say.

I hold Lucy against my chest.

Bishop and Julian argue behind us about who will control me. The consensus is that Julian can have his way with me first, but Bishop will be the one to break me. Bishop thinks he already has control over my mind.

I know what my fate is. Zeke can't save me. He broke his promise to come back to me, although I'm scared to know why.

I won't be able to save myself either.

I look down at Lucy, making the ultimate sacrifice. She's giving up her love—her life. To protect us all from something her mother created.

I don't care what those men do to me. All I care about is this— being here for an amazing woman and letting her love flow through me. I don't care about Zeke's promise. I care about Lucy's.

As I watch Lucy leave this world peacefully, with love in her heart, I realize love is the only thing that can save me. It saved Lucy from living in pain.

I hope love is enough to save me from the pain I'm about to endure...

FALLEN LOVE

PROLOGUE
SIREN

"I know," Zeke says.

Those words haunt me. They dig deep into my heart, piercing my very soul. His words offer me everything I need and nothing I deserve.

"I know, Siren. I know," he repeats again, stepping out of the darkness and into my bedroom aboard the yacht. The moonlight illuminates his face.

My bottom lip trembles. My eyes are watery, but I refuse to cry—I can't cry. Not now. Not after everything we've been through. I won't shed any more damn tears.

Zeke takes a step forward, and my heart wrenches. My pulse is in my throat.

His presence makes me tense. I don't know how to feel about Zeke anymore. His hardened eyes are lost; he doesn't know how to feel about me either.

I look down, twisting the ring Zeke gave me. A ring that represents forever.

A forever we will never have. A forever we both surrendered.

Zeke takes my hand, and I spot his matching ring. A ring that tells the world he's my husband. He's taken. He's mine.

If only those words were true.

"Siren—"

"No," I snap. I can't talk. I can't speak reason. I can't listen to him explain why things ended the way they did. I don't want to hear that he still loves me. Sometimes, love isn't enough. It isn't enough to survive on.

We need more than love. We need air and water and food. We need trust and truth.

We've both sinned too many times.

We've shed too much blood.

There is no coming back from what we've done.

We've wrecked more than just our love. We've hurt every person who has come into our lives.

Every.

Single.

One.

We are alone now. But not together.

Together we destroy. We ruin. Our love destroyed everyone else we love.

Our love has to end. We can't keep being selfish. We can't keep hurting others. We can't keep sacrificing everything to save the other.

I squeeze my eyes shut, doing everything to keep my tears in— keep my pain in.

"I'm sorry," I say. Sorry that I'm crying. Sorry that I hurt you—hurt them. Sorry that I saved you. Life would have been so much easier had I let Zeke die, had I finished my vow to Julian and then vanished myself.

Instead, I was selfish. I saved a man, knowing our love would destroy everything.

"I'm not," Zeke says, pulling on my hand until I'm standing in front of him.

Face to face, hands gripping each other, knowing this is the last time we will touch. The last time we will be in the same room together. *The last time...*

"Our love was never meant to last forever," Zeke says, his own tears dripping down onto our joined hands.

"But we promised. We vowed. We loved—forever," I say, my words broken and painful.

"We kept those promises," Zeke says.

I stare at him. Feeling more love than I've ever felt for another human being. More love than I knew was possible to love another man.

"I'm sorry," I say. I grab his neck, my hand fisting his hair, and I pull him down into one last desperate kiss. A kiss to top all kisses. A kiss to survive on for the rest of my life.

Zeke's lips remain closed at first. From shock. From trying to guard his heart. From trying to protect me. He thinks our departure will be harder if we kiss.

I don't give a damn about what's hard or easy.

I love Zeke Kane with all of my heart. I will never love again like I do now. *Never*.

This is it for me. This is it.

One more kiss.

That's what I need to take with me.

It doesn't take much to part Zeke's lips. My tongue is suddenly inside his, feeling alive again for the first time in weeks. I'm floating on a cloud and doing battle at the same time. That's what it's like kissing Zeke.

Zeke's hands grab my hips, holding me tightly against him until I feel every inch of his hardness. I memorize it all. Everything about him becomes ingrained in my memory, pushing all other memories out until I remember this moment, forever.

I remember the way Zeke feels pushed against me. How hard and strong and protective he feels.

Another snap remembers how his wet lips shoot tingles of electricity through my body. How his tongue on my tongue hits me deep to my core.

I will never forget how his hands hold me like he can't ever let me go.

But then Zeke does let me go.

He ends the kiss, effectively ending us.

We both take a step back; it's the hardest step either of us has ever taken, but it's necessary.

We both know what comes next. We both know our future. We both know this is the last time we will ever be together.

We both touch our rings.

Zeke walks out the door, never to return. I'm alone.

Zeke's gone.

The love of my life is gone.

We promised forever.

What a forever it was.

I don't regret it.

Even if I should regret it, at least for the sake of those who were hurt by our love.

I hoped our forever would last longer, but from the moment it started, we were always destined to end. We wouldn't last a lifetime. We wouldn't have kids and grow old together.

I stare at the engraving on my ring.

I promise...forever.

Zeke kept his forever promise.

Our forever just ended sooner than we could have ever imagined. Love saved us, and in the end, it destroyed everyone we love.

CHAPTER 1
SIREN

Death is only the beginning.

Isn't that the saying?

Maybe that's true for some, but it's not what I've experienced. Death is definitely an end. An end that may lead to a new beginning, if those who are left are able to start again.

But sometimes death is just the end. Sometimes death breaks those who are left so deeply, and there is no coming back. There is no starting over. There's just nothing left to do but wait for death to take you as well.

Watching Lucy die in my arms was the hardest death I've had to endure. I thought she was my enemy. I thought of her as the villain. Watching her sacrifice herself, with a cure in her grasp, was the most selfless thing I've ever witnessed.

She died protecting us all because the cure her mother created also happens to be a contagious cancer that could wipe out continents. If any of our enemies got ahold of it—Julian, Bishop, anyone—they could use it to control the entire planet.

Lucy was the only thing preventing them from getting what they wanted. Lucy protected it. And Zeke protected her. And I protected Zeke. In a way, we are all connected. We are all the reason Julian and

Bishop don't have the viles, the research, the key to controlling the world.

"Promise me," Lucy says, as she lays in my arms.

I suck back tears. Lucy isn't crying. I'm not going to let the last thing she sees be my blubbering face.

"I promise," I say, even though I'm afraid I will never be able to keep it. It's a huge promise I just made. A promise that requires sinning and lying to a lot of people, something I've only just managed to be able to do.

Finally, I can't help it. A tear pools in the corner of my eye, threatening to reveal the pain and fear I'm feeling inside as I hold Lucy in my arms, laying out on the grass in whatever country we were taken to. We're looking out at a beautiful lake, thousands of stars shine overhead, and the moon makes the night sky seem lighter than I've ever seen it.

Lucy finds my hand. I hold it, and she smiles up at me.

"Don't be sad for me," Lucy says, raising her frail hand up to try and wipe my tear. The one tear rolls down my cheek with the speed of a freight train. And then all of my tears are cascading down my cheek.

"How can I not? This shouldn't have happened. You should have had more time. I should have made sure Zeke chose you, not Kai. I should have—"

Lucy coughs. I stroke her back, trying to get more oxygen into her lungs, even though I know her time is dwindling.

"No, I didn't want Zeke to have the burden of watching me die. Someone who loved you, like we loved each other at one point in our life, shouldn't have to be here to see me like this. I want him to remember me as I was, not like this."

I nod, understanding. When my time is up, I hope Zeke isn't there. I couldn't stand for him to be there. I don't want him to ever have to remember me as anything but the woman who loved him deeper than he's ever been loved.

I squeeze her hand tighter. "I'm happy to be here."

Lucy smiles. "Who wouldn't want to watch their competition for the man they love die?" She teases.

I hug her tighter in my lap. "If you had wanted Zeke, you would have won. I can't think of a more incredible woman."

She nods. "I know. But I fell in love with Palmer. I don't want you to think Zeke was the love of my life; he wasn't. Palmer was. Zeke is just an incredible best friend."

"I know."

"Tell me about Palmer," I say.

Lucy does; she tells me everything. Without a doubt, Palmer was Lucy's love. As much as it might have hurt Palmer to have to watch the woman she loves die, she should have been the one here.

"Palmer," Lucy says, looking up at me. She's been out of it for the last hour, hallucinating and barely catching her breath. Her pulse is weak, her face is sweaty, and I swear she only takes a breath every minute or so.

"Yes?" I ask, blinking back my tears. I can be Palmer. I can love her in her last moments on this earth.

"I love you," Lucy says.

"I love you, too," I say back. I don't have to lie. I love Lucy. Maybe I'm not in love with her. But damn, do I love her strength, her courage, her selflessness. It's the most beautiful thing I've ever seen.

I kiss her on the cheek.

I watch Lucy take her last breath. I watch her eyes close. I watch her heart thump one last time, and then she's just...*gone*.

I've seen death.

I've taken lives before.

I've killed.

But I've never seen anything so peaceful as Lucy's death. I hold her body in my arms for a few minutes. A crack of thunder startles me back into reality.

I stare up at the sky, and I see clouds rolling in. The storm had been waiting until Lucy took her last breath, allowing her final few minutes on this earth to be filled with beautiful landscape.

I gently roll Lucy off my lap and stand to gather wildflowers nearby. I form a bouquet and rest it in her hands. Maybe I should have negotiated with Julian and Bishop to take her body back for a proper burial, but I don't think Lucy would have wanted that. She would have wanted to feel free, not buried deep in the ground.

I carry her body to the edge of the lake and softly push her floating body out into the water as the storm rolls in. She looks like an angel before she disappears under the water, the pouring rain forcing her down.

I'm thankful for the rain; it hides my tears as I hear Julian Reed approach and turn to face him. I wish I had more time to mourn Lucy, but there's work to be done to keep my promise to her.

"So, you won? You get to have control of me?" I ask.

"There wasn't anything to win. I'm in charge. Bishop works for me, just like you. He will continue his work training your mind later, but first, we had a deal," Julian says, holding his hand out to me.

Julian is wearing dark suit pants, with a rain jacket over it. He looks put together and proper, even out here in the middle of nowhere. Even as the rain pours down, he's unfazed.

I look up into his eyes, and I see what he wants. It's what he's always wanted—*me*.

I swallow my pride. I push down the desire to punch him in the balls. I made a deal with the devil. I agreed to give him myself in exchange for making sure Lucy died with dignity and love. I don't regret it, and I won't renege on my end of the deal.

I made a promise. I'll keep it.

I always have. That's the main thing Zeke and I both agree on. We keep our promises. If we don't have that, then we've lost our identities.

So I take Julian's hand, surrendering myself to him. I pray that whatever was keeping Zeke away before has been defeated, because I need him to come. I need him to save me, even though I've told him not to before. I told him I'm not worth saving; I don't want him to save me.

I've never wanted Zeke to save me, especially from Julian, because every time Zeke saves me, it risks Zeke finding out the truth.

But without Zeke, I won't survive this time. This time, I need him. This time I need Zeke to save me...

CHAPTER 2
ZEKE

My shoulders are throbbing and tense, that's the first thing I notice before I even open my eyes. My left hand is numb, that's the second.

I open my eyes. A dizziness and splitting headache hit me next.

I blink. I've dealt with all of this before, it's nothing new. I'm not going to let an injured arm and a headache keep me from doing my job. My job is simple: protect those I love.

I quickly take in my situation in a matter of seconds. My wrists are tied, stretching me wide over my head in a V. My left hand is crushed, which is why I can't feel it. And my shoulders are sore from being stretched. I'm not wearing a shirt, and sweat is falling down my neck and forehead.

Drugs are still pulsing through my system—that's why I'm sweaty and my head is so foggy. My ankles are also tied with thick chains bolted to the floor.

I kick, testing the strength of the metal—it's heavy-duty. It's going to take a lot of effort to break free, especially in my state.

I survey the room as well. I'm underground, most likely in a basement from the lack of windows and unfinished floors. There is a lamp in the corner, but otherwise, I'm in the dark.

But I'm not alone.

I can hear the breathing of another person; the breath speeds as the person realizes I'm awake. He or she can now question and torture me.

My brain quickly puts all the pieces together. I was in Julian's house. I was going to get Siren and Lucy back. I went down, into a tunnel, and then a crash...

A boulder trapped me in the tunnel. A woman stepped forward from the darkness.

I look up, and the same woman is standing in front of me now.

She's a small woman, much smaller than Siren. She's probably five foot nothing. Her muscles are thin and long, not like the bulky brutes that normally inhabit my world. It's clear she doesn't usually carry a gun or weapon. She has no skills in martial arts or fighting. I can see it all in the way she carries herself. In fact, she looks like she's about to cry as she looks at me.

Her watering eyes trigger my own suffering. Lucy is dying, and I'm not there to comfort her. Siren is probably being tortured or raped, and I'm not there to protect her.

Please, god, let Beckett, or Enzo, or Kai...let one of them be there to save her. Please. I'll never ask for anything again. I just got Siren. She said yes to marrying me, yes to forever. She said yes.

Now, she's gone.

I failed her.

I promised I would come back when I saved Kai over her and Lucy. I promised. But I failed.

"How long?" I croak, but my voice answers for me. I've been out of it for days, most likely. My throat wouldn't get this dry, my shoulders wouldn't throb this badly, and my hand would still feel the pain if it had only been a few hours.

"Three days," the woman answers me.

My eyes fly open again, and my arms and legs struggle against the chains as I roar in agony.

Three.

Fucking.

Days.

So much could happen in that amount of time. Lucy could have died. And Siren...

God, I can't think of what Julian or Bishop could have done to her in that amount of time. After I got Siren back from Bishop, she was barely able to keep it together. This time...I have no idea if Siren will be the same woman or not. If she'll ever forgive me for failing her.

I'll never forgive myself.

The woman pulls out a cigarette and lights it. "You can struggle against those chains all you want, but you won't get free."

She puffs out some smoke, and I notice her hand shaking. Her eyes are puffy, like she's been crying all three days I've been unconscious. The nicotine entering her system seems to be the only thing keeping her alive.

"Who are you?" I ask, not sure if she'll answer me. She did answer my last question.

"You don't remember?"

She sucks on her cigarette again. I think back, trying to remember if she told me a name.

"I'm Palmer," she says casually.

"What do you want?" I ask. It's obvious this isn't her world. She's not the type with experience kidnapping and torturing someone. I doubt she's ever killed anyone before. Her manicured nails and general frailness tell me that she probably has never even held a gun before. She belongs anywhere except in this basement.

Most likely, she had loads of help to get me here. She's too small to lift my body. I listen carefully, and I hear the creak of a footstep on the floor above. She had help. I don't even know if she is in charge.

"Nothing you can give me," she steps forward, the color returning to her cheeks, but her pain never leaving her eyes.

"Palmer, I don't know what trouble you are in, but I can help you. I don't care who your enemies are. Let me go, let me save someone I love, and I will do everything I can to help you and protect you. I promise." Palmer has to be in trouble. Maybe she's a drug addict. I look at her arms and see no needle marks. Her skin looks healthy, not the yellow-greenish color of most addicts. And her head seems clear.

She's just in pain—incredible, unmoving pain.

"You think you can help me?"

I nod.

She shakes her head. "I've known you for a long time, Zeke Kane. I was told you are a protector, a selfless savior, but it seems to me that you have a hero complex."

I frown, not sure who she knows that has talked about me. None of my friends would say anything about me to a complete stranger.

"Haven't figured it out yet?" Her voice lifts, getting stronger as her pain spreads through her veins into every crevice of her body. I can see it move inside her, her torture turning to anger.

"Who are you? What do you want, Palmer?" I keep my voice calm, hoping it will relax her.

"I want the love of my life back!" Her voice is loud and echos throughout the room.

I still. My heart catches, and my breath pauses. I'm afraid I know the answer—why I'm here. And I don't know how to convince a person who has lost everything to let me go so I can get the only thing in my life back that matters—Siren.

"I want Lucy back," Palmer says, her hand shaking as she grips the cigarette like it's her lifeline. The tears fall anyway.

"What happened to Lucy?" I ask, needing her to keep talking. To get it all out and not break down. I try testing the chains again, but I won't be able to get free without a lot of effort and strength. Strength I don't have at the moment.

"She's dead! That's what happened. She's dead, and I couldn't save her!" Palmer screams, but it's not the volume that gets me. It's the heartbreak.

I feel it—Lucy's dead. Palmer isn't the only one who failed her; I failed Lucy too.

My tears blur my eyes. I lost one of my best friends, a woman I loved. *Did I choose wrong? Should I have saved Lucy instead of Kai?*

No, I shouldn't have chosen at all. I should have found a way to save them all.

"I'm so sorry. I loved Lucy too. I—"

"No, you don't get to speak. You had your chance to save her and you failed," Palmer shakes her cigarette at me.

I close my mouth. No words can bring back Lucy.

"I tried to use you to bargain with them. I tried to trade you for Lucy, but they wouldn't trade."

My eyes darken. They don't want Lucy—they want Siren. They want what Lucy was protecting. What I was protecting.

"Let me go, and I'll kill them. I'll avenge Lucy's death. I'll kill every single person responsible for her death."

Palmer shakes her head. "You're the reason she's dead, not them."

I frown, not following her logic. She's mourning a woman she loves. She hasn't said it, but she doesn't have to. She loved Lucy. I have no doubt Lucy loved her back.

Lucy loved who she loved—man or woman, it made no difference to her. Palmer wouldn't be hurting so much if Lucy didn't love her back.

"Lucy was dying. She had cancer. The treatments stopped working. I stood by her side. I want to the chemo. I loved her through it all. She told me she was cured. She told me she didn't love me anymore. It was all lies."

She sucks on the cigarette, gaining strength from it.

"She wasn't cured. She was sick. She was dying. The chemo wasn't enough. But what her mother created was strong enough."

"You don't know that."

"Don't I? She had the cure, and she wouldn't take it. Even for me." Tears sting her eyes again.

Palmer looks at me with so much damn pain. "She wouldn't take the cure because of you. She loved you. She wanted to protect you. She knew that opening that box would save her life, but it would risk yours —along with everyone else's on this planet. It wasn't just the cure; it was a curse upon this world."

Palmer's head falls. "It was because of her love for you that she wouldn't save herself."

"No," I whisper.

Palmer's head slowly lifts, until she's looking at me. "Lucy loved you more than she did me."

"No, she wasn't thinking about me. She saved the world. If our enemies got it, they would destroy us all."

"Stop lying! She loved you more. She was protecting you. She died protecting you."

Palmer is in my face now, her anger pulsing off her body, her breath hot as fire, and her eyes bulging with rage.

"Let me help you," I say.

She smiles. "Oh, you'll help me. You'll help me deal with this pain." She pounds her hand against her chest, where I know she's hurting.

"You'll help me by giving me an outlet for my anger. You will feel everything I feel, because you took her from me. And when I'm finished, you will tell me where the cure is."

"Palmer, I know you are in pain. That won't go away easily, but you need help. Let me help you. Torturing me won't help. I'm built to withstand torture. I won't break. I've never broke. You aren't experienced with torturing someone. You aren't a devil. You're not a monster. Don't turn into one. Lucy wouldn't want that."

Palmer steps back, and I see the pain turning into full-on rage behind her blue eyes.

"You don't think I can break you?" Her nostrils flare. "That's only because you've never felt torture from someone who has lost someone they love. You've never felt the pain of a person who has nothing left to live for. I lost everything."

"If you keep me here, I'll have nothing to live for either. We will just be two people locked in an endless battle of pain."

She steps closer to me again, calm and confident. Her calmness scares me. I don't cower for me. I can handle the physical pain she's about to inflict. It terrifies me because every second I'm here is a second Siren is at risk.

I can't save Lucy.

But I can still save Siren.

"This is for Lucy." Palmer pushes the cigarette into my skin over my heart.

I don't react to the pain. I don't feel it. All I feel is Siren.

"This is going to be fun. You're strong. You have your own love you are holding onto. I'm going to enjoy taking her from you."

CHAPTER 3
SIREN

I expect to be brought into a dungeon. A room with ropes and chains to bind me, to prevent me from fighting, so Julian Reed can do what he wants with my body.

I expect darkness and pain. I expect him to rip my legs apart and push himself inside.

Instead, Julian holds my hand like we are lovers as he leads me into the large tent-like house in the middle of the African savannah. He leads me past his men. Past Bishop. Past everyone. Until we reach the room at the far end.

When we step inside, it's nothing like the dungeon it should be. This room isn't a cage. This room is awe-inspiring.

Large windows cover two of the walls and the ceiling, giving a perfect view of the starry night and storm clouds rolling in. The floor is white and luxurious, like a cloud beneath our feet. Beautiful candles are lit in one corner of the room, providing romantic lighting. Champagne and strawberries chill on the other side of the room.

This room is meant for honeymooners, for couples celebrating special anniversaries. This room isn't meant for a man to take what he wants from a woman without her consent. This room can't handle what is going through Julian's head right now. It can't take in the dangerous thoughts.

This room is pure. It's beautiful. It's romantic. None of the things that Julian wants. *So why did he choose this room?*

If all Julian wanted to do was rape me, he would have done it years ago. He wants more. He wants me to surrender to him. He wants me to be his.

My lips tighten, and my heart thumps carefully in my chest, looking for an escape route. Julian can want me to be his all he wants. He can rape and torture me for years in this perfect room, but I will never be his. Even if I wanted to be—I'm Zeke's. I gave Zeke Kane everything, and I can never get my heart back.

"What do you think?" Julian asks, his voice husky and dripping with hunger.

"Pretty. It doesn't suit you," I say.

He brings our connected hands up to his lips, and he kisses the back of my hand before he sucks in a deep breath, taking in my scent.

"You smell like wildflowers," he says.

"I smell like mud and rainwater."

He kisses my hand again, and I jerk it away on instinct. I can't stand his lips touching me. *How am I going to let him do anything else to me?*

I'm not.

I take a step away from Julian, expecting this to be the moment where he grabs me and tries to use his force to fuck me. The moment where he snaps his fingers and guards come running in to pin me down.

I'm ready. I don't have any weapons, but I don't need them. I only need the desire to avenge Lucy's death. The desire to save myself. The pull to Zeke, a man who gave me a ring, and promised me forever.

"Relax, Aria. I'm not going to hurt you," Julian says, his voice purring.

I scoff. "You've already hurt me by kidnapping me. By making the man I love choose between the women he loves."

"I thought he would choose you. I really did." Julian walks over to the champagne, pops the cork, and then pours two glasses.

I watch him from across the room, careful to avoid what is sitting in the middle of the room. I refuse to look at it. If I do, the situation will become real, the fear will rise in my chest, fight or flight will kick in.

I won't run; I'll fight. I'll have to fight every man in the house to escape. I could win, but I could also end up dead. Something I promised Zeke wouldn't happen.

I shouldn't fight. I should be smart. I should manipulate Julian into letting me go. I'm just not sure how to do that yet.

Julian walks back to me as my eyes cut to the door behind me.

"It's a metal door. Soundproof. Bulletproof. And I'm the only one who can open it," Julian says, handing me a glass of champagne.

"What do you mean, you are the only one who can open it?"

"Test it."

I reach behind me and push on the door—nothing.

Julian pulls out his phone. "Duncan, try to open the door to my room." Julian ends the call, and we hear a faint sound as a man pushes on the door.

Nothing.

"As I was saying, this is my own little piece of heaven. I brought you here because I knew you would love it. It's beautiful and enchanting, and I'm the only person who has ever been in this room, until you."

I raise an eyebrow. "I know you, Julian. You like nice things, but nothing this beautiful. This room wasn't built for you."

Julian chuckles. "I love how well you know me, Aria. You're right. This room is far too feminine and romantic for my likes, but it's perfect for the woman I love."

He holds out his glass and waits for me to do the same. My hand shakes as I raise my glass in the air. My throat tightens, trying to suffocate me to save me. In my head, I already know what's going to happen next. I know, and I can't stop it.

No, I could stop it, I just won't. The cost would be too great.

"To the woman I love finally finding the man of her dreams."

He clinks his glass against mine, the ring of the crystal hits my ears like a sharp knife to my eardrums. It continues to ring in my ears long after the sound has stopped.

Julian sips his champagne. My weak hand drops my glass to the floor, shattering it into hundreds of tiny pieces.

"Oh, my love, you're shaking. I knew I should have gotten you inside before you became soaked by the rainstorm. Here, let me warm you up."

Julian leans forward, his hand tucking my soaking wet hair behind my hear and gripping my neck in a move all men do when they are trying to comfort a woman before going into a kiss. But there is nothing comforting about his touch. There is nothing welcome about his kiss.

I lean back, just enough for him to notice.

"We had a deal," Julian says in a soothing voice, like he knows he doesn't even have to raise his voice in order to get me to do what he wants.

He's right. We did have a deal. I promised to surrender myself if he let Lucy spend her last moments in my arms, in peace. A promise is a promise. I don't regret it at all, for Lucy's sake.

I also promised to tell them where Lucy's secret is, the box containing the cure and curse, not that I have a clue. But Julian is too focused on fucking me to ask about Lucy's box.

So this time, when his lips move toward mine, I don't move. I literally don't move. I'm stiller than a statue. I don't breathe. I don't twitch. I don't grimace. I swear my heart, brain, and nerves shut down so I don't feel a damn thing when his lips brush over mine.

I feel nothing, but my damn eyes see everything. I see him lean in. I see his tongue lick over his lips, moistening them in anticipation of our kiss. I see his eyes close, and I hear his soft moan as he kisses me.

I see the shit-eating grin on his face when he ends the kiss a few seconds later.

Fuck, what have I gotten myself into? I promised I would surrender to him, and he's not going to stop with a kiss. The kiss is nothing compared to the thoughts in his head. I won't be able to survive everything he plans on doing.

"That's not surrendering, Siren. You promised to be mine. You promised to give me everything. That was like kissing a corpse. When I kiss you, you're supposed to kiss me back," Julian says, stroking my neck with his thumb like he has a claim to me.

"That wasn't part of our deal. Surrendering and giving you everything is not the same thing," I say, taking a step back again.

His hand drops, and I'm free for another second.

"You aren't one to back down on a deal." He raises his brow, and his smirk returns to his disgusting, vile face.

I surrendered myself to save Lucy.

But I gave everything to protect Zeke. Zeke will never know why. He will never forgive me, either.

I twist the ring on my right hand. A ring I doubt will ever move to my left. It would be a sin. I can't give myself to Zeke, not fully, not in the way I want and he deserves. Not without risking everything.

Surrender and live—keep my promise that I traded to give Lucy a peaceful end.

Fight and die—ruining the promise I made to Zeke to stay alive. To let him come save me.

I'm fucked either way.

"I surrender," I say, keeping my promise and ensuring I live just a little longer. But knowing that by giving myself to this monster, I'll probably want to die.

CHAPTER 4
ZEKE

Palmer is pissed.

She's full of rage.

It emanates off her in waves. Her wrath has confiscated every corner of her body. Every nerve. Every blood vessel. Every organ is consumed with her anger.

When she pushes the cigarette butt into my skin, it's not just the pain of the searing fire that I feel, it's her anger. It's impossible not to absorb it. She's shoving her anger into the space between us.

Anger—it's such a complicated emotion. You can be angry for so many reasons. You can choose to be angry. You can be angry because you think life has dealt you an unfair hand. Angry because someone betrayed you. Angry because someone is preventing you from getting something you want.

Palmer isn't angry for any of those reasons. She's angry because it hides her pain. She's lost the woman she loves, the only person who matters to her, and now she's blaming me for her loss.

I understand.

I feel the same way. I feel the pain at the loss of my friend, Lucy. If someone had hurt Siren, killed her, I would kill anyone who could have prevented her death, because anger gives you more control than pain and fear does.

Anger gives you a reason to take action. To do something to feel in control.

Pain leads to mourning. And while it can heal you, mourning doesn't let you feel in control. Mourning is letting yourself feel the loss of the person you love; it's letting it consume you. It's not moving on, but it's accepting what happened.

Palmer isn't ready to mourn. The pain would overwhelm her. But she can deal with her anger. And I'm going to be the one who feels all of her fury.

"You're going to have to do better than that," I say as she pushes the end of the cigarette into a second spot on my skin. I don't flinch. I don't feel anything physical, just the hot pulse of her rage.

I don't let her anger in. That's not how I'm going to win. I could get angry that she's preventing me from rescuing Siren. I could let that anger build inside me and turn it into strength to get free of these heavy chains. I could use that rage to take out the dozens of men on guard us above. I could use it to find a way to hunt Siren down and save her.

But it would require me to kill Palmer in the process, something I can't do. I owe it to Lucy. Lucy left Palmer because she loved her and didn't want her to watch her die. She didn't want Palmer to suffer with her. I can't kill the woman Lucy loved.

So I can't let my anger overwhelm me like Palmer is doing. I have to stay strong. I have to let Palmer break down. Only then will her pain overtake her anger. Only then will I be able to convince her to let me go.

Palmer's eyes drag down my body, taking in all the scars covering my skin like tattoos I never wanted.

"Obviously, you understand physical pain," she says.

I nod. "There is nothing you can do to me that can hurt me."

She bites her lip, and I see that she's not here. She's thinking about something else, not about me.

I could let her be in her own head. It would prolong the pain from happening. But I need her to break, and I need her to break now.

Every second I'm here is another second Julian or Bishop could be hurting Siren. I can't waste one second.

"Palmer? You were saying? Or are you so distracted by my hot body that you can't even imagine hurting me?"

She hisses, her viciousness coming back. "I can see why Lucy loved you. You and I are more alike than we are different. Luckily, that means I know how to hurt you. I know your weaknesses because they are the same as mine."

I look into her muddy brown eyes. I flick past the anger, trying to find the pain, but it's buried so deep within her that I'm not sure I can bring it up to the surface. I have to try—for Siren and Lucy.

"Then do it. Hurt me. Take vengeance on my flesh. Do it for Lucy," I growl.

Palmer snaps. She slaps me across the cheek, her anger pushing her to do something she's probably never done before.

I hear the slap, but I don't feel it. I'm sure it was vicious. I'm sure she used all of her force trying to hurt me. I'm sure my face is red from her handprint. But I don't feel it. I rarely feel physical pain, and right now, I'm so focused on Siren that Palmer could shoot me and throw me into a fire, and I wouldn't feel it. All I want is to go find Siren.

"Don't talk about Lucy," she says.

"Why? She was mine before she was yours. I can talk about Lucy all I want."

Slap.

SLAP.

I huff, my chest rising and falling hard at the double hit. I feel the familiar surge of my own anger taking hold. I'm not used to letting people hurt me without trying to fight back. But I won't fight back. Even if I get free of my chains, I won't hurt Palmer, for Lucy.

"Lucy loved me," she says.

"And before *you*, she loved *me*," I say calmly back. It's true, but I only say it to feed her anger. The only way she'll let her pain in is when her anger is at its height. When all of her walls are down, and her rage is on full display, that's my chance to break her.

This time, it's a punch. My head snaps again to the side, as her force hits my jaw. It's a good punch, but it will hurt her hand more than my jaw.

"Fuck," she curses, shaking her hand.

I raise a brow, staring at her. "Is that all you got? All you are going to do to the man who took the love of your life from you? The man who loved her before you and then discarded her like she was nothing." *Lucy, forgive me. I always loved you, but I'm going to say whatever it takes to get back to Siren.*

Palmer frowns, stepping back like she's considering my words. There is no snarky comeback, and that scares me. My comments are meant to rile her up, to let her inner beast out, not to make her introspective.

She pulls out her phone.

"What are you doing? Can't hurt me on your own?" I ask.

I'm right. I realize it as soon as she speaks on the phone. She's calling down her reinforcements.

Fuck.

I curse, not because I'm afraid of what the men upstairs can do to me. They can physically hurt me more than Palmer can, especially in an unfair fight where I'm chained up. But I need Palmer to be the one to hurt me. I need her to be the one who touches me, to make it personal. That way, she unleashes her anger. If she stands back and watches other people hurt me, I'll never break her.

I hear the men from upstairs file down the stairs.

Palmer grins, thinking she's won.

"Really? This is what you want? To watch someone else do your dirty work? I thought you were stronger than that. I thought we were the same. I thought you took care of your own business," I say.

She leans forward until her breath is on my ear.

"Scared, Zeke? I thought you weren't afraid of anything. Physical pain doesn't scare you. These men can hurt you more than I ever could, so you should be afraid."

She steps back, but she's still less than a foot away from me. I could head-butt her, knee her, hurt her if I wanted to, but I don't. I have to protect her while going after Siren.

My eyes glance behind her at the three men who now occupy the basement with us. One has biceps that make him look like a professional baseball player. I'm sure he can punch like he's hitting a home run. Another is slim and lanky; I don't have to worry about him being able to rip flesh from my bones.

But the third man is a monster. His biceps bulge, his shoulders are built, his thighs thick—he's as big as me. I know what I'm capable of. Even if he isn't as talented as me, it just takes muscles and a little bit of darkness in your heart to be able to do damage to another human being's body. I check his eyes; he has the darkness.

He may not be as skilled as I am at torture, but he doesn't have to be to leave more scars on my body.

I cut back to Palmer, "I'm not afraid of being physically hurt. Your men can torture me all day; I know how to withstand it. But if you prevent me from saving the woman I love, you will regret it. When the anger is gone and replaced with the pain, you'll realize the woman I love was there when the woman you love died. I know in my heart she did everything she could to protect and save her. You'll regret letting her suffer when you come to your senses, when you realize torturing me won't bring her back. You'll regret this."

She grinds her teeth and breathes out her anger through her nostrils. Her eyes flicker side to side.

Did I get through to her?

"I won't regret this," she says, and steps back. All the way back, out of reach. Her eyes never leave mine.

I'm the one who breaks eye-contact when I close my eyes, going to my hardened space that will protect me until the physical pain is over. Palmer may think she's tough, but she's never seen torture. She's never seen what is about to happen to me. Maybe that's enough to break her.

My mind flickers to Siren, thinking I should stay with her to help me get through the pain. My love for her will get me through.

I feel the first punch to my stomach. My body reacts. My abs tighten, my body falls back, but I can't slump all the way back as the chains grip my wrists and ankles, keeping me in place. But the part I hate the most is the sound I make—a wretched sound as my lungs burn trying to get air, and my stomach clenches, trying to keep from vomiting from the force.

I hate that I made a sound.

I hate that I showed that I can feel physical pain.

I can't associate this painful moment with Siren, so I can't let her save me.

Kai is my next thought. The last time I was tortured, she saved me. But I won't let me save her either.

Lucy?

No.

I won't let any woman save me. I won't let any man save me either. I've withstood torture before. This is no different. I just have to go to my dark place, and hope that when this is over, I can escape the darkest depths of my heart and return to Siren.

CHAPTER 5
SIREN

I *surrender.*

I never thought I'd say those words, but Julian did. From the moment I started working for him, he knew. He knew that eventually, I'd be his.

I take a deep breath, gathering courage from all the oxygen in the room. Taking on the strength of any ghosts, spirits, and souls. Gaining power from all the gods and divine beings. Pulling from all the crystals, celestial beings, and deities. Calling on all the martyrs and saints. I need the strength of all of them to survive this, whether I believe in their existence or not. And even then, it won't be enough.

The only person who could help me is the one person who is isn't here—Zeke.

"One step at a time, my little Aria. I wish you just saying the words would be enough and we could fuck like lovers, but you aren't ready yet."

My eyes cut through him.

"Kiss me like you want me. That's the first step to falling in love with me," Julian says.

There it is. He wants me to love him. *Not a chance in hell.*

I step forward. He stays still, waiting for me this time.

I can't do this.

I can't kiss him.

I can't fuck him.

I don't even think I could lie there and let him fuck me, but what he's asking for is so much more than just letting him violate me. He's asking me to give him myself.

I inch closer, except my inches are more like millimeters. At this rate, it's going to take me all year to get close enough to kiss him. *Fine by me.*

"Siren," Julian says.

I freeze. He never calls me Siren. I'm always Aria, never Siren.

"Siren," Julian says again, and I realize what he is doing. He's trying to make it easier for me.

I lean forward, as he says the name that Zeke calls me. I can feel the heat of his breath, but I can't move the final inch.

"I can't," I breathe. *I can't fuck him like he's Zeke. I can't grab him and kiss him. I just can't...*

Julian nods. "I always knew you had a weakness. I just didn't realize it would be a man."

He walks behind me, setting the glass down on the bedside table behind me. I still don't stare at the bed. I can't. I won't. There is no bed. Nothing is going to happen.

"What are you going to do? What do you want?" I breathe out, my voice quieter than ever. I'm usually strong and determined. In a normal situation, I can fight back. But fighting back this time means death to the one person I love above all else. I know in my heart that if I fight, Julian will go after the person I love. He will go after my "weakness." He'll go after Zeke.

Julian doesn't look at me. "I thought you were a romantic candles and flowers type of girl, Siren."

There is a crack of lighting overhead. I jump at the sound and turn my head in the direction. And then I see it—*the bed.*

It's the most exquisite, romantic bed I've ever seen. I didn't think beds could be romantic, but this one is. This one is clouds of white pillows covered in gold trim. Pink and red rose petals are scattered all over it. The candles illuminate it and the stars sparkle down on top of it, making the bed is every woman's dream. This bed would make two people feel like the only two people in the world.

I turn my head, trying to understand how the evil monster behind me could ever want to make love to a woman in a bed like this. I search, but I no longer see Julian out of the corner of my eye.

Fuck.

I turn quickly, but it's too late.

The door opens, and as I expected, four men run in, each grabbing one of my limbs before I can fight back. I'm tied to the beautiful bed that should be my heaven. Instead, it will be my hell.

The men retreat as quickly as they came, and I'm left alone with Julian.

"We will start slowly, with something easy to surrender to. I thought I'd never have you until you gave yourself to me completely, but I realize now, it will take time for you to want me. Which is why I won't discuss all the vows and promises you have made to me, yet. Right now, we will focus on the first step..." his voice trails off. Maybe my brain is shutting down in preparation for what is about to happen.

I begin praying to every god I don't believe in.

None of them come, none of them save me.

Zeke...

I need you. Please, save me.

I stare at the door in the corner, begging it to open. For Zeke to be on the other side. He'd be here if he could, but something is stopping him. Something is keeping him away.

I feel a needle stab into my arm. My mind ignites into a blur of images.

"This will help make you mine," Julian says. At least I think it's Julian.

Fuck, my head is spinning. I can't focus. Between the drugs and being tied up, I won't be able to fight. I won't be able to stop it. I won't be able to tell Zeke I did everything to keep him off of me, to prevent this from happening.

I'm right there, Siren. I'm right there.

I close my eyes, and I hear Zeke's voice so clearly. I feel him everywhere. My anchor keeping me out of the darkness Julian is trying to pull me into.

Don't fight me; you know you love me. You know you want me. Let me make you feel so good.

Suddenly I know how Zeke is going to save me. He's going to ensure Julian isn't the one who fucks me. He's going to take over my dreams, my thoughts, my desires—all I see now is Zeke.

"You want it rough, Siren?"

I shiver at the thought of my big bad man taking me roughly. I love having Zeke both ways. Slow and tender, and rough and fast. I can feel the walls of my pussy tightening at the thought of Zeke entering me fast. Of him pushing me to my limits. Of his teeth sinking into my flesh. His fingers fisting my hair, pulling it hard, bringing all the blood to each part of my body he marks.

"Yes," I hiss. I want it rough. It's been too long since I had Zeke. I need him now. I can't wait.

"Good girl," he says.

"No, I'm a bad girl. Very bad. I need to be punished."

Zeke chuckles, loving who I am. I'm not a good girl. I'm his bad girl. I'm the woman who would kill for him, not caring whose life I had to take to ensure he survives. That's who I am.

"Oh, don't worry, Siren, I'll punish you." His voice sounds darker than it usually is—not just growly, or husky, but heavier than I've ever heard it before.

It startles me, and the haze begins to lift. I remember what I'm pushing down, what my subconscious is protecting me from.

I'm there. It's me, not him, Zeke's voice says again.

I feel the bed dip, and then his hips sink down on top of mine. "God, I've wanted you for so long. How much do you want me?" he says, his hips pressing harder over mine.

I roll my hips up, trying to get him to stop teasing me and give me what I want. He lifts up, preventing me from feeling his cock until I answer him.

"More than I want to breathe, that's how badly I want you, Zeke." He grunts, but still doesn't give me any physical connection except for where his thighs press against my hips.

I feel his hand against my face, stroking my cheek. I close my eyes, leaning against the softness of his hand.

I frown, usually Zeke's hands are rough, cut up, and calloused.

Shh, it's me, Siren. You know it's me, Zeke.

So I keep my eyes closed, my toes tingling as his big strong hands stroke down my cheek to my neck. His face dips to my neck as he presses his lips beneath my ear. So smooth, he shaved for me.

I squirm as the light kisses tingle down my body.

"Zeke," I moan again. I need more. I need him to punish me. I need him to fuck me.

Something deep in my mind says I need this over.

Why would I want this over? All I want is Zeke. Over and over and over.

I arch my back, my wrists and ankles pulling gently on the metal handcuffs, keeping me from touching Zeke.

"What do you want?" he asks.

"For you to touch me, punish me, fuck me."

I feel the blade then, and I smile—finally.

The blade slips under the neck of my shirt, and he pulls down, shredding my shirt.

"Aww," I moan as I feel the blade of the knife trailing down the center of my chest, over my breast bone, digging in just enough to inject into my skin and cause a line down the center of my body that will remind me of this night forever.

Good, I want to remember.

No, you don't.

I push the words in my head out, so confused by all the voices in my head.

"More," I say without him asking.

The knife slides into my soaked pants, soaked from both the rain and my excitement. The knife struggles against the thickness of the material and, at one point, jabs into my thigh.

"Fuck," I cry at the pain, my eyes starting to jolt open. Quickly his lips are on me, and I fall back down, my body relaxing a little as his lips push against mine. His tongue inserts into my mouth, begging for forgiveness for hurting me.

I forgive you, my tongue says back. My mouth opens wider,

inviting more of him in. I can't get enough of Zeke. His mouth takes away my pain, but then I shiver. I'm still soaked from the rain, and although the kisses are nice, they aren't enough to heat my body.

"You're so scared," he says.

"What?" I say, my voice catching, my confusion and embarrassment at being scared instead of flawlessly beautiful for Zeke.

"Don't. Don't try to hide. I love the scars. I love how much pain you can endure."

I bite my lip. "Punish me." I want to feel more pain.

"I'm going to cover every one of your scars with a mark of my own, so when you look at them, you think of me," he says.

"Perfect," I say back, loving the idea of it.

"This mark over your neck is now mine," he says.

I feel the sharp point of the knife. I jolt at the pain, my eyes watering, my stomach heaving trying to get him to stop.

"Fuck, Zeke," I say at the pain.

He kisses me, and I forget the pain.

"This breast is mine," he says, and I feel the scrape over the upper curve of my breast, where a bullet grazed me.

I bite my lip to keep my scream in. I want him to cover my scars with his own, but fuck does this hurt.

"Tell me you want me to mark you."

"I want you to mark me."

"Tell me you want me to fuck you."

"Fuck me, Zeke."

He growls like I said something wrong, but I can't think what it would be.

"Tell me you want me to fuck you," he tries again.

Maybe he didn't hear me the first time?

"I want you to fuck me, Zeke."

He growls, and then I feel his thick cock pushing at my entrance.

Something's wrong.

I got you, it's me. I'm going to fuck you. Think of me.

Zeke, my anchor, my love.

I don't have to open my eyes to know it's him as he pushes inside me in one hard stroke. My body stretches, letting him in, adjusting to him. I wait for him to thicken, for him to consume all of my body, but it never comes.

This isn't Z—

I love you, stay with me.

And then he's thrusting. He's pushing over and over. Drilling inside me with so much force that I hear the bed cracking. That's my Zeke. That's my dangerous strong man who loves me so much that he breaks the bed.

I pull against the handcuffs, trying to grab onto Zeke, to feel his hair, his muscles, but I can't break free.

"Zeke, I want to feel you," I say.

"Shut up, bitch."

"What?" I snap, not believing he said that. I must have heard wrong.

His lips hover over mine again. "I want to hear you scream."

"Zeke," I howl as he hits me deep.

"No, not my name, just scream," he says, and then he's digging his fingers into one of my fresh wounds.

I scream. I scream like I've never screamed before. I like when Zeke punishes me, when he pushes my limits, but this is different. This isn't punishment; this is sin.

"Zeke," I moan, trying to get him to stop. Suddenly, I feel the knife against my nipple. He slices, and I cry out again, the pain making me shake, and vomit rising in my throat.

"You like that, Siren?" he says.

No, I don't like it.

He thrusts again.

Hold onto me, listen to me. I got you. I'm not hurting you. I love you. I would never hurt you.

My eyes fly open, and I see *him*.

The man I've thought of as *he*.

He isn't Zeke.

He is Julian. And he's over me.

No, come back to me. Don't let him win. Let me protect you.

I close my eyes, taking a deep breath as I let my head and heart go back to Zeke. I let him protect me. I think of Zeke while Julian thrusts into me. As he cuts me with a knife, butchering my body like an animal.

I don't cry anymore. I don't moan. I give Julian nothing.

I give Zeke everything.

Zeke anchors me; he keeps me safe. My thoughts stay mine. My body remains mine. Everything is still mine.

I know that Julian pumped me full of drugs. I know that he tricked me into thinking he was Zeke so it would either ruin my images of Zeke or I would do what he wanted. Even with the handcuffs, Julian didn't believe that I wouldn't fight him. That he wouldn't feel in control of me.

Julian isn't in control of me. I'm not his; I'm Zeke's—always.

I feel Julian finishing inside me.

"Scream," he says, needing my pain to finish.

"No," I say, not giving Julian anything.

I feel the knife at my clit.

Fuck, no.

He wouldn't. Would he?

No, he wants me to be his. Julian wants me to give him my pleasure, and he won't be able to if he cuts off my clit.

I scream.

And Julian comes.

I finish in control by screaming the name that will drive Julian insane.

"Zeke!"

CHAPTER 6
ZEKE

Blood drips down my forehead, oozing over my bulging eyes. It seeps into my nose until I'm breathing more blood than oxygen. I taste the rusty sting on my tongue.

My face is bloodied, bruised, and swollen. I can't feel. I can't see. I can't breathe. Blood mutes all of my senses.

I hang from my wrists, where metal cuffs encase them. I'm slumped forward, and the skin around my wrist is cut deep from my own weight. I'm sure the men have more than doubled the scars on my body. My shallow breaths indicate cracked and broken ribs.

From the way the room spins, it's clear I've lost a pint or more of blood.

My legs shake, barely holding me up, putting more weight on my wrists.

I stare down at my feet and see a mix of colors. Red, purple, blue mar my body. Bruises, gashes, welts.

I've gone to the dark place in my heart that knows I deserve this after I've done this to countless other men. To withstand torture, some men push everything out and go to a zen-like place. Others think of the one special person they love to help them get through it.

Some panic and scream, making a big fuss. Others grit and bear it.

I'm different than most. I feel every strike, punch, cut, slice, whip, kick. I feel it and let it become part of me. I let it feed my monster. It hardens me. It ensures I can do my job of protecting everyone. I've never lived for myself. I've never chosen me over someone else. I've never chosen love over ensuring my friends are safe.

The pain should be fueling me to fight back, to seek vengeance, and kill them all for what they've done to me. I should be plotting their deaths so they can never hurt any of my friends.

But I don't give a damn about protecting my friends in this moment. I don't care about protecting Enzo, or Langston, or Liesel, or even Kai. I don't think about honoring Lucy.

All I think about is saving Siren. I promised her. I love her. She's my everything. All I care about is Siren.

So while the pain is feeding the darkest part of my soul, it's also tunneling through toward Siren. Toward finding her, saving her, and loving her.

I can feel it in my bones. Someday I'm going to have to choose— her above everything else. That terrifies me. Not because I don't want to put her first, but because it will mean changing who I am at the most fundamental level. I'll no longer be the enforcer, the protector, the brute strength who is always saving everyone else.

I'll be the man in love. The man selfishly protecting his love.

I'll have to start over. Find a new job. Find a new identity. That transition scares me more than any of the four pairs of eyes staring back at me.

I don't see the people in front of me. The blood and haze of the shock to my body prevents me from actually seeing them, but I feel every single person.

All four people in this room took part in my torment and agony.

The three men took their swings at me, using their preferred methods to pull screams and cries out of me reflexively. Each used a different technique to mark my body.

As I guessed, the large man built most like me did the most damage and took the most pleasure in hurting me.

Palmer was quiet the whole time. She didn't speak. I didn't let myself look at her. I needed to stay strong and focused. I needed her to know I won't engage with her until it's just her and me again alone. The men will see through my plan and stop me. I need her alone.

Now that the beatings have stopped, I pull my head up. It takes all the muscles in my neck and back to lift my head the few inches up so I can glance at Palmer. My head has never felt heavier, and I'm only guessing where she is when I force my head up.

Now is the time. Now is the turning point.

I can't see what my body looks like, but I know I'm not a pretty sight. I'm sure I've never looked worse. If Palmer is going to let her own pain in, it will be now. It will be seeing me so physically damaged, but not giving a damn because there is a woman I love who I have to get to. I have to save Siren.

So I lift my thousand-pound head and find Palmer in the corner, smoking her damn cigarette like she's sitting on the sideline of a fair boxing match.

"Do you believe me now?" I croak out, trying to tell her I won't ever yield. I won't ever give up. She can destroy my body, rip me apart until I'm lying in pieces, but her anger will still be here. I won't let her feel like she's broken me, because I don't give a damn about my body. All I care about is getting Siren back.

Palmer has had her fun. Enough is enough.

I try to speak again, but all I end up doing is gargling blood.

"Should we kill him?" one of the men asks Palmer.

There is a momentary pause, and I think she's going to say yes. Maybe watching me deal with the pain hasn't been near as fun as she thought it would be, and she has no use for me anymore.

"No," she says, shocking the entire room.

I breathe calmly for the first time in hours. Not because I fear death, but I fear dying without ensuring Siren lives a long and happy life.

"Leave," Palmer says suddenly.

My eyes glaze, looking at her through the blood, wishing I could see what is going on in her head.

"But—" one of the men starts.

"Leave!" Palmer's voice shrieks through the room.

The three men stumble and run up the stairs, leaving Palmer and me alone—just like I want.

Now's my chance, *but how can I convince her when I can't even speak?*

My head falls, most likely looking like defeat from Palmer's perspective.

"You don't think you can be broken, do you?"

I moan, but can't speak as my head rolls side to side. I don't have the strength to lift it again.

Palmer walks to my ankles, and I hear the clink of the key going into the lock. She removes the cuffs from my ankles, but I don't move. I'm barely standing on my feet, still putting most of my weight onto my wrists to hold me up.

She stands and undoes one of my wrists, letting me hang by one wrist. I know what's about to happen, and I can't stop it.

She walks to my other side and unlocks the other cuff holding me up.

I fall.

Hard onto the floor.

My body crumples into a broken ball on the floor.

Palmer takes her time. She stands over me, watching me, considering what she wants to do.

She gives me enough time to speak. "Do it for Lucy." Let me go for Lucy.

Her eyes gloss over, and I know I lost Palmer again. "Not until I break you."

She leans over me, grabbing one of the knives the men used, and she goes to work on my bloodied jeans. The knife scrapes into my legs as she rips my jeans from my body. It takes her a while, but eventually, she removes all the clothes from my body until I'm naked on the floor.

I can't fight her.

I can't stop her.

I can't even lift a finger.

She can do whatever she wants with me.

"Lucy loved you," she says.

I moan.

"I've been with men and women. I'm bisexual, just like Lucy. It's time to see what Lucy saw in you. It's time to take the one thing from you that might break you," Palmer says.

It's then I realize what's happening. She's going to use my body. Use me to cover up her pain. Try to force pain into me. Try to take away my control and make me feel like I'm hurting Siren by not stopping Palmer from using my body.

I open my eyes wide and look into Palmer's eyes. The lengths she will go to to prevent herself from feeling her own pain of losing Lucy are immense. Palmer has found my weakness. She knows how to break me.

And there is nothing I can do to stop her.

CHAPTER 7
PALMER

"*L*ucy, is that you?" I ask, my voice catching in my throat at the sight of her. *She's here.*

Some-fucking-how, she's here.

"Yes," her sultry voice says. It's not angelic. It's not perfect. It's gritty and heart-wrenching. That's how I know this is real. She's not an angel. *This is fucking real.*

I feel the wetness in my eyes, sensing the waterfall about to start flowing down my face any second now. These are the last few moments I'm going to have clear vision.

"I thought you were dead," I say, hiccuping on the last word from a lack of oxygen. This is it—the last moment I see Lucy clearly.

She's standing in front of me in dark jeans, a ripped red shirt, and Converse sneakers. Her hair is parted to the extreme on one side, and her lips are painted red.

Lucy looks fierce, like she came here to demand I go into battle with her. I will. I'll do anything for her. I'm just so relieved that she's here. *But is she still mine?*

Lucy runs to me, and our arms fling around each other in a death grip. The fountain of tears streaming down my face doesn't let me see her, but I can still feel her. The curve of her ass against my hand, her soft breasts pushed against mine, our foreheads pressed together.

"Kiss me," I say, not able to even see her bright lips through my tears and joy at her being alive.

Her hands grab my cheeks, and then we are kissing, suffocating, and exhaling. Neither of us can breathe through the kisses, tears, and general lack of oxygen. We can live off each other's kisses, though, forever. Neither of us stop. Neither of us step back to let the other come up for air. We need each other more than we need to live.

I push Lucy back, and she falls to a heap on the floor.

We both laugh at how uncoordinated she is. I straddle her with my legs, pinning her to the floor. Lucy is small, about half my size. I love that I can dominate her. She may be the fierce one, the leader of our two-person team in public, but in the bedroom, I rule.

Lucy's lazy, sexy eyes seem to agree with me.

I wipe my tears on my shirt, hoping I'll stop crying now that she's here and she's still mine.

"You smell like smoke," Lucy says with a frown as she grabs the neck of my shirt and yanks me toward her.

I kiss her again. "Do you care?"

"Yes, because I want you around for a long fucking time."

"Why?"

"Because you are mine."

"Are you sure? Are you sure your heart doesn't still belong to Zeke?" I feel the ache in my chest. This is what I was most afraid of, getting her back only to realize she's still in love with him, not me.

"I love you, Palmer. I used to love Zeke, but that was before I met you. He was my darkness; you are my light. You are the reason I'm alive. You are the reason I live."

"Dammit, stop making me cry. I want to see you when I fuck you," I say through more fucking tears.

Lucy laughs and then palms my breast beneath my shirt. I arch my back at the warm feelings zipping through my body at her touch. "Feel me first; you can look at me the second time. Just feel me."

I moan as she palms my other breast in her small, delicate hands.

This time her thumb brushes over my hardened nipple. I'm gone—my eyes are never opening again. I just want to feel everything.

"Fuck me, Palmer. Take control. Punish me like you're pissed I left you. Fuck me like you won't ever let me leave again."

She doesn't have to ask me twice.

I growl, then I grab her shirt and rip it off over her head as my mouth comes down on her smooth stomach. I start off soft and light, knowing it will drive her wild and prep her for the harsh, teeth bearing kisses I'm about to give her body.

Lucy doesn't move beneath me, probably from the shock of seeing me again. It doesn't matter if she moves, just that she's here. I can do all the work.

My mouth moves its way up her body, tasting every inch, each kiss becoming rougher than the previous. I nip at her nipples, sink my claws into her neck, and kiss her ears. I love every second that I get to worship her skin again.

Lucy moans when I yank on her hair. It's low and deep and unlike her normal sounds. It just drives me to work harder, because I love the guttural sounds she's making.

"I love it when you growl like that for me. I'm going to make you scream like you've never screamed before," I whisper into her ear before biting down hard on her lobe.

She squeals.

I come alive again for the first time in months.

I grab the hem of my shirt and yank it off. I grab her hands and place them on my bare breasts. Her hands somehow seem bigger than they were a minute before, but I ignore the weirdness.

"Rub me," I command.

She doesn't move.

That's how it's going to be. She wants to defy me, so I'll punish her. I grin. I'm going to enjoy this.

I put my hands on top of hers and rub her fingers over my nipples as my hips continue to pin down her narrow hips. I rub myself over her body, but I want more. So much more.

I feel my core heating, my clit tingling in my pants, wanting to feel my skin against hers.

I lean down, my long hair framing her face as I kiss her tenderly. She doesn't kiss me back. So I suck on my lip, pulling another groan out of her.

I grin.

"I want you. All of you."

"Take me."

I scoot back on her body, my hands roaming, and I am delighted to find she's already naked for me. I drag my nails over her bare skin.

She hisses like it hurts, but I don't understand why. I'm not touching her hard enough to leave a mark.

I laugh. "Always the dramatic one." I kiss her inner thigh, and she stops.

I smirk as I begin to undress. I know the way to my woman's heart. I know her body better than anyone, even Zeke. I've loved her longest. Tonight, I'm going to remind her that she doesn't get to leave me just because things get tough. She's mine. For as long as both our hearts are beating.

I struggle to get my pants down over my thighs, but I finally succeed, falling back on my ass on her feet.

We both laugh at how ridiculous it is, but it doesn't change the intensity of the mood. I want her—desperately and wholly. I want to hear her scream my name. Nothing is going to stop that from happening.

I finish shoving my own pants and underwear down, and then I go back to straddling her hips, my hands cupping her head tenderly. As much as I want it rough, as I want to punish her, I can't—not now. I love her too much.

Right now, I just want to celebrate this beautiful moment. Of finding her again. Of her being in my life again. Of being reunited.

"I love you, Lucy, so fucking much," I say, tears falling down my cheeks like lava down a volcano. It burns because I can't see her, filling my eyes and falling slowly. It's not a river that pours out of me, leaving me with only good feelings. These tears hurt.

"I love you, too."

"Make love to me," I say.

"Every chance I get," she says back.

I grin, loving our little saying. It's always the same.

I push Lucy's legs apart and slip my hands between her legs, but what I find surprises me.

"Oh, is that how you want it? You want to fuck me with a strap-on?"

"Mmmm," she moans.

I bite my lip, considering telling Lucy I don't want any toys or devices. I don't want a vibrator or a dildo or any rubber between us. I just want her.

But I can't tell her that. She's obviously thought through how she wants to have me the first time back to already have it strapped on.

"Okay, I'll fuck you however you want me to." I kiss her forehead. I start rubbing myself in slow, methodical circles as I straddle her waist. My eyes are still closed, and the tears are still falling, but I don't need to see Lucy to feel her. She's all around me. She wants to be inside me.

"Please, hurry," I hear her pant. If I wasn't wet before, I am now. I'm soaked, and I rub my wetness all over her belly.

"I'm so fucking wet for you. No one gets me this wet, only you."

And then I grab the plastic cock, and I ride her. I feel myself stretch as the cock fits inside me, I make sure to sink all the way down until our clits are rubbing over each other, and then I begin to rock.

"You like that?"

More moans. She's speechless, that's how much she likes it.

I massage her breasts as I rock over her. It feels so fucking good. Somehow, the rubber cock seems to get harder the longer I pump over it.

Hmm, it must be one of those high-tech cocks meant to resemble the real thing?

I really don't care about how real the strap-on resembles a cock. I just care about Lucy.

I lean forward as I continue to ride her, and then I kiss her again as my hand tangles in her hair. I pull roughly when she doesn't open up for me.

"Going to make me work for it, huh, Lucy?"

I push my way inside her mouth and find her delicious tongue. I massage it, and finally, she gives in, circling my tongue with hers. I feel the moisture building in my walls, fucking the cock. I want it out, though, because I just want her.

"I want you, Lucy. I just want you."

"Then have me. Any way you want me, I'm yours."

I grin. "Thank god."

I go to climb off her and rip the fake cock off her. But I feel her trembling, and I know what that means. She's about to come without me. I don't give a damn that it's our first time together in months and we aren't coming together. I just want her to enjoy this moment. I want her to come as many times as she can.

"Come for me, baby. Come."

I rock harder, knowing the friction on her pussy is what is getting her off. So I ride the cock in longer, faster strokes.

"Come for me, Lucy," I scream, and somehow the thought of her coming brings me right there too. And then we are both coming. I'm screaming, she's screaming. It's the most beautiful, painful sound.

It sounds like coming home, but it also feels fleeting. *How many more times are we going to get to do this?* She came back, but she still has cancer. She's still dying. She still refuses to save herself for me.

I'm about to open my mouth and ask if she is ready to be selfish, do the right thing to save herself, when I feel her coming.

Lucy isn't a squirter. She never comes like this.

Suddenly, everything hits me like a truck ramming into my head.

The tears stop.

The screaming stops.

The fear and anger return, along with a new emotion I've been trying to hold back.

An emotion I dare not name for fear it will become more powerful.

I squeeze my eyes shut, my brain already processing what's happening. It's already telling me I'm about to lose everything I love all over again.

Reality and my imagination mixed in such a fucked up way to try and give me a few more moments of peace, but there is no peace for a woman like me. There is no happiness for a woman who lost the light that guided her way—the beauty in a room of darkness. There is no rest for the wicked, and I am definitely wicked. I'm going to hell for the sins I've committed tonight.

"Shh, it's okay. You are going to be okay," her voice morphs into his, and I realize I'm sobbing again, my shoulders shaking as I still sit on his now soft cock.

What did I do?

And why did I think it would make me feel better to take a man who Lucy once loved?

Why did I think hurting another would heal me? All it did was open a deeper wound.

"Take it one step at a time," his voice says again.

And why is HE comforting me? I had Zeke tortured by three men. And then when he was so broken that he couldn't fight back, I raped him like he was Lucy.

He should hate me. He should want to kill me.

I rest my hand on his chest and feel the unstable beat of his heart. He's conflicted and in pain. The breaths he takes are shallow. If he takes a deep breath, the agony will rip through his entire chest, diaphragm, and gut. He keeps them light and shallow to avoid further injury, but because of his shallow breathing, he never gets a big, healing breath. Never enough to calm himself.

"Fuck!" I scream, my nails digging into his chest.

I pound my hand over his chest in a fist. Pissed at him for not fighting me off. Pissed at myself for turning into a demon. And pissed at the world for taking Lucy.

It should have been me. I should have been the one to die.

Yes, that's it!

I form a plan in my head. A way to end the pain I'm in. This—this heartache, this stabbing, throbbing, loss—I know that no matter how long I live, it will never leave me. Never, never, never.

Lucy was the only person who understood me.

She understood that I hate chocolate but love M&Ms.

She understood that I love the ocean, but hate the sand.

She understood that I loved her, while also loving men.

She understood that I am a complex, misunderstood, broken

woman who shouldn't have been able to heal from the wounds society inflicted at being different, but I did because she walked the road with me.

She was my shield when someone would yell profanities at us, tell us we went against nature, tell us we were going to hell for being ourselves. None of it mattered because of Lucy. She made all of it bearable. Not easy, but she made every profanity worth it.

And now, she's gone.

She's not coming back.

She's just gone.

And I wasn't there when she needed me the most. I wasn't fucking there. She failed me by pushing me away. By not fighting and taking the drugs she needed to survive, screwing everyone else. And I failed her by not finding a way to be with her when she took her last breath.

We both failed.

We both lost.

The only way I can remedy that is to join Lucy in hell. There is no fucking way two badass women like us are going to heaven.

I smile. A genuine full smile. I'm only moments away from ending the pain, from finding peace, from being reunited with Lucy.

Yes, I know what I have to do. I have to end this...

CHAPTER 8
ZEKE

Palmer's demeanor changes from unbearable pain to impenetrable peace in the span of a few seconds. I know what it means—she's found a way to end her pain.

She's planning on killing herself.

I can see it on her face. For a moment, I see it as the right path for her too. She's so fucking happy thinking about joining Lucy that it's hard not to let her die to be with her.

But it's not what Lucy would want, and despite the pain this woman has inflicted on my body, and the amount of heartbreak she has brought me at not saving Siren sooner, I can't condemn her to death either.

Palmer is just in pain. A pain I hope to never understand.

Please, let Siren still be alive. Let her be whole. Let her still love me.

Palmer is still on top of me, my dick is still inside her, and I've never been so disgusted at a woman, at myself. *I fucking came in her! What is wrong with me?* I should have been able to control myself.

I didn't want her, but my body took over. I had no control once she started thrusting over me. The only way to stop myself from coming would have been to push her off me.

I didn't have the physical strength, though. I still don't. That's why until she decides to move, my cock will continue to rest inside her, in a place it doesn't belong.

I feel sick. I want to vomit.

Forgive me, Siren. Please, forgive me.

I close my eyes, keeping the tears in. It's the only part of my body I can currently control.

I can't control my breathing. My broken ribs poking into my lungs only allow me to take short, shallow breaths.

I can't control my heartbeat. It's erratic and racing, scared those men are going to come back into the room and beat me again.

I can't control my muscles. I try. My brain fires, begging my muscles to move. But there is either a break in the connection, or more likely, my muscles just say fuck off because they have taken such a rough beating.

And my fucking cock—don't get me started on that bastard. He's betrayed me more than any other part of me. He had no problem getting hard when a naked woman climbed on top of me and kissed me. He thought it was perfectly fine to enjoy the ride when she sank down over him and milked me dry. He came like it was his right. I want to chop him off for betraying Siren like that.

I swallow hard, trying to push all those thoughts down. There is nothing I can do but go to Siren and ask for the forgiveness I don't deserve but desperately need.

Palmer continues to sit happily on top of me. She bends over, reaching for something I can't make out because I don't have the strength to even turn my fucking head to see.

I'm disappointed when she rights herself on me again, and I see the glint of metal reflecting the light from overhead into my eyes.

"Palmer, don't," I croak out, coughing up more blood.

She sees me, really sees me, since the first time she started fucking me. For the past thirty minutes, she's been in some sort of hypnotic state. She's been seeing me as Lucy, and nothing I said broke her spell.

"I have to," she says, gripping the knife still in front of her. For a second, I think this is going to turn into a murder-suicide, but I don't think she's angry at me anymore. The anger has been displaced by her pain. That's her only focus.

"No, you don't. I know it hurts now, but it won't always be this way."

She whimpers. "Yes, it will. It will always hurt. I'll always feel like I'm drowning, the water will be crashing down on me, but I'll never die. Nor will I ever be able to come up for enough oxygen to sustain me. All I've ever feel is the pain of drowning without it ever ending. I need it to end."

"It will. Trust me. One day, you'll wake up, and the pain will just be gone. It won't be suffocating and trying to kill you anymore. You just have to get through this."

"I can't."

"You can. Let me help you."

"I can't live like this for one hour, let alone the years it will take to get rid of this pain."

"It won't take years."

"How long then?"

I bite my lip. I could lie to her and say only a couple days, but that's not true. I don't know how long it will take.

"More than days, less than years," I say.

"Weeks?"

"Maybe, maybe more, maybe less."

"I can't." She breaks. She can't hold on another second. She slashes her left wrist in one quick sweep. Even if I could move my muscles properly, I wouldn't have been able to stop her, she was so quick.

I stare at her wrist as a small cord of blood drips down her forearm. She gasps in relief, like she can finally breathe for the first time in years. The pain from her wrist takes over from the pain of losing Lucy.

The wound she created is mostly superficial. Sure, if left unattended long enough, she would die from blood loss, maybe. But I'm here. Her guards are here. Right now, all she needs is a bandage, maybe a couple of stitches, and she would survive easily.

I can still save her—for Lucy.

What about Siren?

I can't save Siren until Palmer is dealt with. I'll have a better chance of asking for Siren's forgiveness if I save Palmer and don't let my own anger take hold of me.

"Palmer, give me the knife," I say in the commanding voice I use when I mean business. I don't let the blood clogging my throat prevent me from speaking in my affirmative, dominating way.

Her eyes open, and she stares at me, her hand lifting toward me. She's going to do it. She's in such a state that she just needs me to command her. She needs a leader to follow.

But she stops just short and quickly slices at her arm again, her face lighting up like she just won the lottery instead of having a knife cut into her flesh.

I wince at how deep the second cut is. She could bleed out in an hour from this cut. Not could, will.

I try to move my useless arm next to my body.

MOVE!

My fingers twitch. It's good to know I can feel my fingers, and no nerve damage was done, but that's not reassuring when I have a grief-stricken woman holding a knife that I need to stop. However, knowing that I can move my arm again someday and being able to now, is very different.

I try my legs. One swift kick would knock her off me and hopefully remove the knife from her hand.

Stabbing pain shoots up my spine when I try to move my leg. *Come on, fight through it.*

I get my thigh an inch off the ground before it snaps back.

"Argh!" I scream out in pain.

Palmer watches me yelling, and I can't tell what's going through her mind.

Pain? Sorrow? Heartbreak? What does she feel when she sees me in torment?

"Shh, it's okay," she strokes my cheek. "Once I'm gone, you can call for help. Your body will heal. And then you can find your woman."

This is my chance. "I need to go now, Palmer. Siren is in trouble. Bad men have her—the same men who let Lucy die. I need you to help me. Call your guards down here and tell them we need an ambulance for us both. We need to heal, then together, we can go save Siren."

She stares at me like I just sprouted a second head.

"Palmer, you would like my Siren. Lucy even liked her, and you and

I both know Lucy doesn't like many people." I chuckle, trying to lighten the mood. "But Lucy liked Siren. Help me get her back."

"I can't. I'm sorry."

NO!

This is it—the moment Palmer does something she can't take back.

I have to stop her, or I'll never get the forgiveness I need. From myself. From Lucy. From Siren.

I can't move my limbs, but I realize I can move my core. Palmer moves the knife to her throat. I'm afraid my movements will push the knife into her body instead of knocking it out of her hand, but it's my only chance.

I roll us, my body flipping on my side, my cock finally slipping out of her, and then gravity takes over. My heavy, lifeless body slumps on top of hers.

I watch as her hands drop to my chest, trying to keep me from crushing her or taking the knife from her.

The knife is no longer near her throat.

I did it!

But then...*FUCK!* A sound comes out of me I've never produced. I've been tortured, even been tortured in my sensitive area, but the way the knife slices into my balls is like nothing I've ever experienced before.

I saved Palmer, but as I cry through the pain moments before I blackout, I realize I just ended the Kane line. There will be no little Kanes. No baby Zekes or baby Sirens running around. I thought I was okay with that. I shouldn't have been selfish and wanted to bring kids into our world anyway.

But the moment the knife slices into my testicles, I mourn the loss of something I wanted desperately. Not only do I have to ask Siren for forgiveness for sleeping with another woman, but I have to ask for forgiveness for saving another woman while taking something so precious from both Siren and myself.

We will never have kids. This sealed it. And it's fucking painful. So goddamn painful I'll never be able to catch my breath again.

CHAPTER 9
SIREN

I lie in a cloud of pillows, comforters, and blankets in the center of the most beautiful room I've ever been in. My memories are scattered in my head. Unlike any other time I've been drugged, I want to keep my memories jostled. I don't want to put the pieces back together. My foggy memory is the only thing saving me.

My hand rests on my naked belly stroking up and down to calm the hunger pains. But it doesn't stop my stomach from growling, trying to convince me to go get food.

I can't do anything about my hunger. I'm trapped in this room. No matter how beautiful it is, it's still a cage. I'm still the wild animal that has to be locked inside.

But I don't feel wild anymore. My fight is gone. I don't do anything about the scratches, blood, and sweat covering my naked body. I don't try to cover up with blankets. I don't try to do something about the pain between my legs.

I just lie on the bed face up, bare for the world.

No, for Zeke.

This was Zeke's work. This is all a game. Zeke is in control. He knows what my body needs. I'm not eating because he wants my senses heightened when he fucks me. This isn't blood—this is lube and cum. My body isn't in pain—it's just sore from his touch.

My brain keeps my focus on Zeke instead of the truth. I used to only be able to speak the truth; now, all I can tell is a lie. I can't think of the truth. The truth will kill me. So I'll keep lying to myself. I'll keep hiding from the sin that was created here in this room, and I'll hope that someday, Zeke can pull the truth out of me again, and we will be strong enough to survive it.

I try to take a deep, calming breath, but my breath is shaky and light. Inhaling fully requires me to feel my entire body, something I just can't do.

Instead, I focus on my stomach. It groans. I can focus on hunger. Hunger is safe. Hunger won't lead me to thinking about anything dangerous.

I hear the door open.

No, no, no, no...I'm not ready. I can't handle more.

Zeke and I have fucked twenty-three times. I don't know how many days have passed, but I've counted three moons. Maybe it's been longer than that and I was just asleep, but not many. My body is tired and sore and weak. I can't handle more sex.

"No," I moan, unable to lift my eyelids. I'm so tired. Just let me sleep. I'll be ready for you in the morning after a good night of sleep, Zeke.

But of course, Zeke doesn't leave me alone. His appetite is insatiable. Sex is never enough. He wants me all day, every day.

I feel him standing over the bed, staring down at me with his intense eyes and heavy breath. Even though he's three feet away, I can still feel his warm breath like a fire roasting my body, hoping I'll come alive for him.

My body can't...he broke me. My body is incapable of being turned on anymore. I don't get excited from his kisses, his touch, his gaze.

I used to get excited when Zeke walked into the room, but now, I don't even get turned on when he's inside me. We have to use lube because I'm not wet enough. Even a vibrator doesn't get me off.

Sex no longer feels good to me because of Zeke. The man I love ruined sex for me.

No, he couldn't have. There is something wrong with me.

"What are you doing?" the voice demands. It's not Zeke's, but I don't dare open my eyes. I know I've been hallucinating. I haven't had enough to eat or drink, and I keep seeing things, hearing people.

"Siren, open your eyes," he says.

"No, I can't. I can't fuck you, again. I can't..." I'm crying because I never thought I'd turn Zeke down, but I just can't. My body needs a break. Zeke and I like to play with my limits, but he's pushed me too far.

He chuckles. It's deep and unnerving, enough for me to want to open my heavy eyelids. I open them just a crack, and I realize the man in front of me isn't Zeke.

"No!" I cry, grabbing at the covers, trying to pull them over me and protect myself from this man, this monster.

Bishop grabs my wrist. "I'm not here to rape you."

I don't believe him. I kick, trying to get free. I throw a punch, landing on his neck. My aim is shit right now because I'm so exhausted and can't see. The room spins as I move, but I have to get free. I can't let Bishop touch me.

"Stop," Bishop commands, his voice booming.

"No! I won't let you rape me!" I scream. This time when I kick, my aim is perfect, and I hit him right in the balls.

He releases me, grabbing onto his crown jewels as he doubles over in pain.

I take the chance to run. I jump out of bed and run to the door, my brain becoming clearer and clearer. I grab the doorknob, but the door doesn't budge.

"Help!" I yell, slamming my fists on the door. Surely whoever is on the other side won't want me in here. He won't want to share. He won't let Bishop rape me.

I just don't let my brain name who 'He' is. It's too close to the truth. That truth will destroy me.

"Someone, please, help!" I yell some more, pounding my fists over and over, but the door is thick and soundproof. No one can hear. No one is coming to save me.

My arms are yanked back, and I'm shoved against the door, my face and stomach feeling the coolness of the thick door against my skin.

"Stop. No one is coming," Bishop says. He holds me at my wrists, but otherwise, he doesn't touch me. He doesn't press his front to my naked back. He doesn't drop his head to sniff my hair or caress my neck. He just stands behind me, holding me in place.

"How did you get in here?" I ask, knowing only one man has the ability to enter this room.

"You really want to ask that question? You think he's more powerful than me?"

"I think he's the man in charge and you follow his orders."

"Julian is merely a thug I use to get what I want; he's not in charge."

I wince when he says Julian's name, because it breaks a little of the illusion, but I quickly put my walls back up. It was Zeke. *Zeke, Zeke, Zeke...*

Bishop notices my change and doesn't continue to talk about Julian.

"I'm not going to rape you," he says, dropping his voice until it sounds almost like a lullaby.

"You're a man holding a naked woman hostage, in a soundproof room that only two men can enter. What's stopping you?" I ask, my heart thumping a million miles an hour.

"Did I rape you before?" he asks.

I think back to before, the last time this man held me captive. He didn't rape me. He didn't touch me in any sexual way, but he did fuck with my head.

"No, you didn't." I exhale, knowing I don't have to worry about him raping me. *Maybe he's gay? Maybe he doesn't find me attractive? Maybe he prefers to get his power in different ways?*

Bishop releases my hands and then takes a step back, preparing for me to attack him again.

I turn to face him, watching for his reaction to my nakedness. He doesn't glance down. Not once. His eyes stay on mine, like my eyes alone hold all of my secrets.

"Are you gay?" I ask, needing to know why he won't look at me.

He smirks. "No."

That's it—one word. That's all I get. I know nothing about this man other than he's fit, tall, and handsome in a pretty-boy sort of way. He's muscular, but not as big as Zeke.

He has scars similar to mine on his arms, but that doesn't seem to be where his pain comes from. It comes from a woman. The love of his life that desperately hurt him.

"Who hurt you?" I ask, trying to understand this man.

"You already know."

I frown, racking my brain for the answer, but I come up empty.

"What did you do to me? I know you messed with my head, tortured me, planted your thoughts inside me, and now I think about you all the damn time. When I'm sleeping, dreaming, awake, at the most random times. What did you do?"

"I prevented you from ever feeling the pain I feel," he answers calmly and stoically, like he knew this would be my question, and he's been ready for it.

"What does that mean?"

"I made you mine, instead of his."

"Who? Julian?"

He shakes his head. "The man you think you love. I made sure that I control you instead of him."

"No," I whisper, but I know it's true. Suddenly, a rush of torture floods my mind as I remember every excruciating thing he did to me.

I look at Bishop. "You had no right! I don't care if Zeke eventually hurts me, I love him! I'll love him for as long as I can, even if it's not forever, I'll take the heartbreak later."

Bishop blinks rapidly, like something I said hurt him. Just as quickly as it flashes, it's gone.

I stalk forward, angry and needing to control my own thoughts, my own heart.

"Fix me." My voice is calm, collected, and purposeful. I don't stutter. I choose the exact words I mean.

"No," he shakes his head.

He's a liar.

This is what he wants. He wants me to beg him. He wants me to offer up everything in order to be free again.

I pause, trying to decide my next move. *Do I continue to beg for him to fix me? Getting him to give me what I want, but knowing what he could do to me is so much worse?*

Or do I back off and live with what he did to me? Missing this opportunity would cause me to betray the man I love, again, and this time in a way that I can't take back. A way that is unforgivable. A way I can't live with.

I stare down at the ring I wear on my right hand.

Bishop stares too.

"Forever doesn't exist," he says.

I frown. "Forever is as long as you want it to be. Forever can last years or for a single second. It makes no difference. The promise to love someone forever is a promise I will never break. I love him. He loves me. Our forever might be shorter than most, but we've made it this far. We can make it till the end of our forever."

Bishop walks closer, his eye on the ring. "And how many times have you already betrayed your forever?" He takes my hand, his thumb running over the ring, sending shivers through my body.

"Never," I lie.

"You can't lie to me, Siren. I know you better than anyone. I'm that voice in your head. You don't love him. You don't love anyone."

"Stop!" I yell, trying to push his voice out as I rip my hand from his.

He grins, knowing what he's doing to me.

I hold my hand against my chest, protecting the ring and my heart.

"Fix me," I say again, having to push this. This is why he's here. He wants something from me, and this is the only trade I'm going to be willing to make.

"You are fixed. When you are in love and owned by another man, that's when you are broken," Bishop says.

I shake my head and step toward him, not caring that I'm naked. Not caring how vulnerable I am. I need to be fixed. I still don't know what thoughts Bishop put into my head; I don't know how much control he has over me.

"I want to be free. I want out. I'll make a trade. You came here for a reason. You want something from me. I'll do it. Whatever it is. But get me out of here. Fix me, free me."

A slow grin forms, but his eyes continue to hide his truth. Whatever it is he wants from me will be devastating to give.

I close my eyes, taking a deep calming breath, but I know this is the right choice.

I can't be raped again.

I can't stay here.

And Zeke needs me. There is a reason he didn't come here, that he didn't save me. Zeke needs me, and that trumps everything else. Whatever I have to do, I'll do it.

"Do we have a deal?" I ask, extending my hand.

His eyes flutter down for the first time. He spots my ring, and I'm sure, my naked body. But his body doesn't harden. He doesn't lust after me.

"I'll set you free, if you do a task for me. But you'll have to come back for me to fix you," he says.

I want to argue for better terms. I want to argue for him to fix me now. I want to be free of this man—all of his darkness.

But I feel Zeke calling to me. He needs me. The most important thing right now is getting out of here. I can figure out how to kick this man out of my head later.

"Deal," I say, inching my hand toward his.

Bishop puts his hand in mine, and we shake. I just made a deal with the devil, and I don't even know what he's going to require me to do. But whatever it is, I don't care right now. I just need to be closer to Zeke.

A shockwave jolts through me though when I touch Bishop. Our eyes meet, and I know Bishop feels it too and doesn't understand. Something big just happened between us, but neither of us know what. And I'm not going to stick around to figure it out.

CHAPTER 10
ZEKE

Beep.

    Beep.

    Beep. Beep.

God, I hate that sound. I know where I am—a hospital room.

I'm alive. I should be grateful that Palmer's guards agreed to bring me here. I remember them finding us in the basement.

Palmer distraught and confused, still thinking the best thing for her was to end her life. Me barely able to move with a knife in my groin. I would have bled out in minutes if they had just left me.

"Hospital," Palmer said. *One word; one order.*

Everything went black after that. I passed out. Palmer's order must have been enough for her men to bring me here.

I don't feel any pain. I have so many drugs pumping through the IV in my arm, I could get stepped on by a five thousand ton elephant right now and I wouldn't feel it.

No one else is in the room when I open my eyes. I'm in a sterile white hospital room, with an IV pole, and a fucking beeping machine, waking me up from the depths of a drug-induced coma.

I want to rip off all the cords, the IV out of my arm, and the catheter out of my dick. I want to run away, but I'm not even sure I can sit up on my own, let alone walk out of here. Last time I checked, I could barely move my fingers.

My eyes cut down my body. I'm covered to my chest with a thick white blanket. I have no idea what's underneath. My arms are resting on top of the covers.

I grit my teeth, trying to keep the fear at bay, and then I tell my hand to move—just move. I don't care what it does—even slap myself in the face and yank the IV out.

I raise my arm.

And I exhale the fear.

I hear the door open, and a person silently walks in—not typical of a nurse or doctor entering a patient's room.

I close my eyes and still, assuming it's one of Palmer's guards coming in to check on me. I hear the heavy footprints of his steps in his boots on the floor.

I don't have a weapon. But I don't need one.

I wait patiently for him to approach my bed. He still doesn't speak —he's not going to have a chance to. I'm not becoming Palmer's prisoner again. I'm getting the fuck out of here.

His feet stop, and I attack, even though I don't have a clue if my body can still move the way I need it to.

I punch hard with one hand while I grab for his gun with the other. I swing my legs out, taking his feet out from underneath him. I watch his body fly up and then slam to ground as I aim a gun at him before I realize my mistake.

The man I just attacked is not my enemy.

"Well, I guess that answers whether or not I need to get you a wheelchair," Enzo says.

"Holy fuck," I breathe hard and fast, my body shaking as I stand over Enzo on the floor on his back. But he has a grin on his face.

I extend my hand. He takes it and is back on his feet a second later.

"Glad to know you still have plenty of fight in there." He play punches me on the chest.

"Fuck," I bite my lip as the jolt hits me like he just punched me full out.

Enzo frowns and then looks at my arm and grabs the IV lying on the bed instead of in my vein. I didn't expect the second the drugs weren't continuously running through me that I would be in this much pain.

"We have to go," Enzo says.

I nod, trusting his judgment, even though in about five minutes, ten if I'm lucky, everything Palmer put me through is going to hit me.

I grab the cords at my chest and rip them off, knowing alarms will sound as soon as I do.

"Take a breath," Enzo says.

I don't. I don't need a breath to deal with the pain.

He yanks on my catheter.

I hiss, but still have enough medication in me to avoid registering the pain.

Enzo grabs his gun from me and slips it in his pants. He starts walking toward the door. I follow and stumble from dizziness.

"Hold onto my arm," Enzo says.

I want to argue, but I won't make it out of here otherwise. I grab his arm, using him like a walker.

"Isn't this going to be suspicious, us walking out with me still dressed like this?"

Enzo opens the door. "Definitely." He grins like he did when we were teenagers and about to get into trouble.

I grin back. "Maybe I should hold onto that gun."

"No way in hell. I've always been the better shot, even when your body wasn't beat up," Enzo says.

I'm about to argue again, but he pushes us out into the hallway. I have no idea what country we are in. I have no idea what dangers await us in the hallway. *Are we going to just have to deal with fussing nurses telling me to get back into bed? Or are we going to have to fight our way out?*

Enzo already knows what to expect and is firing his gun the second we exit. I can barely keep up as he shoots down guard after guard—some of them I recognize as the men from Palmer's basement.

I regret Enzo killing them, until I see all of them had guns aimed at us.

Enzo shoots the last one in the hallway. "Come on, let's get out of here."

I nod my agreement and hobble along next to him.

"Palmer's room is on the end. Give me a minute to take her out then—"

"No."

Enzo stops and stares at me. "What? She'll come after you. She'll come after us. We can't let her live. It's not your decision to make."

"Palmer lives," I say, not budging on this.

"She can't. I won't risk my family."

"She has to live."

Enzo shakes his head. Then he grabs the bottom of the hospital gown and lifts it up. "Look what she did to you." He growls, his eyes daring me to look at my damaged body. But I don't.

I can feel all the damage. I can feel it on the surface of my skin all the way down to my bones. Unlike other times where I've been injured, I won't recover. I know instinctively that I will never have kids. I don't even know if I can fuck again.

Now isn't the time to discuss it, though.

I shove the gown back down.

"I'll do it. Just stay here," Enzo says, trying to let me go so he can kill her by himself, but I don't let go of his arm.

"No. Palmer lives. She won't come after us."

"She had dozens of guards outside both of your rooms. That seems like someone who is deep in this world."

I look back at the damage he did to the guards. "Do any of them look like career criminals? Not one of them got a shot off. And you snuck into my room without any of them noticing. They didn't have me handcuffed to the bed. They're amateurs. They are harmless even if they did come after us, but they won't because Palmer isn't a villain, she's just scared."

"What happened to you? Why are you going soft on me? She tortured you. She deserves to be punished. Death is fairer than what we would usually do to repay those sins."

My eyes glaze—Enzo's right. Most people who kidnapped and

tortured me would end up getting tortured twice as bad and then eventually killed. Death would actually be showing her mercy.

I haven't changed. I would still do anything and everything to protect Enzo and his family. This just isn't one of those times where I need to protect them. There is nothing to protect them from.

I don't need revenge for what was taken from me.

I need to show compassion to a woman who lost everything and hope her pain didn't cause me to lose everything as well.

I get in Enzo's face. "I have followed your orders since we were five. I've worked for your company my entire life. I've shown devotion and loyalty to you when I could have gotten free of a mad man much sooner. So I think I've earned the right to make a decision about what to do with a woman who tortured me."

I spit out each word—my anger rumbling through my body. I'm not angry at Enzo. I'm angry at what happened to me. I'm angry I couldn't stop it. I'm angry Lucy is dead, Siren could be as well. I'm angry at what I lost.

"I saved your wife for you. Palmer lives," I say. I let go of his arm, and I start walking toward the door. I know Enzo well enough—he won't kill Palmer.

Sure enough, Enzo catches up to me, and grabs hold of my arm again as I step through the automatic sliding doors.

We won't speak about Palmer again. We've been friends too long to let a fight like this impact us. Enzo will be here for me if I ever want to talk about why, but I don't owe him a reason. He knows how serious this is to me, and that's enough.

We step out into sticky heat; we must be somewhere near the equator. It's too blazing not to be. Even hotter than in Miami.

"Which car?" I ask as I hobble down the sidewalk path toward the parking lot, not wanting to take a step in the wrong direction. Each step I take gets more and more painful.

Enzo doesn't answer me, and I look at him, standing still until he answers me.

He grins and nods in front of us. "That one."

I turn from him to the direction he's looking, and I see a van door open. I see Kai holding Siren back.

"We considered drugging Siren to keep her from coming into the hospital with me. I knew you wouldn't want us to put her at risk to save you. Kai finally convinced her," Enzo says.

My eyes water seeing Siren alive. I can't tell from our distance whether Siren is hurt or not, but I'm thankful Enzo didn't let Siren into that hospital. I need her safe, and I didn't want her to see me so broken.

I straighten my back, trying to look like I'm not completely shattered. I let go of Enzo's arm, no longer allowing myself to use him as a crutch. But the tears, those I can't control—they pour down like rain in a thunderstorm.

"Go get your girl," Enzo says.

Siren is already way ahead of him, running toward me.

This moment is a turning point for Siren and me. I don't understand which way we are turning, but we are. I just hope we can continue to keep our promises while we change course.

CHAPTER 11
SIREN

Bishop put me on a plane the second I agreed to his deal. It was a horrible, awful deal—one I really don't want to uphold. He'll kill Zeke in retribution if I don't keep my end of the deal, though.

Bishop freed me, now I have to do a task for him. One I don't even understand why he wants me to do.

But I don't have a choice—I have to do it.

I'm beyond ready to be done making deals with devils. I have two vows left to fulfill. Two promises stand between me and freedom.

When I look out at the grizzly looking man in a hospital gown that only hits him mid-thigh, I would make all those deals again. I would do anything to be with him.

I touch the ring he gave me. I hope to be making one more vow with Zeke soon.

Kai touches my shoulder. "Go get him." Her smile is tight and sad as she looks out at the two men we love exiting the hospital. She risked her husband's life to save the man I love.

"Thank you," I say to her through tears.

"Go," she says, pushing me out of the van. But I see her tears. Kai wants to check on Zeke as well. She wants to embrace her husband even though it's been less than twenty minutes since the last time we saw him, and this mission was on the low end of risky, compared to most of his tasks.

I jump out of the van and start running toward Zeke. I'm sore, my body aches, my inner thighs are bruised, my body has been cut, and my stomach has been queasy ever since Bishop put me on the plane to Miami to meet up with Enzo and Kai. And I've been sick the entire way here to Bogota, Columbia.

Seeing Zeke somehow just intensifies all those feelings instead of reducing them. As I run, all the fears creep back in.

Will Zeke think I'm damaged?

How hurt is Zeke?

Does he still love me?

Does he still want to marry me?

Why isn't he running toward me? Why was he using Enzo as a crutch?

Zeke takes a step toward me, and I realize why he's not running. He's barely standing on his own.

Relief fills me when it shouldn't. I shouldn't feel any happiness at his pain, but he's not running because of his injuries instead of some emotional issue between us.

I run faster, studying him closer, trying to assess his injuries, so I know where to grab him and pull him into a hug. I decide a hug is better than jumping in his arms, even though that's what I really want to do. When I see the joyous tears on his face, I know he's feeling all the same emotions I am.

Finally, I'm within reach of him.

"Be gentle with me, beautiful," Zeke says, winking at me and holding his arms out.

I jump when I know I shouldn't.

He catches me, even though his body should be too weak.

We fall onto the grass next to the sidewalk, but I'm able to turn us so I bear more of the brunt than Zeke does.

We both grunt when we hit the ground, but don't care as we are finally in each other's arms.

Zeke shakes his head. "Stop saving me." He looks pointedly at my arm where I hit the grass first. His words repeat the plea I've said to him time and time again.

Stop saving me.

I look up at Zeke with a guilty look on my face because I've been wanting Zeke to save me the entire time I was captured. I was begging for him to in my sleep, through the nightmare that was my life, but he was obviously dealing with something much worse.

"I'm sorry," I cry out, the first words I say to him.

Zeke strokes my face. "Don't. If we start with apologies, we will never stop. We have too much to be sorry for. I'm not sorry for what it took to get you back."

"I'm not either."

We grab each other in a desperate kiss. A kiss that we launch at each other with everything we've been feeling—all the pain and agony and heartbreak.

We have a lot to work through. He has no idea what I've been through, and I have no idea what he's been through. He doesn't know what happened to Lucy. He doesn't know what I agreed to get free. And I don't know what it cost him to get back to me.

This kiss is about us, though. It's about proving to the other we still love each other despite everything that has happened. Whatever it is. Whatever horrible things we've done, it doesn't matter. We love each other forever.

Zeke rolls me on top of him, and I panic when I hear the low moans he makes, but he doesn't let me roll off him. He continues to kiss me until we are both suffocating and only living on the tiny amount of oxygen between us.

Neither of us stop, though. We can't pull away. The love we feel is too much. The horrific trauma we've both been through won't allow us to stop.

"Guys, we need to get out of here before the police show up," Enzo says from behind us.

"Fuck off," Zeke says, going right back in for a kiss.

Enzo sighs. "You can keep making out in the back of the van. Just get your ass up."

I giggle and push off of Zeke. I stand as Zeke tries to keep me pressed to him, but I win and stand. I extend my hand, and Zeke takes it, but I realize that he doesn't have the strength to get himself up with my hand alone.

Enzo is already ahead of me, behind Zeke lifting his shoulders up as I pull his arm. Together, we get Zeke on his feet. Enzo throws one of Zeke's arms over his shoulders, and I do the same to Zeke's other arm.

Zeke grimaces but doesn't stop us from helping him. He doesn't really have a choice. The three of us walk back to the open van where Kai waits in the driver's seat. Enzo and I ease Zeke into the middle bench seat, lying him sideways. I climb in after him, lift his head up, and let his head fall on my lap.

I know Zeke doesn't like being vulnerable. He doesn't like looking weak. He wants to be my protector. As I stroke my hand through his long hair and think about telling him what happened to me, how he couldn't prevent it from happening, it's going to kill him. It's going to reopen every wound and make him feel inadequate.

Enzo hops in the passenger's seat, and Kai starts driving away from the hospital and Zeke's looming demons. No matter how fast Kai drives us away, the ghosts will follow. We aren't escaping them. We are just getting to a place where we can learn to survive them. A place where we can get on an equal playing field where we can fight and eventually defeat them.

I take Zeke's hand, needing to feel grounded as we drive. Zeke's hand doesn't feel warm and comforting. I don't feel whole gripping his hand, not like when we were kissing.

When we were kissing, we were able to push everything else out. The bad, the good. Every person. Every nightmare. For a moment in time, it was just us.

Now that we are in the van with Kai and Enzo, we are no longer alone. We have to face reality. Soon, we are going to have to spill everything that happened.

I'm not afraid of hearing what atrocities Zeke lived through. He's strong enough to handle his own physical pain. I don't know if he's strong enough to handle what Julian and Bishop did to me.

My grip on his hand tightens, until I'm squeezing so hard his hand turns white. Instead of telling me to let go, his thumb just traces the back of my hand gently, trying to calm me.

I look down at Zeke's eyes and see the wildness of the thoughts spinning there. We've only just begun our journey. We can say we love each other and want to spend our lives together, but our journey is going to be a lot of work. And there is no guarantee of success.

We drive all afternoon, into the darkness, before reaching the dock where the Black's yacht is tied up. Everyone is tense as we drive, prepared for one of Palmer's team to attack us at any moment. Or waiting for Julian or Bishop to sideswipe and attack us with guns and bombs. Kai parks the rental van as close as we can get to the pier.

Zeke is pretty weak at this point. He's been dosing on and off, and he needs food, water, sleep, and possibly more medical help. There is a team of hired doctors aboard the yacht to help Zeke. The doctors saw to me when I first got on, and I trust them completely.

Zeke needs to talk to them and be examined, that is the first priority, but I can't help but think I need him. One of the most important things for us to heal is to reconnect. And that process is going to be grueling.

Kai and Enzo step out of the van, and as soon as they do, I feel a heaviness lift. It only reaffirms to me that Zeke and I need time alone to figure out where we go from here. But I'll be patient. Zeke needs medical attention first.

Enzo opens the door, and Zeke tenses. Something happened between these two in that hospital that changed the dynamic of their relationship. Enzo helps Zeke out of the van and lifts him in the air, cradling him like a baby.

"I'm carrying your big ass; you don't get to argue with me," Enzo says.

I don't hear Zeke's response, but I smile, watching the two men together like brothers.

Kai takes my hand, and we follow behind our men. Both us scanning the entire walk down the pier, watching for any of our many enemies. I try to push out one of the last times I walked down a pier, having it blown to pieces. *It won't happen again,* I remind myself.

We make it to the safety of the yacht. Enzo and Zeke have already disappeared inside the ship, but I find Nora and Beckett waiting for us.

"You okay?" Nora asks.

I nod, not able to speak.

Kai squeezes my hand, telling me she's here for me. All I want to do is snuggle up next to Zeke.

"Come on," Kai says, still holding my hand like I'm her child she's leading to her bedroom to tuck her in.

I give Nora and Beckett a small tight-lipped smile, and then I'm down in the hallways being led to the bedrooms. I expect Kai to lead me back to my bedroom and let me know the doctors are checking on Zeke. She's going to tell me to get some sleep and she'll have the doctors check on me in the morning.

Instead, she leads me to a different door. The door is already open, and I can see the doctors fussing over Zeke. I can hear Enzo's raised voice yelling at Zeke to let the doctors do their work.

"Out," Kai says forcefully.

All eyes turn to her.

"Everyone out of Zeke's room. Now," Kai says again.

I think they are all going to argue, say that Zeke needs medical attention now.

But one by one, every man files past us. Enzo gives his wife a stern look, but she just raises her brow. He leaves, letting her have all the power over the situation.

I stand behind her, still not seeing Zeke.

"Why did you do that? Zeke needs medical attention," I say, although I don't believe my own words.

"No, he needs you. Just you," she says.

She hugs me. "You have the power to heal him. Trust me." She releases me and tilts her head, telling me it's okay to enter.

"I'll have some wrapped food brought down and left outside the door. You can get it when you're ready."

I nod but don't thank her. I need to save everything for Zeke, for whatever truths are going to be spilled. Once I enter the room, I'm not going to leave again until Zeke and I have fought off all our enemies. Until we are solid in our love and our forever.

I step inside, holding my breath. I see Zeke, and my heart heals instantly, but his bleeds out to me. His heart is in turmoil—turmoil I may not be able to heal.

CHAPTER 12
ZEKE

I'm broken.

That's what everyone's eyes have been telling me. Enzo knows how physically damaged I am. Kai knows I'm emotionally torn up. Nora and Beckett both looked at me with pity. The doctors ran into the room and treated me like I was on the verge of dying.

And then—Siren.

Siren isn't broken.

She doesn't see me as broken.

I thought what we had would be gone after what we just went through. Neither of us was able to protect the other. Neither of us was able to save the other.

We both had to fight alone.

I'm still unsure if that brought us closer together or pushed us apart—a hurricane of evil threw us to the edges of the earth. Can we ever swim the lengths of the earth to get back to each other?

"Hi," Siren says timidly, like we are meeting again for the first time. In a way, this is a second first meeting.

Her single, tentative word sends my heart racing, thump-thumping like a drum trying to call her toward me. She smiles bashfully at my need but takes her time walking to me.

She's wearing jeans and a black tank top. Her arms are fit, but I see the bruises. I see the extra layers of makeup on her face and want to know what she's hiding.

"Hi," I return sweetly.

It causes Siren to bite her lip. She chews on it like I make her nervous, in a flirtatious sort of way. Like we are two people going on our first date. I laugh at that thought because Siren and I have never even gone on a first date. Nothing about our relationship feels normal.

This moment does.

A hospital gown is the only thing hiding my secrets. Siren's wearing makeup and jeans to cover hers. This moment should be awkward. It should feel wrong. But I feel all the flutters of being in love, and I remember the last thing I said to Siren before we were ripped apart—I asked her to marry me.

I search her left hand for the ring but find it empty. My heart drops...

Siren laughs, noticing my reaction.

"What?" I ask, angry that the ring I got for her is gone.

She holds up her right hand. "Looking for this?"

"Come here," I growl.

She jumps onto the bed next to me happily like it's our wedding night instead of the night I crush her dreams. She curls into the crook of my arm, and lays her head on my chest, becoming the missing piece of my body. She fills the void taken from me, but I'm not sure if what is left of me is enough for her.

"Stop," she says.

"What?"

"Just stop. Stop thinking. Just be with me. Hold me. Love me. I love you, Zeke. Nothing that happened to either of us changed that. Nothing ever could. I still want to be your wife. I want our forever—whatever that means. I want it. I'll always love you."

I want our forever too. We never talked about what our forever means, though. *Does it mean this? We will always be running? Always be fighting? Our lives in constant danger?*

Did we want to get out? Settle down in a house with kids?

I realize now that neither of those forevers is going to work.

Neither of them will allow me to love Siren the way she deserves to be loved.

I don't want a life of running and fighting, a life of danger.

But I can't offer her the kids and peaceful life she deserves either.

Siren takes my hand instead of draping her body over mine, sensing she can't be on me without hurting me, even though we haven't discussed all my injuries yet. Or hers.

She traces calming circles in my palm, and I let my thoughts go. I'm present with her. Her warmth is hugging me and reminding me what it means to be happy again.

"What do we do now?" Siren asks after we are both calmer.

I don't know. This isn't a battle against an obvious enemy. I can't just pull out my gun and take down each enemy, one after the other. Our enemies already damaged us. We both have wounds—physical and emotional. We both have pain to share and lingering feelings of anguish, of fear, of loss.

I want to draw a line and start over. Push all those feelings away and begin a new life today with Siren.

I can't, though.

She can't either.

I take her hand in mine and kiss the back of her hand. "We love. We heal—together. We take this step by step, and we find a way to defeat our demons."

CHAPTER 13
SIREN

"Are you scared?" I ask.

"No," Zeke answers, but shudders.

"I'm terrified," I say.

"Me too." Zeke smiles tentatively. "But I don't want to be. I don't want to show you how afraid I am. This should be easy."

"No, it shouldn't be easy. It should be hard. Most couple's relationships don't survive the traumatic. Ours has been tested to the limit."

"Where do we start?" he asks.

This is too big. It's too big to just start talking and lay everything out. Separately either would be too much, but together this becomes enormous. I feel the weight on both of us, weighing us down. We have to do this.

I hear a soft rattling at the door.

Zeke turns his head and then is reaching for a gun.

It scares me that his first reaction is to reach for a gun, even though we're on a heavily guarded ship with his best friends. This time we took no precautions. We are being protected by all of Enzo and Kai's men. Over two dozen superyachts surround us with the highest level of technology. There is no safer place to be.

"It's just Kai. She said she'd leave us some food outside the door," I say, getting up. I open the door and grab the tray of food and carry it back to the bed.

"Grilled cheese," Zeke says without looking at the plate.

"Really? You think?"

He nods with a smile. "It's Kai's favorite comfort food. And she's not much of a chef. And she would have made this herself, not let the chef on board cook it."

I lift the lid, and there are two heart-shaped grilled cheeses underneath.

We both grin. "She makes such a good mom," I say.

He grabs the sandwich and takes a bite, wincing.

"Should you be eating that?" I ask.

"Probably not, but it tastes good."

I take a bite, and I moan. "What kind of cheese did she put in this?"

"I don't know, but it's delicious."

We both eat our sandwiches in quiet after that. I scarf mine down, not realizing how hungry I've been. I haven't eaten a full meal since before Zeke and I were separated.

Zeke barely nibbles on his, wincing every once in a while as the food goes down roughly in his throat. His stomach rumbles, causing him to shift on the bed. Each time he moves, I see the toll it takes on his body. I hear the cracks, the hisses, and the moans he tries to hide. I haven't seen what's underneath his hospital gown, but I know it isn't good.

"Truth or sin?" I ask, thinking maybe a simple question game will help us talk, or at least get us started.

He nods but stiffens. He's leaning against the headboard, picking at the last piece of the grilled cheese, not looking at me.

This is going to be hard.

"Truth," he finally says, his dark eyes meeting mine, begging me not to hurt him. But everything I have to say will hurt him. I start with the easiest topic to tackle. The part that is painful, but in a way we can mourn and heal.

"Lucy died." I take a deep breath and blink back the tears. Maybe starting with her death wasn't the best idea after all. My eyes find Zeke, and he doesn't look shocked. He knew. He already knew.

"Julian didn't kill her. Nor did Bishop."

He exhales a harsh, thankful breath. He was worried her death was painful.

"It was beautiful. One of the most beautiful things I've ever experienced. She died in my arms, outside, looking up at the stars and the water. Lucy was ready to die; she was at peace."

The tears sting now, remembering that moment.

Zeke pulls me to him, and we are both crying silently in each other's arms. Crying, until we drift to sleep.

THE SUN WAKES US BOTH UP.

"Your turn," I start.

"I can't play. I can't do this," his throat clears.

I touch his chin, needing him to look at me so I can understand what he's saying. "You can't play? You can't be with me? What are you saying?"

"I can't play. I'm tired of playing games."

"You want me to tell you the truth? All of it?"

He nods.

"And then you'll tell me yours?"

His jaw clenches, and I know the answer is no. He wants my truth, but he doesn't want to give up his.

"No," I say.

He frowns and tries to turn away from me. I climb on his lap, and he moans loudly. I lift myself up to avoid touching him, but I'm straddling him, looking him face to face so I can get through to him.

I place my hands carefully on his shoulders to hold myself up, studying his reaction. He only flinches, so this can't be hurting him too badly.

"Why don't you want to tell me what happened to you? What are you afraid of?" I ask.

His eyes fill with tears. His teeth grind together until I can hear the clattering sound. The vein in his neck bulges. It's like he's about to burst. If he starts, it will all come out in one explosion that will obliterate us both.

"That you won't want me," he finally says.

I take his face in mine. His glorious, beautiful face. The one with as many scars as mine. He has plenty of battle wounds on his face, but it doesn't make him any less beautiful. It's part of him, as much as his dark, intense eyes, his strong jaw, and long, beast-like hair.

"I'll always want you, no matter what happened to you. No matter what you did or didn't do. It doesn't matter to me, I love you. I'll always want you."

He shakes his head like he doesn't believe me. I grab his face again and press my lips to his through the tears. I suck all his pain away with my mouth and tongue. I'm careful not to push him too far.

He can't handle getting excited and fucking right now. He needs more time to heal, and as much as we both want sex, it won't heal us right now. We need the truth, not sin.

"I'm afraid my pain will be too much for you to bear," I say, spilling my fears.

"Never." He kisses the tears on my cheeks, sucking them off the surface of my skin. "What happened to you will hurt, because once again I failed, not because I can't stand to hear it. I can handle your pain."

I shudder over him, trying not to touch him when I'm desperate to. An idea forms in my head.

"Can you get in the ocean? Will it hurt you?" I ask.

He shakes his head. "My wounds are all stitched and covered. As long as you don't expect me to swim, I should be okay."

"No swimming," I smile. "Do you trust me?"

"With my life."

"Good. What I'm asking you to do will require you to risk your life. Your heart. Your everything." I wiggle my eyebrows, trying to lighten the mood as I jump off the bed.

He chuckles at me. It's deep, but not a belly laugh, which is probably a good thing considering whatever is underneath his nightgown is going to be lots of bruises and scars and agony.

"Get ready to go for a swim."

"Siren," Zeke says in a warning word, reminding me that he can't.

I head to the door. "Trust me."

Zeke does trust me. He loves me too. And he's about to start his forever with me.

CHAPTER 14
ZEKE

"This is crazy," Enzo says as he hands me a pair of swim trunks and a T-shirt.

I laugh. "This is the least crazy thing I've done in a long time."

"Why are you going for a swim when you should be in bed healing?" Enzo asks as he unties my nightgown.

"Because Siren wants me to."

Enzo grumbles. "That sounds like a terrible reason."

The gown falls to the floor, and Enzo gasps. He's speechless looking at me.

"I've looked worse," I remind him of the last time he came for me when I was tortured.

Enzo shakes his head. "You've been through more than all of the rest of us combined."

"I know! Why is it that I'm always the one that gets tortured the worst?"

"Because you are the biggest target."

I laugh. "And what is it about my balls? This is the second time I've been attacked there. I mean, really?"

"They are just big and hairy like the rest of you. People think they are fighting a sasquatch instead of a human."

Enzo helps me step into the swim trunks, and then he slips the shirt on over my head, like one of his twin toddlers.

"You don't have to do this just because Siren wants you to. Does she know about...?"

"No, that's why I have to do this. We need to heal. Siren has a plan to do that. I can't get the words out right now, and she can't either. This is the only way to do this. The ocean has brought us together before. It's where she found me—saved me. It won't fail us."

"I get it. But if your balls get infected and fall off, don't say I didn't warn you," he taunts me.

I nod, remembering the doctors talking about me in the hospital bed when they thought I was out of it—saying how damaged I was. There is nothing I could do to further damage my body. My scars will heal, but only the surface. Everything else will remain damaged, forever.

Forever—a promise and a curse. That's what I should have written on Siren's ring.

Enzo pats my shoulder. "You'll get through this. There was a time I thought Kai and I wouldn't survive, but we did. We figured out how to defeat our enemies and how to love each other. You will too."

"And then I brought new enemies to your doorstep."

"No, you didn't. Julian Reed was always after us. He would have come after us in a different way if he didn't find you. You actually stalled him. This is our fight, now. Not yours alone. We will destroy him like we've defeated all our enemies."

"Boys? You down there? The sun will set soon, and I'm not letting you get in the water if it's not still daylight out," Kai says from the top of the stairs and down the hallway.

"We're coming," Enzo shouts back.

Enzo helps me up the stairs, and then I see Siren preparing one of the dingy boats.

"Really? We aren't even getting in the water? Just going on a boat? I didn't need to change if that was the case," I say.

"Oh, you needed to change. That hospital gown wasn't a good look for you, big guy," Kai says.

I shoot her a dirty look.

"Just get in the boat," Siren says, happy to see me smiling and joking. She thinks it means she has a chance of healing us. The joking is just preventing me from thinking about our unsalvageable relationship. She won't want me when she knows there is no future with me.

Enzo helps me into the boat, and Siren climbs in after me. We are lowered into the water, just the two of us in the small boat.

Siren drives us about a half-mile away from the main yacht. There are several other nearby yachts, all ours protecting us, so I know we are safe. The open water is as private as we can safely be.

"You ready?" she asks.

"Since you haven't told me what we are doing, I guess I'm as ready as I can be. Although my doctors are going to lecture me about how stupid this was and how I'm risking my life."

"It will be worth it, I promise."

"I know."

She lifts her T-shirt off her head, and she's in a white skimpy bikini. The kind that displays every curve, every bruise, every cut.

"Fuck, you're gorgeous," I breathe out, but keep my hands to myself. I have too many feelings at the sight of her. I love staring at her body but hate the new unknown marks. I want her, am desperate for her. I feel the heat rise in my chest at the sight of her curves, the tightness of her stomach, her cleavage spilling out the top of her bikini. But I don't feel my cock stir. I don't get excited in my usual way.

"Down boy," Siren winks at me, thinking my problem right now is that I want to fuck her. I do. God, I want nothing more than to be able to fuck her like before. But I don't even know if I can get hard. And from the bruises on her thighs and arms, I suspect what she went through is preventing her from a romp in the sack too.

Suddenly, she's diving into the water, her body arching like I imagine an Olympic diver would move. Her ass gives me one more tempting view before disappearing under the water.

I stare down at my crotch, willing it to harden, to come to life in any way, but I feel nothing. It's like I'm numb below my waist. I know the muscles and nerves still work in my legs. I can still move, but my cock might as well not exist.

Siren's head pops up. "You coming?"

I nod and jump into the water feet first, nowhere near as gracefully as her dive into the water. This is a stupid idea; there is no way water could heal me.

When my head goes under the cool water, everything changes. I feel alive again. I feel light, like my injuries and pain no longer exist. I remember the last time we were both in the middle of the water like this. I had a bullet in my chest. I was bleeding out. I was going to die. And then...

My head pops out of the water, looking at Siren again in a new light as we both tread water.

Siren bites her lip, trying to keep her growing smile at bay as she looks at me, confident this was the right move.

"You can hold onto the boat," she says.

"No, I don't need to." I don't want to. I just want to feel the water and her.

"You're afraid. I'm afraid. But we are letting that fear go here and now."

I close my eyes, feeling the draining sun's warmth on my face, the ocean water spraying my cheeks with salt, the waves rocking us gently away from the boat. I open my eyes again, renewed. I'll never be able to thank her enough for realizing what we needed.

We will still have a lot of healing left to do when we leave the ocean, but we will have taken the first step, and the first step is the hardest.

So I open my mouth, "Siren, I—"

"Nope, you don't get to tell me anything about what happened to you yet. This is my plan." She winks at me and then takes both of my hands, holding them between us, our kicking legs keeping us above the water.

It's exhausting, but the burn in my lungs and the ache of my legs feel good. It reminds me how much I'm willing to suffer for our relationship. I just don't want Siren to suffer with me.

"Why do you love me, Zeke?"

I frown. "Are you questioning—"

"No, I just want to hear why you love me."

"We would be out here all day if I listed every reason why I love you, Siren. Way past the length of time we are able to tread water without drowning. My love for you is vaster than this ocean.

"I love you for saving me that night in the ocean; you could have easily let me drown. I know you made sacrifices that night that I still don't understand, but you took one look at me and knew I was worth saving. That I was a good man.

"I love that you are my equal, you're able to go head-to-head and toe-to-toe with me on everything. Fighting, wit, and courage. You have it all.

"I love your loyalty to those you care about. Even to those you hate. If you make a promise, you do everything to keep it.

"I love that you still want me even though I've failed you. Even though I'm not strong enough for you. I fail to live up to your equal.

"I love that you held my ex's hand all night, comforting her until she took her last breath." Tears sting again, as the pain at losing Lucy is still fresh. It haunts me that I wasn't there for Lucy, even though I know she didn't want me there. Siren was a good friend in her last moments on this earth.

"I love you because you challenge me. You're willing to fight with me, no matter how hard our life gets." My voice breaks, and I can't. I can't keep talking because if I do, I'll tell her everything that happened. I'll try to convince her she can't be with me. I'll do the right thing, and right now, I can't do the right thing. I can only do the wrong thing—love her, even though I'm going to hurt her.

I see Siren's tears, making me afraid I said the wrong thing, but then I see her smiling and laughing with such joy that her face seems to glow.

"I love you, Zeke Finn Kane. I loved you from the moment I saw you in the water. It hit me in the gut; you were different than every other man I knew in my life. You were one of the good guys, even though you had a rough exterior.

"I love that you forgave me when I hurt you, even though I didn't earn your forgiveness.

"I love that you are selfless and put your friends, even me, above yourself.

"I love how pure your heart is. With you, there is no gray—just black and white. You forgive people of their sins.

"I love your protective spirit. Even now, you are warring with yourself, trying to find a way to protect me from the darkness done to you. You think I won't love you, or I'll want out."

She pauses and lets go of one of my hands, raising her right hand out of the water. The engagement ring I gave her rests on her ring finger, along with a ring on her thumb.

"What are you doing?"

She pulls both rings off her hand and hands me her engagement ring.

"Are you giving this back?" I can't breathe. It's better for her without me, but I can't handle letting her go right now.

"No, I'm not giving it back. I'm giving it to you to put on its proper place. I know this isn't legal. Getting married in the ocean without witnesses, without a marriage license—it means nothing to the world. But to us—it means everything. I don't want to wait until this is over to get married. I don't want to wait until we can find an officiant and get this in writing."

I open my mouth. She needs to know what happened to me. She needs to know what she's agreeing to by marrying me, even just with us as witnesses and nothing but the ocean. If we do this, then to us, we will always be married.

"You should know before we do this—"

"No, I don't want to know what happened to you. I don't want to know what we lost, what we can't get back, what's changed. It doesn't matter. I love you as you. I love you whole; I love you broken. I love you, no matter what happens. No matter how we change. I love you forever. And I want our forever to start now, today. I don't want to wait. I want you to know that no matter what you tell me, I'll always be your wife."

My heart heals, all the wounds stitching together. Sealing any cracks. Mending all scars. I didn't know love could feel like this. I knew it was powerful, but not enough to heal everything.

I was wrong. Loving Siren is enough to fix all of my brokenness. My physical scars will remain, but emotionally, we'll get through this.

"I, Zeke Finn Kane, take you, Siren Aria Torres, to be my wife, in sickness and in health, for richer, for poorer, till death do us part."

I take the ring and grab her left hand, slipping it on her finger.

"You promise to be my husband forever?"

"I do."

I kiss her hand over her ring.

"And I, Siren Aria Torres, take you, Zeke Finn Kane, to be my husband, no matter what happened to you or what will happen to you. No matter if our forever only lasts till tomorrow or for fifty years. No matter how many men you've killed or how many times you try to protect me but don't reach me in time to save me from pain. I take you as my husband, with all your faults, because you are worth it. I love you more than I want to take my next breath. I'm so happy that you are my husband."

I shake my head smiling, loving her unique vows.

"You promise to be my wife forever?"

"I do."

She takes my hand and the ring she was wearing on her thumb and slips it onto my ring finger. I look down at the simple silver ring that I'm sure belonged to Enzo at one point. He's going to have to fight me to get it back now.

"My anchor—forever," she says, reading the hand-done scratching on its surface.

"It's perfect."

"And now you can kiss your bride," Siren says with a smile she won't be able to wipe off her face for days.

The ocean seems to know it's time for a kiss. The waves push us together, and I kiss my wife—something I never thought I'd be doing. I never thought I could have a wife. I never thought I could put one woman above everyone else I love. But as my lips press hard against hers and the ocean pushes us harder together, solidifying our union, I'd let Enzo take a bullet every time if it meant saving this woman, my wife.

The universe in this moment may want us to be together, but I'm shaking, thinking about what I would do to protect Siren. What horrible atrocities I would commit. What lengths I would go to to keep her mine—forever.

Our forever is going to last a lot longer than a few hours or days. I want the next fifty years.

CHAPTER 15
SIREN

We're married.

Not in the eyes of any law or country, but from this moment forward, we will behave as husband and wife. I'll love Zeke as my husband. And he will love me as my wife.

We haven't discussed any of the important details couples should talk about before getting married. We didn't discuss where we'd live, or what job we would do, or if we will have kids. We had no talks about sharing our assets, staying in this dark business, or killing Julian and getting out. We didn't discuss anything.

We're married. We're committed. We will figure everything else out.

"We need to get back in the boat," I say.

Zeke nods as his limbs shake. I knew the water would heal us, even though it also has the power to destroy us. To make us so weak that physically we couldn't recover. It was a risk worth taking because the emotional wounds Zeke is carrying are deep. This was just the start— getting married in the place we started, letting Zeke know that no matter what he tells me, I'm not going anywhere.

I climb onto the boat first, and then Zeke grabs hold of the edge. I lift him over, very much like I did that first night when I met him.

That night he was pretty out of it, already accepting his death, so he wasn't in pain when I pulled him over. This time though, no matter how happy he is that he married me, he's in pain. I help him lay down in the bottom of the boat.

"This was a bad idea. I'm sorry," I say.

He pants, large, heavy breaths, in and out like he just completed a hard workout instead of just treading water and being lifted into a boat.

"No, this was a perfect idea. No regrets."

"No regrets." I smile.

He shivers, and I know he's freezing. I grab towels I brought and wrap him in them. I consider telling him to take off his soaking T-shirt to help him warm-up, but I know he isn't comfortable with that yet. He wore the shirt in the water because he wasn't ready to bear his scars to me.

I won't push him, even though we are married. Healing takes time.

"Ready to head back?" I ask.

"No, not yet." He sits up slowly, wrapping the blankets around him.

"I wish I could help you warm up more," he says.

He eyes something behind me. I follow his gaze and see two thermoses. I grab them and unscrew the top of the first and take a sniff. "Hot chocolate. Kai must have packed it."

I hand it to him, and he takes it in his shaky hands before lifting it to his lips.

"Why couldn't she have packed whiskey? That would have warmed me up better than hot chocolate," he grumbles.

I grin, not that I've been able to stop since we said 'I do.' I stare at him across from me. The sun is setting, and soon all the warmth will be gone.

"I can also help warm you up," I say, biting my bottom lip. I want him. I want to fuck him, snuggle in the bed on the yacht, and then fuck all over again.

His eyes darken, and I swear I see a momentary gaze of fear as his body language changes from relaxed shivering to hard stone.

"You okay?" I ask.

"I'm married to the most incredible woman. What do you think?" It's not an answer; it's avoidance.

It's time. Time for us both to start talking. To tell each other what happened. To rip off the bandaid.

"I was raped," I say, looking at Zeke without blinking, without showing any fear or pain. The words I just said should make me angry, should make me scared, should make me a victim—but I am not a scared victim.

"I'm sorry. I should have—"

"Stop, it's my turn to talk. Julian raped me. He did it with drugs in my system. He wanted me to want him, to give myself to him willingly. So he tricked my brain into thinking you were the one fucking me and not him."

Zeke hisses, his pain pouring through the thick air from him to me. As he does, the sun sets behind him, and we are cast into darkness. The mood changes from joy to terror.

"I'm glad he tricked me. In my head, what Julian did to me was just you. All I felt was you."

I reach across and grab Zeke's hand. "You have nothing to be sorry for because you saved me. You kept me from becoming a victim. From feeling pain. From being scared.

"Someday, I'm sure it will hit me what happened. But I don't look at the bruises now and feel angry. I don't feel like I need therapy to get through this, although I'm sure that would help. I'm still whole. Him violating me didn't ruin me. You were in my head; you were in my heart. Even though I knew it wasn't really you in me, it didn't matter because I knew you'd be waiting for me. That you would help me kill him for what he did to me.

"I'm not a victim, Zeke. So don't make me one. I'm a survivor. I still feel whole. I still feel worthy of being loved by you. I'm not mad at you that you couldn't come before Julian touched me. And I'm not going to let this weight stay with me forever."

I pause, waiting for Zeke to catch up to me. Waiting for his painful reaction. I feel his heart taking the punch my words just dealt him. I feel it hitting him over and over, and I wish I could stop his pain. I can't, though, because it's my pain.

Julian Reed didn't ruin me. He didn't take anything away from me, but he did hurt me. And it's pain we both have to deal with.

"You're a badass, and I'm so honored that you are my wife." He exhales his pain. I've never been prouder of him working through his own grief in such a healthy way.

"I love you," I whisper.

"Bishop? Did he?"

"No, he didn't rape me." I pause. "He just fucked with my head."

"How did you get free?"

"I traded a task Bishop wants me to do for my freedom. He's still in my head. He can twist my thoughts, but if I do the task and go back to him, he'll fix me."

He nods. "Will you do it?"

"Yes, for us," I answer honestly, not telling him what the task is. It's a horrible job, but I will do it for us. I don't want Bishop to control me, and he wants Zeke dead. He wants them all dead for a crime he feels they committed against him.

I need a free head, or Bishop will be able to use me against the people I love. I won't let Bishop use me to hurt Zeke.

"Do you want to know what task Bishop gave me?"

"No. I mean, I do, but I won't ask. I know you don't want to tell me. And I shouldn't know," Zeke says, knowing what I'm going to have to do will betray his friends. Now that we are married, he shouldn't stop me from protecting our marriage, even if it means I'll have to hurt our friends.

Zeke takes another long sip of his hot chocolate, and then he shrugs off the towels.

"What are you doing? You need to stay warm," I say.

"I'm plenty warm." He gives me a look, asking me to trust him. So I do.

But my heart can't stop racing, thinking about what he's about to reveal that he thinks is so bad. That he thinks will make me stop loving him.

"Lucy's lover, Palmer, was the woman who took me. She took me because she was in pain. She was angry Lucy was dying, and she couldn't stop her death."

"Lucy loved her, until her dying breath," I say.

Zeke nods. "They both did. If you want to know what we are capable of doing for love—this is what we are capable of."

Zeke removes his wet shirt over his head, and I see every mark on his body. His body is more black and blue than it is healthy flesh. The parts that aren't bruised are stitched or bandaged, indicating wounds. His chest is the worst I've seen it. Once he heals, there won't be a part of him that isn't scarred.

He stands up, and I feel queasy, afraid of whatever comes next.

He lowers his swim trunks until he's naked before me in the darkness of night. The moonlight illuminates his body, showing me all of him.

If I thought his chest was bad, his legs are worse, and his manhood —it's swollen, red, and damaged.

This is what he was afraid of. This is what he was terrified of revealing to me. That he might be too damaged to ever make love to me again. Too damaged to ever have a chance at us having kids. Too broken.

This is what our love is capable of. This is the type of damage we could inflict on the world, on others we love in order to protect our love—our marriage.

It should terrify me. It should pain me. It should make me feel so many horrible things. Instead, all I see is a man I love. A man I will always love. A man whose love will stay with me forever.

I open my mouth to tell him that, but my stomach can't hold back anymore. I grab the boat and vomit over the side, knowing Zeke is going to see this as a bad sign. He's going to think I'm disgusted by him, even when that couldn't be further from the truth.

CHAPTER 16
ZEKE

Siren's reaction to my body is straight out of my nightmares. I don't know how it could have been worse. She got physically sick at the sight of my disgusting body. I look like a hideous monster.

Sure, my face looks the same, but underneath my clothes, I'm covered with ugly scars twisting over all of my skin. And that part of me that she should be most attracted to is a mangled mess.

Letting her marry me without the truth was a mistake. *What was I thinking? I'm an idiot.*

"We can take it back. We aren't married. We had no witnesses. We didn't sign any papers. We can take it all back." I move to remove the ring as I sit back down, the chill in the air no longer affecting me. All I care about is Siren's reaction.

"No!" she practically screams at me.

"I don't want you to feel obligated to be married to me when you aren't even attracted to me."

She vomits again, and I wince. She's not even looking at me anymore, and she's throwing up her disgust.

"Just—one second," she says.

That one second lasts a lot longer than just one second. In that second, Siren must be regretting her decision to marry a beast like me. We were both raped, both violated. But she came out whole, at least physically, and I came back looking like an alien to her. I look nothing like I did before.

She starts dry heaving, and I can't wait anymore. I move to her, stroking her back, trying to help her to relax even though I'm sure my touch isn't helping. I grab a towel from the floor and wrap myself again so she won't have to look at me.

I hand her the hot chocolate to try and wash out her mouth, but she just shakes her head. I wish I had more to offer her.

Her beautiful eyes sparkle as she looks at me. "I've never been more attracted to you, Zeke. We are absolutely not taking back our vows. We are married. We will always be married. Don't you dare take that back or ruin that moment for me."

I blink. "You can't be attracted to me."

She grabs my hands again. "I am. Being attracted isn't just about the physical. I'm attracted to your physical prowess, sure. I will always love your long hair and curse you to hell if you ever cut it off. But I'm also attracted to your strength. Your courage. Your love for me."

"Then, why did you throw up? I don't understand your reaction."

She purses her lips, breathing again like she's about to be sick again. She holds up a finger, asking me to wait another second.

Goddamn, I can't wait. There is a reason she didn't list patience as a reason she loves me.

"Siren? What is it? What's wrong?"

"I'm pregnant."

My whole world stops—not in a bad way. Not in an 'I've just been shot, and my body is broken and weak, and I can't move' kind of way. My heart skips, my ears tell me I must have heard her wrong, and my breath is swept away.

"How? I mean…really? You're pregnant?" I try to hide the hope in my voice, but it's there. I can't give her a baby. I know it without a doctor confirming it. I've seen the mangled parts hanging between my legs, and there is no way those parts will work properly ever again. But this—this could give us everything. This could give us the kid I instinctively know we both want, even though we've never spoken about it.

Her face brightens at my reaction, and she walks over to me, trying to find a way to sit next to me on the small bench next to my giant ass.

"I don't want you to get too excited. I haven't taken a test, and I haven't had a doctor confirm it yet either. So I might not be—but it's just a very educated guess after knowing my body so well," she says.

Calm down, I tell myself. Don't get too excited. Not until it's confirmed by a dozen doctors. Not until she's gotten through the first trimester. But there is no stopping my excitement.

I grab Siren and jerk her onto my lap.

"Zeke! No, I'll hurt you."

"Not possible, not after that incredible news."

"So, you're happy?"

"I'm ecstatic!" I grab her lips, capturing them with my own, trying to get them to stop grinning long enough to give her a proper kiss. Instead, we both just end up laughing and smiling like idiots against each other's lips.

"I was nervous you didn't want kids. I wasn't even sure I wanted kids, but then I saw Kai and Enzo's twins and—"

"And everything changed. The impossible became possible. If they can do it and keep their kids safe, then so can we," I finish her sentence.

She nods, leaning her head against my chest, her hand going to her still flat stomach. I put my hand on top of hers.

"I've never felt this happy. I never thought I'd be married. Never thought I'd have kids. Never thought I'd be happy. I thought I'd die one day protecting Enzo's ass."

Our smiles stop at that. This changes everything. I mean, sure, the getting married part changed a lot, but the having a kid confirmed it. There is no going back. Our family comes first—the three of us.

"I can't protect them anymore, can I?" I ask.

Siren frowns. "I don't know. We have to put each other first. Which means we won't be doing as good of a job at protecting our employers, our friends. I don't think Enzo and Kai are just going to let you stop working for them. Not because they are cruel, but because they love you and want you in their life."

I brush my hand through her wet hair, lost in thought.

"I love you, Zeke. Everything else we will just have to figure out," she says, pressing a tender kiss against the hardness of my neck.

I stare down at her white bikini and see her nipples harden as she leans against my bare chest.

"Let's head back and stop thinking about our future. At least, what this means for our future in this world. Let's just think about the three of us and enjoy our wedding night," I say.

"Agreed," Siren says. She moves to get off my lap to start the boat up, but I can't let her go. I don't know if I can ever let her go again.

Instead, I'm able to lean back enough to start the engine and steer us back to the yacht.

We tie up at the aft, and then Siren climbs off my lap with a towel draped over her shoulders. Enzo is waiting on the yacht's platform, ready to help me out of the boat and probably to try and tuck me back in my bed.

"I love you, Enzo, like a brother, but I'm naked, and it's my wedding night, so if you'd like to be able to look at your kids in the morning without a black eye, I suggest you go back to bed," I say.

Enzo raises an eyebrow. "As if you could beat me up in your state."

I grab onto the railing and pull myself onto the yacht. The towel around me drops to the floor, and I'm naked standing on the yacht.

"I beat you up in the hospital no problem," I say.

Enzo rolls his eyes and then looks to Siren. "You okay dealing with this ogre tonight, or do you need help?"

"I got this," Siren smiles brightly.

Enzo nods. "I'll keep the happy news from Kai until morning, but expect some extravagant over-the-top celebration in the morning. The twins get up at six. I'll see you at seven."

And then Enzo is gone.

"Bastard," I curse. I pull Siren into my arms. "There is no way I'm going to be done with you by seven."

Siren giggles as I try to scoop her up in my arms and fail.

"Dammit, this isn't very romantic, is it? I can't even lift you up and carry you over the threshold like I want to," I say.

She gets a twinkle in her eye.

"Whatever you are thinking, no," I grumble.

But before I can protest, she's scooped me up in her arms and is carrying me down the stairs to our bedroom.

"This is really emasculating; you know that, right?"

"I do, and I don't care. We are equals in this marriage. Most men don't get the pleasure of having their wives carry them over the threshold, but how lucky are you?" She kicks the door open and plops us down on the bed.

"You're incredible; you know that? The strongest, most badass woman I've ever had the pleasure of knowing. I never thought I'd get married, but if I had to imagine the perfect woman, she wouldn't even come close to comparing to you. I thought I wanted a woman who would drag me out of this world, not one who could fire a gun and throw a punch as easily as I can. But I was so wrong."

"You didn't live up to the guy I pictured as the man I wanted to marry," she says.

I frown.

She grins. "Kidding—of course, you're better, hubby."

"Better than your first hubby?"

She makes a disgusting face. "I was only married to him on paper. It wasn't real."

"And us?"

"We aren't legal on paper, but we are real in all the ways that matter. And tomorrow, I'm going to shout to the world that we're married."

My eyes heat, and I lick my lips in anticipation of tonight. I roll her over onto her back as I prop myself up on my elbow next to her. I don't have the strength to give her an entire night of making love to her body like I want, but I have enough to make her feel good on her wedding night. To give us memories we can keep when things get hard.

"What are you doing?" she giggles, but her voice falls serious when I throw the towel lying lazily on her body to the floor.

"I'm making love to my wife."

"Zeke, I love you, but I don't think this is the best id—" her voice stops when I kiss her neck just above her collarbone. It's tender and sweet, and she makes gasping noises when I do it. Her body curls, her back arches, her hips shift. She can say this isn't a good idea all she wants, but it's the best idea.

"You have to tell me if I do anything that..." I can't finish my sentence. I'm too scared that if I even mention what Julian did right now, it will be enough to ruin the moment.

She looks up at me with hooded lids and a soft expression on her face, like she already came and we are about to begin round two, instead of just starting.

"All I'm thinking about is you, Zeke."

I take a deep breath, realizing I'm the one who's terrified. My biceps are shaking, not from the fatigue of holding myself up, but because if I touch her wrong, she'll be back in that moment with Julian, that moment I couldn't save her.

"Make love to me, Zeke. Put your mouth all over my body."

That's all I need. I kiss her neck again, loving how it makes her squirm. I wonder if I could make her come if I stayed at it long enough. But I'm not patient enough to try, and I want to explore her entire body.

I pull on the string at her neck that releases her bikini top, and then I shove the thin white fabric away. I kiss over the upper curve of her breast before finding her nipple, so ready to be devoured.

I take my time, enjoying every sound. I've been selfish when I fucked her before—teased her to get her excited for when my cock finally entered her. But tonight isn't about me. Tonight is all about her.

I'm going to memorize every sound, every whimper. I'm going to know which spots on her body are her favorites, and which cause her toes to curl.

I take her nipple, licking a slow circle around it before biting it gently with my teeth. I won't be rough with her tonight. Not for a second. I don't want to induce any bad memories.

The gasp followed by the torturous whimpering tell me I could definitely make her come by just stimulating her nipples, but it's not what I want. I want all of her body.

I give both of her nipples ample attention, until they're so hard they could cut through ice. Then I kiss down her scarred stomach. I kiss each scar, and wonder at the thought that there is most likely a baby in there. Tomorrow, we will find out for sure. There are doctors on board. I'm sure they can run a simple pregnancy test.

Siren strokes my hair as I take my time kissing her stomach. It's not turning her on like when I was torturing her nipples, but I need a moment to gather myself so I don't end up crying like a virgin bride on her wedding night.

All it takes is spotting how soaked her white bikini bottoms are to remind me of my mission.

"Remove these, and then ride my face," I say in a deep, commanding voice. I feel my body shaking, even kissing over her body is taxing right now. But I can lay on my back and fuck her pussy. My tongue has plenty of stamina for that.

I lay back on the bed, not covering my own nakedness even though I don't want Siren to see me as her injured anchor. I want her to see me as her knight in shining armor. I want her to know that from now on, I'll move mountains, change the flow of rivers, and jump across oceans to protect her and our baby.

I look over at Siren, now a naked goddess coming out of the water, much like she was the first day I met her. Her hair is still soaked and parted. Her entire body glows from the saltwater, still sticking to her skin combined with my kisses, bringing her blood to the surface of her skin.

"I should have called you goddess, not Siren," I say. "Although, it was your fault I call you Siren."

She grins. "Siren fits better." She carefully parts her legs over my face, not lowering herself yet, but damn, do I have a good view. Her drenched pussy. Her flat stomach. Her gorgeous breasts. "If you thought of me as a goddess, you wouldn't remember that I can lure you to your death as easily as I can save you."

I grab her hips. "Oh, I know my Siren. I know. That's one of the many reasons I love you." And then I yank her down onto my face. I taste how sweet she is, mixed with the saltiness of the ocean.

"Jesus, Zeke. Keep that up, and I'm going to come in like five seconds," Siren purrs as she grabs the headboard above my head as she rocks her hips back and forth, increasing the friction. I circle my tongue over her clit, knowing she likes the unexpected. I switch my technique up again, from fast to torturously slow. The adorable cry of a whimper tells me I'm doing it right.

I smile. "I need to feel you pulsing around me when you come."

I slip a finger between her folds and into her depth. I feel how wet, warm, and perfect she is. She pulls me in deeper, deeper, deeper. So deep I never want to leave. And I never will.

I hear her scream my name, but it seems like she's in another room shouting my name. It's distant, not right above me.

Everything feels isolated for a moment.

Not because I don't hear and feel everything she's feeling, but because I'm hyper-focused on my own body for a second. I can definitely be a selfish, cocky bastard.

But this isn't just about me. It's about our future.

Taking my wife like this, bringing her so much pleasure, hearing her come apart above me has done something to my body. I feel a stirring I never thought I'd feel again—a warmth between my legs, a hardening.

Just like that, I have hope for our future again.

CHAPTER 17
SIREN

"How am I sore, and you didn't even fuck me with your cock?" I ask, stretching as Zeke kisses my neck, trying to get me all hot and bothered for the fourth time since we became man and wife.

He grins. "Because my hands can stretch you as well as my cock can."

"Ahh," I moan as his fingers slip between my legs again.

He's made me come three times already, which may not be our high score for a night, but it was exactly what we needed last night. Each time would end with me coming and then snuggling up in Zeke's arms as we drifted off to sleep with the smell of me on his breath.

Each time he made me come, I'd sneak a peek at him. I'd study him, trying to read all the signs he's not telling me.

I'd notice how his voice changed.

How his nipples would harden, along with all the muscles on his chest.

How his face would flush.

Maybe it was wishful thinking, but I know his cock started to harden and lengthen that last time. We need to talk to a doctor to understand his injuries and his road of recovery. But it sparked hope—

hope that he can heal. That nothing was taken from him. And that not only are we going to be blessed with a baby, but we are going to be a fully functioning family.

"We need to get you a pregnancy test. I'm dying to know for sure," Zeke says, still moving his fingers over my clit before dipping them inside me.

"Mmmm," is all I can manage to get out. I'm sure he's right, whatever he's talking about. I would agree to anything he says right now.

He laughs, realizing now is not the time to have an important conversation.

Two seconds later, I'm coming and screaming, lost to my own pleasure. I really want Zeke to heal so I can fuck his cock again. But if for some reason that's not possible, I won't be missing out on the pleasures of the world. He makes sure of it. I will just have to figure out how to make him feel this good while we are waiting for him to heal.

There is a loud knocking, and we both growl at the door grumpily.

"Wake up, sleepyheads! Although, I know you're already awake. I heard Siren moaning," Kai says from our bedroom door.

"I thought the room was soundproof?" I ask Zeke.

"It is! Well, mostly, but there are security cameras everywhere, and I might have checked it out this morning just to see if you were awake before I came down," Kai says, opening the door.

"Privacy. Boundaries," Zeke hisses at her.

She shrugs. "I know, I know. I'm sorry. I'm just so excited to have a sister!"

Zeke looks from the crazy woman invading our room to me. "You aren't sisters."

"Sure, we are. You're married. And you and Enzo are practically brothers. And you and I are like brother and sister. Either way, it makes her my sister-in-law now!"

Zeke narrows his eyes at Kai like he's going to murder her. "What's happened to you? You are never this bubbly. That's why you and I get along so well."

"Sorry, I had an extra shot in my coffee this morning. Enzo has me drinking cappuccinos now, and I get a little too excited sometimes. But I'm just really, really happy! I have my family back!" Kai comes around to my side of the bed and hugs Zeke, then leans over him to hug me.

I try not to blush as we are both naked and smell like sex, but I guess Kai watched us on the security camera too, so I shouldn't be embarrassed about the smell.

"The first thing I'm doing when I get out of this bed is disabling the security cameras in this room and changing the lock so you can't get in," Zeke grumbles.

"I didn't watch anything, you perv," Kai says, winking at me. *She definitely watched something.*

"Now, get up and get dressed. I want to hear all the details about your wedding and plan something where we can celebrate all our marriages. Enzo and I didn't get to have a wedding with all our friends either. But now you're here, and we can."

"You do realize there is a mad man after us, right? You shouldn't be this happy," Zeke says, but he has a smile on his face now. He's happy for his friend.

"Just get up and get dressed, you oaf. I'm tired of looking at your ugly ass. I've been dealing with unmarried, single guys who only want to talk sports and guns. I'm ready to talk girly stuff, so get up so that Siren and I can become bestest friends."

I smile at that. "You are going to have to fight Nora on that one."

"Oh, I know. I haven't told her that you got married yet because I know she's going to want to be your maid of honor when you do a redo, but I get to be best man, right? You're not going to make it Enzo or Langston?"

"Get out! Or you're going to see more of my naked ass than you've ever wanted to," Zeke growls.

Kai leaves, and Zeke stares at me. "Sorry about her."

I grin. "She just loves you and is excited for you. If you think she's bad, just wait until Nora finds out. She's going to want a re-enactment of the wedding and last night's activities."

He frowns. "I think we should just barricade ourselves in this room and never leave."

My stomach growls.

He presses his hand to my stomach. "I guess we should feed the little guy."

I smile and press my hand over his. "Probably."

"Any chance we can sneak away and find a doctor to administer a pregnancy test without everyone on board speculating or knowing you might be pregnant?"

"Well, we need to get you checked over too, so after breakfast, we'll go see one of the docs on board, and hope they have a pregnancy test. If they don't, we may have to tell Kai or Enzo to stop the yacht somewhere to pick one up."

"Those doctors better hope they have a pregnancy test, or I'm throwing them overboard."

"Says the man who can't even lift me."

"That's it! You're going to get it!" He grabs me and starts tickling me, and I've never been happier that he's able to overpower me. It means he's feeling better and getting some of his strength back.

When we can't laugh anymore, we both get dressed. We both want to shower but decide we don't want to piss off Kai and Nora for making them wait, so we just put on clothes. Zeke struggles to put on his jeans, but I know he's determined to not let his injuries affect him in any way. So if he wants to wear jeans, then dammit, I'm going to support him wearing jeans.

We hold hands as we walk upstairs and into the kitchen, following voices. All eyes fall on us, and the room goes quiet as Kai, Enzo, the twins, Nora, and Beckett all stare at us.

"Well, are you going to announce the news or am I?" Kai asks, grinning from ear to ear.

"Ugh, like you haven't already told everyone, woman," Zeke grumbles with a smile.

Kai rolls her eyes. "I have not told anyone."

"You marry," Ellie says.

The room erupts in laughter, revealing Kai to be the liar that she is. Kai scoops up her little one from the high chair and snuggles her, rubbing Ellie's leftover breakfast all over her white shirt and not caring one bit.

"That was supposed to be our secret, little one," Kai says, kissing her chubby cheeks. She looks at Enzo, who must be able to read his wife better than I can. Suddenly, there are champagne flutes in all of our hands.

"I want to toast the happy, married couple," Kai says. "To Siren and Zeke. We are so happy you found each other, and we look forward to being able to celebrate your love today and forever. We can't wait until you have lots of babies for us all to raise together." Kai winks at me like she knows I'm pregnant. She can't know when I don't even know for sure.

"To Siren and Zeke," the group rejoices.

We all clink our glasses, and I take a minuscule sip to not raise suspicions.

"I can't believe you got married without me there! I was supposed to be your maid of honor, you bitch," Nora says, pulling me into an obnoxious hug.

"Well, it was sudden, and you know, not legal or whatever, so I'm sure if we ever decide to make it legal, we'll invite you to be our witness at the courthouse," I say.

Nora pulls back, looking at me like I'm crazy. "Kai and I will not allow our best friends, who have survived death and murdering devils, to have their love celebrated in a courthouse. When you get married legally, we will be doing it in a big way! Kai and Enzo didn't get to be married in front of those they loved, either. So it can be a joint wedding or a doubleheader or something! I'm so excited!"

I laugh. "Slow down." I squeeze Zeke's hand who looks at Nora like she's insane. "We haven't agreed to a big wedding. We already had everything we wanted. And we can celebrate today."

"Fine, fine. Let me see the rings, though!" Nora grabs my hand around my champagne glass. "Love it! It's so you. You're not a diamonds kind of girl."

"No, I'm not."

"Zeke, let's see it," Nora says.

"It?" Zeke asks, obviously oblivious to my friend's conversation.

"Your ring." Nora grabs his left hand and studies it closely. "It's perfect!"

"It is," Zeke says, bringing my hand to his lips to kiss me, which only eggs Nora on.

"We should have a dance tonight! Everyone could get dressed up, and we could have a wedding reception! Oh my god! I'm so excited," Nora says.

"Are you going to dance with Beckett? He hasn't stopped looking at you," I whisper, wondering how they are doing together.

She sighs. "No, I'll be a single lady going home alone, but it could still be fun. Beckett doesn't seem interested in dating, fucking, or anything fun."

I kiss her on the cheek. "Your happily ever after is coming."

"I know."

Kai comes over, holding Ellie.

"Ooh, give her to me," Nora says, grabbing the toddler and turning from us.

"Congrats, you guys!" Kai hugs us both, and then she whispers in my ear. "It's just grape juice, just in case..." She winks again.

I'm blinking rapidly, shocked she's figured out I might be pregnant.

"I'm right, aren't I?" Kai asks, studying me closely.

Zeke narrows his eyes. "Right about what?"

"Right about everything," Enzo says from behind her. "Congrats, you two."

"Yes, congrats. I know we haven't spoken about how you tried to kill me a while back, but you two make a good fit. I'm really happy for you. And I'm sorry I couldn't rescue Siren, I—" Beckett says awkwardly.

"It wasn't your fault. It was mine. No need to apologize," Zeke says, forgiving Beckett for not being to rescue me just like he couldn't.

"Thank you," I say to everyone trying to move away from the depressing turn Beckett and Zeke started down. "But we don't really have to celebrate."

"We do," Kai and Nora say at the same time.

Zeke and I sigh at the same time.

"So am I right?" Kai leans in so only I can hear her.

"I don't know. But I'd find out a lot sooner if we weren't having to have a weird wedding party breakfast and could meet with a doctor or get a pregnancy test," I hiss back, careful not to raise my voice.

"I can help with that!" She turns to the room. "Alright, enough fussing. Zeke needs to get checked out by a doctor, and we need time to discuss a redo wedding for all of us."

Enzo frowns. "We haven't even eaten the breakfast you cooked yet. Shouldn't we all eat together? Zeke can see a doctor—"

But Kai throws him a look, and he shuts up.

"I'll bring the breakfast to you two later," Kai says.

"I'm sure you will." Zeke fires a warning look at her. If she comes into our room unannounced or looks at the security camera again, he's going to throw her overboard.

"The code is 5523," Kai says.

"Wait, you are giving them our bedroom? What's wrong with theirs?" Enzo asks.

Kai gives him another look, and he shuts up again. She leans into me. "Under the sink on the left. I'll have the doctor come up for Zeke in twenty minutes."

I nod and pull Zeke away from everyone toward Kai and Enzo's bedroom.

"Why did Kai give you access to her bedroom?"

"She has a pregnancy test under the sink."

"Oh."

"Yea, oh." A million little butterflies flutter in my belly, quickly turning into rabbit-sized butterflies hopping around, causing me to jump nervously as we walk.

"Are you feeling okay?" Zeke asks.

"Yep."

"Me too," he says, just as nervous as I am.

We get to the door, and I have to enter the code three times to gain access, but finally, the door opens.

We walk straight to the bathroom. I lean under the sink and pull out the pink box that has one pregnancy test left in it.

I let go of Zeke's hand reluctantly, and then go pee on the stick.

"How long do we have to wait?" I ask, laying the test on the counter.

"Three minutes," Zeke answers, staring at the pregnancy test like it holds our entire future.

It does, which makes this moment so terrifying. This might be our only chance to have a baby that is biologically both ours. Any other kids we have might be adopted, or only me and some sperm guy. This could be our only shot at having something that is part of both of us.

Zeke never asked me if I thought the baby was his or was a result of Julian raping me, but the timing doesn't work for the baby to be Julian's. I know it's Zeke's, but I'm glad I don't have to confirm it to Zeke in that way.

Staring at the test makes me just as nervous to learn I am pregnant as scared to learn I'm not. I'm not sure I would make a good mom. I'm not sure bringing a baby into my world is a good idea, not when I'm constantly being shot at. I'm not the kind of person our kid could look up to. I've done horrible things, things I can't explain to a kid.

Zeke puts his hand in mine, and suddenly it doesn't matter that I don't have all the skills it takes to be a good mom. Zeke is going to make a great dad—he will fill in the holes I'm lacking and vice versa. Together, we will make great parents, and this baby will be loved. That's what matters.

We've turned into a crying, sobbing mess. I don't think we are ever going to stop crying or smiling. Nothing can ruin this moment. This moment has stretched into twenty minutes of just holding and laughing and crying and smiling—pure joy. I've never felt anything like it, but I can only imagine holding my baby in my arms for the first time will be the only thing able to top finding out that my wife is pregnant.

"I can't believe I got a wife and baby in the same day," I say.

She laughs. "You don't have the baby yet. He or she still has another seven or eight months until you meet him or her."

I grab her stomach and kiss it again for the hundredth time. "Nope, mine, now."

There is a knock on the door, and we both quickly grow solemn. Kai said she'd send a doctor in to examine me after we had a few minutes alone, but right now, I want this moment to last forever.

"We can celebrate more after, but we need to know the good and the bad," Siren says.

I nod. Siren takes my hand, and we exit the bathroom and open the door together.

"I'm Dr. Rancor," the gentleman in his fifties says.

"Zeke," I say, shaking his hand. "This is my wife, Siren."

He shakes her hand as well. "Pleasure to meet you both. Mrs. Black has given me a general overview of your condition, but I'd love to do a full examination and hear from you so I can best help you."

I nod as he enters the room with his bag of equipment. He sits in a chair, while Siren and I sit on the edge of the bed. And then I tell my story, while Siren and the doctor listen intently to every word. I didn't think I could talk about it so easily, but finding out I'm going to be a father soon seems to make me brave and push any other emotions away.

"So what do you think? Am I going to be able to fuck again? Have more kids?" I don't mince my words. I want to know the truth.

"Well, we won't know until I examine you. If you could remove your clothes," the doc says.

I do as he says, but my mind isn't on me. It's on Siren. "What do we need to know about the first trimester? I know Siren has been having some morning sickness. What else?"

The doctor chuckles. "First-time parents?"

"Yes," we both say anxiously.

He laughs. "Well, I'm not an obstetrician, so my experience is limited, but for now, unless you are feeling really sick, eat healthily, take it easy, get plenty of rest, and let your body do the rest."

I frown, not liking his answer. I spend the next ten minutes drilling him about everything. Every symptom Siren could have. Every sign of danger we should look for and what to do about it. What we should know about giving birth, especially if we happen to be out at sea on a yacht. When do we really need to get to a hospital? I've picked the doctor's brain of everything I can think of by the time he's finished examining me.

"Well?" Siren asks as I get dressed.

"I wish I could give you all the answers as easily as explaining what to expect while you're expecting," he smiles briefly. "But we just don't know how he will heal or what damage has been done. I would say the initial swelling has gone down. The wounds have more or less healed. You are welcome to try having sex when you feel up to it, but there are no guarantees in medicine or in life. The doctors did a good job stitching you up, but that's all they did. It's hard to know what's going on beneath the surface. Only time will tell."

I frown, and Siren takes my hand, not liking that we got no answers.

"I'll give you the number of the best plastic surgeon and urologist I know in case you need it. But you won't get answers until you try."

"Thank you, doctor," Siren says, leading him out while I sit back down, frustrated.

"You okay?" she asks.

I nod.

"Well, at least he didn't say there was no hope. We have hope and permission to try, so when the time is right, we'll try."

She takes my hand again. "Come on, let's go celebrate with everyone and share the good news."

An hour later, after celebrating, Enzo and I go up to the security room like we used to to get away from everyone. I feel bad about leaving Beckett with the women, but as much as Nora says Beckett isn't interested, he sure does look at her a lot, so I don't feel too badly.

"First things first, block security camera access to my room. And change the code so Kai can't get in," I say.

Enzo laughs but does as I say.

"We need to talk about Julian and Bishop. We have to take them out. We have to destroy them," I say.

Enzo nods. "We do. But Kai and Siren will both want in on the conversation. And we will need Langston and the whole team to take them down."

"Siren stays out of this. She can be involved in the planning, but that's it."

"She won't like that, or agree to it," Enzo says.

"She will."

Enzo studies me closely. "Siren's pregnant."

He doesn't ask it like a question. "Kai told you?"

He shrugs. "Just a guess. That's the only reason I can think of that Siren wouldn't get involved in a fight and you would be that confident she would sit out of a fight."

"Yea, she's pregnant. We were going to wait and tell everyone, but

Kai already guessed, and I'm sure she's down there spilling the beans to everyone else."

"That's my wife and your bestie. She can't keep a secret as good as this one. Although, I'm still pissed she didn't tell me you were alive."

I sigh. "I guess it's good everyone knows. Then we can keep Siren safe."

Enzo nods. "We have a timeline now. We need this mess dealt with before the baby comes. Then we can get back to our usual work."

I shake my head, realizing in this moment exactly what my future holds.

"No."

"No?"

"I mean, yes, we need to kill Julian and Bishop, the sooner, the better. But I won't keep working for you after. After they are dead, I want out. I want a life where my kids can grow up without being afraid."

"My kids are growing up without fear. You can have this life. This life with your friends, your family, and still have kids."

"No, I can't."

Enzo frowns. "Think about it. You aren't going to be happy becoming a security guard at some mall and coaching your kids' soccer games on the weekend. Siren isn't going to be happy as a stay at home mom or waitressing at some local cafe."

"You think those are the best jobs we can get?" I smirk, knowing he's joking.

"You both need a job that involves doing what you love. Wielding a gun, throwing punches, kicking ass, and protecting others. You need this life more than Kai and I do."

I shake my head. "You're wrong. Siren and I don't need this life. And we won't be able to do a good job once we have kids. Once we do, everything changes. We will put our family first—over you, over whoever we're working for, and over anyone else we're supposed to protect."

"I'd never ask you to protect me over your own family."

"I know, but that's the only way I'd work for you. If I'm going to continue to be one of your guards, I need to be able to take a bullet for you. Having a family means I won't."

Enzo nods, understanding spreading on his facial features. "Well, think about it. Kai isn't going to let you go easily. And I'm guessing, neither is Siren."

I turn back to the screen that holds all the information we have on Julian, which is a lot. We have very little on Bishop, which scares me.

"Let's figure out how to kill these guys and protect our families. One last time—together."

CHAPTER 19
SIREN

"Time is up, Siren," Bishop whispers sin into my ear. He knows I don't have a choice but to do what he wants. I can't live like this forever. I can't be controlled forever. I can't.

"No, I need more—more time. I can't do this yet."

"You have to. The time is now."

"No, you never gave me a deadline. You just said to do it, but never when. It's too soon."

"Siren," his voice is a warning. A threat that he will keep getting into my head every night, every morning, every hour until I do what he wants. Until I can't push him out of my head anymore. Until, even when I'm kissing Zeke, I'm thinking about Bishop.

"I need more time. Just a little longer. Please."

He shakes his head in the dark, or maybe those are shadows. I can't tell if he's really here or he's just tricks on my mind. Either way, I need him gone; I'll do anything to rid myself of him.

"Are you dreaming about him?" he asks.

"Who?"

"Julian."

I pause. "No, Julian's not in my head."

345

"Good, don't give him another thought."

"I have to. You know what I owe him. It's as bad as what I owe you."

He shakes his head. "Let me worry about Julian. You just focus on my task. Do as I say, complete your task, and you'll be free of more than one man."

"I don't trust you. If I do this, you'll fix me?"

He smirks. "Do this and I'll more than fix you. I'll set you free; your heart will be yours again."

"But I don't want—"

"Enough. Of course, you want to own your own heart. Don't give it away. Don't let Zeke or any other man take it. It's not theirs. It's yours."

My lips thin into a frown. I don't understand why Bishop always tries to give me relationship advice.

"I'm married," I say.

He pauses, and I can tell what I said shakes him. Not because he wants me, like Julian does, but because he has something against committed relationships.

"All the more reason to do this now."

No.

I don't speak the word. It's in my head. I don't say the word, because I know it isn't true. I'll do the task Bishop gave me; I need him out of my head. I need him gone forever. If doing this one task will get him out, then so be it.

My eyes fly open, and I gasp into the darkness of the room. Bishop's gone. I'm in bed with Zeke, who is snoring adorably next to me.

It was all a dream. Bishop isn't really here. He's not in my head.

I stand up and head to the bathroom to get a drink of water in my panties and tank top. My hair is a disheveled mess, but it has nothing on the nerves shooting through me.

I remember what Bishop wants. I remember what thoughts he's put in my head if I fail. But this task he wants me to do, it's too much. It might not even work.

I grab the cup next to the sink, turn on the faucet, and fill it. But I don't drink the water. I slam the glass down on the counter, watching the glass chip.

I push air quickly through my nostrils, trying to calm the fuck down.

No, it will work. I know what Bishop wants, and I know exactly how to do it. Bishop knows me well. Possibly better than any other man—even Zeke. He's figured out my head, my thoughts, everything.

I wish I could fail. I wish I didn't have the skills to do the task Bishop gave me. If I tried and failed, that would be fine. I would have done what Bishop asked. But I won't fail.

The task will require me to ruin a love—a love I won't be able to heal, mend, fix. I can work stitch by stitch, thread by thread, to put the broken pieces back together, but there will always be one single, broken thread. I can earn forgiveness, but he will never forget. This will become yet another sin that haunts us.

We already have enough sins—enough pain.

So what if I commit one more? Our love has survived before. In some ways, it's survived worse.

No.

Nothing is worse.

"Baby? You okay?" Zeke's voice interrupts my thoughts.

My head is dropped. I never turned the light on, so he can't see my face. I don't want to lie to Zeke, not with my words, but I can let him feel what he wants to feel—reassurance that I'm okay. I just got up to get some water. I'm good. We're good.

Inside my body is in turmoil; my mind is racing to come up with a plan, any plan, that ends with the truth instead of a sin.

I walk over to Zeke and place my hands against his hard, rough chest. I feel my way through his scars, finding his beating heart—so steady, so calm. He's my rock, my anchor. My calm in the storm. Just feeling him now is enough to save me from my future sins.

I stand on my tiptoes, find his lips between his stubble, and kiss him. It's meant to be a reassuring kiss, one to let him know I'm fine. One to let him taste me and realize I haven't spent time getting sick or thinking about Bishop.

But of course, when our lips touch, our fire sparks between us—

that need we have and haven't been able to satisfy zips back and forth. I get the pull in my core, tingling between my legs, the need that only he can satisfy. I grab his neck; he grabs my waist, lifts me high, and tilts my head to make it easier to kiss me.

We stumble back, hitting the counter against my ass. I suck his lip. His tongue teases mine. I want to let my hands wander over his body. I want to feel his biceps, his chest, his ass. I want to roll my hips against his body and find the hardness I seek straining against his boxers.

I don't let myself go there. I keep my hands at his neck, letting my hands grip onto his hair for dear life. I'm like a horny teenage boy who wants to fuck his girlfriend for the first time but doesn't want to push her. I don't want to push Zeke. If I do, I could make him feel worse instead of better. There are no guarantees, that's what the doctor said. But I guarantee you that we are going to love each other forever, so we have forever to figure out how to have sex again.

That's what I tell myself anyway when I keep my hands on his neck instead of feeling over his body. Zeke, on the other hand, has no problem letting his hands roam. When his hand finds my breast beneath my shirt, I gasp like it's the first time I've ever been touched.

"These have gotten bigger," he whispers, his stubble brushing against my cheek. I want his stubble against my thigh. It's not fair for him to keep eating me out and not get anything in return. Not fair to either of us. I want a turn to make him feel good, a turn at licking and tormenting and pulling him to the edge of orgasm.

Zeke keeps going, and I know where this is headed—the same thing that has happened every night for the last two weeks. I'll be riding Zeke's face, or he'll have me spread on the bed as three fingers fuck me. I'm not complaining, I could die a happy woman as long as Zeke kept doing that, but tonight, with Bishop in my head, I need more. And Zeke isn't ready to give me what I need yet.

I grab Zeke's hand and pull it away from my chest. Slowly, I let my body fall down from my high as I break our kiss apart.

Zeke tenses but doesn't say anything. He can't push me to let him touch me when I don't get to touch him.

"Is there anything I could do to make you hate me?" I ask, needing to feel connected to Zeke in any way I can. If words are the only way, then so be it. And I need reassurance that if I do what Bishop wants, I won't be ending us. At least not forever.

Zeke turns me around, so I'm facing the mirror, his chest against my back. His hands go around my waist, and his head drops to my ear.

"No. Nothing you could do could ever make me hate you."

"Nothing? That seems impossible."

He shakes his head, his eyes heating into dark, icy slants piercing through the armor I've put up to hide what's really going on in my head. He knows there is a reason I asked my question. He's probing, testing my walls. I won't let him in. This is as far as he gets. I can't break through his armor to be able to touch him, either.

"Nothing—because you love me. Any choice you make, you wouldn't be doing to intentionally hurt me. Your choices would be made in love, even if I couldn't see it."

It's a good answer, but not the truth. He's going to hate me. At least temporarily. He may forgive me, but hating someone you love is easier than he thinks. He's forgotten how I made him feel before when I betrayed him.

I stare at him in the mirror, my eyes threatening him, calling bullshit.

"Is there anything I could do that would make you stop loving me?" I ask.

He draws in a breath like I wounded him simply by asking the question. He finds my left hand in the dark, connecting it to his own. With our hands intertwined, I see our rings touching. Two pieces of metal barely worth a thousand dollars, but to us, they are worth everything.

"Is there anything I could do to make you stop loving me?" his voice is husky as he turns my question on me.

"No, I could never stop loving you."

I feel his heart thumping against my back. It's sputtering at my words, speeding up at my honesty.

His grip on my stomach tightens where my belly has started to protrude, getting thicker but not revealing my secret to the world just yet. He holds my stomach as possessively as he holds the rest of me.

"I will never stop loving you, both of you. I could be held at gunpoint and told the only way I can live is to stop loving you, and even then, my heart would never betray you. You could murder every other person on the planet, and I would still love you. You could take everything from me, all the money I've ever earned, and I would still love you. You could fuck another man, and I would still love you."

His voice catches, but he forces himself to continue. "You could stop loving me. You could fall for another man, and I would always love you. Our love is different than anything I've felt before. Even Lucy. I loved her, but my love wasn't everlasting. I love my friends, but I would destroy them all tomorrow if it was the only way to keep you. Our love has the power to annihilate entire cities. I would light a city and watch it burn for you."

"I would never ask you..." I say, but I stop myself. We both know it's a lie. I might. I might ask Zeke to do unthinkable things. We have a lot of enemies. I'm sure they all haven't come out of hiding. We will always have enemies. One wrong move means those enemies have power until we destroy them. Those enemies could force us to do horrible, villainous things. We would both do them in a heartbeat to save the other, and to protect our family.

Zeke kisses my cheek. "Don't worry. I'll eliminate our enemies soon. Our family will be safe. We will get out."

He's never admitted he wants to leave this world before. I can't imagine him not carrying a gun every day. I can't think of anything he would enjoy doing more than risking his life to save others. But I understand the desire to get out—to feel safe. I just don't know if getting out will ensure that I'm safe.

Zeke and Enzo have been getting together to plan. This time, I won't be allowed to fight. I have another life to worry about. Risking that life might be the one truly unforgivable sin. But, as Zeke said, it's the one thing I would never do.

"We will get Bishop. We'll drag him here and make him fix you before we kill him," Zeke says.

I nod.

"And Julian—"

"You'll kill him before he says a damn word."

He smirks. "I'm done letting Julian Reed talk. He's a dead man."

I let out a breath, considering telling my last truth when it comes to Julian. But if he's dead, it won't matter. Telling the truth won't change anything—one less pain for Zeke.

Zeke pulls me to him, until my ass is pushed against his hardness.

Wait...

He's hard. I feel it.

My needy eyes meet his. *Does this mean?*

"Soon," he whispers his promise. It's the best damn word he's ever said to me. Soon, I can reconnect with my husband. Soon, we will be whole again. Soon, our enemies will be dead.

CHAPTER 20
ZEKE

"Too slow," Enzo says as he punches me lightly in the jaw.

I growl, my head popping back as I try again to swing in his direction without getting hit. This time he hits my stomach before I make contact with his eye.

He's been pulling all his punches every time we've sparred; my broken body can't take a full hit just yet without crumpling. I need the exercise and the practice, though. We are running out of time to defeat Julian and capture Bishop, and I'm a long way from where I should be physically.

I go for a kick. I'm more a punch with my fists kind of guy, but maybe I need to change my game. Enzo grabs my knee, pushing me to the floor.

"Fuck," I growl when he has me pinned beneath him. I'm beyond frustrated at my weak body. I can't get any part of me to work properly. Not my brain, my fists, my legs, my cock. I've been married to Siren for almost a month now, and I haven't fucked her. We haven't even tried, I'm too scared. Sure, I've felt things, gotten hard around her, but not enough to try. *What if I fail? What if I can't satisfy her the way I used to? What if I'm not enough?*

Enzo sighs and hands me a water. "Your head isn't in it today."

"I'm just out of shape."

Enzo sits next to me, but I remain lying on the ground like the weakling I am.

"No, it's more than that. You may not be in great shape or be able to throw punches as quickly as you used to, but there is nothing wrong with your head. You should still be able to anticipate my throws. We've been fighting since we were six. You know my moves. You know my weaknesses and how to exploit them. You haven't even attempted to avoid a punch or thrown anything I couldn't anticipate. What's going on?"

"Nothing. Just tired and want this fight to be over."

"Bullshit."

I stare up at the black ceiling of the boxing room. The room only has a single light shining, but most of the time, Enzo prefers to have the light off so he can train in the dark. He has the upper hand in the dark, that's why most of our advances happen at night. He can see what others can't.

I don't have the sixth sense he does, but I've trained with him in the dark long enough to know how to fight in the shadows as well as the light.

"We have a plan to kill Julian. And I have a team doing round the clock reconnaissance on Bishop. We won't fail. You don't even need to fight. I can handle it and you know it. If the fight needs to go down tomorrow, Kai and I can take care of it. So what the hell is going on?"

I shake my head. I'm not talking to Enzo about my limp dick problem and how I don't think I'll be enough for my wife.

"Nothing." I sit up and drink the entire bottle of water. "I'm just over this today."

"Bull-fucking-shit."

My eyes shoot at him. "Stay out of it. It's not your concern."

"Do you want me to get Kai, so she can drag whatever is stuck up your ass out of you? You've changed. You walk around like a zombie most of the time. I know you. You aren't scared of a fight, even with a kid on the way. You always thought you'd die for someone you love, dying to protect your kid doesn't scare you. So what is it?"

I push myself up. "I'm not doing this."

"Fine." Enzo pulls out his phone and dials. "Stingray, Zeke needs you. He's in the boxing ring."

With that, Enzo walks off steaming.

Instead of running off, I sit on the bench and wait for Kai. I don't want Siren to worry, and she will if I don't convince Kai that I'm fine.

I hear Kai's footsteps.

"I'm fine, Stingray. You don't need to worry about me. Your husband is just overreacting as usual."

"I'm not your stingray."

My head pops up, trying to find her eyes in the dark. It takes me a second, but I see her standing on the mat in the far corner.

"Where's Kai?" I ask.

"She thought you and I should talk. But if you'd rather talk to Kai, I can go get her," Siren says.

"No, I don't want to talk to Kai."

"Good." Siren stretches her arms overhead and then goes through some practice swings.

"What are you doing?" I ask, watching her every move in the dark. Like a dance, she warms up. I'm mesmerized, but also angry, because I know what she's trying to do, and I won't do it.

"Warming up."

"For what?"

"To fight."

"We aren't fighting."

"Yes, we are."

"You're pregnant."

"The doctor said I could do any physical activity that I had been previously doing. Well, before I was pregnant I fought, I boxed, I did Krav Magra. This is perfectly safe."

"I'm not fighting you."

She smirks. "You fight me, or prepare to get used like a punching bag."

I frown, but I find myself standing and walking onto the mat. *What am I doing? I'm not going to fight her.* But my hands are up, protecting my face.

She throws a punch, but not holding back at all like Enzo did.

"Siren, stop."

Another jab hits me on the forearm. It's strong, swift. It's going to leave a bruise on my arm, and most likely, her hand.

"Stop," I say, trying to keep my cool. *She's carrying my baby and willing to risk his or her life for what? To convince me I'm strong enough to fight?* Even if she weren't carrying a baby right now, I wouldn't fight her.

"No, fight me."

She kicks this time, hitting my hip—too close for comfort to my fucked up groin.

"Siren." I grit my teeth as I say her name, my anger grinding my teeth together until it's painful.

"Come on, Zeke. Throw a punch. You know I'll dodge it."

"No."

"Why not?" She throws another punch, hitting me in the chest.

"Because you're pregnant."

"You don't have to knock me out, just throw a jab in my direction. Something, anything."

"No."

The hits start coming more rapidly now as she dances around me, her footwork excellent like she's actually fighting me in a ring with judges and everything. I've never just watched her skills before. She's practiced a lot. She has incredible technique, perfected over the years. She's more than capable of protecting herself in a fight.

I'm mesmerized by her feet and not watching her hands like I should. She hits me, full out, on the face. I feel myself falling back, and I don't bother cushioning my fall. I just fall until I hit the hard mat.

Siren stares at me, waiting for me to break, to shatter, to feel something she wants me to feel. But I don't have a clue what she's doing, other than pissing me off.

Carefully, she kneels next to me, glaring at me like she's the one who is pissed instead of me.

"You don't get to be angry. You're the one risking our child's life to make some idiotic point," I say.

"No," she snaps, her words harsh and painful. She takes a deep breath, softening. "You are the one hurting our child by not letting me in. I was patient, and I'll continue to be patient. I don't need your cock to be happily married to you, but I do need my husband. I need him to think of himself as whole and not broken. I need him to fight when things get hard, not give up. You're giving up. You're letting them win. I need you to start fighting again. I need you to take what you want. I need you to—"

I grab her, shutting her up with my lips as I pull her to me. Our lips slam together, her mid-sentence and me parted, leaving us kissing in an awkward meeting. Our mouths half open, our teeth crushing, our lungs half-full of oxygen and carbon dioxide. Neither of us prepared for this kiss.

Siren thought she'd have to push me further to get me to break, and I wasn't expecting to break so easily, but our baby pushed me to the edge. I would do anything—ANYTHING—to protect our child.

Although, this kiss isn't just about our baby. It's about me too. I'm tired of waiting. I'm tired of thinking I'm less than, physically broken. It's time to find out. Time to be brave. Time to push the demons out.

Palmer may have had her own issues that led her to raping me, issues I can forgive her for. But I was still raped, violated in a way I never thought I'd be touched. I thought I could stop it, but I couldn't stop it any easier than I could a bullet entering my body.

My cock has gotten hard plenty of times over the last few weeks. That isn't holding me back anymore.

I push my tongue into Siren's mouth on autopilot, splitting her lips, allowing me entrance the way I've done thousands of times. Our tongues meet in a dance, gliding over each other as we do battle. All the normal things happen. Heat spills between us. Her hands roam over my body. Her nipples pebble. Her moans vibrate in her throat.

All the right things happen to me too. Fire shoots to my belly, my body hardens, and I put everything into the kiss. My erection grows against her belly.

But still...I can't...

Siren senses it first. She stops the kiss, resting her thumb on my bottom lip as we both try to calm ourselves down. We both know this isn't going anywhere.

"I don't want to push you. I just want to help you. I want to know that you're fighting for us, for yourself, and that you're being honest with me and telling me what you need. Whatever you need is fine—therapy, time to heal, another doctor's appointment, going slow, facing your demons, forgiving Palmer or killing her. I don't know how to help you, Zeke. You have to let me in. Our child has the right to know his or her father, not just the piece of him that's left."

I rest my head against her forehead. "How did you get through it so quickly? How can you move on so easily? How are you not reliving every moment Julian was inside you?"

She licks her lips. "You. You were in my head. In some way, I'm afraid of what's going to happen later. Maybe someday, it's all going to hit me, and I won't have done enough work. I won't have healed. But you will. Your brain didn't let you cop-out. You have to face what happened to you. Maybe mine won't let me because it knows you need me first, and once you heal, it will be my turn. But for now, you are the one with a broken heart."

"My heart isn't broken," I sigh, closing my eyes to keep the pain in.

"Tell me," she whispers in the dark. When I don't respond, she hands me some boxing gloves.

I put them on wordlessly, still resting my forehead against hers. I hear her reaching for a boxing mitt for me to hit, and she straps them onto her hands.

"Tell me. Let it all out. Give me everything. Lay it all on me. Let me carry some of your burden because I'm strong enough to handle it."

I swing. I can't even tell what I'm swinging at, but somehow, she makes sure I hit the pad she's holding. It makes a soft squishing sound as the two plastics hit and the velcro holding my gloves on stretches.

"Again," she whispers.

I swing again.

Hit.

It feels good. Not like hitting Enzo, this feels different. Cathartic, in a way. It's easier to pretend like Siren's face is Palmer's. It's easier to be vulnerable with Siren.

It's easier to show her my heart is still bleeding from the wound Palmer caused, no matter how much my bruises have lightened and my scars have softened. I've never had to heal from a traumatic experience before. Every other time, I just healed. The torture never went deeper than the surface. Once the stitches came out, I was good to go.

But this time, it's different.

Siren isn't the only one with nightmares.

I don't sleep—I see Palmer's face.

My brain races around the clock, too afraid of where my thoughts will go if I ever stop and let my mind drift in the silence.

I thought I understood darkness. I thought I understood pain. The physical I can handle, but this—this is like flying in the night with no lights. I'm soaring above the tall buildings, weaving through them. I feel alive like never before. I've tapped emotions I didn't know I could feel, but every second of it is a constant fear of crashing into the side of a skyscraper. And when I crash, that's it—I won't survive.

I thought watching Siren get hurt was going to be the worst pain I'd ever feel. I thought I was the protector who just hurt when I couldn't protect others.

But I've never been violated like that. Never felt what it was like to have something taken from Siren and me at the same time. Never knew how being touched in such a twisted way can also wreck you down to your very soul.

Hit.

The impact rattles through my entire body, jostling free the toxins in my body, setting free the ghosts who haunt me.

I feel the ghosts raging. I swing, again and again, trying to get them out. It's a never-ending battle, though, because every time I knock one out, another pops up. The more I swing, the more I hit, the more I let myself feel the physical, the more the internal takes control.

I think about Siren, and that drives me forward. I don't see her anymore through my haze. I just swing and am confident she won't let me hit her. She won't let me hurt our baby. She's right, it's time. My body has healed. I just have to get the dark thoughts out of my mind.

I'm not good enough.

I'm not strong enough.

I should have stopped it.

My cock shouldn't have gotten hard.

I should have fought harder.

I should have pushed her off me.

I shouldn't have come.

I was bigger than her, but I didn't use my strength.

I was smarter than her, but I didn't use my wit.

I wasn't enough.

I was weak.

I gave up.

I let her hurt me.

I gave up power to a woman who wasn't Siren.

I let a woman I didn't love, ruin me.

I let her touch me.

I let her...I let her...it was my fault.

Swing, swing, swing. I let all the horrible thoughts speak.

Every.

Single.

ONE.

The shame takes over, forcing me to sink lower, but there is no going back now. I'm consumed with it.

I should have stopped Palmer.

It didn't matter that I had been tied up without food or water for days.

It didn't matter that my blood had been pumped with drugs, and my brain was foggy.

It didn't matter that three men had beaten me up, spilled my blood, made my muscles throb with the pain of a thousand dragons breathing fire onto my skin all at once.

It. Didn't. Matter.

When I let her touch me, it was just her and me.

Palmer had removed the chains. I could have stopped her. I could have. I should have. But I wasn't enough.

I wasn't strong enough.

I didn't love Siren enough.

Not enough to stop my body from betraying Siren. My cock got hard. Every thrust of her body over me felt good. When her pussy tightened over me, I exploded inside of her.

I felt her wetness. I felt her shudder over me. I let my cock be fucked by her. Palmer used me, and I didn't stop her.

"I didn't stop her.

"I didn't stop her.

"I didn't stop her!"

The last one is a ferocious scream, like a lion letting the whole savannah know that I'm king. Except I'm not a king. I'm letting the world know I'm weak, a coward, an adulterer.

I fall to my knees more broken than I've ever been. I hate myself. I can't look at myself in the mirror. I'm not worthy of Siren.

"I'm not enough," I whisper into the darkness, letting my embarrassing secret out. This is how I die—the pain and shame and guilt of letting that woman fuck me when the only woman I want to fuck is Siren.

I'm sure I'm crying.

I'm sure I look like a dying man about to take his last breath.

I'm sure I've never looked weaker. I've never looked more like a fool than I do now.

I'm sure Siren has never loved me less than she does now.

I feel the boxing gloves leaving my hands, but I don't feel Siren.

"I am enough," her voice sings to me, much in the same way her voice called to me the night she saved me from the water.

She sings it over and over, her voice carrying us, demanding all the attention, all the oxygen down to the tiny molecules. Her voice demands every being, no matter how microscopic, pay attention to her.

The vibration of her voice is what hits me first, smack in the chest. Pounding, pounding, pounding into me. Just like the punches I took earlier, it hits me, letting loose more demons in my body. But unlike before, her voice sings louder than the ghosts' voices.

Siren continues to sing, her voice alone destroying the evil inside me. The evil I allowed in.

"I am enough. I am powerful. I am worthy. I am a king. I am a protector. I am selfless. I am enough," her voice changes tune and melody. It changes pitch going higher and higher, trying to pull me from the darkness of hell and into the light of heaven.

I think she's crazy if she thinks this is going to work, but I'm too exhausted to speak, to move. I've fallen—this is as low as I can possibly go. I've sunk to the deepest parts of hell by betraying the woman I love.

I'm a bad guy.

I deserve it.

This was all just payback for all the men I've murdered, all the women I've failed to save. This is where I belong—suffering, forever.

Siren deserves better.

I shouldn't have let her marry me.

"I am enough. More than enough. I am Zeke. But my name could have as easily been Zeus, the father of all the gods. The strongest, the protector, the one who looked over all the others."

No.

She's wrong.

Her lips are close now, but she doesn't touch me. Not on the lips. Not on the hands. I don't feel her anywhere but in my head.

"Open your heart. Let me in," she whispers before continuing her song. "I am enough. I am love. I am loved. This wasn't my fault. This isn't punishment for my sins. Karma doesn't exist. I'm human, and humans make mistakes. But to Siren, I am a god. I'm her anchor. Her reason for living. The thing tethering her to the goodness in men. I'm a good guy. When I should have punished her, I forgave her. When I should have broken her heart, I married her."

Yes.

I'm her anchor.

I'm her good.

I'm her love.

I think for a minute my heart is going to heal; I'm going to mend. Instead, I feel the pressure building to excruciating painful levels.

"I am enough. I'm worthy. And I'm going to keep my promise to love Siren, forever," she sings again.

That does it—my heart bursts. My world shatters. A dam inside me bursts, and I feel free.

I collapse—the weight gone. Tears are everywhere. I feel like I'm bleeding on that damn floor again with Palmer straddling me about to be taken advantage of.

That should scare me, but it doesn't. When I look up at the gorgeous watering eyes staring over me, when I see the love in her eyes and know that she must have spent hours down here with me in the darkness, I know I am truly loved.

Siren isn't going anywhere. I let her see all of my pain, my shame, my guilt. She understands it all and doesn't care. And now, I know my path forward.

Siren's face watches me carefully, afraid she just lost me again. I grab her hips, helping her to straddle me just like Palmer did in that basement. This dark workout room is mimicking that basement perfectly.

"Zeke, what do you need? Tell me how to help you, and I'll do it," the pain in her voice is still there.

I smirk, grabbing her hair and yanking her down until she can see through my eyes to my soul. "I need you to fuck me, ride me like only you can. I need you to fuck me hard, my beautiful Siren. I need you to remind my cock that you are its master, that I only come for you. I need you to punish me for daring to let another woman touch me."

"Zeke, you have nothing to be sorry for. Nothing I need to punish you for."

"I know." And for the first time since it happened, I believe my own words. I'm angry about what happened to me, but it's not my fault. I need loads of therapy and more time talking about it than I want to admit, but right now, I don't feel my demons. They aren't fluttering around in my heart anymore causing havoc. Siren fought them off.

"But I want you to punish me anyway. I want you rough and hard. I want you to demand my cock to kneel down to his queen and worship you. Fuck me, Siren. Milk me. Remind me of what a stupid ass I've been for not fucking you all these weeks."

Siren bites her lip, and if the lights were on, I know I'd see her cheeks reddening, her eyes dilating. Instead, I settle for thrusting up and hearing the little gasp she makes when my hard cock hits between her legs. I hear her audible gasp.

I grin. *That's right, baby.* I'm about to fuck you like I've never fucked you before. So hold on, and prepare for the ride of your life.

CHAPTER 21
SIREN

I want to jump up and down and scream for joy. I want to run around the yacht and wake everyone up, shouting the good news. I also want to collapse into a ball and sleep for days.

I've never been so exhausted, so drained.

I felt like I just did two Ironmans, a triathlon, and then swam the entire length of the Pacific Ocean.

I never realized the depths of Zeke's pain. He made it seem like it was just his physical body that was hurting. He didn't let me see what was going on inside—the turmoil breaking every cell in his body.

But tonight, I saw it.

I felt it with every punch he threw me.

I heard it with every word he spoke into the darkness.

I tried to take it all away with the sound of my voice. I don't know why I sang. I didn't know if it would work, but singing has always been one of my greatest strengths, my secret weapon.

It worked.

I can hear the change in Zeke's voice. Feel the heaviness lift from the vibrations of his body. His aura is clean again. His heart is mine again. I don't have to fight off Palmer.

Finally, I get what I've wanted for weeks.

What I prayed for.

What I thought might never come.

I get Zeke. All of him.

And damn, is it perfect timing, because I've never needed him more.

I rip my shirt from my body and then tug at his, needing to feel our skins mashed together. We are lying on a workout mat that Enzo and Zeke use to fight each other on. It's covered in sweat, a far cry from the beautiful bed we could be fucking in just a floor above us, but our surroundings don't matter.

I'm not letting anything stop me from having Zeke right now.

"Off," I say, no longer able to form words after singing for three hours straight, singing to his soul and hoping it would listen to me. Hoping my voice would remind him what he already knows inside: he is enough. It isn't his fault what happened. He couldn't have stopped her from taking him any more than I could have stopped Julian from taking from me.

Zeke chuckles as I paw at his shirt in the dark. Our eyes both adjusted long ago, but it's still pitch-black in this room, and my eyes are still human eyes—full of fault, lacking the ability to see much beyond the foot in front of me.

I find Zeke's rough abs, still somehow dipping into deep valleys and high peaks rippling over his body even though his workout routine has reduced significantly since he was injured. His abs are now scarred, but his body refuses to become soft. It refuses to be anything but a brick of muscle, ready to defend me always.

I moan when Zeke's hands push my bra up and find my swollen breasts. They grow larger and more sensitive every day, and Zeke has had plenty of practice finding all the new areas that turn me on now. He works my breasts, molding them, pressing every button before pinching my nipples.

I reach around my back and unhook my bra, needing everything off.

I stand up and shove my leggings and panties down. At this point, they barely fit around my growing stomach. I hear Zeke scrambling to removes his own pants.

I stand over him, listening to him breathe. I'm terrified standing here. I don't know what the end result is going to be. *Am I going to trigger him by trying to fuck him? Especially here, in the dark?*

Did I push him too far? Demand he heals before he is ready?

Even if he's healed emotionally, what if his cock isn't ready? What if he can't perform? Is that going to make everything worse? Undo everything we just healed?

"Siren?" Zeke asks, his voice strong.

"Yes," I try to match my voice to Zeke's, but I know my voice faltered. I know he can hear my fear.

"Get your ass over here and ride me. I've never been harder for you. I've never wanted you more. If you weren't already pregnant, I would fill you with so much of my seed you'd end up pregnant, whether it was the right time of the month for you or not."

I chuckle at his words. They give me strength, just like my song gave him.

I don't think anymore. I'm on the floor, my hips over his, my hands pressed against his chest. My hair is caging in Zeke's head as I breathe over him before going in for a kiss. One final kiss getting us both more turned on and giving Zeke one last chance to back out before we venture into the unknown.

I feel like I'm about to take Zeke's virginity, and I want him to be sure, so fucking sure. I don't want to take anything from him. I want to give him his life back. His strength. His love.

Zeke kisses me, slipping his tongue expertly into my mouth just like he's done a thousand times. There is nothing special about this kiss except what I know is about to follow.

And then, I feel pressure as his teeth roll my bottom lip back and forth between them. My wetness grows between my legs, spilling onto his Zeke's deep V, just above his cock I want so badly.

He presses harder with his teeth and then suddenly releases.

"Fuck me," he growls, gripping my hips and pushing me until I can feel his tip at my slit, but he doesn't push me down. He waits for me to move the final inch.

"With pleasure," I roar as I take all of him at once. His cock rips through my body, and I realize instantly I was wrong when I said I didn't need Zeke's cock before. I was wrong thinking I could live on Zeke's fingers alone, his tongue.

I was so fucking wrong.

His hips rock and mine roll over his, meeting his thrust. It's like the entire ocean is pounding down on top of me. This moment is so intense, in the most delicious, satisfying way.

I didn't realize I was still broken. I was still hurting. I wasn't healed yet. I needed this.

"Why the fuck did I wait six weeks to do this?" Zeke howls as he thrusts in again in long, deep strokes.

"Seven weeks. It was fucking seven."

My nails dig into his flesh.

He hisses.

"I'll never let you go more than seven hours again without my cock."

"Is that a promise?"

"Yes."

"Fuck, we should have put that into the vows."

He rocks again, and I feel him everywhere—all the places I need him.

"Good thing we still need to have another wedding in a courthouse, we can say them then," he grits out. I know he's holding his orgasm back, trying to make this moment last forever.

I rock forward and reach behind, grabbing his balls and squeezing, just enough to punish him.

He bucks like he can't decide if he wants to buck me all the way off him, or if he wants to pull me closer.

"I don't think we can put those in the vows before God."

"Why not?" He breathes deep, his voice so fucking strained.

I open my mouth to speak, but I can't think. My voice doesn't work anymore.

"Exactly," he growls.

And then we are coming. *So. Damn. Hard.*

We both scream so loud that if the room wasn't soundproof,

everyone on the ship would be racing down, thinking we're under attack.

In a way, we did do battle. We both died. And we are now reborn.

This was what we needed.

We needed time.

We needed our bodies to mend.

We needed all our vulnerabilities and shame.

And then we needed to fuck each other dirty and sweating on the floor.

"Thank you," Zeke whispers as I lay on his bare chest. My body is aching for food, for water, for sleep, but I'm not going anywhere. I want Zeke. I want more. One round wasn't enough to satisfy what I've been missing for weeks.

"Thank you," I exhale back.

Zeke strokes my hair, and I grip his.

We breathe a peaceful breath in sync. We did it. We survived. Our horrible past is over.

"My little siren..." Julian says in my head.

I freeze.

"Kiss me like you want me," Julian says, and then I feel his hands on me, touching me...

"Baby? You hungry? Your stomach is growling like I haven't fed you in weeks."

"No, I'm okay," I try to shake Zeke off, but Zeke grabs his shirt, and dresses me in it. He slips back into his boxers. Then he's lifting me, taking me to the kitchen, most likely to feed me.

I shiver, but Zeke just laughs, thinking it was my stomach growling again.

"I'm sorry, little one. I should have fed your mother sooner," Zeke chuckles as he sits me down on a barstool in the kitchen while he goes to work pulling food out. No one is in the kitchen. It's dark outside, probably the middle of the night.

No one sees the moment that Zeke was healed, and mine was torn apart. No one sees the pain I've been fighting down all this time finally got free. No one sees, not even Zeke.

And I won't let him.

I am strong. I am enough. I sing the song I sang to Zeke over and over in my head, but when I hear Julian and Bishop's voice in my head again, goosebumps line my arms, and I know I'm not enough.

CHAPTER 22
ZEKE

We are all sitting out on the top deck—all six of us. The twins are down for a nap in their room.

There are maps and documents spread all around. Laptops on several laps. Guns in most of our waistbands. Ammunition in the corner. Knives hidden beneath our clothes.

This is our world—weapons and strategy. Most people will never see war, but we go to war every day.

Siren is sitting on the loveseat next to me. She's not staring at any of the documents, maps, or laptops. She's barely spoken so far as we discuss how we are going to take down Julian and Bishop, and ensure Palmer will never come after us.

Siren seems tired, there are circles under her eyes, and she looks paler than usual. It's not surprising since she spent most of yesterday fighting my demons for me. She also spent most of last night puking in the bathroom. I've tried to get some food in her, but her body can only handle a few saltines at a time. Kai reassures me it's normal, but I don't know how she's going to grow another life only eating a few crackers a day.

"You okay?" I ask. *Genius, my words are.*

She looks at me and nods, but she isn't really looking at me. She's looking past me, like I'm a ghost to her.

I frown.

I take her hand. "Are you upset you can't fight?" I ask, hoping saying the word 'can't' will stir her up.

"Can't fight? Really? I'm only two or three months pregnant. No one can even notice yet. I sure as hell can kick everyone's ass here," Siren roars.

Enzo laughs.

Beckett snickers.

Both men think I've messed up, saying the wrong thing to egg my wife on. Really, I just wanted to bring her back to life, so my plan worked.

I lean over, grab her neck to keep her from pulling away, and whisper in her ear so only she can hear me. "There's my Siren. I thought I lost her."

Her eyes gleam, but then she kisses me tenderly on the lips. "You'll never lose me."

I nod. We both turn back to Kai, who is leading this meeting. Enzo may have more physical skills than Kai, but my stingray has become the master at strategy, and the men follow her better than they ever did Enzo.

"Where are we on Bishop? We have all this information on Julian. We know where he lives. We know how many men work for him. We have his bank accounts. We know he has one of our yachts. But Bishop is like a ghost. We don't even know if that's his first or last name. He doesn't just go by Bishop."

"You go by Black," Enzo says.

Kai sighs. "Have we found anything more?"

All heads shake.

"Dammit. I really wish we knew something about the man."

"It doesn't matter what we know," Siren says. She's been mostly silent, but since she's the only one who has met Bishop, she's the one who we should be listening to when it comes to him.

I take her hand and give it a squeeze, telling her to continue.

"Bishop isn't a good man. His soul is dark. His heart is broken.

He has nothing to live for. He doesn't believe in love. He doesn't believe in goodness. He's evil. And he won't hesitate to torture you, not in the physical way you are all used to being tortured, but in a psychological way that will stay with you forever. He'll get in your head, shoving a dagger into your brain, and then twist until you bow to him," Siren's voice falls heavy. Her eyes gloss over, and I know Bishop is in her head again. There is nothing I can do to get him out.

She blinks, clearing her head. "When you see Bishop, you kill him. That's what got Zeke and me in trouble with Julian. We hesitated. He offered us something we thought we needed. He struck a deal with us we thought would save us. Instead, it allowed him time to destroy us."

Everyone nods, hanging onto all of her words.

"I need you all to promise me. When you see Bishop, you'll kill him. You won't hesitate. You won't ask questions. You won't try to save him; he can't be saved. Promise me," Siren says.

Everyone nods again.

"No, with your words. Promise me you won't let Bishop's charms win. Promise me you'll shoot and deal with the consequences later," Siren says.

"I promise," Enzo says.

"I promise," Kai says.

"I don't know how to shoot a gun, but I promise if I learn, I'll kill the bastard," Nora says.

"I promise," Beckett says.

And then Siren is looking at me, like my promise holds more weight than all the rest.

"I'll do whatever you want, but don't you need Bishop to fix you first?" I ask so only she can hear.

"Yes, but I'll take care of that soon."

I frown but trust her. I don't have any other choice.

"I promise," I say, the words feeling ominous.

Siren seems satisfied with all our answers and quiets, giving Kai the floor again.

"We need to get the twins far away from here for a while," she says with pain in her voice.

Enzo takes her hand, agreeing. They both look at Beckett, who they seem to trust with their kids more than anyone else here.

"Of course," Beckett answers with as few words exchanged as possible.

"Nora, can you fly them wherever they want to go? Your plane won't be tracked as easily as if they fly commercial," Siren says.

Nora gives Siren a tight smile. Nora knows Siren is just trying to get her away from here and the impending fight. Nora doesn't have the experience fighting like the rest of us do.

"Yes, I'll go with them." Nora looks to Beckett like she's asking permission to tag along, but he doesn't glance her way.

"Where is the box?" I ask Kai. I feel weird not knowing where they are. I was the one who originally hid the box in the Black vault. I was the one Lucy gave the task to. I feel like this is important, like I should know where the box is now. It's the only way I can protect it.

"Hidden," Kai says.

I frown. "Tell me later?"

"No," Kai and Siren say at the same time.

Enzo and I frown at the two strong-willed women in our lives knowing we've already lost, but not stopping us from fighting anyway.

"Why the hell not? We should all know. If one of us dies, the others should know how to protect it," Enzo says, staring at his wife like she's his insubordinate and not his wife and leader.

"It's not safe. The fewer people that know, the better. That way, the information can't be tortured out of any of us. That way, I'm the only one who they can use in that way," Kai says.

"But—" Enzo starts.

Kai gives him a look, and I know she's playing her power card over him. She's the leader of the Black organization. Normally, Enzo and her run the organization together as equals. I've seen them work together well. But every once in a while, when it really matters, Kai uses her power. She won, after all. Today is for her using that power—for her wielding it like it was always meant to be hers.

"I'm the one who should know. Only me. It's not safe. Bishop knows how to play with our minds; if he captures one of us, he could pull the information out. It's too dangerous in the wrong hands. Only I know," Kai says.

Siren exhales a breath and gives a slight nod of agreement to Kai. I don't know why both women feel so strongly about this, but I trust them both. Even though I think this information should be shared, I won't push it.

"So the plan is to gather every last man and woman willing to fight. To call Langston and drag his ass back here from chasing pussy. Then what?" I ask.

"Then I call Julian or Bishop, and tell them where to find us," Siren says.

I grit my teeth, hating the plan, hating that Siren is the one with the closest connection to the two dangerous men. But it's the best plan we have. It gives us control. We get to decide when and where instead of waiting. And neither men can resist the call of a siren.

The meeting adjourns, and we all go our separate ways. All of us have to start preparing for our different tasks. Nora and Beckett to pack to leave. Kai and Enzo to spend every last second with their twins before they leave. And Siren and I to spend every last second together until I convince her to hide somewhere safe.

It's a monumental task, because even though she's pregnant and has our child to worry about, I know she's going to want to be close. She's going to want to do her part to help kill Julian and Bishop and end this war forever.

We get back to our room, and Siren undresses wordlessly, getting ready for bed. She doesn't speak. She doesn't flirt, trying to get me to kiss or fuck her. There will be none of that tonight. The mood is too somber.

I get undressed and brush my teeth silently next to Siren. Me standing in my boxers. Her in her panties and tank top.

We both spit at the same time.

"What's going on in that head of yours?" I ask.

Siren turns on the water, rinses her toothbrush off like she didn't hear me, but I know she did.

"It's time," she says.

I know exactly what she means. It's time to complete whatever task she promised Bishop in order for him to set her free, to fix her.

I want to ask her what task Bishop asked of her, but it doesn't matter. Whatever task it is, I'll support her. I want her to be free of him, and if this is the only way to do it, then so be it.

"The fight is coming, and when I call Julian and Bishop to tell them to meet us, I need him to tell me how to fix me on the phone. I know you don't want me here when the fighting starts. This is the only way to ensure I can get fixed and that you can kill Bishop without hesitation when the time comes," Siren continues.

"What do you need from me?" I ask, knowing the only reason she's bringing this up instead of just doing the task is because she needs my help. I don't ask her what she's doing, or how much pain she's about to bring into our lives. It doesn't matter. Our marriage and love can survive anything. We've already proven that.

"I need you to take Kai away for a couple of hours. Wait until after the twins are gone," Siren says.

I suck in a breath, knowing I'm about to choose my wife over my friends. Siren has to do something to hurt them.

Her eyes are sad and heavy staring at me. Her eyes hold the weight of everything she is about to do.

I step toward her, resting my hands on her hips by her growing belly, holding our child. My eyes stare her down, showing her everything I'm feeling.

"Whatever you need, I'll do it. It's no longer a choice between you and everyone else. I'll always choose you. You'll always come first. Don't ever hesitate to ask of me. Don't worry that you're making me choose—you aren't. When it comes to you and our baby, it's never a choice. You are first. You will always be first."

Her lips press against mine softly, and for a second, I feel like she's poisoning me with her lips, putting me under her spell, softening me to her, bending me to her will. Her lips are that of a siren's.

She's about to use her powers to hurt someone I care about, but it doesn't matter. I've been in love with her from the start. She didn't have to use her powers on me, I've always been her's.

Tomorrow, I'll realize just how deep her talons have a grip on my heart.

CHAPTER 23
SIREN

Everyone is gone.

Well, everyone I need gone is gone.

Beckett and Nora took the twins far away. I don't know where, and I absolutely don't want to know. I don't even know if Kai and Enzo know where they went. I don't know if Beckett and Nora had a plan when they left, other than to take them far way, to hide them. To keep them secret from Julian and Bishop. I'm sure they already know about the twin's existence.

Both men are devils, but I don't think even they would stoop to involving the kids unless they had no other choice to get what they want.

Kai left with Zeke this morning, to make the rounds to all the yachts and prepare them for the upcoming battle. It took zero persuasion from Zeke to convince Kai to go with him. No explanations were needed to convince Enzo as to why the two of them should be the ones to go instead of Enzo and Kai.

Everything has been set up for me to do what I need to do, but instead of getting to work right away, my stomach has been more upset than usual, like my body knows how much this is going to hurt me. How this is going to hurt everyone. Relationships are going to change after this. I'm about to do something unforgivable, something I don't ever want to ask forgiveness for, but something I have to do for my unborn child. My child deserves to have a mother who isn't controlled by a mad man. I can't risk that Bishop could put thoughts in my head that could tell me to hurt my own child. I won't let that happen. I won't.

That's what I think about as I kneel on the tile floor of the bathroom hunched over the toilet. My stomach is twisted, my mouth burns with the taste of my vomit, and my head is sweaty—the complete opposite of what I need to feel and look in order to complete my task.

"Zeke, please forgive me," I say before I push myself off the floor.

I should have already started my plan, but even now, I continue to put it off. I decide to shower first. I spend at least a half an hour scrubbing every inch of my skin, arguing it's important to get all of the vomit smell off, not because I'm stalling.

Then I take another twenty minutes blow-drying my hair.

Another fifteen painting my face with blush and red lipstick.

I waste another thirty minutes finding just the right outfit, even though I end up picking the outfit I started with—a tight-fitting red dress that my black lace bra peeks out the top and that can easily be hiked up. I strap my gun around my thigh, just in case.

Finally, I stare at myself in the mirror—this time the act has nothing to do with me stalling.

This is the last time I'll be able to look at myself and not truly see the siren inside me. It was one thing to use Zeke. I did it out of love for him, and it turned out for the better in the end.

This.

This isn't like that.

This is cementing my place in hell.

I know I chose my outfit correctly from my sharp heels, my skin-tight dress, the color of my lipstick. My hair is stick straight, and when I run my hand through it and flip it so the part is no longer perfectly in the middle but off to one side, I'm a she-devil ready to pounce.

"You're a siren. Aria is gone. You claimed to enjoy being a siren. This is what comes with it. I have to take the good and the bad. My skills can be used against me."

I push all of that out.

Time to go to work.

I step out of my bedroom with confidence. I have a plan to complete Bishop's task, and I know it will work, but it will destroy two unbreakable bonds in the process.

No bonds are unbreakable, Bishop says. *Everyone can be broken.*

I disagree, but I know in my heart he's right. I'm about to prove his point.

I walk up the stairs to the top of the yacht. I had one of the guards bring up the small keyboard piano that I found in one of the twin's playrooms. I sit down at the keys. I stop thinking, and I just play.

I play every tormented love song I can think of, every painful story.

Then I cast the final hook—I sing.

My voice carries throughout the entire ship—calling to the man I seek. I hope the servants are smart enough not to listen to my call, because I just need one man, and I need him alone.

I hear footsteps, but I don't stop. I can't stop. Once I'm in a trance like this, I'm just as much at the mercy of it as the people listening. I keep playing. I keep singing until the last note of the song is over.

"Beautiful," my mark says. I don't turn around. He could have chosen a different word to describe what he heard. He could have said amazing, incredible, wow. Instead, he chose the word I knew he would. He can't help himself. He doesn't realize the importance of words.

Only someone like me who has been careful with words all her life, careful not to tell a lie, would understand the importance of word choice.

I let my hands dance across the keys, but I don't speak. I need him to move closer. I need to pull him in—a word isn't enough.

He clears his throat. "You look beautiful. Waiting for Zeke?"

I turn my head, giving him a partial view of my face, knowing it will draw him in further. Not because he's a man near an attractive woman, but because he's polite and will want to look me in the eyes when he speaks to me.

"Yes. We've never had a date. I thought having one under the stars before we were separated sounded like a good idea. Is it foolish of me to think they will be back soon?" I ask.

Enzo chuckles and moves closer, until he's sitting down on the piano bench next to me. "Yes, those two will be gone for a while still. There are a lot of ships they need to visit."

"And they love each other," I finish.

He sighs, and that's when I notice he has two wine glasses filled with red wine.

"That for me?"

He shrugs. "I know some women still drink a glass of wine, even while pregnant. I thought it was wrong for me to drink and at least not offer you some."

Such a gentleman. And I'm going to play to all his gentlemanly weaknesses.

I take the wine glass and take a sip. Drinking wine is the least risky thing I'm going to do when it comes to risking this baby's life.

Enzo does the same, his heavy eyes looking at me.

"It doesn't make you nervous that your stingray is with my anchor?" I ask, using both Kai and Zeke's nicknames.

"No." Enzo takes a drink of his wine, but his eyes tell me he's lying. They wrinkle in the corners as the truth pulls at him.

"What are you afraid will happen?" I ask, trying again. Drinking my wine so Enzo will drink his. I don't want him drunk; I don't like using drugs to manipulate the men I target. It doesn't seem fair. But I want him relaxed, willing to do things he might otherwise not do.

"The same thing you're afraid will happen."

I laugh like he's ridiculous, even though we both know how easy it is to fall over the line from friends to lovers. From enemies to everything.

I take another sip of wine, then set it on the edge of the piano. My hands are lightly stroking the keys again as I play a soft melody.

"I'm not afraid of anything."

Enzo chuckles deeply. "Now, who's lying?"

"I'm not lying. They could sleep together, and it wouldn't hurt me."

"That's not what I'm afraid they are going to do. You really think Kai and Zeke would sleep together?"

Yes, fall into my trap. Fall so this can be over.

"Don't you?"

"No. I don't."

"Then what do you think?"

I continue to play, knowing this closeness is enough to draw Enzo in. I don't need the sexy clothes. I don't need the wine. I don't need my sultry voice. I need him talking. I need him thinking about Kai. I need him longing for something he thinks he's yet to find.

Humans are simple creatures. We aren't complicated. We all yearn for the same thing—to feel the greatest love.

Enzo and Kai have a relationship that I could only dream of sharing with Zeke. They have a trust in each other that I don't know if Zeke and I can truly have considering our past and how we started.

Yet somehow, Enzo still thinks there is more to be had. He sees the way Zeke calls Kai 'Stingray,' and he thinks he's missing out on some part of his wife. He thinks Kai shares something with Zeke she will never share with him.

She does.

But it's different. It's not Enzo's; it's Zeke's. Enzo and Kai are soulmates, but so are Zeke and Kai. They were all destined to be in each other's lives. All destined to love each other, in the exact way they've come together. There is no Enzo and Kai without Kai and Zeke. No Kai and Zeke without Enzo and Kai.

But the heart can be easily made jealous. Enzo is weak right now. He's worried about his wife, his kids. Scared to death that because he chose this life, a life that involves many enemies, that that means he doesn't deserve his family.

I know because I feel the same way.

For a while, I just play as the dark sky spreads over us. I don't know when Zeke and Kai will be back; I just know my plan will work. It has to for my own kid's future.

"Did Kai tell you where the box is?" I ask, raising my eyebrow at him.

He freezes, his wine glass hovering in front of his mouth.

"I'm not asking because I want to know where they're hidden. I don't." *Please, don't tell me. I don't want to know. Please let Kai have been smart enough not to tell him.* I'll find out if she did, and I can't know. "I'm just curious if she told her husband."

Enzo lowers his wine glass. "She didn't tell me."

He puts the glass down on the other end of the piano. Then, to my surprise, his fingers start playing.

"You play?" I ask, even though it's obvious he does.

"No, but I'm a fast learner."

His hands mimic mine, just an octave lower.

"That's incredible. I was always a slow learner."

"Really?" he asks, surprised.

"Yep, until my twenties. Then all of a sudden, everything I'd studied for years clicked. I learned how to become a fast learner."

He moves his hands differently on the keys, and I copy.

He smiles.

We continue to move our hands over the keys until I can't help but sing the melody in my soul. One of longing to be with the one you love. One I know will speak to Enzo's soul.

Eventually, he stops moving his hands over the keys. He just watches me. With how passionately I'm playing, my dress has hiked up high on my thigh, my straps have fallen off my shoulders, and my cleavage is spilling out of the too-tight dress.

I study Enzo out of the corner of my eye. His sleeves are rolled up, and the top few buttons of his shirt are undone. He's almost as dressed up as I am. It's clear he had the same thought that I'm pretending to have, to dress up for one last romantic moment with the one we love. Instead, we are sharing it together.

"Do you think we share the same kind of connection Kai and Zeke share?" Enzo asks.

No.

Hell no.

But this is the moment I've been waiting for. Enzo isn't drunk, but he's lost. He doesn't hear the voices downstairs. He doesn't know the trap I sprung.

"Maybe. But what is that connection they share exactly?"

I turn sideways on the bench, putting one leg on either side, so I'm straddling it, pushing my dress so high up on my thighs he can see my underwear.

"A deep friendship?"

My eyes seer. *You can do better, Enzo.*

"Really? They are just really good friends? Oh, Enzo, are you really that naive?"

"They aren't lovers!"

"I never said they were."

"You implied it." His face is red. He's angry. He goes to stand up, but I grab his shirt, yanking him down and also to me.

I can do this. We are so close. So fucking close.

"No, but you did. You think they could be. They might, in a moment of weakness, give in to their temptation. Maybe not tonight, but in the past."

He frowns.

"Maybe it's not the past you are worried about but the future. What happens if you and I die? Will they comfort each other through their mourning?"

I curl my hand around his neck.

His brow jumps in shock.

Then he realizes what I'm doing—showing him it could never be true because when I touch the nape of his neck, he feels nothing. How wrong he is...

"Will they accidentally kiss each other in a drunken night, much like this?"

I swing my leg over his lap, my time running out as the footsteps grow louder. His eyes darken in a warning.

"Will they fuck and realize they should have been doing it this entire time? Realize we were never the people they were in love with, it was always each other?"

He shudders, disturbed. I lean toward him. Our lips almost brush.

"If we died, I would want them to find each other. I would want them to be happy. They deserve to be happy if we are gone," he says.

"What if they would be happier with each other now?"

"They wouldn't."

"What if we would be happier?"

"We wouldn't."

"Prove it. You know you need to."

"I don't need to prove anything," Enzo says.

Such a gentleman. I hate doing this, but I don't have a choice. It's now or never.

I grab his hands and place one on my ass, the other on my breast.

"Feel anything?"

"No."

"What about now?" I ask as I kiss his neck.

He stiffens.

"Siren," his voice warns, hating my fire on his neck as much as I hate my tongue licking over his neck.

He tries to push me off him, but he won't dare hurt me since I'm pregnant. So I take what I need from him. I become all the people I hate—Palmer, Julian, Bishop. I take from Enzo, knowing he's defenseless.

I undo his pants and slip inside, avoiding his cock, but accidentally brushing against him all the same. It's not about me violating him; it's about what it looks like to Zeke and Kai.

"You're a liar, Enzo. You want me," I whisper.

"No. Siren, stop."

Forgive me. Please, fucking forgive me.

I see Zeke's eyes. I see them burn into me.

"Want me to stop?" I whisper into Enzo's ear so that Zeke and Kai can't hear the words I speak, but they will hear Enzo's reaction.

"Yes!" he screams. His voice screams everything he wants. He wants me to stop, but to them, it looks like he's begging me to touch him.

My eyes go to Zeke—*I always tell the truth, even when I lie. Find the lie, Zeke. Find the truth. You know this isn't what I want.*

I take the last thing I require of Enzo Black, the great man who can so easily be taken down against his will by a woman. I won't rape him. That was never the goal, but I take everything from him all the same.

He will be able to get it back, eventually. He will be able to remind

Kai that he loves her, that I was the monster tonight, not him. But for now, his life will be broken—as was required of me.

I take the final thing, destroying myself more than I destroy him. I didn't rape Enzo like Julian did me. I won't milk Enzo dry like Palmer did to Zeke. But I fucked with Enzo's head like Bishop did me. And I touched him where I had no right to.

I'm a monster.

A devil.

There is no forgiveness to be had. I won't ask for it either. I keep the tears in. I don't get to be in pain as I do this, as I take everything from the three people on this deck.

I tilt my head, flash Zeke a lustful look so not even he can tell the truth from the lies, and then I kiss Enzo open-mouthed. I kiss him with every emotion I have. I do what Bishop commanded—I kiss Enzo. I destroy two marriages, and I pray like hell we will all survive this.

I didn't understand why Bishop wanted me to do this before, but hearing the collective gasp of the room, feeling the shift in the air, his motive is clear. Bishop wanted us all weak when he fought us. He knew together we could never be beaten, but apart, we are easy targets.

I did this. I destroyed our chance at killing our enemies so I could get Bishop out of my head. I just hope it's worth it.

CHAPTER 24
ZEKE

Siren kissed Enzo.

Yes, my brain is going to be processing what I saw for a long time.

No, it wasn't a dream.

Yes, it was real.

Why? I have no fucking clue what this could have to do with a task Bishop gave her.

My body floods with rage, with anger, with undeniable and uncontrollable pain. I realize this might be my most desperate moment.

Not learning that Siren scammed me.

Not finding out that she was married to another man.

Not having her ripped from me and raped by a man she works for.

No—this guts me worse than all of those. Not because a kiss is somehow worse. Not because the compromising position they were in is too horrible for my eyes to bear. But because of the vows we made, the promises, they mean nothing if we don't keep them. We aren't legally married. The only way we stay married is if we both want to be married. We both dream this dream and want each other more than we want to be apart.

And in one moment of weakness? Of lust? Enzo and Siren threw away everything. Because what? We were fucking gone too long?

Siren told me to take Kai away, so I did. I took her away all damn day. I gave Siren as much time as she could possibly want to complete her mission. I assumed her mission was finding out the location of the box to turn over to Bishop.

I assume that's still what she was doing when she was kissing and dry humping my best friend. She's used to seducing men to get the information she needs, but I'm angry she couldn't come up with any other way to get him to spill.

I can think of a hundred different ways, none of them involve almost fucking my best friend.

The cool air has turned hot, suffocatingly hot, even though we are standing on top of the yacht with plenty of air to be shared between the four of us.

We've paired off in a staring contest of two versus two. I'm staring at Siren. Kai is staring at Enzo. We don't acknowledge the other people up here with us.

My heart doesn't break watching Siren still sitting on Enzo's lap, caressing his head, hiding behind him, using him like a shield to protect herself from me.

I growl, my face turning into a dark shadow. Siren doesn't get to hide. She doesn't get to pretend she was telling the truth while all the time, showing the world a lie. This time, I'm going to make her face the music. She's going to have to own the consequences of her actions.

I put my hands into my leather jacket pockets, though. I can be patient when I want to be. I can wait to get her alone before we talk. So I stand silently.

I'm not going to help her out of this uncomfortable situation. Siren didn't want to talk to me ahead of time and tell me her plan. She doesn't trust me to help her, so I don't trust her with my truth, with my current feelings. She could have told me her plan, and I could have told her she's a damn fool. Then we wouldn't be in this situation.

Kai, on the other hand, doesn't have any patience when it comes to making her vengeance known. All of it is directed at her husband.

"How dare you! After everything we've been through, you do this!" Kai screams, marching over to her husband.

Enzo jumps, so does Siren. Siren is off Enzo's lap as Kai marches over, but her hand gets stuck in his zipper. Siren shoots me a 'help me' glare.

No. Fucking. Way.

You got yourself into this mess, pretty girl, you can get yourself out.

Finally, Enzo yanks her hand free, and Siren stumbles away from Kai just before she slaps Enzo hard across the cheek. He takes it, as he should.

"How could you?" Kai's voice is eerily calm after just being wild.

Enzo stiffens but doesn't speak. There are no apologies or excuses he could give that would make this moment better.

"Are you drunk?" Kai asks, sniffing his breath.

"No," Enzo says. It's clear he isn't drunk. And if he was, he would definitely be sober now. His clothes don't look good, though. His shirt is unbuttoned halfway down. His pants are undone with the top of his pubic hair protruding.

I don't dare look at Siren. I focus on the disaster in front of me. I don't want to see her dress out of place. I don't want to see it ripped or undone. I don't want to see her nipples hard or her panties wet. I don't want to see her flushed cheeks or swollen lips. I don't want to see any evidence that another man touched my woman.

"Did the whore drug you?" Kai hisses, staring from Enzo to Siren.

I growl, "Too far." Apparently, I'll still protect Siren even when I shouldn't.

Kai flips me off, returning her glare to her husband, begging him to give her a reason for this situation. One where he isn't at fault, but he's as much at fault as Siren is. He could have stopped her at any time. He didn't.

"No," Enzo says, sealing his fate.

I don't understand what happened. I know that Siren can seduce. I know her voice is heavenly—it's what healed me. But I don't understand how two married people could end up kissing, with hands in places they shouldn't be. *If we hadn't walked in, then what would have happened? How far would they have gone?*

Kai slaps Enzo again.

"Stingray," he says, his voice begging to let him talk.

"Don't!" Kai takes a shuddering breath. "Don't. You don't get to call me that. Not anymore. Only Zeke can call me that."

I gulp, not liking that at all. With as pissed as Kai is, I wouldn't doubt if she wanted to kiss me right now to get back at Enzo. She stomps over to Siren, and I instinctively go over. I'm pissed at Siren, but I won't let Kai touch her.

"How could you?" Kai says, her heart breaking.

It's then I realize my heart isn't broken. It's just hardened, putting up shield after shield, not wanting to allow Siren back in again. But there's a problem—Siren is already on the inside with me. I should have pushed her out before I started putting my walls back up.

Kai moves her hand up to slap Siren, so I move to prevent her from touching Siren, but Kai's hand falls on my cheek.

I blink rapidly, not understanding.

"I can't slap Siren because she's pregnant," Kai says, like that somehow makes sense for her to instead slap me.

Kai turns in her boots and marches down the stairs. Enzo takes a deep breath like he's gaining courage. He doesn't look at me or Siren. He's focused on his wife. Then he's gone too.

It's just me and Siren alone on the top deck, with nothing but the stars and the sound of the waves.

"I'm—" Siren starts.

"If you end that sentence with 'sorry,' I'm going to jump over the railing and swim until I'm too exhausted to swim anymore. Until I drown in the ocean like I should have all those months ago. I don't want to hear your excuses. I don't want to know why. I don't want some inexcusable apology. Just..." I throw my hands up, but I have no idea how to make this better. No idea what to say or do. "Just..." I try again. But again, I don't know what I need.

My eyes look at Siren, really look at her for the first time. I see her disheveled hair where Enzo's hands touched. I see her smeared lipstick and raccoon eyes from her running mascara. The straps of her dress are halfway down her biceps. Her black lace bra is completely visible on one side. Her dress is still pulled up high on her thigh.

I grind my teeth, my jaw clenching, my veins bulging. I ball up my fists. I need to punch something. I should find Enzo and beat the shit out of him. I don't understand what happened exactly. They both were dressed up. *Why?*

"Did you complete your task?" I ask, carefully and slowly. I need to know this was all for something. That Siren gained some freedom when she kissed Enzo. I need to know this wasn't all for nothing.

She nods.

I can't look at her. I stare out at the dark ocean, but I can still see her out of the corner of my eye. She doesn't look ashamed. She doesn't look scared. She doesn't look angry, timid, or lost. She looks begging. Not for forgiveness, but for something else I don't understand. I thought I knew all of her looks, but this one I've yet to learn. Right now isn't the time for me to study this new one.

"Good," I finally say, and then I'm walking away. I think she might follow me, but as I descend the stairs, I'm alone. I don't hear her foot-steps. I don't feel her presence.

I go all the way to the deepest part of the ship into one of the rooms Enzo and I use to monitor security systems. I unlock the door and step inside. Siren doesn't have the access code to my knowledge. She can't get in if she comes looking for me.

I slam the door, but it doesn't make me feel any better.

"Siren, what have you done?" I fall into the spinning chair and kick my feet up onto the desk.

I listen at the door. She's not coming after me. I would feel her descending already even before I heard her.

Siren would have felt the same. That's how connected we are. When she kissed Enzo, she would have felt us coming. Definitely heard our footsteps and voices. I know she saw me before she kissed him. *But how many kisses did they share before we arrived? Was that the only one?*

Siren knew we were there, and she kissed him like that was the reason for kissing him.

"Stop thinking about it, asshole," I murmur to myself. I need some time to calm down, but I don't know how to do that.

I see a bottle of bourbon sitting on the desk. I grab it and hold it to my chest like I'm going to get the effects of the alcohol simply by pressing the bottle to my body. I pick up my phone and press the number without thinking it through.

Langston, one of my other best friends, is supposedly off chasing down his girlfriend, Liesel. But right now, I need him. I don't give a damn that he hasn't answered any of my other phone calls. I need him, so he better fucking answer.

His voicemail greets me instead, but I still need to talk.

"Langston, you asshole, this is Zeke. Your best friend you left for dead. Yea, I'm alive, you motherfucker. I'm alive, and you haven't come to see me. What the hell is that? I know you are trying to win Liesel back, but I came back from the dead—I think that warrants a visit from my best friend.

"Yea, that's right. I called you my best friend. And right now, I mean it, even though you're on my shit list for not coming to see me already. You have no idea the shit I'm in. Stingray is broken. I can't be there for her this time, because her fucking husband kissed my wife! Yep, you heard me correctly. I have a wife. I'd love for you to meet her, even though I'm pissed."

I stare down at the bottle I want to completely consume. I'm sure the answering machine has cut me off by now, but I keep talking anyway.

"I'm lost, man. I've never felt this lost and scared before. I didn't know what love could do to a man. Now I know. Loving someone makes me crazy. It fucks with my head. It makes me weak and vulnerable. It makes it so she's the only person in the world I care about liking me. I don't even care if I fix my relationship with Enzo, I just want to fix things with her.

"And no, it's not just so I can get some pussy, although having the same magnificent woman to come home to every night is nice. No, I just want...fuck, just come back, man. I don't understand what your deal is, but a fight of epic proportions is about to go down. I need you. We all do. Just get your ass back here and bring Liesel. I know me and her don't always get along, but if you love her, then that's enough for me. I'll go to battle for you to keep her. But I need my best friend by my side, and that's you, asshole. Just don't tell Enzo that. Or Kai. Or Siren."

I end the call and toss my phone on the counter. I should drink the entire bottle of whiskey in my hand and then sleep the rest of the night in here. But after everything we've been through, all the danger we've experienced, I know life is short. There are no guarantees that we get tomorrow. I've waisted too much time not spent with Siren. I'm not going to waist another second.

I set the bottle down and then make my way back upstairs, Siren still waiting. She's sitting at the piano; her fingers curled over the keyboard. She's not really playing; she seems more angry with the piano than anything. She bangs on it roughly, then apologizes sweetly as she moves her fingers over the keys.

And then, she stops. Her fingers are no longer gliding. She's reaching for a wine glass next to her, her head is turned, and I see the mascara lines down her cheeks where her tears have fallen.

She takes a large gulp of the wine, thoroughly pissing me off.

"You shouldn't be doing that," I growl. I guess it's time to show her how angry I am.

CHAPTER 25
SIREN

Zeke came back. *Did he figure out the truth?*

Or is he here to punish me for hurting him? For destroying two relationships with one kiss? For proving that no relationship, no matter how loving, is unbreakable?

"Put the wine glass down," he growls. He's pissed I'm drinking while pregnant.

"No. I'm sure you're drunk off your ass. I think I can have one glass of wine," I spit back. I don't even know why I'm drinking the wine at all. I don't want to hurt my baby in any way, but I'm so damn afraid. I know I'm fucking this all up. I don't know how to help. I don't know how to keep my baby safe. I can't even keep myself safe.

"I'm not drunk." Zeke walks toward me, but I don't give him my full attention. I'm still seated at the piano, gripping my wine glass like a shield.

"Sure, you aren't." I roll my eyes, lifting the glass to my lips again, needing to feel something, but I can't. I don't even feel sorry about what I did. It had to be done. If I really love Zeke and he really loves me, then our relationship will survive. And this is barely a blip on Kai and Enzo's relationship. They will be made up by the morning if they aren't already.

395

Zeke stands over me, breathing down on me. I don't smell a drop of alcohol on his breath.

"I'm not the one who is lying," Zeke says, yanking the glass from my hand and throwing it on the floor, shattering the crystal glass into thousands of pieces.

He knows. He knows why I kissed Enzo. Why I shoved my hand in his pants and made us look like we had been making out for hours instead of just the single kiss.

"Can we fix this?" Zeke asks, his eyes searing down at my flesh, my overexposed skin in this dress.

I swallow hard against the growing dryness of my throat caused by Zeke's intense stare. "We could, but we shouldn't—yet."

"Did you call Bishop?"

"Yes. I'll be fixed tomorrow morning," I say, also indicating when Bishop will attack us. Bishop won't wait, not now that our world is in chaos.

Zeke stares up at the sky like he wants to curse the stars for letting this happen, for the pain he's feeling. He has no idea how hard it was to betray him like that, knowing it was the only way to protect him. He doesn't know what I know. He doesn't know the truth. And hopefully, I will have fixed everything before I have to tell him, before he knows the thoughts in my head.

"I should hate you," Zeke says calmly.

"You should," I agree.

"But I don't."

I nod, already knowing that. It's why Bishop's plan is stupid. His plan will only work for a few hours. The chaos and turmoil we feel will last less than twenty-four hours. Our relationships are too strong.

Zeke stares at the piano like it's his enemy. "Play for me."

"Why?"

"Because you owe me." His eyebrow raises in a snarky way.

He's right. I do owe him.

But I want to burn the piano to the ground, destroying the evidence of my sin. I don't want to play.

Zeke takes a seat on the bench facing the piano, spreads his legs wide, and then pats a spot on the bench in between his legs and the piano.

I move to sit down next to him instead of in front of him, but Zeke grabs my hand and pushes me into the small space in front of him. The back of my dress is mostly backless, so my skin is flush against his front. I can feel the coolness of his leather jacket, combined with his warm breath, on my bare skin.

"Play for me," he breathes. "Not like you played for him. I want a song all my own."

Chills dance over my skin at his words. I bite my lip, trying to keep the feelings at bay. He's not going to let me act on my feelings. He may be forgiving, but he's not going to fuck me after seeing my tongue down one of his best friend's throats.

I rest my hand over the keys, considering what song I want to play.

"Don't get stage fright now. Play for me," Zeke growls impatiently in my ear, taunting me, telling me he knows it wasn't this hard for me to sing for Enzo, so it shouldn't be hard to play for him either.

But it is. Playing for Enzo was about manipulating him. Playing for Zeke is about showing him that I love him more than life itself. That every sin I commit, every truth I tell, is for him.

My hands fall to my lap as I can't come up with a song to play. Zeke puts his hands on top of mine and brings them to the piano. "Play, Siren. Just play," his voice is kinder now, with plenty of begging. He needs this.

I don't think. I play. At first, my fingers just move over the keys in a familiar way, combining several popular songs. I play a little of Bieber, Swift, and Eilish. But quickly, my fingers take on a life of their own. I no longer recognize the melody I'm playing, but it's a beautiful, haunting sound. One that drives me to play faster, to find the next verse, the next melody. I become greedy, wanting to hear the song I've just created. I want to know. I want to hear it.

More. More. More.

I chase the keys, letting the emotions of the song drive through me until I'm consumed by them.

Zeke's hands run up and down my arms, feeling me play in a new intimacy. His head rests on my shoulder. His legs wrap tighter around my hips until it feels like we are both playing together.

"Sing," Zeke says, his throat dry as he speaks the word like a command and a desire.

I open my mouth, having no clue what's going to come out. At first, it's a hum, a single syllable. But then the words come to me, like a gift from the gods.

I step off the cliff and then I'm falling.
The jump is freeing.
I could be flying.
Drifting higher and higher.
A bird in the sky.
I feel so light; I'm sure the air could lift me up.
But I'm not flying.
I'm falling.
Falling through time and space.
Falling through your open hands.
Falling to the deepest hell.
I won't survive the fall.
I don't need to either.
Don't catch me.
Promise, to never catch me.
Just don't let our love fall.

My song is a cry to Zeke to trust me. To love me. To never hurt me. To never betray our love. It's a promise that I will never betray him either, even when it appears like I am.

Zeke lifts my hands from the piano, and my song stops.

"I hate what you did," Zeke says honestly.

"I do too."

"I won't ask you why."

I nod.

"I want to fuck you," he whispers into my ear.

I bite my lip. "Bishop is watching. He has eyes on one of the other yachts."

Bishop told me he had men watching us. Men whose loyalty was to him, not Kai and Enzo.

Zeke stiffens, his eyes searching out in the darkness like he could see the betrayer through the blackness and miles between us.

"Take from me," I say, knowing we still need to appear angry with each other so Bishop will think I did a good job.

Zeke frowns.

"You want me. You take me," I say, needing this so badly. I need him to be rough. I need him to claim me as his.

"You sure?" his voice so damn low and raspy.

"More than I want my heart to keep pumping my body with blood."

His eyes tell me all I need to know. That this is an 'I love you' fuck, not an 'I hate you' fuck, but from the outsider's view, no one would know.

Except us—we will know. This is all about our complicated love story.

Zeke's hands dance one by one down my bare back. I tense with each touch, trying to keep the ecstasy off my face. Zeke has the power to fucking demolish me with one kiss. One kiss could change everything. *If he had kissed Kai and I'd walked in, how would I feel?*

Devastated.

Despondent.

So lost and broken.

The fact that Zeke can sit here and hold me right now, that he wants to kiss and fuck me, just shows that he is the better person. He's so much better than I am. So much better.

His hand continues down until he touches the zipper of my dress. I think he's going to unzip it, reveal more of my skin, but he doesn't.

I lick my lips and lean back toward him, begging for a kiss. I would beg on my knees if it meant he would kiss me.

Instead, Zeke's eyes darken as he grabs my chin. "You think I want to kiss your mouth after you kissed him?" He chuckles darkly. Then his hand goes up my back, until he's fisting my hair, pulling my head back roughly, exposing my neck and chest to him.

His teeth bite on my clavicle like he's a goddamn vampire. Apparently, I'm into vampires because my insides flood with desire and an ache only Zeke can cause.

"Did Enzo turn you on like this?" Zeke asks roughly, even though he already knows the answer.

"No."

Zeke kisses up my neck, and his hand pushes into my bra, finding my nipple and pinching it harshly. "Did he touch you like this?"

"No," I gasp, feeling too good. My head falls back on Zeke's chest. There is no way Bishop's spies wouldn't think I'm enjoying every second of this. But Zeke's dark eyes, gruff voice, and anger might save us. There is no denying his pain etched into every hard line of his face.

Suddenly, Zeke jerks us up off the bench and bends me over the piano. My hands bang against the keys as I hold on. Zeke is bent over me. His hands are gliding down my body, claiming every part of me. "Did you fuck him?"

"No."

Zeke pushes my dress up over my ass, and then he's yanking my panties down, his finger finding how wet I am as he dips slowly inside me, teasing me but not giving me what I want.

"Did you get wet for him?"

"No, only you."

"Damn right. You are mine."

He slaps my ass hard. This isn't for show. This is because he's angry.

I hear his zipper, but Zeke is still clothed. He's going to fuck me with his clothes on. He's going to fuck me without letting me touch him.

"Zeke, I need—" I try to reach back, but he grabs my wrists. He yanks them behind my back, pulling roughly until my shoulders ache at the tension.

And then his cock is pushing at me. But he's not pushing at my entrance. He's pushing at my ass.

"Zeke," I warn. I'm terrified Julian is going to end up back in my head again, all my trauma flooding back. I want to be here with Zeke, not trapped in my nightmares.

He keeps my hands pulled back. My legs are spread for him, and my ass is his for the taking. I feel his cock so hard at my back entrance.

He puts his hand in front of my lips. "Spit."

I do, watching his eyes eat the sight of me. I hear him coat himself with my saliva.

One of his hands grips my hair, the other my wrists, and his cock pushes against my asshole.

His lips find my ear. "I love you, but I need to punish you. Your lips are mine."

"You are such a bastard. You're just trying to find an excuse to fuck my ass," I say back.

His lips cover mine, but he doesn't kiss me. "You know I am." For a second, his face lightens as he winks at me, just for me, not for whoever could be spying on us from the dozens of ships nearby. Kai and Enzo have loyal employees, but I don't doubt that one of them is working for Julian or Bishop, and they're taking pictures to report.

When Zeke removes his face from mine, his eyes have darkened again. It looks likes he's taking from me, raping me, even though he's giving me everything he has. I know when we get to the privacy of the bedroom, he will kiss me sweetly and make me come with his tongue, but this is what is needed now. A show for Bishop. An angry fuck for us.

And then he pushes inside, squeezing his large cock inside my ass, stretching me so damn wide.

"No!" I scream, because it's fucking fun to pretend. Thankfully, Julian isn't in my head. The pain drove him from my mind.

My eyes water for real as he pushes into me, claiming me in a new way. But then one of his hands sneaks between my legs, one finger teasing my clit and another sliding into my pussy. It feels so incredibly delicious. I've never felt more connected to him, more like his than I do now.

"You like that, baby?" Zeke growls his voice torn between the truth and the lie.

"No," I strain back, my teeth tightly grinding together.

There is a flash of worry in Zeke's eyes, so I make mine extra wild to show I'm acting. We should have come up with a safeword.

His jaw ticks as he studies me, finally realizing the truth.

"I'm going to fuck you so hard you won't even dare look at another man."

I nod, and he makes good on his threat.

He fucks and thrusts and pushes so hard that I feel like I'm going to burst.

"I hate these damn names on your neck," Zeke says after a dozen thrusts.

He grabs a shard of glass and slices through my skin, making it look worse for the cameras, but I love him for crossing out the names, his included.

"You belong to yourself, but I hope you freely give yourself to me over and over."

"I do," I say, my finger twisting my wedding ring behind my back so Zeke can see.

And then we both come. His is a ferocious growl of taking what he wants. Mine is a cry of being claimed. Both are an act of love. An act I hope we repeat over and over again.

CHAPTER 26
ZEKE

I don't know how to react when I'm done fucking Siren. I want to wrap her in my arms and never let her go. But that isn't what I should be doing for Bishop's little bitch of a spy watching us.

For him, I should spank Siren's ass and drag her kicking and screaming to my room. I don't want that kiss with Enzo to go to waste. I don't want anything to get in the way of Bishop fixing Siren. I need her whole. I need her brain clear of his thoughts and commands.

If Siren is going to listen to a man, I want it to be me, not that that is likely either. Siren will always be in control of her own life. I will always be chasing after her, hoping I'm enough for her.

But right now, I have to take the lead. So I grab one of Siren's wrists and yank her away from the piano. She tries to smooth her dress down, but I pull her tightly to my body until she is no longer thinking about her dress. She's only thinking about me.

Siren looks at me like I'm her whole world, and I smirk internally. *How did she trick me into so many lies for so long?* She's horrible at this acting thing. It's plain as day that Siren is in love with me, even now.

Then, I'm pulling Siren down the stairs to our bedroom. I yank her inside and throw the door shut before kissing her hard against the door.

She gasps like I'm stealing all of her oxygen.

I moan like she's stealing all of my everything.

Her tongue slices through my mouth, and I know where this is headed, but we don't have time. We have to focus on our tasks at hand.

"Siren, baby, we can't," I moan, not believing that I'm turning down this woman.

She runs her hand through my hair, stroking my face. "I know."

But we don't stop. We kiss and kiss and kiss. I carry her to the shower, turning on the water to clean myself off before I fuck her.

And then, her legs are wrapped around me, my pants are shoved down to my ankles, her dress is hiked up to her waist, and I'm sliding between her wet folds.

"What are you doing to me?" I moan, my brain foggy and unable to remember the important task I should be doing.

"Showing you how good loving me can feel," she whispers back before grabbing my ass and pushing me all the way in.

Her ass felt nice, and it was a good excuse to fuck her there, but there is nothing like fucking her pussy, where I belong.

I fuck her under the water. There is a nice warm bed three feet away, but we never make it that far. We fuck here, in the shower, water beading down our bodies.

It feels like goodbye.

"This isn't goodbye," I grind into her, feeling all of her slickness, all of her tightness, all of her.

"I know," she whispers sadly. Her lips kiss mine tenderly.

I stop. "I'm not going to keep fucking you until I believe you."

Her eyes stop as she takes a deep breath. And then they are memorizing every part of my body. Every scar, every mark, every ripple of muscle. She's watching everything. Her hands move over where her eyes roamed, feeling everything so that if her eyes fail her, her fingers will remember.

I grab her hands. "Siren, stop."

"No, there is no guarantee of tomorrow. No guarantee of five seconds from now. No guarantee of forever."

"We promised forever."

"I know, but we don't get to decide how long our forever lasts. We don't get to know."

I kiss her hand. "That doesn't mean we should just give up."

"I'm not giving up; I'm making sure our forever lasts longer by taking it with me. No matter what separates us, this I will remember."

"Nothing is going to separate us." But it's a lie. I feel it to my bones. I know what we are both capable of doing for love. I know what is coming. I know what dangers are lurking just out our window. And I know this could be goodbye for now.

So I soak up everything about Siren too. Every curve, every line, every soft smile. I feel all of her warm skin. I remember every feminine smell.

I start moving, gliding in and out of her, and I memorize all of that too. I don't need to memorize how she looks or sounds when she comes. I already remember it all. This time will be like all the rest and become a part of me forever.

I try to stall as long as I can. I try to make our orgasms slow and stretch out the release we both want, but it's wishful thinking. There is no way to hold our orgasms back. Our bodies need them as much as we need our next breath. Our bodies will fall over the cliff whether I help us along or not.

I thrust again and we are both orgasming in a beautiful melody that has become our own song.

Just don't let our love fall. Those were the words she sang before. I never intend to. But somehow, when we both come down from our high, it feels like our love is falling down too.

"I need to go warn Kai that Bishop and Julian are coming, so we can put our plan into motion," I say.

"I'll be here," Siren responds.

I kiss her on the cheek, set her down, dry off, and get dressed. Siren heads into the closet with a towel around her body and comes out wearing jeans, a black shirt, and a thick leather jacket. I'm sure she's covered in knives and guns, ready for them to attack at any minute.

"You think they are going to attack tonight?" I ask. "Or are you planning on sleeping in leather?"

"I don't know when they are going to attack, but Bishop wants me to meet him at five in the morning."

I nod. "You aren't leaving this room, though. I'll come get you at five to meet Bishop. Promise me you won't fight unless the battle comes to you. You have our baby to protect."

"I won't leave this room until you come for me. I won't fight unless I have to."

"Thank you." I walk over to her, then lean down and kiss her stomach, where I still can't believe she's growing our baby.

"Go," Siren says, basically pushing me out the door to get me to leave.

Once outside the door, I process what just happened. *Did I just say goodbye to Siren? Is the battle really starting now?*

Fuck, I need to find Kai and get ready.

I don't know where Kai went. She said she was going to another yacht, but I know her. She didn't go anywhere. I wander around on the yacht, not finding any sign of her. I know she didn't go back to bed. And then I spot Enzo, sitting on the edge of one of the decks looking out at the ocean.

I'm not ready to forgive him. I know why Siren seduced him, tricked him, whatever the hell happened. But he let it happen. He didn't know she was doing it to try and get her life back. He let her kiss him, knowing how deeply that knife would hurt all of us.

But I don't want him dead. Tomorrow, I can forgive him. Today, I just want him fighting by me, alive.

"They're coming," I say, giving him a tight look.

He nods. He doesn't ask for forgiveness. He just cracks his neck and then reaches for the gun on him, holding it close.

"Where is she?" I ask.

He nods forward. He's watching Kai from afar, ensuring her safety while giving her the space she needs.

I doubt she'll want to talk to me either, but she doesn't have a choice.

I hop down onto the lower deck and find Kai sitting with her feet dangling over the edge as she leans back against the railing. One wrong move could send her into the ocean below. She has a lit cigar in her hand, but she's not smoking it, just smelling it.

I sigh. Of course, she has to be sitting on the edge of the yacht, where my big ass is going to struggle to sit.

I walk over, and I know she can sense me. "Any chance you want to climb on this side of the railing for this talk, Stingray?"

"No way in hell. Your stupid ass plan is why I'm sitting here in the first place," Kai says.

I laugh and then take my time climbing over the railing. I grip it as I sink down until I'm sitting next to her. I loop my arms through the railing behind me as my ass doesn't fit on the tiny lip Kai is sitting on.

"It wasn't my plan," I say.

She laughs manically. "Don't lie to me, Zeke. I know that plan had something to do with helping Siren. It was something Bishop wanted her to do. Something that would save her. I'm not mad at you for doing it, but don't lie to me and say you didn't know. That's why you went with me to prepare all the men for war."

I sigh. "Yes, I knew Siren was going to do something Bishop wanted. But I didn't realize it had anything to do with Enzo and definitely didn't know it involved kissing him."

She shakes her head. "You would have let them kiss again if it meant saving Siren."

"I guess."

She sniffs one of Enzo's cigars. "I'm not ready to forgive him, or you, or her. I know it was just a kiss, but in this world, we face so many dangers. I just thought I'd never have to worry about Enzo's loyalty. I never thought I'd be faced with him kissing another woman with her hand in his pants. I never thought that was even a worry I needed to have. I thought our relationship was invincible."

"It is. You don't have to worry about Enzo's loyalties. Siren tricked him. That's kind of one of her main skill sets," I say.

"It doesn't matter. He still kissed her."

"No, she kissed him against his will. She manipulated us as much as she did Enzo. She made you believe he was willing; he wasn't."

Kai looks out at the dark ocean, several yachts visible just as dots in the distance.

"You don't have to forgive Siren, or me for my part in all of this. But you do need to forgive Enzo, just not until after tomorrow."

"Why?"

"Because you love him."

Kai shakes her head. "No, I mean, why not until tomorrow?"

"Because they are coming. The battle is here. In the next couple of hours, for sure by morning. They think we are fighting. They think we are weak. Let them think that."

I reach over and give her hand a tight squeeze. "Don't let this affect you, Stingray. The kiss meant nothing."

"You forgave her already, didn't you?"

I nod. "Our lives are too short not to forgive. It doesn't matter what she does. I'm not saying I would stay with her if she changed, if she started abusing me or something. But I will forgive her when she makes a mistake, especially one she did to save my child from herself."

I climb back over the railing.

"Alaska," Kai says, giving me a knowing look, telling me where the box is. She trusts me, and now I carry the burden of knowing too. "I don't forgive you or Siren because there is nothing to forgive. I would kill you all if I had to in order to protect my kids. I don't fault you for doing the same thing."

I nod, and start heading back to Siren, for a few last moments together.

I see the shadow before I hear him. He's here. On the ship. Trying to sneak around in the night.

"We need to talk. We can end this war before it even starts," Julian says. *Don't talk, kill him.*

I turn and fire.

I hear the fire of a gun, and I know Zeke isn't coming back. The battle has started, and I'm stuck here feeling useless until it ends.

It's two in the morning, three hours until Bishop told me to meet him to undo what he fucked up in my head. *What if he's killed before then? What if Zeke is?*

I can't think. I need to shut my brain down. I need to disappear inside myself. I need to focus on finding a way to fight Bishop off from within. That's the way to ensure our victory—by not needing Bishop to fix me in the first place.

But it's not just Bishop I have to worry about.

It's Julian.

And Bishop.

And even Zeke.

All three men have tried to control me. All men have the power to manipulate me.

Julian Reed has taken so much from me, but his power is now limited. He's already used his threat against me, so I know how bad it can get.

Bishop is just getting started, but I have a secret of my own where he is concerned. But that secret will destroy more than just me.

And Zeke Kane is a monster, my monster. He has so much grit and raw manliness inside him. So much darkness that he's always flittering between right and wrong. So far, he's always ended up on the side of good, *but will that always be the case?*

I hear all the men's voices in my head, and I realize Bishop isn't the only one who can control me in this way.

"You're mine," Julian says.

"You're mine," Bishop says.

"You're mine," Zeke says.

But I only want to be one man's.

"Do you? I thought you were a more independent woman than that, Siren? Why should any man own you at all?" Bishop asks in my head.

"No, don't you start. You don't care about me, you just want me to be loyal to you," I say.

"No, I want you to be loyal to yourself. Once you are, the commands I put in your head you will do willingly," Bishop continues.

Fuck.

No.

Stop thinking, Siren. Focus on the sounds. The gunfire. The bombs. The muffled sounds from this soundproof room.

Fuck, why did I promise Zeke I would stay in this room?

Why?

Why?

Why?

If Bishop wasn't already in my head, if Julian wasn't already haunting my dreams, I would think I'm going crazy. I know what crazy looks like, and fearing for everyone I love isn't it.

Yet, I feel myself going mad while I wait for Zeke to come to me. Waiting has never been my strong suit, but I made a promise. I grip my shirt over my stomach; it's not just me I have to worry about anymore.

So I sit on the edge of the bed and stare at the door—praying that it opens to a smiling Zeke.

Instead, I hear multiple men outside. I move to the security camera screen that points out to the door. I watch the men place something against the door, and then step back.

A bomb.

I stare at the camera—a five minute timer starts on the bomb. That's how long I have left in my prison. It's how long I have left to live. Zeke could save me—he could save us. *But at what cost?*

CHAPTER 28

ZEKE

"You missed. I thought you had better aim than that, boy," Julian says.

I frown. *What is it about this guy that I just can't kill him?*

Something deeper is holding me back. Something deep down is preventing me from killing him. *Something...*

"Why can't I kill you?" I ask, not meaning to admit that out loud, but saying it all the same.

Julian snickers. "You haven't figured it out yet?"

I frown. *How should I know?* I never miss. When I shoot, I kill. But with Julian, even when I'm aiming, I miss.

"Don't worry, your wife figured it out," Julian says.

I freeze. *How does he know?*

"I spotted your wedding ring. I assume there is a reason you are wearing it," Julian says.

"What do you want?"

"Just to let you know, I'll blow up your wife's bedroom if you don't hear me out. You and I have a deal, after all. One that you keep trying to run away from," Julian says, holding up his phone, showing me a picture of Siren's room with explosives on the door.

413

I feel the yacht jolt forward. I'm sure it's Julian's doing, trying to separate us from our fleet of men.

I growl, my anger palpating through me as I keep the gun aimed at Julian's head. "Don't touch her."

"I don't plan to. I have other, more important things, to get from you."

"Like?"

"You owe me two more sins or truths. But since you'll never tell me the truth, you can commit a sin," Julian says.

I frown, not liking this.

"Retrieve the box," Julian says, looking past me. I feel more people gathering around us on the main deck, and I don't have to look to know who is standing behind me—Kai and Enzo. Kai is to my left, Enzo my right.

"Welcome, everyone," Julian says.

I swallow.

"You're not getting away, not this time," Kai says.

"You thought your little games could break us up, not going to happen. We fight together," Enzo says.

"I'm always up for a good fight with my friends," Langston says.

Langston's voice gets me to turn. He's standing next to Enzo. He looks good, although a bit worn down and unshaven. He winks at me when I turn.

I exhale a breath. Everyone who needs to be here is here. We can figure out how to take him down, then hunt down Bishop and do the same to him. This time, they will all end up dead. We all point our guns at Julian.

"It's over. Let Siren go, and we'll make your death quick," I say.

Julian laughs. "I won't be the one dying tonight. But if I do, Siren will die at the same time."

I stiffen. He's holding his phone, showing a countdown until the bomb detonates.

I can't kill him until the bomb is disarmed.

"Go," I say to Langston.

And then he's gone to hopefully disarm the bomb in time.

Julian looks at his watch. "He has three minutes. Do you think he's fast enough? Because if I don't enter in the code by then, the bomb will go off."

"What do you want?"

"You have two sins left. Finish them, and I won't harm Siren. Finish them, and I'll let her live."

Julian is careful with his words. He doesn't promise me my life, just hers—it's enough. He knows that. He knows all I care about is making sure that she lives, that our baby lives.

"These last two sins are different than the rest—darker, more dangerous. Requiring more loyalty than you've given me so far," Julian's eyes seer.

Hurry up, Langston. I need Siren safe.

"Whatever it is, I'll do it," I say, no words I've ever spoken have been truer.

Julian nods. "Prove it."

"How?"

I cringe, knowing Kai and Enzo need to run because whatever he's going to have me do involves them.

"Kill Enzo," Julian says.

This is about loyalty. And time is ticking down. I turn and shoot, not giving Enzo or myself time to think. I aim for the shoulder, hoping it's enough to appease Julian.

Julian laughs as Kai shrieks.

"What's the final sin?" I ask, knowing we've already wasted a minute. I only have two minutes left to get this madman to turn off the bomb.

"That wasn't your sin. Just the test. And you failed."

"I shot him."

"I said *kill* him."

"If I kill him, that completes one of my two sins," I say, trying to come up with a way to save Enzo and Siren. An idea forms in my head for how to save Enzo. I don't love it, but it gives him a fighting chance.

Julian looks behind me. "Fine, kill Enzo Black, the leader of the great Black empire, and you'll only have one sin left."

I turn and look at Kai's pleading eyes as she holds onto the wound in Enzo's shoulder.

"Disarm the bomb, Julian," I say.

"Not until Enzo is dead."

A tear waters my eyes, knowing what I'm about to do. I turn, counting down my final sixty seconds that I have to do something until Siren dies. Julian will kill her this time if I don't do this, but I'm hoping Langston found a way to stop this before I get to her.

Sixty.

Fifty-nine.

Fifty-eight.

I walk over to Kai, who is leaning over Enzo's body. I look at her, searching her eyes for any solution that she has. She wants to fight. To shoot Julian and call his bluff. We were supposed to shoot him and Bishop the second we saw them. Well, Bishop isn't showing himself, and Julian, as always, is one step ahead of us.

Fifty.

Forty-nine.

Forty-eight.

I look down at Enzo, who gives me a tight nod avoiding his wife, knowing she's not going to let me do what I'm about to do easily. If she's pissed at Siren for kissing Enzo, she sure as hell will never speak to me again if I kill him.

Thirty.

Twenty-nine.

Twenty-eight.

"I'm sorry," I whisper to them both. I used to think I would never betray them. I would never choose anyone else above them. I was wrong.

Siren and our baby are the only things that matter to me. I'll save Kai and Enzo the best I can, but if I have to trade their lives to save Siren's and my baby, I will.

With a swift punch, I knock Kai back onto her ass, hitting her hard enough to temporarily knock her unconscious. I raise my gun and fire into Enzo, ensuring plenty of blood loss and show for Julian as I hit him in the gut. I pray I don't hit any vital organs.

Enzo growls as his eyes go to his wife, who is knocked out cold behind me.

"Bastard," Enzo curses, already weak from blood loss but still caring more about his wife than he does himself. *If I survive this fight with Julian, Enzo will kill me himself. Even if Enzo doesn't survive this, he'll come back as a ghost to kill me.*

I grab Enzo's hand and pull him to the edge of the yacht.

Twenty.

Nineteen.

Eighteen.

"We always said we'd die for those we love," I say.

Enzo nods. I push his almost lifeless body into the fast ocean current, much like when I was shot on his yacht and fell into the ocean. I was left to die. To drown.

I was inches away from death before Siren found me. I just hope Enzo doesn't have to wait as long as I did to be found.

Fifteen.

Fourteen.

Thirteen.

"Enzo's dead. Now disarm the bomb. Let Siren go."

Julian tsks. "He's not dead."

"Yet," I finish. "He's not dead yet, but I thought you'd prefer the great Enzo Black to suffer a long, torturous death. That's the death he deserves, not a clean bullet to the heart."

Ten.

Nine.

Eight.

God, please work. If I have to shoot Enzo in the head, though, I will. Just please don't make me.

Julian lifts his phone, considering.

Five.

Four.

Three.

Julian types in a code and then shows me the phone.

I exhale. He disarmed the bomb. Siren's safe.

"Now, where is the box? Get me to the box and unlock it, and I'll never lay a hand on Siren again," Julian says.

"Alaska, the box is in Alaska," I say, grateful that Kai told me a location, so I could use it now to save my wife.

Kai sits up, now wide awake. She glares at me as she dives overboard, racing to find Enzo.

"You're going to take me to Alaska and lead me to that box."

"I will," I say, betraying everyone but Siren. This is why I shouldn't have fallen in love.

Siren is my everything. I just ruined years of friendships. I possibly ended my friend's life. Siren tried to destroy a marriage. All to protect our own love.

I just chose a side. I chose Julian's. I am no longer loyal to the Black name. I'll do whatever Julian or Bishop want in order to protect Siren and my baby.

Julian ensured my loyalty, and I've never hated myself more.

"I'll take you to the box. I'll be loyal to you. But Siren stays here under Langton's protection. And if you lay a finger on her again, you'll wish you were dead."

Julian nods as I march downstairs.

I'm devastated by what I did, and even more wrecked by what I'm about to do.

CHAPTER 29
SIREN

I'm usually a fighter.

When I'm put in a horrible situation, I fight. But this time, I sit silently. I meditate, I pray, I hope.

I don't pray for myself.

I don't meditate for Zeke.

I hope that when we both die, this life inside me finds a way to live, to forgive us for not being enough.

The only way we save each other and this baby is by burning every city, every friend, every person to the ground. We turn them all to ash. Our love is too big. Our sins too great. We were never meant to love each other. I was wrong—I thought finding Zeke in that vast ocean was fate.

I thought it meant that we were meant to be.

That our love was supposed to find each other.

But it wasn't fate.

It wasn't destiny.

It was the devil taking a stab in the dark and pushing two people who have just enough darkness in their hearts together and then sitting back and watching the carnage they would inflict evolve.

I may not be able to see the future, but I can see ours. It ends in destruction—of us or our friends.

We've chosen us.

Over and over again.

It leaves us alone and in pain. Sure, we have each other. We love each other. *But is that enough? Is our love enough to survive on?*

No.

But if we choose our friends, can we live without love?

No.

We are at an impasse. We should have never found each other. We should have never have created this life.

I wait, trying to figure out which option Zeke chose—us or them.

I wait for the bomb or the quiet.

The door unlocks, and Zeke appears. He chose us.

My eyes water, not able to imagine the destruction he just caused and is yet to cause.

"I have to go," he says.

I nod, unable to speak, but agreeing. I break.

"I know," Zeke says, knowing what's already in my heart.

"I know, Siren, I know."

He steps closer.

"I'm sorry," I say, breaking more inside.

"I'm not." He lifts me until we are both standing together.

"Our love was never meant to last forever," Zeke says, his own tears dripping down onto our joined hands.

"But we promised. We vowed. We loved—forever," I say, my words broken and painful.

"We kept those promises," Zeke says.

We kiss. One last kiss to last the lifetime never meant to be.

Our rings touch, rings that represent a marriage that was never real. One that was only ever real to us.

He walks toward the door, and it's then that I realize I don't know the truth anymore. I don't know if he's doing this on his own accord or because Julian demands it. *I don't know if this is a truth, a lie, or a sin?*

I'll find out, though. If there is a chance this is all a sin, then I still have a chance at my happily ever after.

Tears are falling fast now, so painful and real they wreck my entire body, shaking me until I can barely stand.

"I have to go, but you'll be safe—always and forever. Nothing will ever change that." Zeke moves his head, and then he's pushing a man inside my room. "This is my best friend, Langston. He'll protect you, no matter what."

I freeze.

I can't think.

I don't hear the rest of Zeke's words.

I can't process them.

I can't believe what is happening.

I can't believe what I'm seeing.

I can't...

I try to find Zeke. I try to find the words to tell him. To explain to him what is happening. But I can't.

I fucking can't.

By the time I do, Zeke is gone. All that is left is Langston—a man I know very well.

A man who isn't Langston at all.

Langston is dead, at least, his soul is.

Langston is the man who has been haunting my dreams.

He's the man who can control my thoughts.

Bishop—Langston Bishop—my own personal nightmare.

I run to the door and try to get past him. Zeke couldn't have gone far.

But Langston Bishop grabs me as I try to move past.

"Zeke!" I yell and cry. He either doesn't hear my call or chooses not to listen.

My entire body trembles with fear and pain. I'm having a panic attack. I can't breathe, as Bishop throws me on the bed.

"Zeke's gone. You're finally free. Free of love, of pain," Bishop says.

I don't feel free at all, though. I feel loss. Zeke just sacrificed everything and left me alone with the one man who hijacked my mind.

My eyes widen at the thought of everything else we're about to lose.

BROKEN ANCHOR

PROLOGUE
ZEKE

How far will I go for love?

That's the question that stays with me as I float, bobbing up and down over waves that could easily consume me. I've been here before; been in this same dire situation. Felt like I can't breathe, like this is the end.

My blood is slipping from my body. My ribs are tightening around my lungs like a vise grip. My head is raging in a bone-spitting headache from all the pain I feel.

The only pain I care about, though, emanates from my heart.

Last time I was here, in the darkness of night, in the middle of the vast ocean, I was content. I was dying to save Kai and Enzo, my family, those I love.

This time, I'm dying to save my one true love.

I thought I knew what dying for someone felt like. But this—this is so much more. This is different. This is what I was put on this earth to do—to die protecting someone I love.

I've always been a protector.

That is who I am.

I could change careers, but it wouldn't change who I am. I, Zeke Kane, am a protector. I am only me when I'm protecting others.

I've protected many people in my life—sacrificed over and over again. But I've never risked it all like I did to protect Siren.

I've never hurt someone I love in order to protect Siren.

Never sinned like I did to protect Siren.

I would do it all again.

I would end up right here back in this ocean if it meant I got to love Siren like I did. That I got the honor of protecting her, saving her, even though she didn't need me to save her. She never did; she was always enough for herself.

She tried to tell me all along—trust her, let her save herself. That way, I wouldn't have to give up myself.

Siren didn't understand that I wanted to give up everything for her. The only way I could love her was to love her with everything, even knowing that our love would destroy everything.

For a moment, Siren thought I turned my back on our love. She thought I was ashamed of what I did. It took her all of five minutes to figure out my lie.

I would never turn my back on our love. And I would do all the horrible sins over again, if it were the only way to keep her and our unborn child safe.

My only regret is that I can't love her forever. That I have to give her up. That one day she will find another man to make her happy. And when I haunt her ass from hell, I won't even be upset that she found happiness. She's made so many sacrifices; she deserves all the happiness in the world.

It makes dying easier—knowing that Siren gets to live. I will take her sins with me when I die. She will get to live in truth, in love, in happiness.

How far am I willing to go for love?

Too far.

How much am I willing to break?

All the way.

We've all sinned.

Enzo.

Kai.

Langston.

Liesel.

Siren.

Me.

All of us.

We've all hurt each other in unforgivable ways while protecting those we hold dearest. And that's the way it should be. None of us hold grudges for what Enzo did to protect Kai. What Langston did for Liesel. Or what I did for Siren.

In the end, we protect our own.

We all do what has to be done to protect the love of our lives.

We are all a family. And we fix our mistakes.

I'm leaving this earth knowing my family forgives me for the sins I've caused.

And I forgive them. All of them.

In a game of truth or sin, we all chose sin.

The truth broke us.

Love destroyed us.

Sin saved us.

How far will I go for love?

As far as it takes...

CHAPTER 1
ZEKE

Siren is safe.

My child is safe.

They are safe.

That's what I repeat over and over again as I step into the helicopter following Julian. That's the only thing keeping my feet moving.

I walked away from Siren. We hardly spoke before I left her, but we both knew what it meant. That I wasn't coming back—either because I'll die protecting my family or do something so horrible that Siren won't want me back.

It's a lie.

It's all a lie.

I can pretend all I want that I'll die in battle with Julian, or that the best thing for Siren is to live without me. I tell myself I can stand to leave her to find a new man—one who hasn't murdered for her.

Lies.

Siren is my everything. The reason I'm still alive. The reason I'm getting into this damn helicopter.

And as for the sins I've committed, I would commit them all again. I would shoot Enzo again. I would betray my friends again. I would betray every person on this planet in order to protect Siren and my child.

If that makes me a monster, so be it. I'm a monster. I'm a horrible friend. I've betrayed everyone who was ever good to me.

I look at the man standing in front of me—a man smirking like he's won. Julian Reed is the devil. But when I put a bullet into Enzo, not knowing if he was going to survive or not, I became the devil too. It doesn't matter that I was doing it to save us. It doesn't matter that I shot him to protect Siren. It doesn't matter that I did everything in my power to ensure that Enzo lives.

I shot one of my best friends.

Then I shoved him over the edge of the yacht and left him to die.

My stomach tightens, threatening to spill at the thought.

No, Enzo Black is alive. I did everything I could to protect my friend. He's alive. Kai will find him. She'll realize what we did.

I won't have to ask for Enzo or Kai's forgiveness this time, but what if there's a next time? How far will I go for Siren?

As far as it takes to keep her safe.

Which is why I'm here, on Julian's helicopter, committing my loyalty to him. It's why I left Siren alone—to fulfill my destiny to protect her and our baby at all costs.

So I'm going to do this. I'm going to help Julian. Then, I'm going to kill Julian, Bishop, and any other man who threatens to hurt Siren or my baby. Finally, I'm going to spend the rest of my life loving Siren like it's my job, my reason for existence. And I don't care how many people we burn with our love.

I strap myself into the seat next to Julian in the second row. The propellers spin overhead, buzzing loudly in my ear. I pick up head-phones and cover my ear, muting the sound.

We lift off, and my heart cracks, leaving Siren behind.

She's safe.

Our baby is safe.

That's why I'm doing this—to keep her safe.

Langston will protect her as well as I could. He'll get her the fuck away from all the danger.

Kai and Enzo will come. They will fight. They are too invested not to.

But Siren will be safe with Langston. He promised me he would keep her safe. He has no one else to live for, so he'll live for her. Protect her like he loves her.

I thought Langston was in love with Liesel. I thought he would be the next to get his happily ever after. I guess I was wrong.

But I trust that Langston will keep his word.

I glance down, my first mistake. Siren is on the top deck of the yacht, staring up at me with so much pain and sadness in her eyes.

I had to, baby. I had to give up myself to keep you safe. I had to turn into a monster, the devil. You can be a little devilish too. And when I return, our darkness will blend together. We will heal each other.

She grips her biceps as if holding herself back from running after me. It's not like she has another option; she can't chase after a helicopter on foot. Although, I wouldn't put it past her to dive into the ocean and swim stride for stride keeping up with the helicopter. That's how incredible she is.

I look at her sternly out the window. *This sacrifice will all be for nothing if you follow me. Stay safe. Protect our baby.*

Her eyes tell me I'm wrong. Her eyes tell me I've made a mistake.

She screams, I think, or maybe she sings. I can't tell from the whirl of the helicopter blades. But I can feel her pain hit my heart.

I know, baby. I know. This will all be over soon, though. Just wait a little longer.

I watch as Langston walks up behind her.

She's safe. I glare at him with my most dangerous threat. *If you survive and she doesn't, the first thing I'm going to do is kill you.*

Langston smirks, but there is a heaviness behind his eyes.

What am I missing?

Nothing. I'm just being paranoid—Siren is safe with Langston.

Julian leans his head to look out the window, and then he looks back at me. He does this over and over again. And then he's chuckling, wildly, madly. His wretched chuckle rings in my ear thanks to the headphones we are using to communicate with each other.

"What's so funny?" I ask, assuming he's not going to tell me.

"Who is that man standing behind Aria?" Julian asks.

I frown. "Langston."

"Bishop," Julian says simultaneously.

It all clicks.

Everything I've been too stupid to see. The reason that Langston has been gone this whole time. It's not because he was chasing after a girl. It's because he was busy working with Julian. He was busy turning on his friends, betraying us all in a way that makes me shooting Enzo look like exchanging friendship bracelets instead of the stark betrayal it was.

Langston is working with our enemy. What he did to Siren's head. What he could have done to her body. Tricking me into thinking he will protect her instead of using her in some grand scheme with Julian Reed.

"You bastard," I curse as I try to figure out my next move. Apparently, my next move is choking the man next to me; consequences be dammed. I can't actually kill Julian, though. This was his security plan all along—have Langston, or Bishop, whoever he is, watch Siren and hurt or kill her if I don't do as Julian says.

So I can't kill Julian, but I can hurt him a little.

Julian shakes his head, and that's when I realize the man sitting next to the pilot has a gun on my head.

I release him.

"You promised Siren would be safe," I bark as I unhook my seatbelt even though a gun is still pointed at my head.

I have to get to Siren. She's not safe. Not with that lying asshole. He hurt her already. He fucked with her head. I never thought I would want to kill a man who I grew up with. A man that a few moments ago, I would have done anything to protect. Langston is like a brother to me. But Langston is dead. Bishop took over.

Why? What happened to turn him into this cruel man?

I don't know.

And I don't care. I just want to put a bullet in his head for hurting Siren. Just like I want to burn Julian at the stake for raping her.

Before I think it through, I have the door of the helicopter open, and I'm staring down at the ocean below. We've flown far enough away from Siren and Langston that I can barely make them out in the distance. We are flying too high above the ocean. If I jump, there is no guarantee that I'll survive.

Fuck.

I grab the gun out of the asshole's hand in the front seat and have it aimed at Julian so fucking fast.

Julian just grins. We've been here so many times. And he knows just like all the others, I won't pull the trigger. If he dies, there is nothing stopping Bishop from killing Siren a second later.

"Turn this helicopter around," I say.

"You really think I planned this?"

"Yes. You two have been working together this whole time. Turn this the fuck around. I didn't agree to work for you while you let your guard dog watch Siren and kill her if I put one toe out of line."

Julian considers his next words carefully, which puts me on edge. *Is he concocting a lie? Or trying to figure out some way to prevent me from killing him?*

"Turn this helicopter around now. Or I'll kill you and your men, then turn the helicopter around myself. This wasn't part of our arrangement. I work for you; Siren is safe. This is the opposite of Siren being safe."

"Bishop doesn't work for me."

"Bullshit."

Julian laughs. "Really? Bishop, or Langston, whatever his name is, was loyal to you a lot longer than he's ever been loyal to me. What makes you think his loyalty lies with me and not you?"

"The fact that he hurt Siren."

A sly grin works its way over Julian's features. His words only had one goal—get me to remember just how dangerous Bishop is; realize just how much danger Siren is in.

"Shoot me and find out whose side Bishop is on."

I hold the gun right up to his forehead. He doesn't try to bat my hand away. He knows that even though Bishop is definitely on Julian's side now, I can't shoot Julian. It's too risky. I can't kill Julian, kill the two men in the front of this helicopter, and return to Siren before Bishop kills her.

Bishop staying with Siren is their insurance policy that I behave. That I do what they want. That I hurt everyone I love for them.

"Tell Bishop to let Siren go."

Julian cracks his neck. So cavalier with his own life. So sure that I won't kill him. I won't kill him today, but it doesn't mean I won't kill him soon. His day is coming. And then I'll commit the ultimate sin, and I'll enjoy every second of it.

"Tell him," I command, my threat clear in my voice.

"No."

I fire, purposefully grazing the top of his head, so the bullet only burns over his hair, searing it and leaving a permanent mark on the top of his head, but not seriously wounding him.

But it does what I intended—send fear into him. Fear that I will actually kill him.

I kill the man in the passenger seat, and then I shoot the pilot before I jump out of the helicopter, grabbing the landing gear under the helicopter and hanging from it.

I know that if Siren can see me, I'm probably causing her a heart attack right now. So I hope that she can't. For once, I hope that Bishop has her tied her up in a bedroom or the yacht has turned and driven far enough away that she can't see me.

I don't have time to think about Siren right now. I'm dangling from the bottom of a helicopter that is going down, at least until Julian gets into the pilot's seat and takes control.

I have to time this just right. I have to wait until the helicopter has descended far enough down that it is safe for me to jump, but not wait too long so that Julian has gained control again and started ascending.

I stare at the dark ocean beneath me getting closer with each second. I know we need to be at least 200 feet in order for me to jump safely and have a good chance at survival.

Just a little lower.

Come on.

I glance up, but all I can see is the bottom of the helicopter. I have no idea what is happening inside. I don't know how close Julian is to getting control of the helicopter.

So close. Just...

The helicopter starts yanking up. This is my chance.

I'll do anything to keep Siren safe. Including risking my own life.

I let go.

Falling, having no idea if I'm close enough to the water to safely jump, but I risk it.

I don't have a choice.

If I don't jump, if I don't do everything I can to protect Siren, I might as well die. Siren is my only reason for living.

The three-second fall seems to last a lot longer. In that time, I think about everything.

Every sin Siren and I have committed against each other.

Every sin we've committed for each other.

I think about our unborn child.

Cayden.

He has Siren's eyes. And my chin.

He has the name of a hero. A name that gives him the power to fight.

Siren and I haven't talked names, and I don't even know if the child she carries is a boy or a girl. But the name is clear in my mind when I hit the water.

It's clear when I sink twenty feet under the water.

It's clear when I kick my legs, propelling my body up.

It's clear when I take a deep breath after I crack the surface.

Cayden.

The name means fighter.

He's my fighter.

If fighting to protect Siren wasn't enough, now I have a second reason. I may not be strong enough to protect everyone—Siren, my son, and my extended family. But my son is. Siren is.

I'll do everything I can to protect them—everything.

CHAPTER 2
SIREN

I stand on the deck, watching the helicopter fly away with Zeke and the devil. I'm left with a man who might be worse than the devil.

"Come on," Bishop says.

I laugh at his craziness. "Just like that, huh? You think you can control me because you've fucked with my head. Given me endless nightmares. You're going to have to do better than that."

"No, I won't."

"Yes, you will. You'll have to drug me. Tie me up. Because unless you are taking me to go after my husband, I'm not coming with you."

"Your husband, huh?"

I frown, folding my arms over my chest as I glare at Bishop, flashing him my wedding ring.

Bishop doesn't react. "So sure of your love. So sure of his." It's not a question. He says it because he knows it's how I feel. He's mocking me, acting like I shouldn't be sure about anything, definitely not my love for Zeke and his love for me.

We stare at each other in an unspoken standoff.

"Have I ever hurt you, Siren?"

"Yes."

"You sure about that?" His brows raise, and a wicked grin flicks across his lips.

What is he getting at? Have I imagined everything he's done to me?

I try to think, but as soon as I do, my head clouds. The more I think about what Bishop did, the foggier it gets.

"You hurt me. You tortured me. You fucked with my head."

Bishop nods. "If you are sure..."

He's playing games. Don't fall for it. He's fucking with my head. I need to do the same back.

"How could you do it? How could you betray your best friend?"

He gets in my face. A gentle rage flows from his body as he crowds me, but doesn't touch me. "How could you betray the man you love?"

I suck in a breath.

My world spins on its axis. *Have I judged Bishop wrongly this whole time? Has he just been doing what he had to do to survive? To keep us safe? To make Julian think he was on his side? Or is he manipulating me now to get what he wants? To get me to go with him without a fight?*

"Who are you?"

"You already know." Tension leaves him as he speaks.

"Are you Bishop or Langston?"

His lips thin, and he turns, walking away from me as he heads inside the yacht.

I follow.

He goes into the bridge, starts the engines, and starts driving us away. I don't try to stop him.

"Are you good or evil?"

He chuckles. "Really? What are we, five? You of all people know there is no such thing as a person being all good or all evil."

I do, but I also know that every person still thinks of themselves as all good or all evil. Good people sometimes do bad things, and evil people sometimes do good. But in our deepest hearts, we all see ourselves as one or the other.

How does Bishop see himself?

He isn't going to tell me, at least not right now.

"Where are we going?"

"Where do you think?"

I shrug. "I honestly don't know. I don't know who you are or what to think of you."

"We are going to get the box with the vials of cancer virus and cure in it."

I frown.

"No."

"You're not the one in charge. You won't be making the decisions. All the decisions you made were wrong anyway."

"What's that supposed to mean?"

"You working for Julian and hurting Zeke—it doesn't seem like the kind of thing a person does if they love someone."

My blood boils. I charge at him.

"How dare you!" I hit him. I meant to just slap him, but it becomes a punch. I don't think about all the reasons I shouldn't be punching him. I just punch. I fight. *How dare he question my love for Zeke!* He has no idea how hard it was. No idea what I've done to save Zeke.

"I love Zeke with everything! Everything I've done has been to protect him! Don't you understand that? The only two men I've ever made a vow to were my ex-husband and Zeke. I promised Julian every-thing to keep Zeke alive. Julian can't kill Zeke!"

Bishop grabs my wrists, stopping me from throwing another punch. It dawns on me that he never punched me back. He never stopped me. He took every punch. He let me hurt him.

Why?

Who is Langston Bishop? I doubt Bishop is Langston's last name. Zeke and Kai and Enzo would have gotten suspicious at the first mention of Bishop's name if so. But in my head, this man standing in front of me is both Langston and Bishop. Both good and bad. More bad than good, but there is a part of him that was once good. A part that was once loyal to Enzo Black. To Kai Black. To Zeke Kane.

I just have to find that man again.

Who are you? I think as I stare up at the man still gripping my wrists with force, but not hard enough to hurt me, just enough to prevent me from hitting him again.

"A man you are going to have to trust if you want to survive this," he answers.

I thought I asked the question in my head, but apparently not. That, or he can now read my thoughts.

I jerk my wrists out of his. "There is no way I'll ever trust a man who has hurt me."

Langston Bishop looks at me with a stern gaze. Somehow he seems taller, his shoulders broader, his intensity deeper. Zeke is a giant among men. Langston's blonde hair, fair skin, and slimmer build make me think he was once the light. The casual man. The playboy, if I understood correctly from everyone's stories about him.

Right now, Langston Bishop is the opposite of light. He's darkness.

But so are you, Siren...

He shrugs his shoulders and rolls his eyes at me, pretending to not care whether or not I trust him, but it's a front. The darkness, the pain is covering something deeper. It could be darker, more evil than the shield he's wearing like armor, or it could be the light that he long ago buried.

He shakes his head. "This is all your fault, you know?"

I frown. "My fault. Really? I was blackmailed by Julian. Basically sold to him by my ex-husband. I was tortured by you. Raped by Julian. Trust me, none of this is my fault."

He snickers as if he has a secret so obvious he can't believe I haven't realized it yet.

"What?" I ask, needing to understand, needing the truth.

"It doesn't matter that you didn't want any of it. Neither did Helen of Troy, and yet a war was fought for her."

"I'm not Helen of Troy."

"No, you're a siren—much more dangerous. You are capable of destroying us all if you wanted to."

I frown. I agree. I could hurt them all. Kill them all. I know how powerful I can be when I'm angry. I know the depths I will go if I'm pushed. If I had wanted to kill them all, then they would already be dead.

I was the only one who could have killed Julian Reed in the beginning. Instead, I found a different way to save Zeke, and in the end, it could cost us all our lives.

"Which is why I'm glad you're on my team," Langston Bishop says, turning back toward the helm, and we start moving again.

"I'm not on your team."

"Yes, you are. We all want the same thing—the box. Whoever has it wins the war. I know you wouldn't have chosen me as your partner. Trust me, you are the last person I would have chosen as well, but this is where the cards lay. We all go after the box. Julian and Zeke, Kai and Enzo, you and me. Once we win, then we can figure out which of us gets to use it."

"I'm not on your side. And I'm not going to help you steal the box. It belongs to Kai and Enzo."

"You'll help because you love him. There is no way you won't help."

Langston Bishop doesn't believe me. He's going to drag me into the middle of a fight I have no business being in. I can't fight when I have another life to worry about.

"You're wrong."

"I'm not."

"I'm pregnant."

Langston cuts the engine at my words and slowly turns to face me with shock on his face. His brain is working into overdrive, trying to figure out what to do with this information—with me.

"Who knows?" he asks, staring down at my stomach, and trying to figure out how he missed the swell of my stomach before.

"Everyone."

His teeth grind together. I don't know why it matters who knows. Everyone knowing is a good thing. It means that only the cruelest would attack a pregnant woman, and I'm not even sure Julian is that evil.

"Julian?" he asks.

I shrug. "I doubt it unless Zeke told him."

Langston Bishop's eyes move side to side as he thinks. "Good, make sure to keep it that way."

"Why? Why does it matter if Julian knows?"

"Because he'll either try to claim it as his own or kill it." His words are solemn like it hurts him to say them, which confuses me even more. He turns back and starts moving us away again.

He doesn't order me around.

He doesn't tell me what to do.

He said we were teammates.

I'm more confused than ever.

I need to remember everything that Langston Bishop has done to me. I need to remember how he fucked with my head. I need him to fix me. I need to run and hide until the danger is over.

I brush my hand over my stomach, where my baby resides. It still doesn't feel real.

I will protect my baby with my life. But Langston Bishop is right; there is no way I'm going to stay out of this fight. Not when Zeke's life is on the line.

CHAPTER 3
KAI

I hit the water minutes after Zeke shoots Enzo. I already know the outcome before I jump into the water. I know—I feel Enzo's vibration the second my body hits the water. I may have a strange, unreal connection with Zeke, but my connection with Enzo is otherworldly.

Enzo Black is my husband, my best friend, the father of my children. He's the strongest man I know—a man who is strong despite having an equally strong wife who technically holds more power than him.

We've always been able to take down our enemies together. As long as we are together, we are strong. Unstoppable. Together we win. But apart, that's when we lose. Being together isn't about being physically together. Being together is about sharing our hearts. Enzo and I share one heart, one set of lungs, one of everything. We are one person in two bodies.

Despite the pain and turmoil it seems we have caused each other, this is far from the worst day of our lives. This doesn't even scratch the surface.

Our greatest enemies are our friends. Those who love us, also have that one special person that they love more. That they have to protect above everything else. That's when our lives are at risk.

Which is why we're prepared—for everything. Even the greatest betrayal.

It doesn't ease the anxiety ripping through my chest and taking over my mind. Even though I know the outcome, my anxiety doesn't, and it's the part of me in control. It's driving me forward, propelling me to swim faster when there is no need.

Finally, the sight I needed to see to crush my anxiety for good comes into view—Enzo.

He's in the water, floating on his back, looking up at the dark sky.

I take a deep breath and swim toward him. I may have had a temporary moment of anxiety and fear, but I won't let Enzo see that.

"You're a good actor," I say, keeping my voice light and playful when I approach him.

Enzo continues to float on his back for a second longer. My words didn't startle him. He felt me coming before I spoke. Before the waves my swimming created washed over him, he knew I was coming.

"And you're a terrible actor," he says, smirking as he comes to face me.

I pout, hating being terrible at anything. "I am not! Julian thought I was concerned about you dying."

I try to keep my hands to myself as I tread water instead of checking him out all over like I want to, but the fact that he's joking with me tells me he's more than fine—our plan worked.

Enzo smiles at me as his hand brushes my hair from my face, finally giving me the touches I'm desperately craving.

"I'm not talking about then. I'm talking about now," he says.

I shudder. "I'm not acting."

"Yes, you are. You're pretending you are strong. That you were one hundred percent certain that our plan worked and you just calmly swam over here. When in truth, the second you started acting in front of Julian, your anxiety hit a new level, and you couldn't squash it. Even though you knew deep down that I would be fine, your anxiety took over, and you're afraid and pissed and need me."

I scowl at him. But of course, he's right.

"Yes, I fucking need you! You're my husband, my everything. And I had a full-on panic attack swimming to you that I would find your corpse instead of finding you relaxedly floating on your back. I—"

Enzo's lips crash down on mine. They are desperate, hungry, and tells me I wasn't the only one acting. I know him letting Zeke push him over the edge of the yacht was hard, because it meant he left me unprotected.

Apart we are vulnerable—together, we are unstoppable.

His tongue pushes into my mouth, and my hands grip his face before sliding down his neck. I need to make sure that he's okay.

"You're okay? You're not hurt?" I ask, before diving in for another kiss. If he isn't okay, if he's really hurt, I shouldn't be kissing him like this. I shouldn't be stealing all his breaths. But I can't help myself. I need his kisses. I need to know that we are more than okay.

"Yes. Are you okay?" he asks, his voice deepening into a protective beast that will swim the length of the ocean to kill Julian if I'm hurt.

I grin against his lips. "I just swam a good hundred yards. I'm kissing my husband. I'm good."

"Thank fuck."

And then we are kissing and kissing and kissing.

We are still treading water, while our hands confirm what our words said—that we are okay.

I start first, yanking off his shirt that is covered in what I hope is fake blood. Enzo's hands slink under my shirt, rips apart my bullet-proof vest, and then feels the skin over my stomach before cupping my breasts.

I gasp as he does. "I'm fine."

He smirks. "I know. But I think I need to fuck you to be sure."

My body heats. *God, I need to fuck him.* I need to feel connected to him completely. I need to know that the connection we share is still as strong as ever.

"Yes," the word is a plea, a promise, a cry. I need Enzo inside me. I need to feel connected. I need us to be us again.

No more pretending.

No more acting.

No more lying, scheming, betraying. That's not who we are. We tell each other the truth. We share everything. And that's not going to stop now. No matter how we hurt each other.

I kiss him again hard, but we can't fuck here in the middle of the ocean while treading water. So as much as I want to keep kissing and kissing, we need to stop and come up with a plan to find land or a boat, something.

But before we go anywhere, I need to know...

Enzo growls, seeing the concern etched on my face. I know I got a dozen more gray hairs and a couple more worry lines in the last hour alone.

"Look, I'm fine. The bullet hit the armor and exploded the fake blood bag just like we planned."

He's fine.

The bullet didn't hit him.

The blood is fake.

He was just acting when he wheezed.

He's just bruised from the impact of the bullet.

Zeke didn't shoot him.

Zeke is his friend.

He knew.

He knew about the bulletproof vests and jackets.

He was wearing one himself.

Enzo was never in any danger.

He's fine.

"Stingray, look..."

Enzo grabs my hands and runs it over his jacket. He shows me where the bullets are lodged in the armor. He shows me the fake blood oozing from it. Then he removes the jacket and puts my hand on the spots where the bullets should have entered his body but didn't.

I find no holes.

Enzo is fine. He's alive. The bullet didn't even break his skin.

And then the tears fall.

The anxiety, fear, panic all take their toll, and finally, I burst in one big release. I clutch onto Enzo's neck as the tears cascade down my face, and my cries fall from my lips in waves that I'm sure can be heard for miles around.

Enzo holds me tight to his chest as he kisses my cheeks, catching each tear before it falls to the ocean.

"It's okay, I got you," Enzo says.

I can barely process his words, but somehow we are moving. We are swimming. And then I'm being pulled up onto a boat. One of our yachts, I realize.

"Where to?" Ethan, one of our men, asks me.

"Miami," Enzo answers.

"Do you need medical assistance first?"

"No, we'll be in the captain's room," Enzo answers before lifting me against his bare wet chest and carrying me through the yacht to the captain's room at the back.

"We shouldn't kick Griffin out of his room," I say as Enzo enters in a code and the door opens.

"It's the most secure room on the ship. We are kicking him out of the room," he growls.

When the door shuts, we collapse on the bed. Enzo's lips collide with mine again, and I forget about kicking Griffin out of the room. I forget about the new danger we face. I forget about our friends that we should be worried about protecting. All I can think about is Enzo and our kids.

"Ellie, Finn?" I ask, trying to be a good mother, but Enzo is making it hard as he kisses down my neck.

"They are safe. Nora and Beckett have them. They would call if there was a problem."

They are safe.

My shirt is off, and then he pauses over me.

I shiver underneath him, not because we are both soaked, but because of Enzo's stare. Even after all this time together, after everything we've been through, one look from Enzo still makes me feel like an inexperienced virgin about to be taken for the first time. One touch from him sends my toes curling, my heart racing. One kiss and I become consumed by him.

And Enzo knows it.

But just because he makes me feel alive and protected in a way that I've never felt before, I'm still pissed at him.

"You let Siren kiss you."

My fingers rake down his front, my nails teasing his skin before I get to his soaked jeans.

He sucks in a breath when I roughly undo the button on his jeans, followed by the zipper.

"Stingray," he says my name like a warning. I know how this works. We both like it rough. And we have no problem taking what we need from each other—punishing each other when it's deserved—loving each other sweetly when the mood is right. And right now, this won't be about making love. This will be a fierce, intense grind of punishment, sin, and love. Once I start, once I declare that punishment needs to be given, I'll unleash his monster inside him—it's exactly what I want.

"You. Kissed. Her."

I reach into his pants and grab his rock hard member.

"Kai," he growls, his voice so gruff and husky as he tries to keep control of the situation.

I'm not mad. Not really. I know that Enzo loves me. I know I'm the only woman for him. I know that he only let Siren kiss him so he could understand who Siren is, what her intentions are, how far she will go. But right now, when my emotions are this high, I want a reason to give him everything I have—my good and bad.

I squeeze too hard.

"Do you deny it?"

I bite my lip as I meet him eye to eye. I know what happened. I was there. I saw. But I want him to say it. I want to hear him speak his crime. Even if he committed the crime for the right reason, it still needs to be punished. Just like Zeke will one day pay for shooting Enzo. Even though it ultimately saved his life. Even though he did it to save Siren. All sins catch up to us eventually.

We all sin.

We all lie.

"No, I don't deny it."

I slide my hand up and down his cock, letting him know that I have all the power. I'm in complete control here, not him, as I let my nails dance over the skin of his cock.

He hisses but doesn't stop me, even though he's bigger than me. He lets me hurt him. He sinned. He let Siren kiss him. He let her lips touch what was mine.

And now, I'm going to make him pay. I'm going to commit my own sin against my husband. And we are both going to enjoy every minute of it.

CHAPTER 4
ENZO

Kai strokes me again. Her nails dig deeper into my flesh.

I've hurt Kai before.

I've done unimaginable things, betrayed her too many times, but never with her as my wife. When we took those vows, she became mine, and I became hers. We've never seriously threatened the vows we took, never tested the wedding bands we wear, never pushed the limits of what it means to be married.

But I did.

I let another woman kiss me. I hurt my wife. Now I'm going to let her get her revenge. I'm going to do everything I can to let her heal. She needs this. I need this.

I need my stingray back. I need to be worthy of her love again.

Suddenly, she stops. Her hand is no longer on my cock, and for a second, I think she's changed her mind. We aren't going to fuck. She isn't going to punish me for hurting her, even for a good reason.

"Stingray, please."

She bites her lip at my soft plea. Then she runs her hand through her dark hair as she lays on the bed.

"What are you doing?"

She's silent. It takes me two seconds to realize what she is doing. I may have fucked up, but I'm still her husband. I still know her better than anyone. I know what she's thinking, sometimes even before she does.

This silence, this unspeaking, this untouching—this is my punishment.

It's her punishment, too, though. She can pretend she can hold out as much as I can, or that she doesn't want to fuck me after I let another woman kiss me. She's wrong. She wants to fuck me. She wants to feel our connection again. She needs it as much as I do.

"You can punish me all you want, Stingray. Dig your nails into me. Deny me orgasms. Whip me. Beat me. Pour hot wax onto my body. Tie me up. Do your worst. But don't you dare deny what you deserve. Use my body. Take care of yourself. Take out your pain on me. But don't you dare feel a second of pain in the process."

One.

Two.

And then, a smile. This is what she was waiting for—me to surrender, me to give her my full permission to do her worst.

I grin back even though I know what my stingray is capable of. I don't know how upset she really is about the kiss. I only let the kiss happen to find out what Siren was up to. Kai knows that, but she needs to hear it from me. She needs to understand how much letting another woman kiss me hurt me, and how much it felt like nothing compared to kissing her.

Kai needs to know I will never want another woman; I only want her.

Forever.

Nothing will ever stop me from loving her.

I stand up and let my pants drop until I'm completely naked in front of her. My chest is bruised from where the bullets hit me, but the way Kai's eyes are eating up my body, I know I must not look too bad.

I smirk.

"You want me."

She frowns and then stands, removing her own pants until she's naked in front of me.

"I shouldn't." She gives me a stern look. Her eyes narrow, her lips tense, and her jaw hardens.

I put my hands out in front of her. "Tie me up. Hurt me. Make me pay for what I did to you."

Her fingers trace over my wrists lightly, imagining ties around them, I'm sure. It drives me mad. I feel her light touch warm my body. Her touch ripples over my skin and hardens my cock.

I don't know what we will find in Griffin's closet, but I'd guess we could at least find a tie. If we are lucky, some rope or handcuffs.

"No," she snaps, removing her hands from my skin.

"No?" I step closer into her space, practically begging her to touch me. She can't resist my rockhard body, just like I can't resist her soft curves.

She bats her eyelashes at me as heat fills her cheeks. "I don't need to tie you up. You're my husband. You'll do what I say. You'll take your punishment without moving."

She's right. I will. I'd rather be tied up though, it would be easier. It's going to drive me crazy to let her touch me and not touch her back.

"On the bed, hubby."

I swallow the knot in my throat. It's not fear, I feel, but regret. I should have found a different way to find out what Siren was up to. I shouldn't have fucked with our wedding vows. I shouldn't have tested Kai's love for me.

I walk to the bed and lay down face up.

"Turn over."

I give her a suspicious look but do as she says. I roll onto my stomach.

"You do realize that thing you need to make yourself feel good is on the other side of my body, right?"

She chuckles. "I understand geometry. I know that I can't ride your cock with you on your stomach. I'm not ready to fuck you yet."

Her words slice through me. I don't know what she has planned, but I saw a twinkle in her eye, and I know that look means trouble.

Outside I growl, but inside I'm smiling. This is the woman I married—a woman stronger than me. A woman who knows what she wants and expects of me and will settle for nothing less. I love this woman with everything I have.

I let my eyes wander around the room, trying to find something she could use to punish me. I see a lamp, a pen, a remote. Not really what I was hoping to find. No candle. No rope. And not shockingly, no whips.

Kai moves onto the bed and then straddles my hips before her hands come down on my shoulders like she's about to give me a massage. I tense because I know better, rather than relax.

"Why so tense? You have no reason to feel tense, baby. Just like I had no reason to be tense after seeing your lips pressed against another woman."

She massages for a second before her claws dig into my skin like daggers. My shoulder is sore from being shot there. Even though the bullet didn't impact my skin, the deep bruise hurts when she squeezes.

She leans down until her hot breath is on my neck, and I groan. It feels so good. For a second, I forget she wants to punish me as she kisses down my neck. When her kisses get to my back, she changes from kissing to sinking her teeth into me.

My groans turn painful as she bites me over and over, all over my back. I'm going to have dozens of bite marks all over my back.

"You. Are. Mine."

I smile, loving how possessive she is of me.

She moves down until she is at my ass, and when she bites down on my cheek, I can't help but yelp.

She smacks over where she just bit me. "Mine."

"Yours, baby. I'm all yours."

"You sure about that?"

"Yes."

"Every inch of you?"

"Yes."

"What about this part of you?" She licks her fingers before circling them over my asshole.

I clench, not wanting her to touch me there. She never has before. We are pretty wild in the bedroom. We've done almost everything, except that.

But if she needs to know that all of me is hers, I'm up for trying anything with her.

"Yes, all of me is yours."

And then her finger is pushing inside me, claiming all of me. At first, it feels incredibly uncomfortable. My eyes even water at the intrusion. She doesn't give me time to get used to the feeling until another finger is inside and then another.

She finds my prostate and strokes me until the pain turns to pleasure.

Holy fuck, it feels good.

My cock hardens, and I'm desperate for her.

I move, trying to grab her. To feel her. To make her feel good.

But she slaps my hand away.

"Don't move."

She continues to push into me until I'm so close to coming. And then suddenly she stops.

"Turn over."

I do, resisting all my natural urges to touch her.

"Your ass is mine, but what about your lips? Are they mine?"

"Yours. They are all yours."

"You sure about that? Because I'm pretty sure I saw you kissing another woman with these lips."

"Let me show you how much I didn't give her. I didn't give her what matters."

I grab her hips without permission and pull her until she is straddling my face, and then I drive my tongue between her legs until I taste her sweetness. She rides my face as I lick her lips slowly with my tongue, spreading her wider.

"Jesus," she purrs as I find her clit and flick it with careful precision.

She's lost control as I remind her how much she owns my lips and tongue, show her what I haven't given to any woman but her.

Her back arches, and she grabs the headboard behind me as I devour her. She reacts so quickly to my actions. I can feel all of her wetness cover my lips and tongue just like I wanted. Her lips swell, along with her clit, and her sweetness spills onto my tongue.

But it's not enough. I want to make her scream. I reach up and grab her breasts, flicking over her nipples in a circular way that I know drives her mad.

"Enzo!" And then I claim her. I remind her that she alone owns my lips as she comes all over my face.

Slowly, she comes down from her high. She remembers that she is supposed to be punishing me, not letting me enjoy myself. She carefully climbs off my face and moves back until she is just above my cock.

Yes, please fuck me. Feeling her come over my face is one of my favorite things—watching her come undone like that.

But there is nothing like being inside her. I don't need to come. I don't care about my pleasure. I just need to feel the connection between us.

"What about this?" She grabs my cock. "Is this still mine and mine alone?"

Her voice has changed. Gone is the lightheartedness. Gone is the teasing. She's pissed.

I frown, hating that I made her feel this way for even a single second.

"My cock is always only yours. I've never strayed, and I never will."

She grabs it again, holding it rougher than usual as she pumps me hard.

"She touched you."

"She didn't."

"I saw. Her hand was in your pants."

"She didn't touch me. Her finger grazed me on accident, but that was it. She. Didn't. Touch. Me. I wouldn't have let her. That would have been too far. It would have crossed a line that even I wouldn't have been able to forgive myself for."

She hesitates for a second, watching me closely trying to tell if I'm telling the truth or a lie.

"Truth," she finally says, and then she sinks down on top of me in one powerful stroke.

"Stingray!" I cry out, finally feeling the connectedness I need. I don't touch her like I want. I let her decide what I get to do. I'm just thankful to be connected to her in any way.

She doesn't move at first. She just lets the connection be only my cock inside her pussy. And for a moment, that's enough.

Our eyes hold, unspoken words pass between us.

She forgives me.

And I love her even more for it.

Then I'm grabbing her, and she's thrusting over me with everything she has. Our bodies connect in a wild fury. She grinds her body down on top of mine, and the love we share for each other flows freely between us, just like it has since the moment I realized I loved her. She is the missing piece of my life I thought I would never have.

She rides me like this is going to last forever, like we will never experience another moment after this one. This is the last instant that matters.

I watch my wife come undone on top of my cock. Her body changes from pain to love. Her eyes roll back, her hair falls freely down her back, her cheeks flush bright pink, her nipples harden, and her hips roll over mine as her orgasm approaches until she can't hold on anymore. She lets go.

I'm so lost in her that I don't realize my own body is coming right with her, exploding inside of her, giving her all of my cum.

Slowly we both stop—neither of us speak. We don't have to after what just happened. Our bodies already did all of the talking. We love each other. We forgive each other. We would forgive each other for anything. That's how much we love each other. There was never a question about forgiveness or reconciliation. We were always going to end up loving each other forever.

"Come here," I say, pulling her against my chest.

She falls on top of me as my cock slips out of her. We are a mess. We should shower off the seawater, cum, blood, and sweat. But we won't.

Being clean right now doesn't matter.

I hold Kai against my chest. Her hand traces slowly over my heart.

"I love you, Stingray."

"I love you, too."

"What are you thinking?" I know her. Even though we just shared that incredible, mind-blowing moment together, she still has dozens of thoughts racing in her head.

"I'm still mad at Zeke. And unfortunately, I can't fuck him and make it all better."

My head swivels to her, and my hand grabs her hand, forcing her to stop tracing circles on my chest.

"Damn right, you can't fuck him," I growl.

She smiles. "I didn't mean I want to fuck Zeke. I just meant that making up with you is easier than making up with him."

Our fingers dance together as I hold her hand. I can feel her heartache from being angry at Zeke flow through her. It will eat at her until she can see him again, which is exactly what she doesn't need. She needs to be focused on protecting herself and this family.

"There is nothing to forgive," I say.

She leans on her elbow and sits up. "What do you mean? He fucking shot you! He needs to crawl on his knees and beg for my forgiveness and hope I don't shoot him for what he did to you."

I smile, loving how far she would go for me. She just needs someone to blame for the fear she felt in the moments when she didn't know if the plan had worked or not.

"No, you have no reason to be angry with Zeke, and you know that. Zeke knew we were all wearing the bulletproof armor. He knew they would spurt fake blood, so our enemies thought the bullets were hitting us and not our protective gear.

"He knew that by shooting me himself that I was most likely helping him complete Julian's task. He knew that pushing me into the ocean was more about saving me than killing me. He knew. He knew that I would survive. He knew.

"He did it to protect me, to protect you, and get you the fuck off the boat and after me. He did it to protect Siren. What Zeke did doesn't need to be forgiven. What he did needs to be thanked. The only reason we are all here is because Zeke saved us."

Kai narrows her eyes, her lips jut out a little as she pouts adorably. She kisses me sweetly on the cheek.

"You're a good friend," she says before trying to pull away.

I yank her back. "And you're a better one. Don't hold this against Zeke. Not after everything you two have been through. Your friendship shouldn't change because of this."

She sighs but kisses me again before she tries to climb out of bed, again.

"Why do you keep trying to climb out of my bed, Stingray?"

"Because we need to go get to the box I hid before anyone else finds it."

I shake my head.

She folds her arms over her chest.

Both of us in a standoff position, ready to fight.

"We need to sleep. We can get the box in the morning."

"That's bullshit, and you know it. Julian could have already reached the box by now."

"Where did you hide it?"

She closes her mouth tighter like that will make it harder for her to spill the truth.

I can't help it. I laugh a little.

"We need to go, right now."

"No, we don't. We need to rest. We need all our strength to fight off Julian and his men. We've lost too many times already. I'm tired of losing."

She gnaws on her bottom lip, and I can see the worry lines forming around her eyes again. There is something she isn't telling me.

"Spill," I command.

She takes a deep breath. And I prepare for her to say something stupid.

"I hid the box in Alaska."

Fuck.

I jump out of bed so fast. In record time, we have both rinsed off, dressed, and are headed upstairs to tell the captain our new coordinates.

I love my wife. I know why she hid the box there. It's safest there.

I just hope to God that Nora and Beckett didn't choose it as a place to hide our kids.

We are in this together, though. Together, we are going to stop this bastard, destroy the box, and keep our family safe.

CHAPTER 5
ZEKE

I hear Julian's helicopter turning around and know I have limited time to get to Siren before he kills me.

I'm a sitting duck here in the ocean. There are no boats around. All the yachts that were here before have left, including the one Siren was on.

I don't know how well Julian can fly a helicopter, but my time is limited.

I start swimming in the direction I saw Siren's yacht go. I don't have a plan. There is nothing I can do but swim and hope it's enough.

The ocean has not always been my friend. Ultimately, it has never taken my life, and the ocean did bring me Siren. The ocean may be an obstacle, but as much as it has threatened my life, it has blessed it just as much.

I don't know what the ocean will choose this time. I don't know if I'll be able to get to Siren or if the ocean will finally take me.

As the buzz of the helicopter gets closer, I have a sinking feeling that the ocean is not going to be my friend. There is no one to save me. No one knows I'm here and is going to come back for me.

Kai has long ago found Enzo. And Siren is gone.

The helicopter gets closer. All I know is that I won't follow Julian's orders. I won't go back. I have to be free. It's the only way I have a chance at saving Siren from Langston.

As the helicopter approaches, I make a decision.

Ocean, now is the time to save me.

I take a deep breath.

Then I dive under.

I kick as far down as I can get my body to sink.

I stare up at the sky and watch the helicopter buzz around. I won't be able to survive down here long. I'll run out of oxygen soon, and then I'll have to surface. When I do, Julian will spot me.

As my oxygen evaporates, I scramble, looking for something, anything that can save me. A boat to come by. A floating piece of driftwood to hide under—something.

Instead, my foot tangles in a damn plastic bag. *Fucking people acting like the world is their garbage can and not throwing away their recycling properly.* I untangle my foot from the plastic and am about to kick for the surface when I spot something in the bag.

I realize the bag is a McDonald's takeout bag, and inside is a cup and a straw.

A straw!

I have no idea if it will work, but I'm willing to try anything to get Siren back safely. I was stupid to take Julian's deal. I should have known he would never honor it. He would send Langston to watch over Siren and somehow persuade him to eventually kill her.

I grab the straw and put it between my lips as I head for the surface. I'm careful to keep my body under the water, hoping that even though I'm at the surface, Julian can't see me. The straw sticks out above the waves, and I take a cautious breath.

It works.

I can breathe.

Albeit, in short, painful breaths—breaths that don't fully satisfy my lungs. Breaths half-filled with salt water as the waves bump into my straw. But breaths that keep me alive and hidden from view. Breaths that get me one step closer to helping Siren.

So I'll hover here, at the surface of the water, and wait until Julian has to head for shore to land. Then I'll surface. Then I'll swim all night, and the next night and the night after that, until I find land or a boat. I'll find Siren, and I'll kill everyone who threatens her life, even my ex-best friend, Langston.

Julian hovers for twenty minutes until he finally heads toward shore to land.

I break the surface, gasping and coughing hard, expelling the water that slowly entered my lungs with each breath. It takes a solid minute of coughing until I can breathe semi-normally again.

The ocean spared me.

But I still have a long way to go to get Siren back.

I start swimming, not thinking about how exhausted and tired I am already, not thinking about it being smarter to conserve energy and float here until a boat comes.

I swim like I'm Michael Phelps in an Olympic race.

I swim as hard and as fast as my arms and legs can move. I'm a big guy, but not in the way Phelps is. My wingspan is big, but more in a giant grizzly bear sort of way. My legs are more like tree trunks than flippers. But right now, if I were racing Phelps, I'd put money on me swimming faster. Phelps never had to chase after the woman he loved to keep her safe before.

I swim all night, and when the sun rises, I have hope when I see a boat in the distance headed straight toward me.

It could be Julian's, but I don't have a choice but to get on it. So when the boat approaches and I wave it down, I climb up hesitantly. I don't have a gun on me. Physically, I'm in no shape to fight, but tell that to my heart.

When I hit the deck, I know the men are dangerous. They don't have their guns pointed at me, but I see the outlines of them beneath their clothes.

"You okay, man?" one man says.

"Yea, I could use a towel, though," I say.

The man nods and turns like he's going to go get me a towel. He doesn't get a step in before I've grabbed him by the neck, pulled his gun out, and aimed it at his head.

All the men tense. Some grab their guns and point it at me.

"I'm Zeke Kane. And I have no problem killing this man and every single one of you if I have to. My wife is in danger. I've survived an entire night chasing after her in the ocean, and no one is going to stop me. Now, put your guns down."

All the men immediately drop their guns to my surprise. Either they all love the man I'm pointing my gun at, or they are all pussies.

"Mr. Kane, we are at your service. We didn't recognize you at first, but we work for Kai Black. We will take you wherever you need and fight by your side," the man standing in front of me says.

I look around at all the eyes staring back and me. I recognize a few men and even know a few by name.

I found one of the Black organization's ships. *Thank God.*

I release the man I'm holding.

"I'll go get you that towel," the man says, scampering off.

I chuckle. I don't give a damn about a towel. I can stay dripping wet and cold. The only thing that will truly warm me is getting Siren back.

"Where to, sir?" Dustin, a man I recognize, says, looking at me for direction.

"I need to get to the security system," I say now that I recognize this as one of the Black's boats. We put a tracking system on all the yachts. We can track the one that Langston and Siren are on.

An hour later, we pull up to the shore of San Salvador Island. I spot the yacht parked at the end of the pier, and I don't wait until our boat is tied up to jump onto the pier and run to their boat.

"Siren!" I scream as I run to the yacht.

I don't get an answer. I pull my gun out in case I face Langston. I realize now why Siren wanted us all to shoot first as soon as we were faced with Bishop. She knew Bishop was Langston, our supposed friend. She knew but couldn't break our hearts. She warned us in the only way she knew how.

I failed before. I won't fail this time. If I come face to face with Langston again, I'll shoot him and ask questions later. That's what he deserves after what he did to Siren.

"Siren!" I yell as I run through the top deck.

Nothing.

I move up to the top decks.

Nothing.

I run down to the bottom decks and yell. I open every door slowly, through the painstaking security process that Kai and Enzo installed on their yachts so each room could act like a safe room when danger approached.

Nothing.

They aren't here.

I emerge and walk back onto the pier, where the men have now disembarked the boat.

"Did you find her?" Dustin asks.

"No, but they couldn't have gone far," I say, although my words are more of a hope than a truth.

Dustin nods. "We will canvass the town. We will find her, Mr. Kane."

"Call me Zeke."

"Of course."

"Let's go."

I don't bother putting the gun away. I don't give a fuck if the police try to arrest me, or if I'm putting fear into people around me. I need the gun to shoot Langston or Julian if I see either of them.

Most people don't notice the gun, or if they do, they don't question it. They look at me and feel like it belongs to me. And no one dares take it away.

I search the island, and everywhere I look, I see Siren. Every woman with long brown hair and a thin muscular frame must be her. But she's not here.

Where are you, baby? Call out to me. Use your voice. Tell me where you are.

If I can't find them in town, I'm guessing they went to the airport. I'm about to tell the men that's where I'm headed when I stop dead in my tracks.

Walking casually down the sidewalk like two friends are Siren and Langston. She is talking quickly, and he is shaking his head, which makes her laugh.

She's laughing.

I don't know how to process this scene. My brain expected to find her tied up with a knife or gun to her throat. I expected to find her hurt, hanging onto life, not walking downtown like she's headed to get a coffee or pick up a souvenir at one of the local shops.

What.

The.

Fuck.

I want to run across the street and grab her. I want to shoot Langston and beat him until he answers every question.

Instead, I watch. I try to understand what is happening. Why she is walking with him so calmly?

Maybe I was wrong? Maybe he isn't Bishop? I did tell her to trust him after all.

No.

Julian confirmed he was Bishop.

Langston is Bishop.

I'm about to shoot Langston when I hear the click of a gun behind me. I don't have to turn around to know who is standing behind me with a gun pointed at my head.

Julian Reed.

I was too focused on Siren. It gave him the opportunity to sneak up on me.

"Come with me or Siren dies," Julian says.

He's threatened our lives before, and every time I've fallen for it. I've not killed him because I thought it was the right thing to do. I thought the best way to protect Siren was to make a deal with Julian. Not anymore. Siren is pregnant. The only way to protect her and my baby is to kill the man behind me.

CHAPTER 6
SIREN

I take another step and try not to puke. Apparently, my morning sickness decided to kick in now, at the worst possible time. I'm stuck on a yacht with a man I have no idea if I should trust or not, while trying to avoid another madman who might kill me or my baby, while also trying to figure out how to save my husband from dying to protect me.

Perfect timing.

"Do you have what you need yet?" Langston Bishop asks next to me.

"No, I told you I need Sprite and crackers. That always helps when I feel sick."

He sighs. "You do realize that sugar water is not going to help you. It's crap."

I chuckle. "It will help me. It always helps."

He rolls his eyes. "Let's try this store. If they don't have it, though, we are buying what they have and getting the hell out of here."

He grabs my bicep and guides me into the fifth store we've entered on the island. I was surprised when I started puking last night that Langston changed course and directed us to the nearest island. He did it to get me medical help. I said I didn't need it, just Sprite and crackers.

"Look, they have 7-Up and oyster crackers," Langston says as he leads me to the back of the store.

I keep waiting for him to pull a gun on me, to lose his patience, and say he's done with my silly mission, but so far he hasn't. We just keep going from store to store, him humoring me like my mission is going to actually help me, when actually each store we enter is another chance for me to escape.

He knows that, but still, he allows me to do it.

I scrunch up my nose. "I said Sprite, not 7-Up."

"Isn't that the same thing?"

"No, it is most definitely not. Sprite is heaven from the gods. 7-Up is like dog piss."

Langston shakes his head. "I don't know how Zeke puts up with you. You are the most frustrating woman."

"If you don't want to put up with me, you could just let me go. I'll stay here and keep up my search for Sprite, while you can go look for the box that holds the weapon to take down the world in it."

"I think I spotted another store on the corner. Maybe they have your precious Sprite and crackers."

I frown, not understanding why he hasn't grabbed the supplies and marched my ass back on the boat.

But I can't think about that for long before my stomach is queasy again and I'm going to be sick in this cute seaside store, if I don't find a bathroom soon.

Langston springs into action. He picks me up honeymoon style and carries me to the bathroom before depositing me on the floor in front of a toilet, seconds before I'm sick.

I don't know at what point in me throwing up that he leaves, but when my stomach finally settles, I realize I'm alone in the bathroom. I walk to the sink and wash my hands before splashing water on my face and deciding that when I exit, I'll take the 7-Up.

When I leave the bathroom, I find Langston Bishop standing there.

"How you feeling?"

"Like death. I'll take the 7-Up."

It's then that Langston holds out the items in his hands—Sprite, crackers, and a bag of something else.

"You found Sprite?"

He nods with a smug smile.

I take the items from him and immediately start sipping on the Sprite. It feels like fizzy heaven going down my throat. I tear open the crackers and munch on them as well, instantly knowing that I'll be able to get through this now that I have the items I've been desperate for.

"What's that?" I ask about the bag.

"More crackers and Sprite. I made sure to stock up."

"Good thinking."

"And some ginger." He pulls the item out and offers it to me. "Munch on this, it will help more than that disgusting carbonated death drink."

"Hey, the Sprite is helping."

"Sure, it is. Just try it." I take the piece of dried ginger from his hand, and I pop it into my mouth, deciding I should be nice.

We walk out of the store with the items in hand.

"Better?" he asks as we walk.

I feel much better, so I nod.

He grins, thinking the ginger is helping. But it's definitely my Sprite.

Langston Bishop starts guiding me back toward the yacht.

"I'm not getting back on that thing with you. I have my Sprite, but it's not a miracle cure. It won't keep me from getting sick again."

"You're sick because you have morning sickness, not because of motion sickness from the yacht. Come on."

"No, I'm not going anywhere with you."

"You don't have a choice, Siren. Trust me."

I scoff, still munching on my crackers. "You want me to trust you?"

He nods.

"Then fix me. Fix what you did to my head. Make it so that I don't dream about you anymore. So that your words aren't in my head. Fix me. Earn my trust. Then maybe I'll go with you willingly."

He stops walking, so I do too. His eyes narrow, trying to read my thoughts to determine if he gives me what I want if I'll really work with him willingly. Doubtful. I just want him to fix me, so I can be free.

My head starts spinning the longer he looks at me. I feel him creeping back into my head, my thoughts...

Come with me.

Don't fight me.

Do what I say.

It's easier.

I shake it off and try to focus on the man in front of me, instead of the version of him who has been haunting me and demanding my thoughts.

We continue our stare-off. Neither of us budge or move. I hope like hell that Langston Bishop doesn't realize how much he can still control my thoughts, and that he can't tell how weak I am. How easily he can win.

"Come with me," he says.

"No," I say firmly, surprising myself when the word I'm thinking is yes.

"Fine."

Wait, did I just win?

Langston Bishop grabs my arm, and he's lifting me in his arms again.

Nope, I definitely didn't just win.

I fight. "Let me go! You can't just do whatever you want to me!"

"I told you to come with me. To get on the boat. You chose not to; your decision has consequences."

I beat against his chest as he climbs onto the yacht, but I don't struggle too much. I'm afraid he'll drop me and hurt the baby. He knows that. It's like fighting while handcuffed. I only have limited ways that I can fight.

But I am a fighter. I won't give up just because I'm pregnant, especially when this man thinks he can bully me around after doing horrendous things to me.

So while I'm yelling and beating against his chest, I'm also making a plan.

I search for his gun with my eyes. I find it. As soon as we are firmly on the deck of the ship, I grab it and then kick hard, forcing him to drop me. I'm prepared and land on my feet, aiming the gun at his head.

Langston doesn't react like I expect him to. He doesn't put his hands up. He's not afraid of death, not in the least. *Or is he not afraid of me?*

"Now, fix me. Tell me how to get you out of my head, or I'll shoot you."

"Shoot me."

"What?"

"Shoot me, it will make you feel better."

I frown. *Why does he want me to shoot him?* I glance over my shoulder, but there is no one behind me. We were the only ones on the yacht when we arrived, but I don't trust that he doesn't have other men here. That must be the real reason we stopped, not to get me my damn Sprite.

"No one is here. Shoot me, Siren."

I smirk. "If I shoot you, I'll kill you. I'm not some weak girl who has never held a gun before. This is what I do for a living. This is who I am. I shoot you, I kill you."

"You won't kill me."

"Yes, I will."

"No, because if you kill me, you'll never know the truth. You'll never know how to fix your head. I'll always be there, even when I'm gone."

Dammit. Dammit. Dammit.

Continuing to aim the gun at Langston Bishop, I'm more confused than ever who the man standing in front of me is. *Is there still a piece of him that is Zeke's old friend? Or is he all monster now?*

What should I do?

Shoot him.

Kill him.

Or surrender.

Surrendering doesn't seem like an option. Killing him isn't one either.

But I could shoot him. I could hurt him.

I could make him pay for everything he's done to me.

Would it really help?

It would make me feel a tiny bit better to know that I got a little piece of revenge. And maybe it would strike a tiny bit of fear into him.

I don't think.

I fire.

One single shot.

It hits him in the shoulder, just above his heart.

He doesn't react. He doesn't flinch. He doesn't reach for his shoulder. He stands there as solid as ever.

I frown, and my head drops to the side, annoyed. "You're wearing a bulletproof vest."

He grabs the back of his shirt and yanks it over his head. His abs ripple into my view. He's not wearing a vest. With the shirt off, I spot the bullet wound in his shoulder with blood dripping out.

"Now that you got that out of your system, go rest while I set sail. And eat more of the ginger," he says before storming away.

He doesn't wait to make sure I head toward a bedroom. He's not afraid of me running off. Letting me shoot him was another attempt at gaining my trust.

Fuck him.

I'm leaving. I'll find the box myself. I'll go after Zeke. I'll save the motherfucking world. And when I do, I'll come back and kill him.

"LET ME GO TO HER FIRST," BISHOP SAYS.

"Why? So you can fuck her first? I don't think so. I've waited a long time for this. She's mine," Julian says.

"Getting the information is more important than raping her. Let me talk to her."

"You can talk after I have her."

I hear a loud sound.

"You punched me, you bastard."

"Don't touch her. Don't rape her. She doesn't deserve that."

I BLINK RAPIDLY. *DID THAT REALLY HAPPEN? OR WAS THAT ANOTHER dream?* Another thought Bishop put in my head.

My head is throbbing. I need to lie down.

The engines start up. I have limited time left to make my decision —jump now or stay with Langston Bishop on this yacht.

I watch the gap between the yacht and pier grow bigger until the space becomes too big to jump. If I jumped now, I'd end up in the water.

I choose to say. I need to rest. More importantly, I need answers...

CHAPTER 7
ZEKE

I knock the gun out of his hand in one swift motion. I get Julian in a headlock, intent on killing him, when I see Siren and Langston exit the building and start walking down the street.

I can't lose them. I need to get Siren. I need to make sure she's safe.

I raise my gun to finish Julian when Dustin rounds the corner. He looks at me holding Julian in a headlock.

"What do you need me to do?" he asks.

I should stay and make sure Julian's interrogated and then killed, but I have to be the one to ensure that Siren is alive and safe.

I want Julian Reed interrogated. I want to know everything he knows. I want to ensure there are no other people he's working with, but I want him dead more. Every second he's still alive is a second that he could escape and kill us.

I throw Julian into Dustin's capable arms.

"Kill him and then meet me at our yacht."

He nods.

Then I'm running out into the street, trying my best to think that Julian is dead. That he won't escape this time. That it doesn't matter that I'm not the one to put the bullet in his head. I just need to keep Siren safe. That's what I do—protect. And protecting others doesn't mean that I have to be the one to kill him.

When I round the corner onto Main Street, I don't see Siren or Langston, but they couldn't have gone far. I scan quickly through the crowds of shoppers casually strolling down the sidewalks, through the cabs and cars honking at each other.

Where did they go?

My heart says the pier. I run down the street, and I see several more men who work for Black and were with me on the yacht.

"Go to the alley between Second and Third Avenues. Make sure that Dustin kills the man he's holding," I bark.

The men nod and run in that direction, while I continue on to the pier.

I spot the yacht at the end—it's moving.

"Fuck."

I run down the pier, moving as fast as humanly possible. And then I'm at the end of the pier. The yacht is still creeping along, but soon it will be in deep enough water that it can pick up speed.

I have two choices. Either get in my boat and chase after them again or jump in the water and swim.

I choose the latter, as they're not going very fast yet, and I need to be as quiet as possible.

I take a deep breath as I prepare to jump back in the water. "Fucking hell."

I jump back into the cool water. I hate this ocean right now, but it gives me a chance at saving Siren.

Their yacht continues to pull away as I swim, but there is no way I'm letting it get away. I push my arms through the water and kick hard with my legs, ensuring that I swim as fast as humanly possible.

Catching up to them, I grab onto a loose floating buoy at the back of the yacht. I exhale a deep breath in relief. I'm not on the boat yet, but it won't get away from me, not this time.

Hand over hand, I pull myself up the rope until I can grip the railing of the boat. Then I pull myself out of the water and over the railing onto the deck of the yacht.

I'm huffing hard, my chest expanding and deflating wildly when I stand up. My body is fatigued, but I don't care. I don't know what danger is on this yacht. I don't know if it's just Siren and Langston or if Langston has more men on the boat, just like I do back at shore.

I should have called and had my men get on the yacht to meet me here, but I don't have time for even a phone call. I need to get Siren. I need to protect her. I need her in my arms.

And I need to kill Langston.

Fuck, I can't think about that. That's going to wreck me, no matter what he did to Siren. Shooting Enzo was bad enough even though Kai eventually got word to me that he's alive after making me suffer first.

Although, I just now realize that his bitchass has all my money since I had to buy Siren from him. That will make it easier to shoot him.

I pull my gun out as I creep through the yacht.

It's eerily quiet.

Someone is obviously steering the yacht, but that is one of the most secure rooms in the yacht. If it's locked, I'm not getting in. Hopefully, that's not where Siren is.

I make it to the stairs where I have to decide. *Do I go up or down?*

Downstairs are bedrooms with locks that I will have to manually unlock. If Siren is downstairs, she's most likely tied up and locked away.

Something tells me to go up, even though it makes no sense to me.

I keep my gun pointed in front of me as I climb the stairs, not having a clue what I'm going to find.

When I reach the top deck, the wind of the yacht speeding up brushes though me, but that's not what takes my breath away.

Siren.

She's leaning against the railing as the sun beats down on her. She's wearing tiny shorts and a flowy tank-top that hides her growing belly. She looks like sunshine in the middle of the darkest storm.

The second both of my feet are on deck, Siren turns and faces me. For a second, we just stand, not sure what we are seeing is real. We only just saw each other last night. It's been less than twenty-four hours since we've been apart, but it feels like a lifetime.

I said goodbye to her. I thought I was going to die, or even if I did survive, I would do such horrible atrocities to protect my family that she would never want me. I thought I was leaving her with the best person possible. I couldn't have been more wrong.

"I'm really here," I say when tears water her eyes.

Then we are running at each other like we haven't seen each other in years.

I grab her in my arms before we collide too hard. I don't want to hurt the baby, but I can't help but spin her around a second before I kiss her hard on the lips. My joy at seeing her safe and kissing her again overtakes all other feelings.

"You're here. How? Why? How?" Siren starts.

"Shh," I say before kissing her again. Langston must be on the bridge, but I don't know for how long. Once we are out to sea, he can set the autopilot and come search for her.

"We need to go," I say.

"Go?" Her eyes dart out to the ocean. She's right. We aren't going anywhere. I might brave the seas and swim the mile to shore, but I would never allow Siren to. And as we pick up speed, that option becomes less than ideal.

"I need to get you somewhere safe; then I can deal with Langston."

She laughs, not the reaction I was expecting.

"Oh, so you're going to tell me your plan this time before you leave me somewhere safe? Not like last time where you left me with the enemy and didn't let me talk about the plan first."

I frown. She's right, but I don't care right now. I just want her safe.

"Are Enzo and Kai safe? Alive?"

"Yes," I say.

"What about Julian?"

I suck in a breath. "Dead."

She narrows her eyes. "What does that mean?"

"It means he's dead."

"You're lying. Why?"

I bite my lip as my veins pop out of my head and blood swishes through my body like raging rivers. "Because I had him. I could have killed him, but instead, I came after you. I needed to know that you were safe."

"So, why do you think he's dead?"

"Because men who work for Kai and Enzo found me. They are working for me. They ran into me when I got Julian. I told them to kill him."

We both stare at each other. Julian Reed could be dead. Or he could have escaped again.

"He's not dead," we both say at the same time.

"At least we need to assume he's not dead until we know for sure," Siren says.

I nod reluctantly.

"I think I'm going to be sick." Siren grabs at her stomach. "Can you help me to a bathroom?"

I take her hand. I want off this boat immediately, but I'll go along with what she wants. And we don't have another option at the moment. She'll be safe enough in one of the bedrooms with me as her guard.

I hold my gun in one hand as I lead her down, hoping like hell that Langston doesn't pop out, and I don't have to shoot him. I've shot enough of my friends to last me a lifetime.

When we make it into one of the bedrooms, I quickly lock the door, praying Langston hasn't overridden the security system already. I help Siren to the bathroom just before she vomits.

I rub her back, hold her hair, anything I can do, but I don't feel like I'm doing enough.

Finally, she sits back.

"I need my Sprite."

I frown. *Sprite?*

"Is there some up in the kitchen?"

"No, it's in the bag on the bed."

I get up and return with the bag and hand her a Sprite. Then I pull out crackers and ginger.

"You should really try the ginger. It would help."

She rolls her eyes. "Don't get me started."

I sit next to her on the bathroom floor, as it doesn't look like we are leaving anytime soon. I still hold the gun, but Langston hasn't come searching for her, so I have no idea if he knows I'm here or not.

"How did you get these supplies anyway?"

"That's why we stopped at the island. I was getting sick and said I needed them. Langston agreed to stop." She nibbles at the corner of a cracker as she looks at me.

"Why would he do that?"

She raises her shoulders.

I frown, staring at my hands that are folded above my knees with my gun in my hand. "I should call my men, tell them to meet the yacht, and then attack."

"No."

"Why not?"

"Because I need Langston Bishop to trust me."

"Langston Bishop? You know Bishop isn't his last name, right?"

"I know, but until I figure out who he is, I call him by both names."

"He's Langston, the monster who tortured you."

She's quiet.

"What aren't you telling me?"

"I'm just not sure about him. I'm not sure I remember correctly what he did to me."

"What do you mean?"

"I mean that he may or may not have tortured me."

"That's pretty black and white. How do you not know?"

She stands up suddenly. I follow as she walks into the bedroom and begins to pace. "My head is all fucked up. I don't know what he did. The memories I do remember are clouded. They keep coming back to me in short bursts that don't make sense."

"Which is why we need to leave, now."

"No, I need Langston to fix me."

"He won't. He's too far gone. He's evil now."

She raises her eyebrows. "Don't you start. By that measure, we are both evil, too."

I take her hand and place it over her stomach. "We are."

She smiles.

"That's why we have to destroy our enemies—to protect this little guy."

"Guy, huh?"

I shrug. "Our little warrior."

"Better."

I keep my hand on her stomach.

"Langston Bishop trusts me. I think he does, or he wants me to trust him. And I think I can trick him into fixing me, by guaranteeing I'll work with him if he fixes me."

"No."

"We don't have a choice. I can't live with him in my head. It's not safe for our little warrior. I've had thoughts, dark thoughts. I'm afraid I'll go crazy."

Fuck.

"What do you suggest then?" I say.

"Langston Bishop doesn't know you are here. You stay hidden and prepared to protect me, while I convince him to fix me. It's the safest plan."

"I don't like it."

"You don't have a choice."

"Fine, but if he puts one hand on you, I'll kill him."

She nods, agreeing.

"I'll sneak into the security room and get it wired so I can watch the feed on my phone. Then I'll stay hidden but close so I can protect you. I won't let him hurt you. I promise."

"I need to go check on him."

"Check on him? Why? Won't he come find you?"

She bites her lip as a blush spreads. "Probably not."

"Why not?"

She kisses me once more on the lips, and as much as I want to fuck her right here, she was just sick and needs to go deal with Langston. The sooner she can convince him, the sooner she'll be safe.

"He's been shot and is probably in need of stitches. I'm guessing once he set the autopilot, he either took a pain pill or alcohol to pass out from the pain."

"Who shot him?"

Siren walks to the door and opens it with a grin. "Me."

I smile back as I follow her out to head to the security room. "That's my girl," I whisper in her ear before kissing her hair and disappearing into the shadows.

She doesn't need me to protect her, but I'll be here, waiting in the shadows. Waiting for the moment when I can finally save her for good.

CHAPTER 8
SIREN

I walk up the stairs, feeling Zeke behind me in the hallway. With each step I take, I feel Zeke's presence less and less. I don't know if I'm making the right decision. I don't know if convincing Langston to trust me is a good move or not. Or if I should just have Zeke kill him, as horrible as that sounds.

Right now, all I can focus on is putting one foot in front of the other. It's an impossible task as it means each step I take is further away from Zeke.

"I'll be watching you. I'm with you. You got this," Zeke says from behind me.

His words feed me. I take another step, then another. Then I'm on the upper deck. Zeke is no longer with me, but he'll be watching from the security cameras.

I'm safe.

I rub my stomach. *We're safe.*

I head to the bridge and knock on the door.

There is silence at first, but then I hear the door unlocking and crack open. I push my way inside.

I find Langston Bishop shirtless as he holds some gauze to his shoulder where I shot him. There is an open first-aid kit lying on the counter next to where he sits staring out at the ocean out the front window.

I smile; I can't help it. He looks young and innocent as he fumbles with the supplies trying to pull out the tweezers.

"Your stomach better?" he asks.

I nod.

"Good."

He removes the gauze from his wound without a drop of pain on his face. Then he begins digging into his wound to pull out the bullet fragment. He starts to pull something out, but it's not the bullet, instead, it's pieces of his flesh.

"Fuck," he curses under his breath. I don't think it's from the pain, just the frustration of not being able to find the bullet.

"Need some help?"

He ignores me and digs the tweezers in. Again, he comes up empty.

I sigh. I can't watch him struggle.

I march over and grab the tweezers from his hand, dig them into his wound, and pull out the bullet. I drop it into the trash bin.

I don't bother asking if he needs additional help. I just go to work. I swab the wound with alcohol and then find a staple gun that I can use instead of doing the stitching by hand.

"Do you need any pain medication or alcohol first?" I hold the staple gun up, letting him know what I'm about to do.

He grunts.

"I'll take that as a no."

I start stapling.

"So considerate of you to ask if I need pain medicine before you staple me up, but not before you shoot me."

"You told me to shoot you!" I insert another staple. This time he hisses.

"So you can feel pain. I thought you might be immune to feeling anything," I say smugly.

He rolls his eyes. "Of course, I can feel pain. But there is no use reacting to it; it doesn't make the pain go away. It doesn't make it any better."

"I agree," I say as I put the last staple into his arm.

Our eyes meet in a weird moment of understanding each other. I don't know what happened to Langston that turned him into Bishop. I don't know what pain he felt or horror he experienced, but I can understand how someone can let pain turn to anger. Although, Langston doesn't seem angry.

I finish working on his arm, adding more gauze and then wrapping it around his arm to hold it in place.

"Thanks," Langston Bishop says suddenly.

I freeze. I wasn't expecting a thank you. Julian sure wouldn't say thank you after I stitched him up. He would have expected me to like I was his private nurse.

"You're welcome. Thanks for letting me shoot you. I feel better."

"Anytime," he says with a smile as he wiggles his eyebrows.

I laugh. "Really? I can shoot you anytime?"

He shrugs. "If you really need it. A bullet wound in an extremity is hardly anything unusual for me."

I let my eyes roam his chest for the first time, and it's then that I notice all the scars. Similar to Zeke's. Similar to mine.

I move the tank top straps on my shoulder, where I also wear the scar from a bullet wound.

He stares at it a moment. "We are more similar than we are different."

"Probably. But I didn't torture you. I just shot you after you told me to."

"You would have if given the chance." Langston closes the first-aid kit and puts it back on the wall.

"Of course."

He smiles at that and then moves back to the helm, looking at a navigation screen.

I consider asking him to fix me, or to take me home, but what truly matters right now is gaining his trust. I earned some of it by fixing his shoulder, but I need to use this moment to get more. I need something to continue the trust that is slowly building between us.

"Where are we going?"

His head turns to me, and I can see all of his thoughts turning behind his bright blue eyes. Between his eyes and blonde hair, he seems like light instead of the darkness toiling beneath the surface. It's the same darkness I feel inside Julian, yet it's different somehow.

"Spain," he answers.

My eyebrows raise, surprised he told me and not afraid to hide my shock to him.

"I have a house there. We need to put some distance between us and everyone else."

"Is that where the box is?"

He shakes his head.

"Then why are we going there?"

"We need some time and space for us to figure out where the box is."

His words tell me hardly anything, and yet they seem important, like a hidden message hides in his words only I can decode. Except I don't have the code key.

I don't have a clue how to interpret his words or why we need time and space to find the box, when to my knowledge, Kai Black is the only person who knows where the box is because she hid it.

"Go get some rest. And try not to get sick. The Sprite we have has to last you all the way to Spain." He winks at me.

"You're not worried I'll escape between now and then?"

"How are you going to escape? We are in the middle of the ocean. We are all alone, just the two of us. I'll make sure we can't be tracked before I go to sleep."

"You can do that?"

"I helped build the security system. I know how to disable the tracker. And I know how to use the system to keep an eye on you."

"So sure of yourself."

He nods. "Go to bed. You aren't going anywhere. We both know that. You won't go anywhere for the same reason you won't kill me."

"Goodnight, Langston Bishop."

He frowns as I say the name I've been calling him in my head.

"Goodnight, Siren Kane." He uses Zeke's last name, and it warms my heart.

I head downstairs, anxious to talk to Zeke and to verify he's really here. I pray he hasn't left me, or that I didn't imagine him earlier.

I don't feel unsafe anymore around Langston Bishop, but I don't feel safe either. I feel on edge. I feel unbalanced. And I can't understand why.

I open the door to my room and look around. The room seems empty, except for the bed. I don't feel Zeke's presence.

I frantically move around the room, hoping he's come back from the security room before Langston Bishop headed there himself. I move to the bathroom but don't find him there either.

My shoulders slump. My heart squeezes. I need my husband. I need him, and I don't know how to call him back to me.

I lean against the counter in the bathroom, exhausted and anxious. If he comes face to face with Langston Bishop alone, Zeke will try and kill him, which will ruin everything. Zeke won't be able to forgive himself if he kills his friend without understanding his motives first. He won't forgive himself if my head never heals.

"Looking for someone?" Zeke says from the doorway.

I catch my breath seeing him here.

"Don't do that to me," I say as I race into his open embrace. His arms fall around my back, and he holds me tight against his chest.

"You're the one making me. If it were up to me, I'd shoot Langston now, and we could get off this yacht."

"How about you fuck me instead?"

CHAPTER 9
ZEKE

How about you fuck me instead?

My body instantly hardens at her words. I'm so desperate for her. I need her. I need to fuck her. I need to feel connected to her in every way.

I feel selfish for wanting that when she's been sick and having to deal with Langston, while I hide like a silent bodyguard. Watching her help Langston while he stood shirtless in front of her drove me mad.

If we are going to keep this up, he better keep a shirt on from now on, because I won't survive otherwise.

And now she wants to fuck.

"I need you, Zeke."

"You have no idea what that does to me."

She smirks. "I have an idea." Her hand pushes between us until she's gripping my hardening cock.

"What about the security system? Are there cameras in the bedrooms?"

"No."

Siren smiles. "Lock the door then."

"Already done."

She lifts her arms and steps back, waiting for me to lift her shirt with a seductive bat of her eyelashes.

So I do as I'm silently told, and I'm rewarded by the most beautiful sight of her naked stomach and breasts. Siren has always been strong and muscular, but still very feminine. Now where her muscles once were flush against the surface is a softening, growing belly bump.

"I've never seen a more beautiful sight."

She blushes. "Take off my shorts."

I step forward. The button on her shorts is already unbuttoned. Soon her clothes won't fit over her stomach at all. I unzip the zipper and shimmy her shorts and underwear off her body until she is completely naked.

I'm speechless watching her.

"Your turn," Siren says as I stand in front of her, still completely clothed.

"Get in bed," I order.

Siren frowns.

"Bed," I command.

She pouts but does as I say, brushing past me and swaying her hips as she does. She's begging me to follow her with her body, but she doesn't need to beg; I'll be coming willingly.

I remove my clothes quickly and then turn off the lights before I walk to the bed. Siren is lying on top of the covers, her legs spread, her nipples pebbling for me.

"Under the covers," I command.

She frowns, thinking I'm turning her down. I'm not. I just don't want to fuck her. I want to love her like she's the queen. And if I touch her before getting her into bed where I want her, I'll lose my control and fuck her like an animal.

Once Siren is under the covers, I slide in next to her.

"Face the window."

Again she gives me a dirty look but rolls on her side.

I take a deep calming breath, trying my best not to let my need for her overtake me and turn into a devouring monster. I put my hand on her back, trailing my fingers down her spine slowly.

I watch her breath speed up at the gentle gesture. I add my heated breath, too, as I continue to trace her spine with my fingertips.

"Zeke," she breathes, her voice achy and needy.

I know what she wants. I'll give it to her, but first, she needs to relax. She needs to feel safe and loved. And I want this to last as long as it can, which means taking things excruciatingly slowly.

She takes a deep, calming breath. Her shoulders slump. I want her as relaxed as possible. I'm tired of making her tense and anxious. I'm tired of putting her through all of this. This needs to end. I need to stop this.

For now, the only thing I can help ease is her stress. Soon I will ensure that our enemies are gone, no matter the cost. No matter what I have to do, I will protect her and our baby.

My hands grip her neck, rubbing gently, then I move down to her shoulders and back, massaging every tense muscle. My hands slide lower, over her ass. I massage her ass too, then down her legs.

She moans, her back relaxing into my hands as I massage her back.

"Zeke," her voice grows more desperate.

"Shh, just feel. Don't think. Don't worry. I've got you."

Her head rolls back against my shoulder, and her arm reaches back, trying to pull me closer to her.

I grin, watching how relaxed, yet needy, she is.

Who am I kidding? I can't hold back much longer, either.

I push my body flush to hers until I can feel all of her back against my front. My cock pushes between her legs as I reach around and tease her nipples and kiss her neck.

"I love you. I want to protect you," I whisper.

She moans as I flick her nipple with my thumb.

"Let me protect you. Let me find a way to be the one to put myself in harm's danger, not you. I can't stand it. I love you too much to ever lose you. I wouldn't survive."

She takes my hand in hers, as her legs part and my cock slips closer to her entrance.

"Just like I couldn't lose you. It's not fair to think that you would be the only one to lose something if either of us fails," she says.

I push my hips forward slowly, so close to being inside of her, but knowing I won't last the second I am.

"Promise me you'll let me protect you."

She moans. "Promise me you won't risk your life to protect mine."

I can't promise any more than she can.

I reach between her legs and tease her clit.

"Promise me," I say, teasing her more, my cock taunting her entrance but not pushing inside her like she's begging.

She moans.

Neither of us can stand it anymore. I start thrusting inside her, giving her all that I have—all my dreams, desires, wants. I slide in and out, our bodies gliding together.

And just like I knew we would, too quickly we come.

We both muffle our cries. The rooms are soundproof, but it's still hard not to want to quiet our moaning when we don't want Langston to know.

I kiss over her ear, knowing she will never promise to let me protect her, but I'm going to promise her anyway. She needs to know how far I'll go, what I'll do to protect her. When she's scared or worried, she needs to know that she is safe. I will never let anyone hurt her again.

"I promise I'll protect you." I put my hand on her stomach. "I'll protect both of you—always."

CHAPTER 10
SIREN

I'll always protect you.

Always.

Those words play over and over in my head as I fall to sleep.

You're safe.

I'll protect you.

I'll keep you safe.

Zeke?

No, it's not Zeke. He can't keep you safe. I can.

I sit up abruptly as memories start flooding my head. I gasp hard and fast, unable to catch my breath. My lungs are burning, and my chest is tight, but I don't feel it, not really. I'm too focused on trying to remember the fleeting images.

Zeke sits up abruptly next to me, grabbing his gun before he realizes how flushed I am. He puts his hand on my forehead.

"You're burning up," Zeke says, trying to hide the worry in his voice, but I can sense it all the same.

He runs to the bathroom and returns a minute later with a cool washcloth, a glass of water, and a thermometer.

He puts the thermometer in my mouth, giving me a few more seconds before I will have to speak.

Who was the man?

The thermometer beeps, and Zeke removes it from my mouth with a slight relaxation of his facial muscles. "No fever."

He shoves the water into my hand. "Drink."

I sip, but I'm not worried about having a temperature or an illness.

"A nightmare?" Zeke asks.

I take another sip and then hand Zeke the water.

"More like a memory."

"A bad one?" Zeke's forehead brows until lines form around his eyes.

"No."

Zeke rubs my back, helping me relax.

"Want to tell me what it was about?"

"Just a man telling me that he'll protect me, but it wasn't you."

Zeke frowns. "Enzo?"

"No, I don't know who the man was. He didn't have a face, and he didn't have a voice I recognized. At least the memory didn't."

A knock on the door startles us both.

"Langston Bishop," I say as Zeke aims his gun at the door.

Zeke sighs. "I don't want to leave you. Not until I'm sure you are okay."

"I'm fine." I stand up and head to the closet. I pull on a T-shirt and shorts and throw a robe over my body to stay warm.

Zeke is dressed but otherwise sitting on the edge of the bed.

"Hide," I hiss at him.

He frowns but eventually heads to the closet.

I open the door and find Langston standing in the doorway.

"What would you like for breakfast?"

I frown at him as I tuck the robe tighter around my body.

"Breakfast. Are you an eggs and toast kind of girl? Pancakes? Oatmeal?"

I continue to stare at him. I don't understand this man.

"Siren?" He waves his hand in front of my face.

"Sorry, um...oatmeal."

He nods. "I'll fix it. Do you want to eat upstairs or in your room?"

I want to eat here with Zeke, but something tells me I need to spend as much time as I can with Langston Bishop before we get to Spain. We need intel to decide on a plan. *Do I continue to go with him? Or do I let Zeke kill him?*

"I'll come up," I say.

His eyes dilate in slight surprise, but then he's gone.

"You should have eaten here," Zeke says from behind me.

"I need to figure out why he did what he did to me. Why I'm here. Is he still working with Julian? Is he more evil than good? Something happened, and I'm the only one he might talk to."

Zeke cracks his knuckles. "He'd talk to me."

"Yea, and then you might kill a man you shouldn't."

"There is no excuse for what he did to you." He tucks a loose strand behind my ear.

"There is more to Langston Bishop than you realize. I just have to figure him out."

I kiss him tenderly. "I'll be back. And I'll make sure to sneak you some food."

"Don't worry about the food. I'll sneak some. Just make sure Langston keeps his shirt on."

"What fun is that?" I tease.

Zeke frowns. "Not funny."

"I might just have to shoot him again to see those rippling abs."

Then I disappear out the door, preventing Zeke from saying anything back without chancing that Langston will hear him. I assumed wrong.

Zeke follows me out. He catches my hand before I make it to the stairs and then pulls me back to him.

Zeke, I mouth, motioning my head upstairs. Langston could come down any second, and I'd ruin all the trust I've built with him so far.

Zeke presses his lips hard to my mouth, capturing me and reminding me who I belong to. Like that is even a question.

I belong to Zeke. I always have. I always will.

I promise, I mouth to Zeke when we finally break the kiss. I run up the stairs knowing Zeke will be protecting me nearby while I figure out what is going on with Langston.

I spot Langston putting a bowl of oatmeal and an orange juice at a table, and my nerves catch up to me. *What am I doing with this monster? A man who has hurt me? A man who threatened my life?*

However, he didn't rape me when he could have.

He tried to stop Julian.

And he's been nice ever since I've been on this boat.

"Anything else you need?" he asks like he's about to leave.

I walk over to my table and sit down. "Are you not going to join me?"

"Do you want me to join you?"

"No, but then again, I would prefer not to be your captive in the first place. But since we are both here, I think it's best we make the most of this and talk to each other."

He sits down in front of me, and I'm surprised that he also has oatmeal in his bowl.

"Is oatmeal what you usually eat?" I ask, staring at him.

"No."

"Then why are you eating it?"

"Because that's what you wanted, and I didn't want to cook two things."

I smile.

I can see why Langston Bishop and Zeke used to be friends. There are a lot of similarities between them. *But what changed? What happened that threw him down this path so far diverged from Zeke's own path?*

"Tell me a story about you and Zeke," I say before I take a bite of my oatmeal like we are two friends reminiscing about the good ole days.

"No." He shoves a bite into his mouth.

"Why not? How much longer do we have until we get to Spain? Another week at least? Why not make the most of it?"

Langston Bishop puts his spoon down. "You aren't asking to pass the time."

My heart stills. He knows Zeke is here. I grip my spoon tighter; maybe I could somehow use it as a weapon if I needed to.

He stands up. "You're asking because you think I'm a good person, and you think you will be able to manipulate me by talking."

I stand up too. "I think there is more than the evil I saw when you first bought me. There is more to you. The old you is still there."

He looks at me gravely. "I'm not a good person, Siren. I never was. Stop trying to find that part of me."

I step in front of him, so he will have to physically move me if he wants to leave the kitchen. It's probably not a smart move, but in order to figure out what his motives are, I need to push him to his limits.

"Are you going to kill me?" I ask.

He doesn't answer. "Move, Siren. I don't want to play games with you."

I smile thinly. "You're a good person, Langston Bishop."

"Why do you say that?"

I move out of his way. "Because you aren't going to kill me."

"I never answered you when you asked that."

"Exactly. If I had asked Julian Reed that he would have answered yes immediately. You clearly have no plan of killing me."

Langston Bishop leans toward me, giving me his most menacing snarl. "Maybe I'm just not as obvious as Julian Reed."

I step aside, and then he leaves me standing in the kitchen.

I cross my arms and huff in frustration.

A few seconds later, Zeke appears. He grabs Langston's uneaten bowl of oatmeal and scarfs it down.

"What do you think?" I ask Zeke.

"I think you should stop this whole thing and let me go take him out."

I return to the table and take another bite of my oatmeal. I'm not hungry, but I know the baby needs food.

"What do you really think about him?"

Zeke looks out the door where Langston left. "I think I never knew my best friend at all." He doesn't look at me when he continues. "But I think we need to find out his motivations. I think we need to convince him to fix you. I think we need answers."

I kiss Zeke on the lips, knowing how hard it is for him to stand by and watch me try to manipulate his friend. It's tearing him up inside to watch me put myself in danger when he could easily get rid of the threat, even if it meant we would have to face bigger threats down the road.

I take both of our bowls to the sink and rinse them out, rinsing down the evidence of Zeke's presence.

"Where is he?" I ask Zeke.

He stares down at his phone that has the security feed on it. "The gym."

I crack my neck. "I could use a workout."

CHAPTER 11
ZEKE

Every time I let Siren go back with Langston, I feel sick. My stomach knots, my chest tightens, my heart races. I'm sweaty and clammy, anxiety rising in my throat. My body reacts to the danger with a full-blown anxiety attack.

Even though I can protect Siren, save her in a moment, I'm sick because I'm the reason she's in this situation in the first place. If it wasn't for me, she would be safe. She wouldn't know who Langston is. She wouldn't have been tortured by him.

This is all my fault. She shouldn't be the one to fix the problem. I should. But Langston is talking to her. Slowly, and painfully. She can get him to talk without shedding any blood.

If I did this my way, Langston would be dead before he spoke a word.

Siren heads to the gym, where Langston is lifting weights in front of a mirror.

I stand outside the gym door. I caught the door at the last second to keep it from closing so I can listen through the door and watch on the screen as Siren enters the gym.

At first, she just walks over to Langston but doesn't say anything.

She picks up some dumbbells and starts lifting them next to Langston like he isn't there.

Of course, they fall into sync, lifting the dumbbells up to their shoulders at the same time.

Jesus, I'm not going to survive this. I'm giving her until we get to Spain. That's it. Then this ends.

Langston's shirt comes off, and I almost come unglued. I want to break through the door, but I stop myself.

"Really? You can't workout with a shirt on?" Siren asks, rolling her eyes at him.

"I didn't ask you to join me. You were the one that followed me, remember?" Langston says.

"And you are the bastard who took her memories from her," I say, quietly to myself.

She throws her dumbbells down on the floor in frustration. "I'm not the one holding me captive here."

Langston watches her silently as she walks over to the boxing ring and starts putting on some gloves.

"What are you doing?"

"Punching you, so I don't shoot you again." Siren continues to strap the gloves onto her hands as Langston climbs into the ring.

"Punch away," he says, holding his arms out like he is just going to stand there and let him hit her.

Siren grins slyly, and then she throws a punch. Langston steps out of her way. He's the fastest of all of us. She's fought Enzo and me, and we all fight differently. I use my brute strength. Enzo uses a combination of speed and strength. Langston uses his speed and brains. He outsmarts his competitor. She's going to have to change her strategy if she wants to land a punch because he's too quick to be hit.

"Good, I thought you were just going to stand there and let me punch you. If that was the case, I could have just as easily hit a punching bag," Siren says.

Langston smirks. "You won't hit me. Not without me blocking you."

"I shot you, didn't I?"

"Yea, that required zero skill. This requires a lot."

She throws another punch. It's slow on purpose to trick Langston into thinking she's slower than she actually is.

I grin. I know how well they both fight, but my money is on my girl.

As much as it puts me on edge that she is fighting while pregnant, I've seen her do it before and be fine. For some reason, Langston isn't fighting back, just dodging or blocking her punches.

"You're going to have to do better than that," Langston says.

Siren throws another punch, barely missing Langston's nose. "You mean, like that?"

Langston shoots her a dubious look. "I look forward to the day when we can fight fair. You have me at a disadvantage since I won't fight a pregnant woman."

Siren swings again. "And why is that? Julian would have no problem fighting me in my condition."

Langston's feet dance as he moves out of the way once again with a frown on his face. His muscles tense, and for once, I'm glad his shirt is off. It gives more clues as to what he's thinking.

"Come on, if you think this is so unfair, fight back," Siren goads him.

I tense, not liking this. If she succeeds in getting him to fight back, I might not be able to move fast enough to stop him from making contact.

"You're a good person, that's why," Siren says.

Langston grinds his teeth together. His muscles turn into a brick wall, and I think she's going to be able to make an impact now.

But she swings, he dodges.

"Why am I here? Why me?" Siren pleads as she swings in rapid succession.

"Why do you work for Julian when you hate him? I remember the hate in your voice when you were together. I remember you pleading him not to rape me. You tried to save me. You did everything you could."

More swings, more dodging.

"Why is that? You care about us? You care about your friends?"

Swing.

Dodge.

"What made you pretend to be someone you're not? Was it a girl?"

Swing, dodge; this one closer than all the rest. So close she actually brushed her glove against his cheek.

"Liesel? Is that the girl that broke your heart? Turned you evil?"

She struck a nerve, and this time when she punches, she hits him square in the jaw. She doesn't let up. She keeps punching him in the face again and again. She suddenly kicks hard to his stomach, bringing him to his knees.

Langston never retaliates, no matter how angry he gets. He won't hurt her, even though he's hurt her before. *What am I missing? What happened? What changed from before?*

She kicks again, and this time, her ankle seems to twist as she kicks, and she grabs her stomach.

She moans loudly and falls to the floor. I start to run through the door, scared to death something happened. She's in pain; maybe she lost the baby.

But as she falls, she looks into the corner of the room where the security camera is and winks. That wink is the only thing that keeps me back, reminding me this is a game to get Langston to tell us the truth.

Langston runs to her. "Are you okay? Is it the baby?"

"I don't know; my stomach," Siren cries dramatically, too dramatically. I know her well. Langston doesn't. He buys the lie.

Langston sits over her, worry filling his eyes. "I'll redirect us toward the nearest hospital, put out a mayday call, and see if there is a boat with a doctor nearby."

Siren smiles at his reaction.

"What?" Langston practically yells his worry in her face.

"Why are you worried about me? Why are you trying to protect me?"

"You're not really hurt. The baby's fine?" He falls back on his heels.

"Yes, the baby's fine. I'm fine. I played you to show you how much you care about me."

Langston sits down next to her. He stares at the floor and then finally up at her.

"I protect you because you are the only one who knows the location of the box. Your memories hold the key to finding it," Langston says.

Siren looks at him with confusion. "That's not possible. Zeke put the box in the vault. And then Kai moved it. She is the only one who knows, not me."

Langston is shaking his head, and my phone buzzes in my hand, and my view of the security cameras vanishes.

"It's a fake," he tells her.

My phone screen updates to show an incoming call—Kai.

Something tells me that I need to answer the phone. Kai wouldn't be calling me otherwise.

"Hello," I whisper as I step away from the door.

"We have a problem," Kai says, not bothering with pleasantries.

"I think I know."

"The box I hid isn't the real one. I opened it to destroy it. There was nothing in it."

I stare at the door, realizing there is so much I don't know.

"We have to find it. If it gets into Julian's hands—"

"He won't get it."

"How do you know?"

"Because Siren is the only person who knows where it is."

My memories.

I'm the only one who knows where the box is.

None of this makes any sense.

I continue to stare at Langston Bishop, more confused than ever.

"Maybe we should make some tea or get you another Sprite; then I'll explain everything," he says.

"Tea would be nice."

He stands and then holds out his hand to help me up.

"And put a shirt on."

"Why? Am I too distracting?"

"No, but I'm married, and it's weird to be around you without a shirt on."

He pauses for a second; maybe I gave away that Zeke is here. Instead, Langston walks over to his shirt and puts it on. We walk back upstairs to the kitchen.

I try to force my brain to remember what Langston Bishop thinks I know, but all it does is give me a headache while Langston makes two cups of tea.

"Don't do that," he says. He carries the cups outside, and we sit, looking out at the ocean. He hands me my cup, and I take it mindlessly.

"Don't do what?"

"Force yourself to remember. It's not good for you."

I stare at him incredulously. My heart beats rapidly, realizing how much I might be connected to him.

"Tell me the truth," I say.

"The box in the vault is fake."

"It's not in the vault anymore. Kai hid it."

"Well, wherever it is, it's fake."

"How?"

"Your parents and Julian's parents worked together."

I gasp. "No, there is no way. My parents were missionaries. They were religious and not always kind to me, but they would have no reason to be involved in something like this."

Langston sighs. "They wanted to rid the world of its evil with the viral cancer, and only use the cure on those they deemed worthy. Those who hadn't sinned."

I freeze, remembering their conversations. It sounds like them.

"Julian's parents felt much the same. Julian's mother worked with Lucy's mother in a lab in Miami. She realized what Lucy's mother had discovered, but it was too late to steal. Lucy had already given it to Zeke to hide. The vault was too hard to get into themselves, and the Black name was too strong. If they were caught, Black would kill them all."

I process all of his words, realizing just how connected all our families are and have been this entire time.

"So they had me steal it," I say. I can't remember ever stealing it. I don't remember breaking into the vault, but I'm sure that's where I fit into this puzzle.

"Yes. No one would suspect a young twenty-something girl. One who could seduce and fight better than they could."

"How did I steal it?"

"You've met Zeke and me before. You flirted with us both in a bar. Zeke took an instant attraction to you; it was like nothing I'd ever seen before. He was still in love with Lucy at the time, although that relationship was ending, but you—he couldn't help but fall for you."

We didn't meet in the ocean. We met before in a bar.

"You flirted. You danced with Zeke. You stole his key to the vault."

"How could I have forgotten meeting you both?"

Langston Bishop ignores me and continues his story. "You broke into the vault and switched the boxes. You didn't know what you were doing or stealing, just that you were promised your freedom if you did this task.

"Zeke searched for you everywhere for days, hoping to find the woman who enchanted him and stole a piece of his heart."

Zeke. My heart beats for him. "How did Zeke forget me when you clearly didn't?"

"It hurt too much to remember you."

I nod, understanding. If Zeke was ever taken from me, the only way I could survive was to forget him, erase him from my memory.

"What then?"

"Then you opened the box. You realized what was inside and that you couldn't give it to them. So you hid it and killed them all. You realized it wasn't enough. Others knew of its existence. The Black family. Julian. The mystery would spread. So you started drinking, doing drugs, shock therapy—anything to make you forget so they couldn't use you to get to the box."

I blink rapidly. I forced myself to forget. Everyone Julian has done has been to get me to remember. He put Zeke into my life, hoping I would remember.

"Did you forget, or are you just a really good liar?" Langston Bishop asks.

"I can't tell a lie."

He waits, knowing that is a lie.

"At least, I couldn't tell a lie. I think all the lying and hiding of the secret maxed out my abilities. My brain couldn't process anymore lies. But lately, I've been able to lie more and more. Whatever you did to me, it started unleashing memories and allowed me space to lie again."

Langston Bishop nods.

"I think your voice in my head has actually been my father. All the words I thought you were saying were words he's said to me when he was alive."

"How do you fit into all of this? How do you know so much?"

"I needed to leave, get away for a while, my own pain was too much."

"Because of Liesel?"

Langston Bishop doesn't answer me.

"I experimented much like you did with forgetting. I needed to forget the pain. I did all sorts of horrible things—trauma can make you forget."

"Just like the trauma of killing my own parents helped me forget."

He nods.

"We're monsters."

"Yes, we are."

We both sip our tea silently before he continues.

"I ran into Julian Reed and realized he was trying to hurt my family and friends. So I stepped in, wanting to prevent Julian from hurting them. I pretended to be on Julian's side to protect my family.

"When your husband sold you, I realized who you were. I didn't trust you initially, but then I realized you had forgotten everything. But I knew you had to remember, so I could destroy the box along with the virus inside. It was the only way to protect my family. I didn't realize at first whose side you were on. I didn't know you had hidden it to keep it safe. So I started methods to try to regain your memories. Some were painful. Remembering can be painful."

"You were trying to save us all, Langston."

He nods slightly.

He's good. He was the ultimate protector. He was trying to protect us all. He wasn't torturing me; he was begging me to remember so we could destroy the thing that could kill us all.

"Langston," I say.

He looks up at me. "Just Langston?"

I nod. He's Langston. He's good. Not evil. Bishop doesn't exist. He's just a man he was playing as he tried to save us.

"Thank you," I say.

"Don't thank me. I don't have the power to save anyone. And

getting your memory back is going to hurt like hell. Only you can decide if you want to do that."

"Still, you've done a lot to help us while taking all the blame for being a monster."

Langston smirks. "Don't think I'm not still a monster. Trust me, I am. A bigger monster than all of you. I won't be accepted back into the Black family with open arms when this is all over."

"But you are on my side, Langston. You're my teammate."

"Zeke is your teammate. I'm just the man who will do what it takes to help you remember. The man you will hate for hurting you."

CHAPTER 13
ZEKE

I lie down in the bed while I wait for Siren to come back. I consider making my presence known and kicking Langston's ass after learning that Langston has been protecting us this entire time.

But I don't trust anyone but Siren right now. I don't know if she believes everything Langston said or not, but I do know that I only trust her.

The bedroom door opens quietly and then closes.

I jump up when I see her. She's in as much shock as I am.

I don't know what to say. I can hardly think of a plan. And I'm about to spill more bad news on her. All I can do is hold her in my arms, so that's what I do.

I pull Siren tight to me, wishing my arms alone could be enough to protect her.

Time passes, probably only a few minutes, but minutes feel like hours when you're living with so much uncertainty.

"Did you hear everything Langston said?"

I nod. "Most."

I don't miss that she now calls him Langston instead of Langston Bishop. She's decided who he is—just Langston—the good man who was once my friend. He's still my friend, just an asshole for trying to save us all instead of letting us know the truth and working with us.

If we have all learned one thing, it's when this is over, we need to learn to work together better.

Gently, I lead her to the edge of the bed so we can sit down and discuss everything that happened.

"I heard that you alone know where the box is. That it's in your memories. That's what Langston was trying to do, help you remember."

She nods.

"Did you hear the part where we met before?"

"Yes, I don't know how I could have forgotten you. Even if we only met for a second, I can't imagine ever forgetting." I take her hand and kiss it. "But I can understand the pain I must have felt at only knowing you for a moment and then losing you."

She bites her lip and tucks her hair behind her ear.

"What are you thinking?"

"Do you think everything Langston said is true?" she asks.

"Most likely. Kai called. She went back to get the box she hid. She opened it with plans to destroy it, but it was empty. Wherever it is, it's gone."

"So that means it's up to me to remember." She stands suddenly and paces as she bites her nails.

I stand to stop her from pacing, blocking her path, but she turns to pace in a smaller circle, so I grab her.

"It's going to be okay. We will make a plan. And now that you know what the dreams are about, you don't have to be afraid anymore. You can relax and let the memories come. You'll remember. And then we will destroy it."

Siren takes a deep breath, washing away some of the pain. I can't help but wonder if she's hiding something that I'm not putting together.

"I promise you, everything is going to be okay."

She puts my hand over her heart. "Tell that to my anxious heart."

Fuck, her heart is beating so fast.

There is so much more to be said. The worst hasn't even been spoken yet, but I can't stand to see her anxious.

"Undress and get in the bed," I say, deciding we need another calming round of sex to get her to relax.

"No."

"No?"

"I don't need a massage. I don't need slow and loving. I need hard and fast. I need passion and emotion. I need you to make me forget. I need you to remind me of how much my husband enjoys fucking me."

I spin her around until her ass is against my front, so she can feel my erection growing in my pants against her back. I tilt her head up and kiss her harshly, my tongue pushing past her lips, tasting every sweet drop of her.

"You want the beast inside?" I ask.

"Yes, I want my beast-man."

I give her a wicked grin. "You're going to regret saying that when you are so sore you can't walk straight for a week."

She bats her long eyelashes at me. "It will be worth it."

I tug on her hair and nip at her neck, and she moans so loudly that I'm afraid I hurt her. But I know she's just loud because she's anxious and needs to put everything into this. She needs a distraction to relax. The room is soundproof, but I've barely touched her, and she's already moaning at the top of her lungs. I've got to keep her quiet.

"Siren, baby, you are going to have to be quieter. The room is soundproof, but I'm not sure the walls can withstand your beautiful cries."

"I can't be quiet," she moans louder as I kiss her neck again.

She may want me to let my inner demon out on her, but we will definitely be caught if I do.

So instead, I decide on a different move.

I kiss her mouth, blocking some of her moans with my own mouth as I walk her into the bathroom. I flick on the shower behind her, and then I push us under the spray. The cold water chills us both, causing us to gasp before the water turns warmer.

The reaction Siren gives me is what I was hoping for. She's focused entirely on the water and me, but not as loudly as she was before.

I peel her shirt off and kiss every spot of flesh I can find on her body before caressing her breasts and pinching her nipples harshly.

She yelps at the sharp pinch of her nipple.

"Shh," I say as my hand slides down her smooth stomach and into her shorts.

"I can't. Everything feels heightened right now."

I slip my finger inside her and find her as wet inside as out.

I bite down on her shoulder to keep from screaming out myself at how perfect she is.

"I need you, Zeke. I need you, now."

"Yes."

I undo my pants and push hers down as I slide my cock between her legs, teasing her clit with my tip.

"Zeke," she cries, moaning, and I'm not even inside her yet.

I push inside her and listen to the heavenly sound leaving her throat as I pleasure her in a way only I can.

I thrust inside, and our combined ecstasy is loud enough to wake someone up a mile away. I must have left a window or the door open, because the door to the bedroom swings opens, and I hear Langston run inside.

"Siren! Are you okay? I heard screaming," he yells as he enters her bedroom, but doesn't find her.

I whisper in Siren's ear. "Tell him you are okay."

I stroke her back, but don't move my cock. She needs to tell him that she's okay to make him go away.

"Yes!" she cries, but it sounds too euphoric, there is no way he's buying that. "I'm fine!"

"You sure? Are you sick?"

"No!"

"You're scaring me. What's happening?" I hear him try the door. Even though there is no key to the bathroom, it wouldn't take much to break the lock open.

Although, it wouldn't be the worst thing for him to find me here, but until we've discussed a plan, I'd rather him not.

"Just go with it," I whisper into Siren's ear before I thrust hard into her, making her cry out.

"I'm making myself come! Go away!" She cries out as I thrust harder and harder.

She grips the side of the shower as I pump into her over and over, harder and harder with each stroke.

I hear Langston eventually retreat. I'm not sure if he believed her or not, but he's gone, and I can fuck her in peace.

So that's what I do. I drive in and out of her, watching her come more and more undone until she's screaming my name so loudly I'm afraid Langston is going to come back in here to check on her.

I finish right after her.

We don't speak as we dry off and get dressed, but I can tell she's more relaxed than she was before.

I go and double lock the bedroom door so Langston can't get in while we sleep. Then I lie down in bed with Siren, unable to keep holding my words back. I have to tell her everything.

CHAPTER 14
SIREN

I snuggle into the bed with Zeke, trying to enjoy the last few moments of lingering sex bliss. I try to mark everything in my memory, now that I know how easily my memories can be taken from me.

I remember the feel of the water raining down on my face. The feel of Zeke at my back. His hands on my body. His cock slipping in and out of me. The gruff sounds he made. The screams I made.

I memorize it all, solidifying myself for what's to come. Zeke's energy has changed to anxiety, signaling challenges we're about to face.

"Now Langston can't get in again," Zeke says.

I blush, thinking about Langston walking in on us, the sounds I was making, and what I said I was doing...

"Langston knows you are here," I say.

Zeke shrugs. "Maybe, maybe not. Does it matter anymore?"

"No, it doesn't. He told me the truth. Now we just have to decide what to do with the truth."

Zeke pulls me to him as he strokes my hair, and we lay on our sides, staring at each other. "I have another truth to tell first."

I nod, knowing this was coming.

"Julian Reed isn't dead."

My heart shutters, but it doesn't come as a surprise. I knew deep down that Julian couldn't be killed easily. The only way is by Zeke's or my hands.

"I knew he wasn't dead."

"I'm sorry. I should have stayed. I should have killed him myself. I should have—"

I put my fingers to his lips. "No, you have nothing to apologize for. I needed you here with me."

I remove my fingers. "I wish I could have killed him and been here with you. I feel like I'm failing you."

"You aren't. You're loving me. You're protecting me. It's enough."

Zeke kisses the back of my hand. "But I can't stay and protect you here forever. I have to go back—"

"I know." I don't want Zeke to risk his life. I won't survive if something happens to him.

"We will be in Spain tomorrow. We need to make a plan," Zeke says.

I nod. "I need to stay. I need to figure out my memories with Langston."

"And I need to go kill Julian Reed."

Our fingers tangle together. Who knows how long we'll be apart this time.

It breaks my heart.

When I look into Zeke's eyes, I can see the fear in his.

"It's just temporary. A few days, maybe a week. We will be together again."

"I know, and you'll be safe. Langston will protect you; I'll make sure of that. You will take your time remembering. There is no rush. Once Julian is dead, we will recover your memories and go destroy the box forever."

"You have to promise me that you won't put yourself at risk. That you will stop giving yourself up to save me. You will go with Kai and Enzo, and together you will all take down Julian. Promise?"

"I promise I will not put myself in excessive danger. But if it comes down to your life or mine, I will do everything I can to protect you. Don't ever make me promise differently."

I suck in a breath. I don't want to let him go. I don't want to let him risk his life without me there to fight by his side. But I can't risk my baby's life.

He tilts my head up until I can stare into his deep dark eyes. "Promise me that if you remember where the box is that you will wait until I've killed Julian and returned to go after it. We will go after it together. Your job is to remember if you can, but most importantly, your job is to stay safe. Promise me."

I kiss him. We've promised so many things. We've broken more promises than we've kept. The only promises that matter are the marriage vows we made.

"This is it. We just have to get through this final battle. This final fight, and then we will be safe," I say.

He nods. "And we will win."

But what happens after? We can't keep risking our lives like this. I can't keep risking our child's life. When this is over, our lives are going to be very different. We will have to start over, find other ways to make money, to be happy. Fighting and killing people won't work.

"So it's decided. Tomorrow I will fly to Kai and Enzo to go hunt down Julian and kill him," Zeke says.

"And I'll stay with Langston, hiding in his home, safe and doing my best to remember."

Zeke's face is filled with worry. I know how much it pains him to leave me.

"I'll text and call you as much as I can. You have the tough job. My job is just to eat and keep this baby growing," I say, rubbing my hand over my stomach, which makes him smile.

I memorize his grin. The small dimple that forms in his cheek. The light in his dark eyes.

Zeke leans down and kisses my stomach while I stroke his hair.

I try to spare him as much pain I can because he feels my pain worse than I feel it myself. I lie even though I know it's a sin, but it's a worthy sin to spare him.

The truth is, I will try to get my memories back, but it will be incredibly painful. I remember what Langston tried to do to get me to remember before. It's going to take a lot more to remember now. I have to remember to protect my family.

As long as the box is out there, my family isn't safe. The Black family is the most powerful organized crime family in the world. Hundreds of others will try and hunt the box down if they know they can use it to take down the notorious Black family.

I have to remember, no matter how painful. I have to destroy the box. But I can't let Zeke know how painful it will be, which is why Langston has to be the one to help me. I have to be strong enough to let Zeke go, and pray that he comes back.

CHAPTER 15
ZEKE

We've stopped moving, and I don't hear the purr of the engines anymore, which means we've made it to Spain.

Siren is still asleep in my arms. I want to spend every moment with her, hold onto her until the very last second, spending our last moments together kissing, hugging, and fucking.

But I have something important to do to ensure that she is safe. As much as I'd love to lay here holding her in my arms and watching her sleep, I get out of bed, shower quickly, and get dressed in my only attire of jeans and a T-shirt.

When I come back to the bedroom, Siren has stirred.

I walk over and kiss her on the head. "Shhh, sleep and take your time getting dressed. I'll be back in a few minutes."

"Where are you going?" she says with a soft smile on her face.

"I'll be back." I kiss her again. I don't have to tell her for her to know exactly what I'm doing.

I don't know how this conversation is going to go. If this conversation doesn't go well, I may need to put Siren on a flight by herself to the farthest ends of the earth after I kill Langston.

For now, I don't want to talk about it. I just want to go deal with it and get back to our last few moments together as quickly as possible.

I head upstairs after quickly looking at the security feed to see where Langston is.

He's making breakfast in the kitchen.

I walk into the doorway of the kitchen, and Langston immediately senses me.

"Are we going to finally talk, or are you going to continue sneaking around and monitoring me on the security cameras?" Langston says, not turning around.

"When did you figure it out?"

"I suspected it when I set up the security system, but couldn't find any evidence of tampering. But after last night's show...there was no way the sounds she was making came from a vibrator."

I chuckle but try to keep it quick. We aren't back on good footing at the moment.

Langston turns around and stares at me wordlessly. He's wearing a dark grey T-shirt and jeans just like me. He looks like the same Langston I've known since I was a kid, but so much has changed. We are both different men.

"So you're married now. I never thought I'd see the day. I thought we'd both be bachelors forever," Langston finally says.

I walk forward silently.

Langston stiffens. He knows what's coming. And he deserves worse.

I punch him hard in the jaw. His head snaps—blood spills from his broken nose when he turns back to face me.

"That was for hurting my wife," I say.

He stares at me with his arms at his side. He won't fight me. He knows he deserves it, and he's preparing for another hit.

"And this is for protecting her." I grab his shoulder and pull him into a hug.

He relaxes a second and then hugs me back.

Finally, we step back, staring at each other. "Are you going to tell me why you lied to us? Why you pretended to be Bishop?"

"Partly to protect you all," Langston answers.

"And the other part?"

"My own personal shit you don't need to be concerned with."

I frown.

"I'm trying to trust you, Langston, but when you say shit like that, you don't make it easy."

"I'm not trying to make it easy. I'm just doing what I have to."

Langston's nose is still bleeding. I walk over to the sink and wet a hand-towel before tossing it to him. "Here."

He snatches it and wipes the blood from his nose. "Thanks."

"I'm going to assume the personal stuff has to do with your own woman problems?" Liesel, to be exact, if I had to guess.

"I'm not going to tell you. So if that's why you are here, you can drop it. I'm not ready to share anything except what you need to know."

I walk over to the bar and pour us both a scotch.

Langston raises his eyebrows as I hand him the drink. "I'm guessing this isn't to toast your impending fatherhood? Although, congrats, by the way. I always thought you'd make a good father."

"No, we have other things to discuss. Come on," I sigh as we walk to a table on the top deck. We sit and look out at the city beyond the pier where we are parked.

We both sip our scotch, even though it's early in the morning. We need the drink to get through this conversation.

"Julian Reed has to be killed," I say.

Langston nods. "I agree, but you can't just kill him. You have to kill the man financing him."

"Which is who?'

Langston sips his drink. "I don't know. I tried investigating, but I never figured it out."

"We need a plan to make Julian think I'm on his side," I say.

"I thought that was what you were doing when you went with him in the helicopter."

"Yea, I was until I realized that you go by the name Bishop." I give him a dirty look.

He sighs. "Don't blame this on me."

"You hurt Siren. I blame you. You could have told me the truth when you bought her."

"I didn't realize she was yours. I recognized who she was. I knew she was the girl who flirted with you and that you fell for in the bar that night all those years ago, but I didn't realize she was yours until you bought her back from me."

"Speaking of that, you owe me the money I paid you to get her back. Don't think I forgot."

Langston chuckles. "That was fun. But it showed me just how much you love her. How far you're willing to go for her."

"Well, it wasn't fun when I didn't have the money for protecting my friends. And why did you need to test my love for her?"

"So I knew how to handle her to get her memories back."

"Now that you know, hands off her."

Langston puts his hands up mockingly. "Have I touched her since you've been monitoring me?"

"No, but it doesn't mean I trust you around her. It doesn't mean I even trust you completely yet." Although, I need to trust him in order to leave Siren with him. We all know I need to be the one to go and kill Julian, but I'll only do that if I believe in my heart that Siren and our baby will be safe.

Langston drinks his scotch wearily, leaning back in his chair as the sun rises higher behind him. We don't have much time until Siren decides to join us.

"What do you need from me to trust me again?" Langston asks.

"Show me how far you are willing to go to protect her."

Langston finishes his drink, already preparing to do whatever I ask him to do. He's one of my best friends. I don't want to see him in pain. I just want to test his loyalty. I want to see how far he's willing to go to protect Siren.

I pull a knife from my pocket and hand it to him. He takes it carefully, knowing I'm going to ask him to use it against himself.

"Cut off your finger so I know you'd be willing to lose a limb for her. That is how far I need you to go if you love her."

He sucks in a breath as he processes what I'm saying. He holds the silver knife in his hand expertly, like he could hit a man in the heart with it. He could.

But that's not what I'm asking him to do. I'm asking him to cut off a finger. Remove part of himself that he can never get back.

I don't know exactly what Langston did to try to get her memories back, but no more. The pain and torture stops now. Only slow, gentle methods from here forward. This is payback for what he did, and proof that he will do what it takes to protect her.

"Which finger?" Langston says, casually flicking the knife around in his hand.

I give him a stern look. "Your choice."

He glides the knife over each finger of his left hand, considering. I assume he'll choose his pinky, but instead, he lets the knife stop on his pointer finger.

He takes a deep breath. We have both been through plenty of pain and torture before, but none that was self-inflicted. We've hurt each other fighting and training, and been hurt countless times by our enemies, but that is as far as it has gone.

It's different inflicting physical pain on yourself rather than it being inflicted upon you. When you are tortured, you fight back. You have adrenaline pumping to keep the pain from becoming too much.

That's not true right now.

"I regret ever hurting Siren. I regret pushing her as far as I did, but Siren is a part of our family now. You love her. I will protect Siren with my life. I will do whatever it takes to keep her safe and alive. I will protect your unborn baby with my life." Langston lifts the knife above his index finger and is about to slam down. He looks me straight in the eye. "I promise to protect Siren no matter what it costs me. No matter how much I lose, I'll ensure that she lives. I vow."

And then he's slamming his arm down, intent on slicing off his finger in one quick movement. My hand catches his wrist just as the knife hits the flesh on top of his finger.

Langston exhales harshly, surprised by my sudden movement to save his finger. The knife draws some blood, but his finger is still intact.

Langston slowly looks at me, his blue eyes dilating in surprise. "Why did you stop me?"

"I don't need to maim you for no reason. I just needed to know you were willing to do it. You'll be able to protect Siren better with all ten fingers."

Langston's shoulders relax. He gives me a curt nod in understanding.

"But if you let anyone hurt Siren, yourself included, I'll do the same thing to the woman you love." My words are harsh and cruel. And exactly how I feel.

He can deny that he loves a woman all he wants, but if he doesn't love Liesel, he definitely cares deeply for her. He wouldn't want me to lay a finger on her.

"Did I pass? Do you trust me?" Langston asks.

"Yes, I trust you. Don't make me regret it."

Langston stands and fetches the bottle of scotch, before refilling our glasses. His hand shakes as he pours, his nerves still a bit shot. He could have been faking his attempt, but based on how he's acting, it seems like he truly believed he was going to cut off his finger.

"So, what's your plan? Find Julian's financier and kill them both?"

I think for a minute. "Are you still in contact with Julian?"

"Yes," Langston says, drinking all of his scotch before he pours another glass. His hand shakes less this time.

"Does he still think you are working together toward the same goal?"

"Yes, I believe so."

"Good."

"What are you two planning without me?" Siren asks, smiling in the doorway. When I look at her, I'm glad that I didn't make Langston cut off his finger. She would be disappointed in me.

I hold out my hand, and she takes a seat on my lap. I hold her tightly, looking across the table to Langston. I'm putting everything I love in his hands.

Don't fail me, asshole.

CHAPTER 16
SIREN

We have a plan, and as usual, I hate it.

One of us has to sacrifice too much to save the rest of us, but I can't think of a better option.

We are doing this as safely as possible. Kai and Enzo will be there to protect Zeke, but Zeke is still going willingly back into the lion's den. And as much as I want to be his shield, I can't.

Instead, I sit on his lap while Langston pulls his phone out to arrange everything. I'm thankful that the two of them are getting along and trusting each other again. I don't know what Langston had to do to gain Zeke's trust again, but he did. Otherwise, Zeke wouldn't be leaving me here with Langston.

Langston puts the phone to his ear, while Zeke and I sit silently by.

"Hello," Langston says.

A pause.

"I have a trade I'd like to make," Langston says.

We wait patiently for Julian to talk.

"I want in, fifty-fifty, on the box when we find it. In exchange, I'll give you Zeke."

Another pause. Langston looks up at both of us, waiting for us to stop him.

"Deal," he says and then ends the call.

"Where is the trade happening?"

"He said to meet him in Belize. I'll send my men in my place to travel with you. He knows my task is to make Siren remember, so she's safe with me. He won't interfere with trying to learn her memories."

Zeke kisses my hair.

"Good," Zeke says.

"I'll help you understand his security system and give you ideas on how to infiltrate the system before you leave," Langston says.

Zeke nods.

I stand up, and then Zeke stands. "Go get ready. I'll be right down," I instruct.

Zeke kisses me again, and then he walks downstairs.

I look at Langston. "What did he make you do to earn his trust?"

"Nothing."

I shake my head. "Liar. I know Zeke better than you do."

"Truly. In the end, he didn't make me go through with it."

"Good."

Langston stands and stares at me, looking through to my soul. "You haven't told him what you plan to do to get your memories back, have you?"

"No, I haven't."

"Why not?"

"Because if I did, he wouldn't go."

Langston frowns.

"Are you going to tell him?" I ask.

Langston looks past me. "No, I won't tell him. He feels other's pain worse than any of us. He physically can't stand to see you hurt, and I don't like hurting him."

I nod, and then I head downstairs to find Zeke preparing to leave. He's gathered all his weapons and hidden them as best as he can beneath his clothes.

"I'm not sure I'm ready for this," I say honestly. I don't want him to leave. I'm too afraid he won't come back.

Zeke holds out his hand, and I take it.

"Me neither." He pulls me to him for the hundredth time in the last few days. We're bound together like magnets, and it's going to hurt like hell when we are pulled apart.

"It's for the best, though. You need to go. Kill Julian and protect this family."

He rests his hand on my stomach. "And you need to protect our little one."

"I will."

"Kiss me."

Then our lips are smashed together, our tongues pushing and striking to bore deeper into each other's mouths. Maybe if we tangle ourselves together further, then we won't be able to be ripped apart.

It's a lie.

We both know it.

It's just going to make the separation harder.

But neither of us cares. We need this more than we need air.

Our hands find their way under each other's clothes. We don't have time to fuck, but that doesn't matter. We need each other too much to stop with just a simple kiss.

Our time is running out. These are our last moments together. Zeke may never come back. We may both fail in our missions.

That only makes my heart beat faster, my pulse race, and my breath catch in my throat as I kiss him. I'm sure I'm a flushed mess. My hair is tangled in his fist, and my clothes are out of place, but I don't care. I never want these kisses to end.

"It's time," Langston says sadly from the doorway. Even he can't stand to make this end. But Langston's men are here to pretend to take Zeke as their prisoner to Julian, and if I don't let Zeke go, he'll miss his flight. And if that happens, I'll never let him go.

So I grab onto Zeke's shirt with my fists, as I peel my lips from his, still staying close. This is going to take everything in me to step away from him.

Zeke tucks a strand of hair behind my ear, knowing how hard this is for me as I still clutch onto him.

"This isn't goodbye," he breathes.

"I know." But I feel the tears and fear welling. We can't promise that this isn't goodbye. We can never make that promise.

"I'll come back. I won't miss the birth of our child."

"That's months away," I breathe. He better be back long before our child is born.

"I wish I could promise more. If all goes well, I'll be back in a few days, but if it doesn't..."

"It could take months." I kiss him firmly on the cheek. "Just come back to me."

"I promise."

Zeke looks down, where I'm gripping his shirt.

"I'm going to need your help," I whisper.

He clutches his hands over mine. "I'll always be with you, even when I'm not physically here."

"I'll hold you in my heart forever."

"Close your eyes, baby."

I don't want to. I know what's going to happen when I do.

"It's okay. Close your eyes."

I look at Zeke one last time, and then I close them.

"Imagine me in your head."

I do.

Zeke loosens my grip on his shirt, and then he kisses me, one last time.

"I love you," he whispers over my lips.

"I love you, too."

And then he's gone. I keep my eyes closed for as long as I can. I pretend he's still here with me, that he isn't risking his life to save our family.

Finally, I open my eyes. And as I guessed, Zeke is gone.

Langston is standing in the doorway, giving me my space. But when he sees how broken I am, he rushes over and pulls me into his arms. It's comforting, but nothing like being held by Zeke.

"You're going to get through this—you're strong." He doesn't say Zeke is going to survive, or that he's going to come back, but that I'm going to get through this. I'm strong.

His words are the truth, but it still hurts. It hurts that he can't promise me Zeke is going to be okay.

"Zeke is the strongest man I know. If anyone can survive this, he can."

I look up at Langston, and I see the truth of his words in his eyes. He believes them. That's enough for me.

I step back out of his arms and realize that I've been crying. I wipe my tears on the back of my hand. Crying isn't going to help anything. I need to be strong. I need to get to the task at hand. Zeke isn't the only one with a mission to save this family.

I need to remember where I hid the box. I need to find it and destroy it. That way, there is no reason for anyone to ever come after us again. After this is over, we will move the country and learn to raise sheep or something. We will leave this world. But first, we have to find a way to win.

I look at Langston. "How do we do this?"

He looks at me cautiously, afraid to rush me. Maybe today should just be about resting and trying to not worry, but I can't wait. I need something to do, and the sooner we figure out my memories, the sooner this can end. If I'm safe, Langston wouldn't have to watch over me. He could go help Zeke kill Julian and his men.

"Trauma can take away the memories, but it can also trigger them," Langston finally says with a serious tone.

I straighten my shoulders, standing as tall as I can. I'm not going to be defeated. I'm going to fight. I'm going to ensure my husband returns and has a family to return to.

"Then, trauma is where we will start."

CHAPTER 17
ZEKE

I step out of the doorway of Siren's bedroom, and immediately the tears start.

I asked Langston to cut off his finger to show how much he would protect Siren. Walking away from her feels worse than that. It feels like I've lost an entire limb.

I know in my gut that it's the right thing to do. I know I need to leave her to protect her, but each step I take away from her still kills me.

My only comfort is that I finally believe that Langston will protect her with his life. It's not just because of all the things I've watched him do these last few days, nor because he was willing to cut off a finger for her. But because of the water tearing up in his eyes, watching me and Siren say goodbye.

Langston knows how important Siren is to me. He finally gets it. He witnessed it. I have no doubt that he will do anything to protect her.

Two men are waiting on the pier.

"You must be Zeke," the man says, extending his hand to me.

I shake it. "Yes."

"I'm Donovan. And this is Pedro."

I shake the other man's hand.

"We better get going, we have a flight to catch to Belize."

I nod and follow the men to the waiting blacked-out SUV. On the ride to the airport, we discuss strategy for how we should all behave when we meet with Julian, which keeps my brain occupied. But on the flight over, there is nothing to do but think of Siren and the life we will eventually have.

That is until the end of the flight. Donovan comes back to my seat on the private jet we chartered.

"Ready for this?"

I nod and grip the armrests to keep from reacting.

He punches me, twice in the face. Once in the stomach.

"Thanks, Donovan," I say.

He nods and then takes his seat again.

I add a couple of small rips to my shirt. The masquerade is complete. I looked like I've been through a fight, and they captured me.

Finally, we land, and I have something to focus on again other than my sorrow.

Pedro slaps some handcuffs onto my wrists that I'm more than capable of getting out of. Then he leads me to a waiting SUV to drive us the short ten-minute drive to where Julian is.

Once Pedro stops the car, Donovan takes his gun and points it at me.

"You ready?" he asks.

"Yes."

Pedro steps out of the driver's seat, drawing his gun as he opens my door and then pulls me out by the arm. Donovan steps out behind me and grabs my other arm. They both keep their guns trained on me as we walk into the soccer field and wait for Julian to show up.

A moment later, another blacked-out car pulls up. To my surprise, Julian climbs out of the driver's seat. I don't see anyone with him.

He pulls off his sunglasses as he walks over to us.

"Here's the down payment you can give to your boss, good faith money that we will split the profits we make from the sales of the vials fifty-fifty," Julian says before tossing the bag at our feet.

Donovan picks it up and unzips it. He flicks through the money quickly, all for show.

Then he pushes me forward. "He's yours to deal with now."

Donovan and Pedro head back to the car, and I hear the spit of the gravel as they drive off. Julian and I are left to stare at each other.

We both know I could run and break free easily, so I expect Julian to draw his gun to try and control me. Then again, that's not really his style.

Instead, Julian walks to me and grabs the handcuffs around my wrists. He pops them open with his hands.

I frown, not understanding what he is doing.

"You saw Siren was with Bishop?" Julian asks me.

"Yes."

He grins. "Well, now we have our answer. Bishop is on my side, not yours."

I growl. "Tell me why I'm here, or I'm leaving. We both know those handcuffs were the only way you were going to defeat me. And now that you released me, you have no chance."

Julian laughs. "Now that you know that Bishop has Siren, I don't need handcuffs to control you. You tried going after her, but from the looks of you, you clearly lost. Bishop still has Siren. The only way you are getting her back alive is if you help me. If you run or kill me, Bishop has been ordered to kill Siren."

I shove Julian hard against his car door.

"You bastard. Don't ever threaten my wife's life."

"Help me get the box. I know you know where it is. Lucy gave it to you to hide. Tell me where it is. Help me get it back, and I won't kill Siren."

I release him.

"If Bishop so much as lays a finger on her, I'll make you wish you were dead."

"If he so much as lays a finger on her without my permission, I'll be the one making him wish he were dead." Julian turns and opens the driver's door. He doesn't pat me down. He doesn't check to see what weapons I have on me. He just climbs inside the car, knowing I will join him.

And I do. I round the car and climb into the seat next to him.

"Where to?" Julian asks, testing me.

I frown, even though inside I'm smiling. This is exactly what I wanted. I know precisely where we are going—Kai and Enzo and their team are waiting to ambush us. They will torture Julian for information about his financier, while I'll break into his phone and find out that way. We have it all planned out. It will work.

"Alaska," I say.

"Clean yourself up." Julian tosses me a towel and first aid kit. And then he starts driving.

CHAPTER 18

SIREN

Langston drives me through the countryside toward his house in his convertible, with me in the passenger seat. We're headed to the same house where he held me after being captured.

Langston looks over at me. Even with his sunglasses on, I can tell by the set of his jaw and intensity flowing off him that he's nervous.

"Just tell me, Langston. After everything we've been through, I don't think anything you need to say should make you nervous."

He pauses then says, "I should warn you."

"About what?"

"You might be triggered when you arrive at the house. Last time you stayed with me, I did everything I could to make it the worst experience possible without actually hurting you in any long-lasting way. I didn't beat you. I didn't rape you. But it will still jog haunting memories most likely."

I sip on my Sprite as I gaze at the countryside, taking in what he said.

"Why do you think, when Julian raped me, it didn't trigger my memories? I had nightmares, but I still didn't remember the thing I'm desperate to remember."

537

"I'm nervous about that too. It should have."

"What is your theory on why it didn't?"

"It wasn't traumatic enough. As horrible as it was, it still wasn't on the same plane as you killing your own parents, as you burying a secret so deep in your brain and locking it away. It's going to take something big to unlock it."

Langston grabs my shoulder and squeezes it. "I'll be by your side the whole way. And if you would rather wait for Zeke to get back to be here with you, then we can."

I shake my head. "No. If I have to relive any trauma, it will be too hard for Zeke to bare."

"Probably," Langston agrees.

"What trauma did you live through that you were hoping to forget?" I ask, hoping that we have been friends long enough that he will tell me.

He never gives me an answer. Instead, he nods forward.

I turn and get my first glance at the place I once thought was a place of torture, but now realize was the first place for my healing.

I wait for the daydreams to haunt me, but they don't come, which almost makes it worse.

We both step out of the car, and Langston opens the door, drawing his gun.

"It's just a precaution. The security system is still up and running, but I want to be extra careful."

I nod and follow Langston in, using him like a bodyguard. He leads me to the security room, where he double checks the system and then tells me it's safe.

Only then do I explore the house a moment on my own, before Langston shows me to my bedroom next to his.

I sit on the edge of the bed. Even though today has been long, and I've had to deal with a lot, sleep won't be coming for a long time, so I might as well get to work.

"What have you tried before to get me to remember? My memory of my time here is wrong," I say.

"We don't have to start today. There is a tub in the bathroom. Why don't you take a long bath, read a book, and relax tonight?"

"No, I don't want to rest. I want to do something, try something."

If I were speaking to Zeke, he would be fighting back and ordering me around. Langston is different, though. He doesn't bark orders. But then he understands what I've been through. He knows the pain I've faced. And he, like me, wants to do something to fix this as soon as possible.

Langston sits on the edge of the bed next to me.

"I tried withholding food, putting you in a cell where you thought others were being tortured next to you, shock therapy, and drugs. I tried making you hate me, making myself into a monster that you could fight, but all it gave us were flickers of your memories. None of them were even related to the one memory we are trying to remember."

"I wish I could just make myself remember. Zeke seems to think if I give it enough time, I'll remember."

"I wish I had an easier way to help you. I've talked to all the experts, done all the research myself. The best way to remember is through a traumatic experience, something that triggers your memory.

"Although, I don't want to try any of the methods I tried before. It was one thing when you were healthy to push the limits of bringing you into a traumatic experience. It's another thing now that you are pregnant."

"So, what do you suggest we try first?"

"First, we should try the gentlest method we can."

"Which is?"

"Hypnosis. We'd bring you back to the night you met Zeke and I. Your mind may allow you to remember that happy moment, then maybe you'll remember the rest."

I nod several times. "I think that's a good idea. If for no other reason than I would love to remember the first time I laid eyes on Zeke. I would love to know if it was love at first sight or not."

"Well, it was on one side." Langston winks at me. Then he stands and holds out his hand to help me up.

I take his hand, and he helps me stand.

"Find a spot in the house where you feel calm and relaxed. I'll get my phone and play some music that will help with the hypnosis."

"Thank you, Langston."

"Don't thank me. I have no idea if this will work."

I shake my head. "Thank you for ensuring my safety." I put my hand on my stomach. "Our safety."

"Come on," he says, but I see a hint of pink cross his cheeks.

I follow him out of my bedroom, and we walk through the house to a library with gorgeous floor-to-ceiling windows.

"Will this work?" He asks me.

I nod, feeling very safe in this relaxing room.

Langston sits in the middle of the floor, so I mirror him by sitting across from him.

"Close your eyes and clear your mind," Langston says.

I do as he starts playing soft music on his phone.

I try to calm myself as I listen to the soothing music.

"Take slow, deep breaths," Langston says.

I try to slow my breathing.

"In."

I do through my nose.

"And out."

I exhale through my mouth.

His voice is calming, similar to Zeke's.

"You are safe," Langston says.

I am safe.

"Relax into your breath."

I do.

"Now think back to the first time you met Zeke. What was he doing?"

I take a deep breath and don't let the memory of finding Zeke in the ocean fill my brain. Instead, I leave my mind blank, trying to let the images come to me.

I KNOW WHO MY TARGETS ARE. TWO MEN, BOYS REALLY, SIMILAR IN AGE to me. They work for the younger Black. They know how to access the vault. They all have access. They all have keycards and fingerprint access. The finger-

print is easy. Just get one of the many drinks they are holding and slip it into my purse. But the keycard will take more finagling.

When I step foot inside the bar where the two boys are drinking, I assume the bar will be crowded, and I won't be able to spot them easily. To my surprise, it's very easy, even though the bar is crowded, because there are only two men in the entire bar.

I thought I would have to work to figure out who they were. All I had to go by are their names—Langston and Zeke—and that they frequent this bar. I wasn't expecting that my main competition would be twenty other females all vying for their attention.

It's like they are royalty the way the women are treating them.

They are seated in a corner booth of the bar with four women around them. The rest of the women flirt or dance from afar, hoping to be summoned.

I roll my eyes as I walk to the bar and try to form a plan. I can't see the two men through the crowds of women very clearly, so I won't be able to study them from afar. I need a plan to get close.

"What can I get you?" a male bartender asks me.

"The most expensive scotch you have," I answer.

"Are you buying the guys a drink?"

"No, it's for myself."

The bartender nods at me with an impressed look.

"Can I get a credit card to open a tab for you?"

I smirk. "Who says I'll be the one buying?"

He shakes his head. "Good luck to you."

I cross my legs and watch his eyes drop to my exposed thighs. I know how to seduce like it's my job, which it is quickly becoming. I seduce men to get what I want. Or, more often, what my parents want.

"I don't need luck," I say when his eyes finally reach my face again after raking over every inch of my body. I may be wearing a dress like every other woman here, but no other woman knows how to use her curves like I do.

The bartender gapes. "You're right; you don't need luck. I'll put it on their tab."

I smile and wait for my drink before I make my move. The bartender ignores everyone else waiting and pours my drink first.

"Thanks," I say, lifting the glass as I make my way around the crowded bar. There are many seats left, which will make my ploy work even better.

There is one empty seat left at the guys' booth; they just don't realize it's empty.

I walk over like a whirlwind and drop onto one of the boys' lap.

"Excuse me? What do you think you are doing?" he asks.

"Sitting, there are no chairs open. This was the only spot I could find."

I turn my head to get a good look at the kid whose lap I'm sitting on, and my jaw drops.

This boy is all man. I was expecting a kid; instead, I got a beast. He has long dark hair, a scruffy face, dreamy eyes, and muscles for days. If he wasn't my target, I'd be head over heels in love with him right now. I can feel how fast my heart is beating, and it takes me a minute to adjust. All I know is I'm going to love using this man tonight.

"SIREN? SIREN, ARE YOU OKAY?" LANGSTON'S VOICE SAYS.

I blink rapidly, looking at Langston. "I remember."

"You remember where you hid the box?"

"No, I remember meeting you and Zeke the first time." I gasp as I stand up abruptly from the ground. My head is light, and I'm dizzy as I try to process everything.

Langston grabs my elbow, keeping me steady and on my feet.

"Thanks," I mumble.

"Sit down and let me make you some tea, then you can tell me what happened."

I let Langston lead me to a large sofa, and I sit. Langston studies me closely for a second before leaving me alone.

I've met Zeke and Langston before. I can't believe it. I can't believe I have memories that I can't remember.

"Here, drink this." Langston hands me a cup of tea. I take it and sip it all down quickly, even though it's hot and burns my throat.

Langston sits next to me, takes my cup from me, pours more hot water in, and returns it to me, saying, "Slowly this time."

His eyes give me a warning to drink slowly, so I take a sip.

"What did you remember?"

"I remember coming to the bar. I remember sitting on Zeke's lap." I blush and look at Langston. "I remember falling for Zeke instantly."

Langston smiles back at me and leans back, drinking his own tea.

I raise an eyebrow. "You know drinking tea isn't the manliest thing you could be doing. You could drink alcohol if you want, I don't mind."

"I don't want to drink alcohol, and I'm perfectly comfortable in my own manhood."

I smile at that.

"I'm glad you remember meeting Zeke. I've been so annoyed that neither of you could remember while I'm stuck remembering witnessing you two exchanging sappy words and constantly flirting."

I tuck my hair behind my ear as I lean back on the couch with my cup of tea resting in my lap. "I can't believe how much our lives have been intertwined this whole time. I can't believe how different my life could have been if I decided to take a chance on Zeke then, instead of now."

"You can't think like that. If you and Zeke had started dating then, you would have been on the yacht when Zeke was shot. You would have thought he was dead along with us. No one would have been there to save him. You couldn't be together then because you needed to save him so you could be together now."

I look at Langston sitting next to me. I don't know how I could have ever mistaken him for a monster, when he's clearly a kind man who truly cares about his family.

"Thanks for saying that. I needed that."

"Don't," Langston tenses.

"Don't what?"

"Don't think I'm a good man. I'm not your savior. I'm barely your friend. Don't ever mistake me for more than I am."

"Who are you, then?"

"I'll protect you, but I'll also look out for my own interests. I'll do horrible things that I'll never explain to you or anyone else. I'll protect you, but don't think that protection lasts forever like Zeke's."

I nod, but I don't believe his words. I don't think Langston could ever stop protecting me. The only thing he would ever let get in the way of protecting me would be his love for another woman in a situation worse than mine.

"I love you too, Langston." I wink at him.

He blinks rapidly like he's never heard those words spoken to him before.

I laugh. "I'm not in love with you, but I love you like a brother. And I will do everything in my power to protect you too."

He rubs the back of his neck. "How could you love me when I've been so cruel?"

"Have you been that cruel?" I throw his own words from earlier back at him as I smile behind my cup of tea.

He shakes his head, and I decide not to push the conversation further.

"So what do we do now? I remember meeting you, but I don't remember anything after that. I don't remember stealing the box. I don't remember hiding it." I don't remember killing my own parents.

"Now, we try to get some sleep. Tomorrow we will try to push you further."

I shudder, but I know he's right as I yawn.

"We should go to bed," Langston says.

I agree. However, I don't want to be alone right now. Zeke is gone. He hasn't texted or called. We don't know if he's still alive or hurt. We don't know what's happening.

So I set my cup down on the end table and then curl my legs up beneath me and lean onto Langston's chest. He stiffens at first, but slowly he puts his arms around my back, holding me against him.

"Zeke is going to kill me for this."

I laugh. "He would until I told him that you were just being a good brother and helping me keep the nightmares away."

"I can do that."

I close my eyes and try to sleep. The nightmares will stay away as long as Langston is here, but I'm afraid what I need to do to remember is let the nightmares in.

CHAPTER 19
ZEKE

We arrive in Alaska at Kai and Enzo's house up here. I feel weird about using their house to attack Julian and commit murder when this place is such a sanctuary for them, far away from all the evil in their lives. But we know the area and the land, so we'll have an advantage here.

"Where is it?" Julian asks as he parks the SUV we rented in front of the house.

"In a security box in the basement."

Julian pulls out his gun and motions for me to do the same. "Remember what will happen if you turn on me."

"I get the box, turn it over to you, and Siren goes free. I got it. I won't betray you. I tried that, and I failed."

Julian snickers.

God, I'm going to enjoy killing Julian more than any other man I've killed. I hope Enzo and Kai don't kill him before I get a chance to hurt him.

I keep my eyes peeled for any sign of them or their men as we walk up to the front door. I haven't texted or had contact with them since Langston's men turned me over to Julian, so I don't know where they are hiding or when they plan on attacking Julian. But I'll be ready, and I can't wait to finally give the bastard what he deserves.

I pick the lock on the door and open it, sticking my gun in first before stepping inside.

Julian follows right after me, practically using me as a human shield —*coward*.

I continue through the house, but I don't see any sign of anyone. Enzo and Kai are very talented assassins, so they won't make themselves known until the last second. Still, it unsettles me to have no hints as to where they are.

"Where is the basement?" Julian asks.

I scan the room. "This way."

I start heading down the hallway, toward the basement door. I open it, and we walk downstairs carefully. I don't bother with the lights, and neither does Julian.

"There," I say, pointing to the safe sitting at the far end of the room.

"Good, now unlock it."

I snarl. Of course, he won't be doing any of the work himself.

I walk to the safe and tuck my gun away, going to work on picking the safe. I only know how to do it because the Black family deals in security systems. Otherwise, a system like this can't be opened.

I take my time, assuming now is when Enzo and Kai are going to choose to ambush Julian.

But when I hear the final click of the lock before the safe pops open, there has been no ambush.

"The safe is unlocked," I say, stepping away from it.

Julian steps forward after putting his gun away. I take mine out and scan around the darkness, trying to look for Kai and Enzo to give them the signal.

Finally, I see the whites of men's eyes staring back at me. I see guns. They aren't pointed at Julian.

Fuck.

Julian opens the safe and pulls out the box that Siren hid here after stealing it from the vault. The box once held a secret weapon; instead, the box is now empty.

Julian opens it easily. The latch is already broken open from Kai and Enzo.

Julian doesn't seem surprised to find it empty. Instead, he whistles.

The lights flick on, and two dozen men step forward with their guns aimed at me. Then I see them, Enzo and Kai, tied up with guns trained on them.

Julian tosses the box to the ground. His eyes have darkened, but otherwise, there is no sign of anger as he walks toward me.

"I thought you cared more about your wife's life than this. But I guess I was wrong; you don't care about Siren at all."

My body fills with rage. "All I care about is Siren."

"Then stop lying to me. Stop trying to trick me!"

"Stop trying to kill my family!"

Julian shakes his head before he walks over to Enzo. It's the first I've seen Enzo since I shot him. I'm glad the damage I did was minimal. My eyes skim to Kai, who doesn't seem upset with me in the least, even though deep down she'd love to have my balls for daring to hurt her husband.

I flick back to Julian, who is patting Enzo on the cheek. "Look at that—he isn't dead. Isn't that what I asked of you? For you to kill him?" Julian punches his shoulder where I shot him. Enzo doesn't flinch, restricted by the restraints around his wrists, arms, and ankles. Julian grabs his shirt and rips it open, finding no bullet wound.

Julian turns to me and hisses through clenched teeth. "Lies...all you lot can do is lie."

He walks over to me, getting in my face, even though I'm a foot taller than him.

"You do realize that I hold all the power? I have everything, and you have nothing. If you don't do exactly as I say from here on out, you'll lose everything you hold dear."

My chest rises and falls as I focus on my breathing instead of snapping his neck. It would make me feel better for a split second, before the rain of bullets his men would send down on me and my friends a second later.

"What do you want?" I ask.

Julian tsks. "No, you don't get to ask that. First, you have to be punished for what you did here today."

"Whip me, beat me, torture me. You can do whatever you want to me. It won't leave a dent on me. It will be nothing compared to what I've already experienced."

Julian pulls out his cell phone with a grin.

I stiffen but remember Langston is on my side. He won't let anything bad happen to Siren. There is nothing to fear. I just have to let Julian know how afraid I am.

Julian dials a number, then puts the phone to his ear.

"Don't," I beg.

He laughs. "You lied. You get punished."

He turns his attention back to the phone. "Bishop, I need you to do something for me."

I wait for Langston to speak back.

"I need you to punish Siren for Zeke's disloyalty. I need you to make her scream now on the phone so we can all hear."

My eyes widen, and my heart stops.

Langston won't really hurt her. Whatever screams Siren makes will be fake. *They will be an act. They won't be real.*

Julian pulls the phone from his ear and puts the phone on speakerphone. Thank God he didn't ask to video chat and show him beating Siren, that would be harder to fake. And if Julian saw Siren, he might realize that she's pregnant.

There's a scuffle.

Then I hear Langston say, "Come here, bitch."

It's an act. It's all a lie.

I look over at Enzo and Kai, who both fight against their bindings to stop Langston. They, too, know it's fake, but it's still hard to not react. It's also what they would be doing if they didn't know it was fake. I need to let myself react more to sell this.

"Julian, stop this. I'll do whatever you want. I'll help you find where the real box is. Just don't hurt Siren," I beg.

"I have Siren tied up. Should I continue, Julian?" Langston says.

Julian's grin turns up slowly, and it looks the devil himself is possessing his body.

"Yes," he says.

"No!" I scream, running to Julian.

But it's too late.

I hear a whip-like sound, followed by Siren howling. I don't know how he made the noises without striking actual flesh, which scares me.

Siren is fine. Langston promised. He promised.

Another whip, though, and the scream from Siren this time is horrific. It echoes through my ears and lands in my heart. I never want Siren to hurt. I can't stand for her to hurt. It feels worse than a thousand whips hitting my back all at once.

"Please, stop this," I beg Julian.

Julian just cocks his head and licks his lips in enjoyment. "Three more," he says into the phone.

Three more. I can't stand it, even though I know it's fake. I can't listen to her scream three more times.

"Please!" I get down on my knees in front of Julian, begging him to stop this, to end this.

I hear another strike, another scream. Her voice is high-pitched, and it sounds like she's losing her voice or crying.

She can't be, though, not my strong Siren.

Another strike. Another scream. Another piece of my fragile heart breaks, and I feel tears watering my eyes. Apparently, I don't need to act at all. As much as I thought I was certain that Langston was on our side, this is Bishop. And Bishop, I don't trust.

I close my eyes as the fifth and final strike is delivered, followed by a scream that splits my soul.

It's not real. She's not in pain. The baby isn't in danger. This isn't real.

"That's enough for now," Julian says into the phone before hanging up.

He walks over to me.

"Stand up," he commands.

I do. We always had a plan that if we failed, I would fall in line. Get him to trust me, figure out his financial backer, and then find a way to kill them all.

"Now, one of you three knows where the box is. Tell me, or we will go through that entire exercise again."

CHAPTER 20
SIREN

I didn't have to fake my screams or tears. If Julian wanted Langston to hurt me, it could only mean one thing—Zeke failed. He got captured for real, and I don't know if he's going to survive.

My emotions ran high as Langston handed me the whip and told me to strike his back each time Julian asked. I didn't hit him very hard, just enough to make a horrible sound over the phone. It was enough that Langston had to bite down on a belt to keep from making a sound.

But my cries of pain were real. They weren't because of the physical pain I was in, but because of my fear of losing Zeke, of my child growing up without a father. I can't stand the thoughts.

I made the wrong decision in letting him go back to fight Julian Reed alone. I should have sent Langston with him. I should have gone with him. Or he shouldn't have gone at all.

Langston ends the call, and instead of worrying about the pain I inflicted on his back, he holds me close in a deep hug as I collapse to the floor.

"Julian has Zeke. He failed. He's going to die. I can't lose him," I sob into Langston's shoulder.

"Shhh, Zeke isn't going to die. He had a plan for this, remember? He's strong. He's not going to let anything stop him from coming back for the birth of his first child."

"That's months away."

"Yes, and I suspect he'll be back a lot sooner than that. But you have to stay strong, so Zeke can stay strong."

I nod vigorously—Langston's right. I'm being ridiculous. Zeke is obviously still alive or Julian wouldn't call. And I heard Zeke's voice in the background. Zeke is alive. He'll win this war in the end.

"Let me look at your back." I turn Langston around. "Oh my god!" I gasp. "I didn't mean to hit you so hard." Red welts pop up on his back.

Langston brushes me off. "I'm fine. You shot me, remember? That was much worse. You just got into it a little when you were feeling all the pain."

"Let me get you something to soothe your back, though." I'm off before Langston can stop me.

I run to the bathroom, catching my breath before finding some salve to rub on his back. Zeke is strong. He's going to survive. I have to remain calm for my baby.

I grab the bottle of salve and then run back to find Langston still sitting shirtless in the living room.

"This should help," I say as I squirt some into my hand and then rub it on his back. He doesn't flinch or react when I touch him.

"Is that better?" I ask.

"Yes. Thanks, Ren," Langston says.

"Ren, huh?" I sit down on the couch while Langston stands from the floor, puts on his shirt, and then sits next to me.

"I know Siren is the name Zeke calls you. It feels as much as an endearment as it does your real name. And no one seems to call you Aria. What do you prefer I call you?"

I smile. "Ren sounds perfect, Lang."

He laughs at my shortening of his name, but I notice him wince slightly when his back hits the back of the couch. I hurt him more than I intended.

"Wait here, one sec." I rush off and come back with a bottle of whiskey and a glass for him. I pour and hand him a full glass.

"Thanks," he says, staring at the glass a second before drinking it quickly. I pour another shot into the glass, and this one, he sips slower.

He looks at me, studying me closely. "Did it trigger any new memories?"

I shake my head sadly.

"What do we do now? We've tried hypnosis and meditation. They haven't worked."

He bites his lip, and I know what he's thinking but doesn't want to suggest.

"What is it?" I ask. "It can't be as bad as you think it is, just tell me."

"You killed your parents right after hiding the box, right?"

"Yes, I assume so."

"Then maybe killing someone is the answer."

I frown. "But I've killed people before. It didn't trigger anything."

"True, but you are in a very emotional state right now. Combine that with killing someone, and it just might do it."

I nod, it makes sense. "I'm not just going to go kill an innocent person in hopes that I can remember where I hid a box. Even if finding the box first might save millions."

"I'm not asking you to kill an innocent person. Your parents weren't innocent."

I take a deep breath. It's a better idea than Langston trying to torture me, but Zeke will kill me if I put myself into danger trying to remember.

"I won't let you be in any danger."

"I know," I exhale a deep breath. "So, where are we going to find a bad guy who is easy to kill and doesn't put me at too much risk?"

Langston downs his drink. "Come on, we have a bad guy to hunt down."

He holds out his hand, and I take it.

"Where are we going?"

"You still got your gun and knife on you?"

"Always."

"Good, then let's go." He drags me to his car before I have time to process what we are doing. Then we are driving down the road, destination unknown.

"What are you thinking about?" he asks.

"Zeke."

"Good, keep thinking about him."

So I do. I let the fear of losing him in, even though I know it comes with some anxiety. I let it in. I let all my emotions in. I feel all my worry as we drive.

Finally, Langston stops in an alleyway.

"Where are we?"

"A local bar."

"I don't think anyone deserves to die just because they like to drink."

"We aren't killing someone because they drink too much. We are killing a known rapist."

It's like Langston hit me with a bolt of lighting. Rage erupts in me to be near a man inside this bar who raped other women. That is not something that should ever happen.

"How do you know?"

"He paid the judge to throw out the case. I've seen the evidence; it was all over the local papers here. He's guilty. He owns this bar, and not a single woman will enter for fear of what he will do to them."

I let my anger flow through me.

"Name."

"Fred Parry."

"Do you have a picture?"

"No, you aren't going inside the bar. You'll wait here, and I'll drag him out—"

"No, I'm going. We are trying to trigger my memories. I need to be as involved as possible."

"It's not—"

"Safe? This man is a rapist, not an assassin. I have a gun and a knife. I have a badass bodyguard. I'll be fine." My eyes shoot into Langston, not giving him a choice in the matter.

He nods.

We jump out of the car and start walking toward the bar side by side. I'm focused on my mission. There is nothing that gets my adrenaline going more than killing an evil, vile monster. I'm going to enjoy this a little too much.

We walk into the bar, and as Langston said, there are no women. The scene is the exact opposite of when I found Zeke and Langston in their bar all those years ago.

"I never asked, why was there only women in the bar when I met you?"

"We were stupid playboys who didn't realize that women like you and Kai existed. Otherwise, we wouldn't have been wasting time just getting laid every night."

"Good answer." I look around as all the men's eyes stare at me with a silent hunger.

"I'm looking for a Mr. Fred Parry," I say loudly. I suspect that if I killed several men in this bar, it would all be deserved.

None of the men answer me.

I look to Langston, who they will answer to.

"Where is Fred Parry?" Langston says, his voice booming with an aura of authority.

A man points in the direction of the back.

"Carry on," I say as we walk through the bar like we own the place. Langston stops at the back door and steps through first with his gun raised.

I follow after. I would prefer to walk in first, but it's safer to enter second.

We walk through a short hallway to an open door that leads to a cramped office. Two men are smoking a cigar around a desk.

"Fred Parry?" Langston asks the man sitting behind the desk.

"Yes, who the bloody hell are you? You aren't supposed to be back here. Get out!"

Langston shakes his head and then grabs the other man by the back of the shirt. "You, get out."

"But—" the man mumbles.

"Get. Out." Langston growls to the man who finally spots the gun he's holding. The man scurries out so fast that you'd think his feet were on fire.

I step inside the office next, shutting the door behind me with a thud.

"What the hell is this?" Fred yells at us, his voice gruff from years of smoking, no doubt.

"We are here to deliver justice," I say.

Fred laughs, turning into a cough of smoke. "Justice? Like there is such a thing."

"Well, you are about to find out how justice works," I say.

I walk over to his desk, grab him by the back of his neck, and turn him in his chair to me. He tries to fight me off him, but I only hold on harder.

"Did you rape a woman in this very bar?"

He narrows his eyes. "Go to hell."

I slam his head down on the desk.

"Did you rape someone?"

His throat tightens, his face now bloodied from a most likely broken nose, but he realizes that I'm serious.

I move to slam his head down again.

"Yes!" he screams. "Yes, I raped her."

"Just her?" I ask sternly.

"No, I've raped six other women."

So much emotion pours through me. The thought that Zeke could die from a man who raped me has me on edge. Holding this rapist's neck sets me on fire.

I want to burn this whole place down. I can feel the energy in this room. He brought the women here. He raped them here, most likely on this very desk. After I kill him, I will burn this bar to the ground. I will ensure the women have their justice.

I slam his head down again, and the man screams like he's being tortured. He has no idea what torture feels like—yet.

"Please, I have money. I can pay you," the man pleads.

God, he disgusts me. Like I would want to take money from a man like him.

I look to Langston, who is leaning against the wall watching this happen.

"Leave us. I'd like to have a little chat alone with Mr. Parry here."

Langston frowns. He doesn't want to leave me alone, but I can handle this vile man. He's not dangerous, and I need to let all the feelings flow if I have a chance at getting my memories back.

"I'll be right outside," Langston says before stepping out. He'll be listening and will barge back in at any second if I need him.

I nod. He shuts the door to the office, leaving me and Mr. Parry alone.

I consider torturing the man. He deserves it, but I don't think it will help me get my memories back, and it won't heal me.

But Fred won't be walking out of this office alive.

"What do you want then?" Fred asks with a shaky voice.

I consider his question. I want his death. I want to spill his blood on the table where he tortured people. *But other than that, what do I want?*

"Why? Why did you do it?" I ask, realizing that's what I want. To know why a man rapes. *Why was I raped? Why, when Julian could have convinced any number of women to sleep with him? Why, when he could have paid for the pleasure? Why take from me? Why am I not more hurt by the pain I experienced?*

The man stares at me, blinking like I can't be serious to ask such a question. That's when I realize that there is no reason. There is just something dark inside that drives some men to do bad things.

I close my eyes and let my own rape fill my head. I let all the dark images of Julian being on top of me, hurting me, taking from me. I remember it all. Not the images of Zeke that I filled my head with to hide my pain, I let the real truth come through.

Until my hands are clammy and shaking. Until my breath has sped up. Until I'm afraid this man standing in front of me could do the same thing to me unless I stop him.

Only then do I open my eyes and pull the trigger.

The man falls dead in front of me in a single shot. I stare at his lifeless bloodied body. He got off easy.

I close my eyes and try to remember my parents, my pain then. My horror at finding out that the box I stole for them was dangerous to the world, and what their intentions were.

But all I see is Julian.

"Damn," I curse under my breath, knowing that this trauma isn't close enough. I don't know what is, but this isn't.

The door opens, and Langston looks from me to Fred then back to me with a question in his eyes.

I shake my head.

"We can try again."

"No, I need to think more about it. As much as I'd love to scour the entire city, ridding it of all the rapists and murders, I need to find something else, something that doesn't remind me of my own rape."

Langston nods. "Let's get out of here."

I follow Langston out into the hallway. I find the fire alarm and pull it, ensuring the bar empties out. Then I walk into the main bar, now empty, and pull out a bottle of rum. I drench everything in sight. Then light a match and toss it on the bar.

It immediately catches fires. The bar will burn. This place will be lost to history. The women will get their justice.

"Come on, we should go," Langston says as sirens sound in the distance.

I follow Langston out the back, the heat of the fire warming our backsides.

I stop suddenly, an unusual cold washing over me.

"What is it?" Langston stops abruptly, holding my biceps as he stares down at me.

"I don't know. Just a coldness washed over me. A dark chill. Something's wrong."

I meet Langston's eyes, and I don't have to tell him what I think it means. *Something has happened to Zeke.*

Langston pulls out his phone, and we both look down at the missed call flashing on the screen.

It's from Julian.

Fuck.

CHAPTER 21
ZEKE

"Who wants to tell me where the real box is? Hmm?" Julian asks as he looks from me to Enzo and Kai. They're bound still, but standing on their own.

I'm the only unrestrained one, but with a dozen guns aimed at me, I'm as tied up as they are.

None of us speak. I need a plan. *If we give him a random destination and there is no box there, then what?* We are no better off than we are now. And he might kill us and go search for it himself. He doesn't realize Siren knows. He thinks we have it and hid it.

I could kill Julian now, as I still have my gun, but I'd be risking my friend's lives. No, now isn't the time. I need to give them a chance to break free first. Then, I can figure out who Julian's backer is and kill them both.

"No one wants to speak, huh? Should I get Bishop back on the phone?" Julian takes his phone out again and dials a number.

"Rot in hell," Kai yells at Julian, drawing his attention to her. He holds out the phone, and we all watch it ring as he walks toward her.

Don't pick up. Don't pick up.

I can't handle listening to Siren screaming again. I'll lose my mind.

The phone stops ringing, playing a voicemail recording.

559

Julian ends the call as he licks his lips, staring at Kai like he's just realized she's a woman.

"Too bad for you," Julian says to Kai.

Enzo and I lose it at the same time. Julian will not touch Kai. He will never touch another woman who doesn't willingly give herself over to him.

I charge at Julian from behind, while Enzo trips Julian up, keeping him from touching her.

I grab onto Julian, and we tumble to the ground. I punch him hard. My rage overflows in me, rage at what he wanted to do to Kai, at what he did to Siren. All other thoughts of how to keep everyone safe fly out of my mind.

I punch him viciously in the face, drawing blood from his mouth. I probably knocked a tooth loose. I punch three more times before arms go around me, pulling me up.

Guns are pointed at me, but no one shoots. They may torture us, but they won't kill us. They don't know which one of us has the information. They think we are protecting ourselves by not spreading the information through our group. They don't realize that none of us knows. The only person who knows is Siren, and her memories are locked away at the moment.

"Shoot me. Kill me. None of us will ever tell you where the box is," I taunt Julian.

He glares at me with a bruised and bloodied face. It felt good to punch him.

Julian approaches me when his phone rings again.

He stops and pulls it out of his pocket.

I try to fight to get free from the men holding me back, but I can't. From the timid look on Julian's face, it's not Langston calling him back.

"Yes," he says sternly.

Pause.

"Not yet, sir."

Sir. This must be the man financing this whole venture.

"Yes, sir."

Julian hangs up. "Everyone out." His eyes hang on me, letting me know I'll be staying.

The guards start dragging Kai and Enzo out, which is a good thing. They will be safe away from Julian.

"Tie him up first, then leave us," Julian says to the guards holding me back.

They tie my wrists behind my back, and my ankles together, before leaving me standing in the room alone.

"Coward. You can't even fight me without me being tied up," I spout.

"I'm not going to fight you. I'm going to make you see reason."

"Yea, and what reason is that?"

"I need the box. And you need Siren to survive. We need each other."

"No, you need me. I don't need you."

"You have until Bishop calls me back to tell me where the box is, or who among you knows. If you don't, I'll have him rape Siren. If that doesn't do the trick, I'll have him kill her."

"If you do that, you'll have nothing to hold over me."

"Time is running out. I don't have any choice anymore."

"You mean, your boss has grown impatient and wants results."

He growls at me before taking his phone out. He types a quick text message to Langston and then hits send. He holds up the phone to show it to me. *Tie up Siren and then FaceTime me.*

Fuck, no. How is Langston going to be able to hide what he's doing to Siren if it's on video?

"Tell me, and this all ends. Tell me where the box is. Tell me who knows where it is hidden, and I won't give Bishop the order."

I grit my teeth. I don't know how to stop this.

"Your problem is with me, take it out on me like a man."

"No, you've been tortured and near death too many times. The only thing that even comes close to bringing you pain anymore is when I hurt Siren."

"You care about Siren too, don't let another man hurt her."

"I don't take enjoyment in having another man touch a woman who I feel is mine. But since I had her first, I think I can make an exception."

The phone rings. I stare at it—a video call from Bishop.

I squeeze my eyes closed and then open them again, hoping to God this isn't happening, that it's all a nightmare.

But when I open them again, Julian is answering the phone call.

"Hello, Bishop, so happy you could call me back."

"Since I don't exactly work for you, I don't have to be at your beck and call or tell you what I'm doing. This is a partnership."

"Yes, of course. But I think you're going to like where our partnership is headed. Is Siren tied up?"

"Yes," Langston says, moving the phone so I can see Siren tied in a similar fashion to me, except she's seated. She's wearing a loose sweatshirt that hides her belly with black leggings underneath.

A beautiful and heartbreaking sight.

"Zeke here needs a little motivation to tell us where the box is," Julian says.

The camera is still pointed at Siren. "Don't tell him anything!" she shouts at me.

"Siren! Baby!" I cry out.

"Hush," Julian orders, muting the phone so that my voice can no longer be heard. When I'm quiet, he unmutes it and speaks.

"Slap her."

Langston does. I hear the slap of her cheek. The redness is growing. It was a real slap. There was no way to hide it. No way to fake it.

"One last chance," Julian says to me.

I'm sweaty. I'm broken. I can feel every bit of her pain. I can't watch Langston try to fake his way through hurting her. He'll have no choice but to hurt her or reveal the truth. It's best if Julian still trusts Langston. And if for some reason I'm wrong, and Langston really is on Julian's side and not mine, then I need to protect Siren.

"Stop this, and I'll talk," I say.

Julian walks over to me. "Start talking."

"I need to know that everyone is safe. Release Kai and Enzo in good faith that you will release Siren and me when the time comes."

"No."

"Then I'm not giving you the information," I say, and hope to death that Julian won't push Langston any further to hurt Siren.

Julian studies me. Both of us need to win this war, not wanting to back down.

Whoever blinks first will show weakness. *How far will I push this before I crack and protect Siren at all costs? How desperate is Julian to know the information?*

"I'll leave Kai and Enzo here tied up with two guards. It will take them some time to break free, but they are more than capable of getting them untied and taking down two guards while we go get the box. That is the best I will do."

"Deal," I say, knowing that is as far as I can push him while also protecting Siren's life.

"So, where is it?"

"I don't know."

"Who knows?" Julian gets in my face.

I have to make a decision. I've tried fighting Julian apart and failed. And as much as I don't want to let Julian anywhere near Siren, I think the best decision is to be together. Together we can take him down. Langston can help. It's the only way I can think to save us all.

Julian reads it on my face. I don't even have to tell him.

"Siren knows," he says after muting the phone.

"Yes," I say. At least it keeps him from killing her if he thinks she knows where the box is. But it doesn't save her from being tortured. Although, maybe he'll torture me to get her to speak. So I add, "And her only weakness is me."

Julian grins. "I'm going to enjoy torturing you while I persuade my Aria to talk."

Good. As long as you don't touch her, do whatever you want to me.

Julian picks up the phone and unmutes it. "We are headed to you. We will be there in twenty-four hours."

"Do you know where the box is?" Langston asks back.

"No, but we will soon," Julian says and then hangs up before calling in his guards to carry me to the car still tied up. Julian thinks he needs to keep me tied up, but he doesn't. I won't fight him, bringing me back to Siren. That I will never fight.

Langston, you better be ready to take this motherfucker down. There is no way I'm going to let him touch Siren.

CHAPTER 22
SIREN

Langston hangs up the phone.

"I'm so sorry," Langston runs over and unties my ankles and wrists while staring at my face where he slapped me.

"I had to make it look real. I'll go get some ice."

"No, I'm fine. I can handle a slap. I'm just thankful he didn't ask you to do more."

We both still, knowing how far Julian could have asked Langston to go. He could have had him whip me, or even rape me. And short of telling the truth, that Langston is on our side and not Julian's, there was nothing we could have done.

We both know it—how close we came.

"I'll do everything I can to protect you; you know that, right?" Langston says.

"Yes, I do."

"The good news is that Zeke's alive. Let's focus on that."

"Except we can't focus on that. They are coming here. We have to unlock my memories, find the box, and destroy it. Our time has run out."

Langston runs his hand through his blonde hair. "Unlocking your memory isn't something we can rush. We've tried everything. I don't think there is anything left to try."

I tilt my head. "We haven't tried everything."

His eyes narrow as he tries to make sense of my words. "You're right; we haven't. You killed someone you loved. You did it to protect the world, but you still did it."

"I'm not going to kill anyone I love, not again."

I stand up and walk out of the room, through the door to the back deck, needing some fresh air. I know what Langston is going to suggest, and I'm not doing it.

Langston gives me a minute before he steps out onto the deck and leans against the railing next to me as we both look out at the garden below.

"We don't have a choice."

"I'm not going to kill you in hopes that I might remember."

"Then what do you suggest?"

I bite my lip as I rack my brain for any idea other than killing Langston.

"We should think about where I might have hidden it. What choices I had available to me at the time. Send someone to search in those places if we can't look ourselves."

Langston turns around and leans his elbows on the railing. "Okay, you were in your early twenties. What resources did you have? How much money did you have available to you?"

"I didn't have much money."

He nods. "That's good. Then it's probably still in Florida somewhere. Or St. Kitts, where you met Julian and your ex-husband?"

I frown.

"What?" His brows furrow.

"I didn't have money. But my best friend, Nora, had endless amounts of money."

"Okay, but would she have lent you money?"

I nod. "It gets worse."

"How could it get worse?"

"Nora has her pilot's license. She owned a private plane. She could have flown me anywhere."

Langston stares, his eyes widen.

I could have hidden it anywhere. Literally, anywhere.

"Nora," we both say at the same time.

We run back inside and grab my cell phone. I dial Nora's number.

"Pick up, pick up," I mutter. I know her and Beckett are in charge of keeping the twins safe. Calling her on a phone that might be traceable is dangerous for them, but not finding the box first is more dangerous.

"Siren, what is it? What's wrong?" Nora answers.

I exhale a breath as Langston stares me nervously.

"I need to ask you an important question."

"Okay, what is it?"

"Do you remember back when I made a trip to Miami just before my parents died?"

"Yes, I remember. You were so despondent afterward. You wouldn't talk about it. And then shortly after you got married."

She remembers. Thank goodness.

"Do you remember me asking you to fly me anywhere or borrow any money? Maybe I asked you to fly me somewhere after Miami or right after I returned to the island?"

"No, you couldn't have asked me to fly anywhere. I didn't get my pilot's license until the following spring."

Dammit.

"What about money? Do you remember me asking you to borrow any money?"

Nora sighs. "I wish you would have asked to borrow money. But you never did, you hated being a burden."

I run my hand through my hair as I sink down in the chair. I was so hopeful that Nora would be able to give us a clue, but once again, I come up empty.

"Can you remember me talking about hiding something? About a trip somewhere? A new security box I purchased? Anything like that?"

"I wish I could, but you didn't talk much during that time. You started down a bad path, and then you found Hugo. And then everything else spiraled after that."

There's a pause.

"You don't remember that time, do you?" Nora asks.

"No, that's what Langston was trying to do, spark my memories."

I'm about to hang up the phone when Nora says, "I don't know if this helps at all, but I do remember something weird that happened a year later."

I sit up, hopeful.

"I was talking about all the places I wanted to go for my birthday and trying to convince you to go with me. I mentioned that we should go to Scotland, and the look you gave me was like all the blood had been sucked out of you.

"I asked you if you had you been there before. You said no, but your reaction was wrong. You shouldn't have had that strong of a reaction. We never talked about it. But we also never traveled to Scotland."

"Scotland," I repeat.

"I don't know if it's helpful, but maybe start there. Something bad happened there."

"Thank you, Nora. I want to ask how you are doing, but I shouldn't know anything about where you are or how you're doing. It would put you at risk. Tell Beckett that I called and to make sure your phone isn't traced."

"Ugh, I can't stand Beckett."

I frown. "I thought you had the hots for him."

"I do, but that doesn't mean he isn't the most insufferable know-it-all, who even wants to lecture me on how to take care of two little ones."

I smile. "Is your problem that he is right and does know more about babies than you?"

She sighs. "Yes, but I should be the one who knows more. I'm the woman!"

I laugh. "Beckett spent weeks taking care of them on his own before. He's been their uncle for months now. The babies are named after him. I don't think it's wrong that he knows more than you."

"He doesn't have to rub it in my face, though."

I bite my lip to keep from laughing again.

"I need to go, Nora. Stay safe. And don't forget to tell Beckett about this call."

"Yea, yea, so he can come to my rescue and save me."

"He's saving the babies, not just you."

"I guess." I can practically hear her rolling her eyes. "Stay safe. Hope to see you soon."

We end the call, and I look at Langston.

"Scotland, that's all she could give me," I say.

Langston runs off, returning a minute later with his laptop. He pulls up Scotland on a map and starts zeroing in different places.

"Anything look familiar to you or stand out?"

I stare at the map, a cold feeling washing over me. I take the computer from him and place it on my lap. I roam the cursor over the screen, hoping that something will trigger my memories.

I could have hidden it anywhere in the country—anywhere.

By the sea.

In the cities.

Buried in the sand.

Or in the mountains.

Locked in a lockbox.

Secured in a safe.

Getting a country to focus on is no more helpful than knowing that I hid it somewhere in the world. There are simply too many places to search.

I zoom in and put it on satellite view so that I can see the buildings and streets, hoping something will help me to remember. The familiar look of a building. The name of the street. Anything.

"Siren?" Langston eventually says, taking the laptop from me and closing it.

I blink rapidly and then stare at him.

"You've been looking at the screen for over an hour. If you were going to remember something, I think you would have remembered by now."

"I'm sorry. I'm just terrified that I won't remember, but that Julian will. If he figures out where it is before us, then we are all doomed."

"Don't put this all on yourself. We are in this together. You did your best to hide it away, and you've kept it safe all this time. Now it's time we all protect it."

"Why didn't I destroy it?" I ask.

Langston shifts in his seat. "Maybe you did?"

I rack my brain, but I don't have a clue. "Well, unfortunately, we won't know until we find the box and confirm it still exists."

"Time is running out, Ren," Langston says, taking my hand in his.

A knock at the door startles us. It looks like time has already run out.

CHAPTER 23
ZEKE

I never expected to be at Langston's place so soon, yet here I am, standing tied up in the doorway while Julian knocks on the door. Six men stand behind us with guns pointed at me to keep me in check.

The door opens, and Langston stands in the doorway.

"I'm surprised to see you here. This wasn't part of the plan," Langston says to Julian.

"Plans change, you know that. Are you going to invite us in?"

"You and Zeke sure, but I don't need my house overrun by your calvary."

Julian frowns. "My men stay with me."

"Why? Don't you trust me? My security system is the best in the world."

Julian steps inside, pushing Langston out of the way, before snapping his fingers at his men to follow. Two of his men shove me inside, not that they need to. Siren is inside. I need to see her.

Langston gets in Julian's face. "Your men can stay in the front of the house. The rear is off-limits."

"Fine," Julian says, grabbing my ropes and pulling me after him as we walk into the living room.

I see Siren—similarly tied up. She's still wearing an oversized sweatshirt to hide her growing belly. Her legs and arms are tied to the chair she's sitting in, and her mouth is taped shut.

I look at Langston and growl through the bandana tied around my mouth. *Why did he have to tie her up? Why use tape on her mouth?*

He glares back, not giving away whose side he is on at all.

I turn my attention back to Siren. She doesn't look hurt. I don't see any visible bruises or scars. There isn't even a mark on her cheek from when Langston slapped her face.

She's fine, I tell myself.

Julian yanks on my ropes as he takes a seat on the couch. Langston sits opposite him, while I continue to stand. Both men ignore Siren and me.

"I came here because I need to speak with Siren alone," Julian says.

Langston laughs, crossing his leg over his knee as he leans back. "No. I have my prisoner. You have yours. That's how this works."

"Except, Siren isn't your prisoner. I already bought her months ago," Julian says.

"Actually, I bought her months ago," Langston says.

"And you sold her. She wasn't yours to buy. She has always been mine. Maybe not physically, but her life belongs to me."

"What does that mean?" Langston leans forward in his chair.

"She traded the rest of her life for Zeke's when she saved him from the water and brought her to me. She's mine. She has no choice but to tell me where the box is. Otherwise, I'll take Zeke's life."

Siren's eyes widen, and she fights against the constraints.

Shhh, baby, it will be okay. If anyone is going to die, it should be me, not you.

Langston looks from Julian to me. He doesn't know how to get out of this.

I tear the bandana from my mouth with my teeth. "I'll take her debt."

Julian looks at me with a smirk. "Do you realize what you are offering?"

"Yes, I'll take Siren's place."

"You are offering to be my loyal servant for the rest of your life?"

I gasp and look at Siren. I didn't realize she had promised Julian her life in order to save mine.

"Yes," I say.

"Then it looks like Siren is my prisoner. And Zeke is yours," Langston says.

Julian frowns, and I can tell he isn't sure he likes the trade.

"Regardless who belongs to whom, you and I have a deal. Together, we need to find that box, and she is the only one who knows where it is," Julian says, staring at Siren sadistically.

"Don't worry. I'll make her talk," Langston says.

"You have until morning to make her talk. Otherwise, it's my turn to try," Julian says with a smirk.

Langston nods in agreement.

Fuck.

Langston walks over to Siren and rips the tape holding her to the chair from her ankles and legs, before twisting her arms behind her back, forcing her to stand, and leading her away.

Langston brushes her hair off her neck and then puts his lips on my woman. I buck against my restraints trying to get to her, but Julian holds me back.

"I'm going to enjoy making you talk," Langston says against her neck.

I lose it. I run at Langston, but three of Julian's men quickly tackle me to the ground.

Langston and Julian both chuckle.

"Come, my beauty." Langston pulls on Siren's wrist. She fights him gently, not really struggling as hard as she can.

Langston isn't going to hurt her. He's on our side.

Langston and Siren disappear down the hallway to his bedroom. I wince when I hear a thump and a light scream.

Julian notices my reaction. "Don't worry, Bishop is a gentle man underneath all that hard exterior. Tonight, she'll sleep easily. Tomorrow is when the real pain begins."

Julian heads down the hallway to one of the spare bedrooms.

His men tie me up in the chair Siren had just occupied, and then make beds for themselves on the couches and floor.

A man to my left starts snoring almost immediately, but it's a welcome sound. It drowns out a little of the screaming, yelping, and whimpering coming from down the hallway.

It's all fake, I repeat to myself.

But what if it isn't?

♡

"Zeke."

The voice jolts me awake, and I almost yell, I'm awoken so abruptly with a hand over my mouth.

"Shh, come on," Langston says.

My eyes widen when I realize Langston is standing in front of me. I look down and see that my hands and ankles have become untied.

Langston motions with his head to follow him, so I do. The men in the living room sleep soundly as we tiptoe away. We continue toward the open back door and then outside into the garden out back.

Siren is sitting on the edge of a fountain, waiting for me. When she sees me, she jumps up and runs toward me.

Our arms tangle around each other as soon as we reach each other. If I have it my way, we will never let go again.

"I was so afraid that Julian killed you," Siren cries into my shoulder.

"Never. You know that bastard can't take me down."

I glance behind me and realize that Langston has disappeared. Hopefully, he's standing guard, so Siren and I can have a few moments together.

And I'm going to make the most of every second we have together.

I grab the hem of her sweatshirt and lift it over her head. She's wearing a tank top underneath, and I lift that next. She's not wearing a bra, so I can see every bit of her under the moonlight.

I run my hands down her arms, then across her chest, and finally over her stomach. I turn her around and then run my hand over her smooth back. There isn't a mark on her body.

Finally, I turn her back to me.

"Satisfied?" Siren asks.

"Yes."

"Langston didn't touch me. He protected me."

"Thank God for that." I grab her cheeks and pull her lips to mine so I can kiss her like I want to. Her arms go under my shirt, feeling me over to check that I'm all in one piece too.

"Satisfied?" I ask with a smirk.

"Yes," she breathes.

"God, I need you, Siren. I'm not going to be able to sleep tonight without fucking you first."

She bites her lip. "Neither will I."

There aren't many places to fuck in the garden. I wish we had a bed or even a shower. But all we have is a garden of flowers, a fountain, and a small bench.

I grab her hand and pull her toward the bench, but when I sit down on the bench to pull her into my lap, it creaks. There is no way we are going to sit, let alone fuck on it, without breaking the small wooden thing.

Siren laughs. "Come here." She pulls my hand, and I stand and follow Siren as she leads me through the garden to a small patch of grass. Then she yanks me down to the grass with her.

I laugh along with her as I situate myself on my elbows over her.

"I feel like a kid again," she says.

"You'll feel all woman once I get done with you."

Her eyes light up at my words before I reach between her legs and rub her gently. Her eyes roll back, and her body writhes beneath me as I rub over her pants. I can feel her growing wetter.

"Zeke, fuck me, please."

I pull her pants down and slip my finger between her folds.

"So wet, so ready."

"Yes," she breathes.

She fumbles with my jeans, trying to get the button and zipper undone as quickly as possible. I understand her need to move quickly. Time has been taken from us too many times. There is never a guarantee that we will have more than a few minutes together. Never a guarantee of more time than the present.

I shove my jeans down as soon as she gets the button undone, and then she's pulling me toward her wet entrance. My cock doesn't need guidance—inside her is all it ever wants. I could find her with my eyes closed, and all my senses turned off.

I push her thighs back, spreading her wider as I push into her.

She gasps as I fill her.

"I remember you," she says suddenly.

"Did you ever forget me?"

She grins. "I forgot our first meeting in the bar when I sat on your lap."

I thrust in and out of her until she's unable to speak, too focused on how incredible she feels.

It gives me a moment to study her. To let my heart fill. To remember all my moments with her. *How could I ever forget?*

"Fuck me, my beast-man."

I grin wildly, remembering her sitting on my lap and calling me her beast-man, even then. I remember her flirting with me.

"You kissed me that night. That was our first kiss."

"I did not," she breathes again as I slow my thrusts.

I wait for her to remember.

"Oh my god! I did kiss you." She bites her lip, remembering that delicious kiss. We didn't know each other at all. It was just an instant connection. We both knew that the moment wouldn't last, but one day we would be together again. We needed one sweet moment to take with us forever.

I bite her bottom lip, pulling it into my mouth like she did to me when we kissed the first time.

Her eyes meet mine. She remembers.

I grab her hips, and she tugs my neck holding me close to her. I thrust in and out. Over, and over, circling her clit with my groin, until she's ready to scream my name and I hers.

I crash my mouth over hers to muffle our screams as we both come together. I spill into her as she clenches down on me.

We stay locked together for a moment, knowing this could be the last time.

"It won't be," I say, reading her mind.

"No, our forever has to last a lot longer than this." She kisses my wedding ring.

I nod and help her off the grass before we both get dressed again. And then I pull her onto my lap as we sit and relax, our time together fleeting.

"How close are you to remembering?" I ask.

"That's as much as I've remembered. I killed my parents just after I hid the box, so Langston and I both think I need to experience a similar trauma in order to trigger the memory. We found a rapist and killed him, but it barely triggered anything."

Siren is silent after she speaks, fidgeting with the strands of her hair as she pulls a piece of grass out of it.

"What aren't you telling me?"

Her eyes look behind me, and that's when I spot Langston standing over us.

"She didn't remember after killing the rapist was because the violence wasn't personal. She didn't know the man. She needs to kill someone she knows and loves. Someone like me," Langston says, with his hands in the pocket of his jeans.

I look from Siren to Langston. "You can't kill him."

"She wouldn't have to actually kill me. Just make her think she did. Stop just short of killing me," Langston says.

I'm still having a hard time forgiving Langston for what he did before. But offering to let Siren almost kill him, knowing that it could result in his actual death, washes the slate clean instantly.

"You can't kill him," I repeat again, and I feel Siren relax in my arms. It's clear she doesn't want to kill him either.

"You can't kill him because you are going to kill me instead," I say.

CHAPTER 24
SIREN

"**N**o."

I stand abruptly, removing my hands from his.

"I'm not asking you to actually kill me," Zeke.

"Then what are you suggesting?" I turn toward Zeke with fear and pain.

"Just that you could—almost kill me."

I frown. "No, it's too dangerous. What if you actually died?"

He shrugs. "Then, you'd be no worse off."

"No. I would be devastated, and I wouldn't recover."

His lips thin. "I know, but there isn't any other choice."

"You could kill me, instead," Langston offers again.

"No, I'm not killing anyone," I say.

Zeke grabs my arms and forces me to look at him. "You won't kill me. We will make sure of it. We'll put fail-safes in place. Trust me. Langston will be here to ensure you don't kill me. But we have to find the box. Julian will torture you to get the information if we don't find it tonight."

I exhale my stress. "What is your plan?"

He reaches around me and pulls my gun from my waist. "Well, I won't let you shoot me again."

"I second that," Langston says.

I laugh, giving them the reaction they were hoping for.

But Zeke's own smile falters. "Drown me."

"What? No—"

He nods. "Drown me. It's personal and physical, but even if you go too far, there is a good chance you can bring me back. You know CPR?"

"Yes."

"And there is AED in the hall," Langston says. He jogs off to go get what we might need.

"I don't like this," I say.

"I don't really either, but we are out of time."

I don't know what to say.

Zeke grabs my hand and starts leading me toward the fountain.

Jesus Christ. I can't do this.

But Zeke looks at me with so much determination. He's willing to do anything to help me remember. I can't just say no. If I ever doubted Zeke's love for me, I can't anymore.

I can't doubt Langston's either. He was just as willing to die for me.

Langston sets supplies down next to the fountain—a towel, the AED, and rope. And then he looks at Zeke. "It should be me."

"No, it should be me. She loves you. I can see that, but Siren and I share a deeper love. If anyone is going to trigger her memories, it's going to be me."

I frown at the rope Langston picks up.

Zeke pulls off his shirt, and as much as I want to take in his muscles and run my hands over them, I'm too focused on what I'm about to do.

Langston hands me the rope as Zeke turns around and puts his arms behind his back.

"Tie them together, Siren."

"I can't. Can't Langston do it?"

Langston steps back, out of view. He won't help me with any part but making sure that Zeke doesn't die. That's his role. My role is to carry out every bit of the violence, to remember.

"I'll do my best not to fight you until I can't stand it any longer.

But if you don't tie me up, I'll fight too soon, and you won't feel like you are actually killing me," Zeke says.

"This is outrageous," I protest, but I tie his arms together.

Zeke kneels in front of the fountain. I stand frozen behind him.

"Siren, please."

I step forward, my arms and legs shaking. My mother's face flashes in my head. Water comes next.

More flashes of memories flow.

Blood.

Tears.

Please...

The memories move me forward; I need to try this. This could be what helps me remember.

I walk up behind Zeke, reluctantly, just like I did when I was killing my own mother.

I push Zeke's head down, until it's submerged in the water. And then I hold him there, forcefully.

At first, not much happens.

It's peaceful.

I focus on the water—the moonlight shining down on me. I let my fear spread.

I have to do this.

Suddenly, then everything changes.

Zeke starts thrashing his head. Bubbles pour out of his mouth. It takes all of my strength to hold him under.

"MOTHER," I GASP, AS HER FACE COMES INTO VIEW.

"Please, don't kill me."

"I don't want to. But I can't let you have the box. Do you understand what it contains? What power it wields?" Please say no. Please say that you didn't realize, that you don't want it.

"Yes. The world needs to be rid of monsters. This is the only way to erase half the world. To get rid of the evil."

"By unleashing uncontrollable evil onto the world?"

"We can control it. We have the cure. We will be able to give the cure to those deserving."

"No, you don't get to play God. You don't get to decide who lives and dies."

"What did you do with the box, Aria?"

"I hid it."

"Where?"

I shake my head. "Please, don't make me do this. Please, surrender. Give up. Let me save you."

"Give me the box, Aria." My mother attacks, running full force over me.

I move out of the way at the last second; it's too late for her momentum to stop her, she goes overboard into the water. I jump in after her, knowing what I have to do. She can't come back up. She has to stay under.

"SIREN! STOP!"

I blink rapidly as Langston yanks me away from the fountain and grabs Zeke's lifeless body.

"Oh my god!"

"Shh," Langston hushes me. He grabs a knife and swiftly rips through the rope tying Zeke's hands together. Then he puts Zeke on his back and begins chest compressions.

"Get the AED ready," Langston says.

I tear my eyes away from Zeke, who is lying lifeless on the ground. I open the AED box, pull out the application pads, and press them to Zeke's chest while Langston breathes a breath into Zeke's mouth.

The AED machine starts. "No heartbeat detected," the robot voice says.

"No, please, no," I say.

Langston grabs me and pulls me away from Zeke's body before the AED delivers a shock.

"Continue chest compressions," the robot guides us.

Langston restarts chest compressions, and I move to Zeke's head. "Breathe, Zeke. Come back to me. I need you. Come back."

The machine starts up again, telling us to step back.

We stop touching Zeke so the machine can deliver another shock.

"No heartbeat detected, continue chest compressions."

Langston continues.

"Zeke, please!"

Another zap from the machine, more chest compressions.

"I'm so sorry." I grab Zeke's head, breathing air into his mouth, hoping something will bring him back.

"No heartbeat detected."

The machine shocks him again. And then shuts off.

The machine has given up, but there is no way I'm giving up. I can't have killed him. This can't be happening.

I push Langston out of the way and pump down over his heart with all of my weight. I'm cracking ribs and crushing him, but I'll do anything to get his heart started again, including trading my soul to the devil if he will save him.

"Please," I beg to the silent night. "Don't let him die."

And then...I feel something—a fluttering of his heart beneath my hands.

"Yes, come on, Zeke. Wake up. Come back to me."

I continue doing hard compressions, while Langston breathes into Zeke's mouth.

Then, Zeke coughs.

He coughs!

He's alive.

I stop suddenly as he coughs up what looks like a gallon of water before falling back to the ground, exhausted.

"You are alive," I say through my tears.

Zeke's wipes my cheek dry with his thumb with a soft smile. "I couldn't stand Langston giving me anymore mouth to mouth. I would have thought you would be the one to do that, Siren."

I collapse on top of him, hugging him tightly.

"I'm so sorry," I cry into his chest.

He strokes my back. "Shh, I'm okay. You didn't do anything wrong."

I see tears in Langston's eyes when I look up. He was just as worried that he had killed his friend. He looks away, though, when he notices me staring.

How could I have ever thought that Langston was a bad man?

I focus back on Zeke. "I'm just so thankful that you are alive. Your heart stopped, and we didn't think we could get it started again."

Zeke holds my cheeks in his hands, wiping my tears with his thumbs and tucking my hair behind my ears, trying to comfort me.

"My heart will always beat for you."

I smile through the tears as I try to catch my breath.

Zeke takes a deep breath, and I realize I'm squashing him. I roll off him and help him sit up.

"How are you feeling?" I ask.

"Like the luckiest man in the world to be married to you."

"Seriously, how does your chest feel?"

He takes a deep breath in and out. "It burns a little, but I can get a good breath, so I think I'll be fine."

I nod.

"I hate to end this, but we should get back soon before any of the men start waking up," Langston says, and then he starts walking back toward the house to give us a chance to say goodbye once again.

"I'm so tired of saying goodbye," I say.

"This isn't goodbye. We are together, now. I'm not letting anything stand between us. Not again." Zeke leans down and presses his lips to mine. I return the kiss fiercely. We don't let our tongues slip into each other's mouths; we just seal our lips together like we've become one person.

Slowly, Zeke pulls us apart. As much as he says we will be together, that this isn't goodbye, my heart can no longer escape the dreaded feeling.

"Did it work?" Zeke asks.

"What?" I ask, not understanding his question.

"Did your memories come back?" he asks.

My mother flashes in my head. She came back, but nothing else. I still don't remember where the box is. There is nothing Zeke can do about it now, though. He won't let us go back inside if he thinks I don't remember, and we have to go back inside. If we run, Julian will hunt us down and kill us. We aren't running, not anymore. We will face this, now.

"Yes," I say. It's the truth—I do remember. But it is also the most horrible sin, because I don't remember the important part—where the box is.

Zeke nods. "Good." He kisses my temple.

He takes my hand and leads me back to the house, where Langston is standing guard. I notice Langston has a roll of tape in his hands, reminding us that Zeke has to be tied up again, while I will be sleeping in Langston's room.

I quickly kiss Zeke one last time. I keep it short; otherwise, I wouldn't stop kissing him.

"Ready?" Langston asks us.

We nod and silently follow him into the house.

Zeke holds my hand for as long as he can before he has to take a seat again. Langston reties Zeke to the chair, none of us speaking for fear of waking up the sleeping guards.

Zeke winks at me with a wicked sultry grin, and I bite my lip and blush in return.

Once Zeke is retied, Langston walks over to me. He gives me a stern look that tells me we have to go, but I can't get my feet to move.

Langston tugs on my hand, but I'm frozen, watching Zeke.

Eventually, Langston picks me up and carries me down the hallway, away from Zeke.

Once in the bedroom, Langston locks the door and sets me down on the bed before he sits next to me.

"Did you really remember?"

"I remembered my mother, but not where I hid the box."

Langston takes my hand in his, trying to comfort me as he rubs his thumb over the back of my hand.

"What are we going to do?" I ask.

"We will think of something. I won't let Julian hurt you; I promise you that."

We sit on the edge of the bed in silence for a while. We should be sleeping.

Suddenly, out of nowhere, Langston slaps me.

I turn and look at him as I grab my cheek, more from shock than pain.

"What are you doing?"

There is no remorse in his eyes. No apology. And no reason for this that I can see.

He grabs me by the arm with such force I'm sure he's going to bruise me and throws me back on the bed. He ties me up roughly while I'm lying on my back, still in too much shock to fight back.

He takes a piece of tape and moves to put it over my mouth.

"I thought you were my friend. Why are you doing this?"

He puts the tape on my mouth, silencing me.

"The truth is I was never your friend. I just pretended to be to get what Julian wanted. I'm on Julian's side. I'm a monster." Langston walks to the bathroom, while I lay in bed tied up. A single tear rolls down my cheek.

How could I have been so wrong about Langston? He really is Bishop. He really is a monster.

CHAPTER 25
ZEKE

Somehow I sleep, even though my lungs burn from being filled with water.

I've never been so terrified in my life. I've been near death before; that isn't what had me panicked. What I feared was that Siren would kill me, and then she'd never forgive herself.

Siren brought me back to life even after I was dead, but my body is paying the price for it. Even though I'm tied up in a chair and in a ton of pain, I was able to sleep because my body demanded it.

However, the noise coming down the hallway is what woke me up.

Julian marched toward Langston and Siren's room, and as soon as he started down that hallway, the sounds started up again from Langston's room—smacking, yelping, crying.

I tried to block it out. It's not real; I saw it all before. They did this dance earlier, and I got to see Siren after. She didn't have a mark on her. I hope they find a way to make her look beat up without having to mark her at all. Julian will know something is up if she comes out looking untouched.

That must be what they are doing now.

Please, be careful. Don't really hurt her.

Julian knocks on the bedroom door. "Time's up. We need to talk."

He then walks into the living room; his men wake to attention.

The noises coming from their bedroom quiet for a minute, and then Langston appears, dragging Siren behind him by the hair.

I come unglued. She looks a disheveled mess. Her clothes and hair are all awry. Most of her clothes are heavily torn, revealing bruises and scratches.

They aren't real. Or if they are real, they are mild. Just enough necessary to make it appear that Langston raped and tortured her all night.

But there are tears in her eyes. Real. Genuine. Tears.

I fight against my restraints. *Damn Langston for taping my arms and legs so tightly that I can't break free.*

It's not real. She's acting.

Jesus, does it look real.

Langston releases Siren, and she scoots away to the corner of the room like she's terrified of him. She's not tied up, cowering in the corner against the wall.

What the hell is happening? What did I miss?

"Where is it?" Julian sits in one of the chairs, motioning for Langston to sit opposite of him.

"Scotland," Langston answers, naming a country and not a specific place.

Julian narrows his eyes. "Where exactly?"

Langston doesn't answer. *Does he not know? Did Siren keep the information to herself? Or does he not want to tell Julian?*

"Fine, don't tell me. I'll make her tell me," Julian stands and moves toward Siren.

Fight, baby. Kick his ass.

She doesn't move, though. She slumps to the floor, practically curling into a ball, so unlike my Siren.

I fight against my restraints, but I make no progress.

Julian goes to grab Siren's hair, but Langston grabs his wrist.

"She's mine. Until we have the box, she's my assurance that you won't betray me. I know you want her," Langston says, throwing Julian's hand down.

Julian studies Siren closer, and I see the secret revealed a second before he does, but it's too late.

"You're pregnant?" Julian says, blinking at Siren.

She stares down at the floor, not looking at him.

"Answer me! Are. You. Pregnant?"

Siren finally looks up at him, the heat and fire returning to her eyes. "Yes."

"Whose? Whose is it?"

Julian studies her belly, like it holds all the answers, like it can tell him whose baby she's caring.

I fight the scarf off from around my mouth. "MINE," I growl.

Everyone's attention turns to me when I speak.

Julian turns to me. "How do you know for sure? I raped her several weeks ago. It would make sense if the baby were mine."

There is a small chance the baby is his, but I'm not letting him know that. He will never be a father. I will ensure that.

"We had a DNA test run to ensure I was the father. If not, Siren was going to terminate the pregnancy." It's a lie, but I don't care. I don't want Julian to have any claim to the baby. Siren assured me she doesn't think it's him. She's too far along for it to be his. But I want him to know definitively that the baby isn't his.

Julian's reaction is blank. He doesn't blink, and he doesn't show emotion on his face. Instead, he walks into the kitchen and then returns a moment later with a roll of tape.

I snarl at him as he takes a piece of tape and wraps it over my mouth, assuring my silence.

"I'll find out if the baby is mine or not. If it's mine, I will enjoy raising it with Siren. If it's not, I will destroy it."

I fight so hard that I break the chair I'm sitting in. I've never wanted to kill a man more than I do now. The second I get my legs free, five men dive on top of me. They quickly tie more ropes around me and hold me down, taking two men per rope to ensure I'm immobile.

He threatened my child. I'm going to kill him and then bring him back to life and kill him again, over and over.

Julian's phone buzzes, and he frowns before looking at it. He answers, "Yes."

There's a pause.

"We're close."

Another pause.

"I understand."

And then he ends the call. He looks to Langston. "Where exactly is it located?"

"All I've gotten is a country. But if I spend the day with her, I'm sure I'll get the exact location," Langston says. "Why don't you head to Scotland, and we will follow as soon as I finish breaking her."

"No, we are out of time. It has to be today. Get her to tell us now, or I will."

Langston looks like he wants to object, but decides against it. I plead with him with my eyes to save Siren. I don't care about me. Just get her and get out of here. I'll find a way to kill Julian. We can hunt his financier down after Julian is dead.

Langston walks over to Siren, who coils back like he's about to strike out at her. Her reaction terrifies me.

He grabs one of her wrists and starts dragging her to his bedroom.

Julian sits down in his chair and flicks on the TV as Langston leaves. Then Julian flicks the channel to Langston's security system.

"Put on a good show," Julian says, winking at Langston as he drags Siren out of the room.

Fuck.

I give Langston one last plea with my eyes. *You can escape. Take Siren out the window and make a run for it. Kai and Enzo will be here soon to help me. Just save her.* There is no way to fake torturing her on a live feed. And I know Siren, she won't give up the location when she knows Julian is listening.

Langston gives me no indication of what he's thinking as he drags Siren down the hallway away from me once again.

I stare at the TV, waiting for them to come back into view. I take in the wrecked room on the screen. The comforter and sheets are half on the bed. The furniture is all messed up with drawers out, and lamps thrown to the floor.

Please don't let any more damage happen. Please let Siren and our baby be okay.

Langston and Siren come back into view. She tries to pull away and get him to let go of her wrists, but the way he's gripping her wrist, there is no way her arm can slip through.

"Let me go!" Siren cries, her legs are kicking against Langston to let her go.

Langston ignores her pleas, her suffering. The pain she's trying to inflict on him doesn't even phase him.

Siren pulls hard on his grip, throwing her entire body to the floor to try and make it as difficult as possible for Langston.

I know my girl; she can escape any man. If Langston is truly hurting her, Siren will fight back until she escapes.

This is all fake, a show.

Langston drags her through the room to the bed.

Do not get in that bed.

Then he's yanking her up by her wrists and throwing her into the bed.

Siren immediately tries to roll off the other side of the bed, but Langston grabs her ankle and yanks her back. He throws his weight on top of her, pinning her body underneath him.

Julian snickers next to me.

I scream beneath the tape over my mouth. I don't understand how he is okay with another man raping a woman who he feels is his.

Julian looks at me and laughs. "Don't worry, Zeke. She's not Bishop's. He's just borrowing her. She's *mine*."

I fight harder against my restraints and yell through the tape, hoping Julian will want to talk and remove the tape, but his eyes have turned back to the screen. Mine follow, although I wish they hadn't—because what I see will never leave my mind. Not ever.

Siren's pants are around her ankles. Her wrists are pinned together in one of Langston's hands above her head, and his body is pressed between her legs.

I can't watch this, even if it's fake, but I can't tear my eyes away from it either. I'm trapped in a horror movie.

There is no audio from the security camera; the only sounds we hear are when Langston makes her scream or cry loud enough that we can hear down the hallway.

We can't see their mouths move at this angle either, so I don't know if they are talking. I don't know what sounds Siren is making.

Langston's hand roars back, and there's a slap.

"Hit the bitch again!" one of the guards shouts at the TV.

"Strip her and turn her around so we can see her. This is better than free porn," another guard says, and then they are all chuckling together, shouting out what they want Langston to do to her like they are watching an HBO fight or something.

Come on, baby. Kick him off you. Do something. Show me you still have some fight left in you.

Then I see a knife that Langston has pulled out and pushed against her neck. She's breathing heavily but doesn't move. Her eyes dart down, trying to get a look at how he's holding the knife to her neck, but otherwise, she's as still as stone.

This is fake, I repeat to myself for the thousandth time. This is just an orchestrated dance to please Julian. This is just so Langston can still pretend he is working with Julian; so that he can get close to him and eventually help us kill him.

But the way he's holding the knife against her carotid has me nervous. He's pressing harder than necessary. It seems real, so fucking real.

Make up a lie about where the box is, and end this—please.

I watch carefully, every movement.

Langston continues to hold the knife to her neck as he reaches down and works on his pants.

My eyes widen, watching in fear.

This is fake.

Fake.

Fake.

Fake.

He's not going to rape her. He's not going to hurt her.

A single tear drops from Siren's eye, landing in the corner. She looks disgusted at Langston, like she hates him worse than any man she's ever hated.

Siren hates Julian. He raped her, violated her. But I know that thinking about me saved her from the pain.

She's not thinking about me, now. She's hating Langston—a man who she thought was her friend. Who I believed was my friend.

"No!" I scream through the tape as I watch him position himself between her legs, keeping the knife at her neck, her hands stay above her head, likely because he's told her he'll slit her throat if she moves.

Julian's eyes darken.

The room quiets as they watch with fascination.

And then I watch him thrust his hips.

I watch her cringe in disgust.

That single tear that was caught in her eye rolls down her cheek and off her chin.

That tear tells me everything—this is real.

This isn't fake.

Langston played us both.

He's not our friend.

He works for Julian.

From the smug expression on Julian's face, this is why he was willing to let Langston rape Siren. He wanted to show me, once and for all, whose side Langston is on—his. Julian won the war. He got Siren. And he turned my best friend against me.

I fight with all my might against the bindings, but I can't break free. I'm locked where I am with nothing to look at, but my beautiful wife being violated.

I feel bile rising in my throat. I'd vomit if there wasn't tape covering my mouth.

I'm going to kill him.

I'm going to kill them all—burn everyone in this house, send them all to hell.

I watch Langton thrust into Siren like she's his, like he has the right. No one has the right.

I failed.

I failed to protect her.

This is my biggest failure. The only reason she's with Langston right now is because I told her to trust him. I thought he was my friend. I was so wrong.

I will never forgive myself.

But I can't keep letting this go on. I have to stop it. *I have to.*

I fight harder, pushing again and again and again against the bindings. I get one ankle free then the other.

The men are too focused on the TV to notice.

I pull hard on my wrists, but I can't get them free.

I stare at the TV, gaining strength from Siren to save her. Siren must have decided this is the moment to fight back, too, because I see her and Langston struggling instead of him thrusting.

Yes, we have to fight back. We won't take this without fighting. Together, we are going to destroy them all.

I rip my arms free and then rip the tape from my mouth. This gets everyone's attention, but it's too late. Nothing will stop me from running into the room, ripping Langston off of Siren, and squeezing the life out of Langston.

A guard comes at me, but I punch him, knocking him down with one hit.

Two more attack from the side with guns firing at me. I dodge the bullets, grab a gun from one of them and use it to fire at the other before turning it on the other guard. Both men drop.

Then I turn and fire the gun at the other three men. I move to turn the gun on Julian when he gasps at the sight on the TV before shouting, "You're a fucking dead man!"

He starts storming down the hallway before I have a chance to fire at him.

I glance at the TV, scared of what I will find.

Blood.

So much fucking blood covers the white sheet, droves and droves of blood. Langston continues to lie on top of Siren, so I can't figure out where the blood is coming from on the TV.

The sight only amplifies my speed. I run down the hallway, knocking Julian aside so I can be the first to burst through the room.

The moment in front of me almost makes me faint. I've never seen anything worse; nothing could be worse.

Siren dead is the only imaginable thing that could be worse.

The blood I see is unimaginable.

I can't tell where it's coming from.

I grab Langston by the back of his neck and throw him off of her. I have to get to her. I have to end her pain. I have to protect her from any more evil.

When I rip him off her, I see where the blood is coming from—from between her legs. I look over at Langston, who has pulled his pants up, blood all over him as well.

I look back at Siren with so many tears and pain in my eyes. I can't breathe. I can't think. My heart stops. And unlike last time, I don't think it can be resuscitated. It will never work properly again.

What I see can't be true. I can't have let this happen. I can't have.

I open my mouth to ask, but my voice doesn't work, only my tears.

My tears fall freely, pouring gallons of water out of my eyes. My very soul escapes through my tear ducts.

The pain I see on Siren's face isn't physical. It's not because Langton physically hurt her. It's because of what she knows is true, the loss she's experiencing.

I open my mouth again, my lungs still burning from being drowned, but now my throat has tightened, making it almost impossible to speak. But I have to; I have to know the truth, no matter how painful, how horrible, how unthinkable. I have to face it. I have to be strong for her.

I hear Julian behind me. Langston is moving toward us. I need a moment to understand that truth. After that, I'll turn into the monster I need to be to destroy the men behind me. But right now, I need to connect Siren and my's pain. I need it to fuel me through my heartache and make the men pay who did this.

I take Siren's hand in mine through our tears, and then I push through my pain.

"The baby?" I ask above barely a whisper.

Siren purses her lips, letting all the air out of her body, like that will somehow let the truth out, but it doesn't. She has to speak. She has to tell me.

"Gone," she yelps as she says it, like speaking the truth makes it true.

My head drops to hers as our pain mixes. Our hearts break. I don't know how we survive this pain. I don't know how Siren can ever forgive me for letting this happen.

But I know that I will make every man responsible pay.

CHAPTER 26
SIREN

Gone—the word burns through me. Just like the pain. I never thought I'd experience such trauma, such loss. But here I am, experiencing the worst thing possible.

Zeke's head rests against my forehead. The pain flows through him as powerfully as water over rapids. I feel every sharp intake of his breath, every rip of his heart, every vibration of his pain. I sense it all.

I feel his pain worse than I feel my own. It's intolerable to him. He won't recover from this. The man I knew is gone. I've destroyed him with my news.

My truth.

My sinful truth.

I close my eyes, and I remember. The trauma, the worst trauma I can imagine short of Zeke dying, is what spirals me into the past. What causes me to remember everything. All the truths I've hidden.

I WALK UP THE LARGE HILL COMPLETELY OUT OF BREATH. I LOOK BEHIND me, afraid I'm being tracked, but of course, I'm not. Everyone who knows about this is either dead or thinks the fake I swapped it with is real. There is no one coming after me. At least, not yet.

But someday, I know they will. A great evil will come for it. And when that happens, I will have this box as hidden as humanly possible.

So I keep climbing, even though I'm exhausted. My feet burn, my heart aches with the pain I've endured to protect the box. This is my destiny; this is my purpose—to protect the world from this danger.

Finally, I step foot on top of the large hill. An old fashioned castle straight out of the fourteenth century sits on top. I take a deep breath.

I'm doing the right thing.

I walk to the door, and before I have a chance to knock, a man opens it. A man I've never met before but who I instantly trust.

"Are you sure you want to hide it, instead of destroying it?" he asks me, not even giving me an introduction. He knows why I'm here, and he knows that finishing the task is more important than small talk.

"Yes, I can't say exactly why. Mostly a feeling that it's going to be needed someday."

He nods. "You don't have to explain it to me. You are the one who should make the decision. I trust you."

I pull the box out of my bag and hold it out to him. "Just as I trust you."

He takes it from me. "I'll guard it with my life."

"Even from me?"

He hesitates but then finally agrees. "Yes, I'll guard it, even from you."

"Thank you. I know what I'm asking."

"Nothing more than is required."

He doesn't invite me in. Even if he did, I can't come inside. I need to leave. I need to forget. I need to finish my task and figure out how I can forget, so no one can ever use me to find such evil.

"I should go."

"I would say until next time, but if we did this right, we will never meet again," he says.

That saddens me, that I'll never get to know this man. But it's for the best. He's the only person I feel I can trust. And I don't have anything to say. There is nothing I can say. I have to leave. I can't communicate with him. I can't come back here. Even to step foot in this country would be putting the world at risk.

But I can't bring myself to say goodbye either. Instead, I turn, and I walk down the hill, away from the only family I have left.

. . .

I open my eyes and find Zeke staring at me.

"Baby?" he asks, trying to understand what just happened to me. He thinks I already knew the location of the box, so I shouldn't tell him I didn't know until just now.

Instead, I just bite my lip, like the pain I'm feeling is too much for me to bear. He pulls me into a hug, and then all hell breaks loose.

Gunshots ring out all around the room and house.

Zeke falls on top of me, shielding me with his body as the bullets fly.

My eyes cut under Zeke's arm to see to the door. "Kai and Enzo are here," I whisper to him.

"Don't trust Langston!" Zeke shouts to them.

A gun is tossed on the bed. Zeke grabs it and turns, keeping his body over mine as he starts firing at the men coming into the room. I don't know where all these men are coming from, but half work for Enzo and Kai, while the other half work for Julian, or at least Julian's financier.

Another loud boom rings out, causing Zeke to yank me off the bed with him, and then use the bed as protection while he shoots over it.

"Stay behind me, no matter what, okay?" Zeke asks.

"Yes," I say.

"Let's go," Zeke says, when there is a break in the gunfire.

I peer around him and find only one man firing toward us from the door. I don't know where Langston or Julian went, or where Enzo or Kai went, but it appears the fighting has moved to another part of the house.

Zeke grabs my hand, and we move around the bed. Zeke kills the man at the door, and when we get to the door, he grabs a gun on the ground and hands it to me.

He gives me a warning look. *Stay behind him. Only fire when necessary. Stay safe.*

I nod. Then we are moving through the hallway. By the time we get to the living room, I realize that half the house has been blown away. It saddens me for a second to see such a beautiful house destroyed, but that thought is gone the next second as we come across the main fight.

Men are shooting everywhere, smoke billows around us, making it impossible to see clearly.

"There is a car in the garage. If we get separated, meet me there," Zeke says.

"Okay."

And then we push through, firing and slinking low through the smoke.

I cough as smoke enters my lungs, but I keep pressing on; I have to. We can't stay in this house much longer.

Zeke keeps moving forward, but I lose him.

There is more smoke toward the direction of the garage. I have to get out of the house before I head to the garage, or I won't be able to breathe much longer.

I end up crawling on all fours, searching for someone I trust.

I cough over and over. It burns, my eyes are watering, my nose dripping.

I collapse on the floor, unable to get enough oxygen to breathe. Gunshots ring out in the distance. Apparently, the battle has moved away from the smoke. I'd rather deal with a barrage of bullets than this thick smoke, too.

I start crawling again, unable to see my hands in front of me as I move. I have to keep going, though.

I consider calling for help, but I'm afraid it could draw the wrong attention of the wrong people. And from all my coughing, I probably wouldn't be able to yell very loudly anyway.

Must.

Move.

Forward.

I have to get out of the smoke. Of all the ways that I envisioned my death, dying in a house filled with smoke with people just outside who could save me, if they could just find me, was not the way that I thought I would go.

My head spins, and I start seeing spots.

I cough again as I try to suck in any oxygen, but there seems to be none left in the house.

I refuse to die like this. I will find a way through this even though my body is shutting down; my heartbeat is growing weaker; my chest has tightened.

I collapse, my arms are unable to move me forward any further. Maybe if I hover close to the ground, I'll be able to get enough oxygen until the smoke lifts.

So that's what I do while praying for a miracle.

"I got you." His voice is strong, despite the smoke. His arms scoop me up, and then we are running through the smoke. I cough against his chest; he grips me tighter.

We are through the smoke a moment later, but he doesn't stop running. I suspect he won't until he gets us somewhere he deems safe.

I continue to cough as he runs for what seems like miles before he finally stops. He unlocks a car and then places me in the back.

"Take a deep breath. In and out, slowly. You're safe now. There is plenty of oxygen for you to breathe. Just take some deep, slow breaths."

I try, but cough.

"Try again," he says.

I do.

I wheeze, but I'm able to get more oxygen this time and only cough a tiny bit.

"Good, again."

I take another breath, then another. The pain in my lungs eases a little with every breath.

"We need to go," he says, hopping in the front seat and putting the car in drive.

"I—" I say, starting to tell him everything that needs to be said, but my voice is hoarse.

"Shhh, Siren. Don't speak. You can tell me once we get to the airport," Langston cuts me off.

I need to speak. I have so much to say, but after everything that happened, I'm too weak. Too weak to talk. Too weak to fight. So instead, I drift off to sleep.

CHAPTER 27
ZEKE

"Siren!" I yell as I cough just outside the band of smoke that has filled the house. I don't know where all the smoke is coming from; there doesn't seem to be a fire.

"Siren!" I scream again at the top of my lungs, but that only makes me cough worse.

A bullet buzzes by my head, and I turn and fire. I have to stay alive so I can save her. I will not fail her again. I will not. *I can't...*

"Don't move," Julian says.

I look up and see that Julian has Kai in a headlock with a gun pointed at her.

Fuck.

Enzo runs up beside me. I look around at our small group, but I don't see Siren or Langston.

My heart races, thinking they could be together.

No.

I just saw Siren a minute ago. She'll make her way out through the smoke the same as I did. Hopefully, she's made it to the garage as is hiding, waiting for me to get to her.

And no one seems to know where Langston is. Right now, I have to focus on Kai, on saving her.

"Let her go," I say through a cough.

"I'd be willing to make a trade," Julian says.

I sigh and hold my hands up, dropping my gun. I turn to Enzo beside me. "Take Kai and find Siren. Keep her safe and away from all of this. Don't trust Langston."

Enzo nods at me.

I step forward while Enzo keeps his gun aimed at Julian. When I get close, Julian pushes Kai away and aims his gun at me.

Kai looks at me with such pain. "Go," I tell her.

She hesitates a second and then Enzo says, "Stingray, we have to go."

Kai gives me one last look, and then she runs off with Enzo.

Please go find Siren. Let her be safe.

"They aren't going to find Siren," Julian says to me.

"Siren will lead them to her."

He shakes his head. "Unlikely, since she isn't alone."

"What do you mean?" But my heart already knows. I know it isn't smart, but I have to know she isn't here. I take off to the house behind me. Somehow, most of the smoke is gone when I enter the house.

"Siren!" I yell as I step over fallen men. I run throughout the house, even back to the bedroom I found her in, but she's not there.

I run through the house again. *Please, be in the garage.* I open the back door and step into the garage.

"Siren!" I yell again, looking through the cars and under them for her. She's gone.

"I told you, he has her," Julian says from the doorway.

I turn with all of my rage and face him. "Tell him to bring her back, or neither of you will find the box. Call him and tell him right now, or I'll kill you. The only reason I've kept you alive is because I know you aren't the one in charge. There is another man paying you, pulling all the strings. And I thought you could lead me to him, but I'll kill you now if you don't have Langston bring her back right now."

"I have no doubt that is true, but there is just one problem."

"Which is?"

"I want Bishop, or Langston, whatever his name is, dead too."

I blink rapidly.

"I want him dead for what he did to Siren."

I scoff. "You raped her too, you know. You're no better than him."

"You're right, I'm not. But he killed her child, possibly my child, and I won't forgive him for that. I want him dead. He knows that. We aren't working together anymore."

I frown.

"This is what I suggest. You help me find the box, and I'll help you ensure Siren is safe," Julian says.

"Not likely, since you've tried to kill her more than most."

"I'll tell you a truth. I could never kill Siren. I love her as much as you do."

"No one loves her more than me."

Julian shakes his head. "I get the box. You get Siren. Do we have a deal?"

"And what happens to Langston?"

"The first one to find him gets to kill him."

Julian holds out a gun to me, and I take it. Then he's pulling out his phone. "We are going to need a private jet at the Bilbao airport immediately."

Julian hangs up and climbs into a speed car. I climb in after him.

We haven't agreed on anything, but he has a car and a jet. I need both to get to Siren since Langston hasn't returned my money yet.

"How are we going to know where to go once we get to Scotland?" I ask as Julian starts the car.

Julian's eyes narrow. "Because Siren isn't the only one who just got her memory back."

CHAPTER 28
SIREN

I open my eyes. I sit up and take in my surroundings. I'm lying on a couch on a private jet, surrounded by oval windows that frame fluffy clouds we are already flying through.

"Careful, don't sit up too fast," Langston says as I start pushing myself up. I cough as soon as I do.

"Here, breathe through this," Langston holds up an oxygen mask to my face that I realize is strapped around my neck and must have fallen off my face. I take a couple of deep breaths, and my lungs feel a bit better, yet I still cough a few times before I settle. When I feel better, I remove the oxygen mask.

"Here." Langston holds out a cup of tea to me.

I take it and sip.

"How are you feeling?" Langston asks. He's sitting on the couch next to me, staring at me with such intensity.

I cough again. "My chest and throat hurt, but otherwise, my main feeling is guilt for betraying Zeke."

He nods and then coughs as well.

I frown, not realizing that he might have inhaled as much smoke as I did when he rescued me.

"How are you feeling?" I ask.

He coughs again before clearing his throat. "Like I ruined a friend-ship forever."

I want to reassure him that he and Zeke will one day heal their relationship, but after what we did, I doubt that it will come easily. I'm going to have my hands full making sure Zeke doesn't kill Langston the next time we see him.

So I don't say anything.

"You didn't have a choice, you know. You had to do it. You had to hurt him," Langston says, knowing that I'm beating myself up for what I did to Zeke.

"I know, but I still hate hurting him. I hate lying to him. I hate all of it. When this is over, I hope I never have to lie again."

"Someday soon that day will come."

We both sip our teas. Unspoken questions linger between us. *Was it worth it? Did I get the information I needed?*

"We need to go to Inverness," I say, letting Langston know it was worth it.

"I'll go tell the pilots."

Langston stands and walks to the front of the plane to discuss flight plans.

The weight of what I did crashes down upon me.

I watched Zeke break, fully and completely. Zeke is devastated because of what I did. He shattered into a million pieces before my very eyes because of what I let him think, because of what I did.

My anchor is broken. He's hurting, and I can't comfort him, not until this is all over. He will never be the same. I don't think I'm able to put the pieces back together.

Tears start falling again, and my cough returns. Zeke isn't the only one; I'm broken too.

Zeke holds a part of me, and I won't be whole until we are together again.

I feel arms going around me as I cry. I swear I feel his tears wet my shoulder, but I don't pull away from his chest to verify.

"I've got you until you can be with Zeke again."

I shake in Langston's arms.

"I've got you," he repeats again.

"I know. Thank you for protecting me, even when I didn't realize that was what you were doing."

"I'm sorry I had to hurt you at all. I'm so sorry. I wish I could have come up with something different, something easier, to protect you. But—"

I pull back and wipe my eyes. "No, you did the right thing. Just like I did to Zeke."

"Forgive me?" Langston asks.

"There is nothing to forgive. But I forgive you, if that's what you need to hear."

I hug him again. Zeke is my husband, but Langston has quickly become someone special in my life. I don't know how to label our relationship. It's not a friendship, not like Nora and me, and it's different than a brother and sister relationship. I can't think of a term, but I imagine it feels a lot like how Kai and Zeke feel. Because of what we've been through, because of our shared pain, we will forever be connected.

He smiles at me. "Thank you."

"How long will it take us to get to Inverness?"

"Eight hours."

"We will beat them all there. We will find where you buried the box. And we will destroy it before anyone else can get there. We have a good couple of hours head start. After it's destroyed, I will make sure you are safe, and then I will help Zeke, Enzo, and Kai kill Julian and his financier."

"I didn't bury it," I say behind my eyelashes.

"What did you do with it then?"

"I gave it to a man."

He frowns. "Who? A man you trusted? How could you ensure it was safe? How do you know that it's still there?"

"Because the man is my brother."

Langston's eyes widen. "You have a brother?"

"I didn't know it either. He's thirteen years older than me. He was out of the house before I was old enough to know him. He lived by himself, away from the world. His heart is like mine. He knew how important it was to keep it safe. It's still there in the castle with him."

"Okay, good. We will get the box from him, then."

"He won't give it to us."

"What do you mean? I thought he was your brother? You trusted him to protect it?"

"I did. I do. But he promised to protect it, even from me."

Langston sinks back, realizing what it's going to take me to get the box—fighting my own brother. My own blood. I may have never known him, but it's still going to hurt trying to defeat him.

"We will find a way," Langston says, as he stares down at my stomach where I'm rubbing it. He puts his hand over mine, and we watch as we both feel a kick.

"We always find a way."

CHAPTER 29
ZEKE

I sit on the plane headed to Scotland.

I try not to think about everything that has happened.

My friend's betrayal.

My wife's suffering.

My child's death.

I wait for the tears to come, but they don't. The tears have vanished, and in their absence, I've hardened into a man capable of untold sin. My wrath will be felt throughout the world. I will not rest until every man who had a hand, no matter how small, in my child's death pays for his sins.

I've made a deal with the devil to keep Siren safe and ensure that Langston pays for what he did, but the devil will also die for his part.

I'm tired of playing games. Today, the world burns.

Julian is sitting at the front of the private jet, staring at his phone, while I sit in the back, as far away from him as I can get. Several of his men sit in between us.

But I'm tired of waiting and not knowing all the players. I want to know who the men are that I will be burning to the ground.

I get out of my seat and march to the front. If Julian's men were smart, they'd try to stop me, but they aren't the most intelligent bunch. They can't see a threat coming when they need to.

Julian doesn't seem to think of me as a threat either because he doesn't so much as blink when I walk over to him.

I grab him by the shoulders and throw him hard against the other side of the plane. His head bashes into the wall, and then I shove my arm against his throat, making it hard for him to breathe.

"Who finances you? I've seen your bank accounts. I know you are wealthy beyond imagination. Those stupid tasks you sent me on were nothing more than a game to you. You haven't made your billions from smuggling drugs and people. Who finances you?"

"You think I'll tell you, just like that?"

"If you don't want to die."

"I won't be dying." His eyes dart around the room to his men, who finally caught on and have their guns aimed at me.

I lean in close. "My child is dead. My wife broken. You think I care about dying right now? I only care about wiping the earth of evil."

"Thomas, get us two whiskeys," Julian snaps at one of his men.

I narrow my eyes. "What are you doing?"

"We have a partnership. You want to talk? Let's talk."

The man brings over two whiskey glasses.

Julian raises his eyebrows, waiting for me to decide how to handle this.

I let him go and grab one of the glasses.

"Everyone out," Julian says.

The man who brought us the glasses directs everyone to the back and then closes the door between the front and the back of the plane.

"Enzo's father," Julian says.

I frown. "Enzo's father can't be financing you, he's dead."

"No, he's not financing me. He's the reason for all of this, though. He originally made a deal with Siren's parents and mine. They had all agreed to work together, sharing resources and working together in drug and weapons trade. Eventually, Enzo's father, Mr. Black, cut our families out and ensured we were powerless."

"So, this all started because your parents and Siren's parents wanted revenge against the Black family?"

"Yes, our families wanted to ruin the Black family. The box contains the ultimate tool to do that—a cancer that spreads like a virus with us having the only cure. We could control who lived and who died."

I nod, it makes sense. "But then Siren killed them all."

"Did she?" Julian sips his drink.

I frown. "She did. She told me herself."

"She tried to. And she almost succeeded, but one man survived."

"Who?"

Julian grins. "Her father."

"Siren's father is financing you?"

"Yes. He invested some money in oil. He made a killing. He wanted me to hire her so I could keep an eye on her. We never realized that she was the key to finding the box all along, though."

"If her father survived, wouldn't he have known the truth?"

"No, he thought Siren had failed in stealing the box from the Black vault. We thought you knew where the box was. We were wrong; she succeeded. We were too stupid to realize that a woman like Siren doesn't fail."

I smirk. "No, she doesn't."

"That's what I remembered. That Siren doesn't fail. I also know that you know Siren better than anyone. We may not know the exact location where she hid the box in Scotland, but you know her. If you want to find Langston before he hurts her again, we will have to work together to find her."

"Where is Siren's father?"

"Why would I tell you that? It's one of the few things keeping me alive."

"Where is he?" I threaten again.

"I'll tell you as soon as I have the box and am safely away. He's at the top of your death list, and since I want him dead too, I have no problem letting you do the dirty work."

"You're scum."

"I know. But soon, I will hold the power of the world. You could have had it, but instead, you will trade it all away for love. Who's the fool?"

I don't answer, but I know what he thinks—I'm the fool. A fool that would do anything for love.

CHAPTER 30
SIREN

I take a deep breath and gasp as I struggle to walk up the hill toward the castle at the top. Where I last saw my brother. Where I hid the box with him.

"Are you okay? Do you need me to carry you?" Langston asks.

I stop and grip my waist. "No, I'm fine. It's just this damn body armor underneath my shirt. It's not built for pregnant women. It's very tight around my chest."

Langston laughs. "You don't look pregnant anymore with how tight that thing goes around you. I can imagine it's hard to breathe in."

"Yes, but it keeps me and the little one safe, so I'll deal with it."

I take another step, and a large boom explodes right next to me. Langston jumps on top of me as he draws his gun and looks around, but there doesn't seem to be anyone nearby.

I look over to the right where the bomb went off. Close, but more of a warning than an actual attempt on our lives.

"That would be my brother," I say.

Langston frowns. "Are you sure you don't have his phone number? We could just call him and tell him we intend to destroy the box and avoid all of this."

"I wish it were that simple, but Easton promised to protect it with his life, even from me. He hoped that someday someone would come along with a pure heart, someone who could break the cure from the cancer and use it only for good."

"But that person never came along."

"No. We could drop a bomb; blow the whole castle up and then search in the wreckage to ensure it was destroyed," I say, my voice sounding cruel and harsh.

"Could you really do that with your brother inside?" Langston asks.

Maybe—that's how far I'm willing to go to protect my family and the world. But I don't say that. It's an option if it comes to that, but first, we will try to get it by convincing my brother to destroy it.

"Stay behind me," Langston says as we continue up the hill. Zeke said the same thing to me back in Spain, and we ended up separated. I hope that doesn't happen again.

More bombs rain down around us, but none of them come close enough to cause us any danger, so we continue on up the hill. I hope that as much as I don't want to kill my brother, he doesn't want to kill me either.

We make it to the top of the hill in one piece, standing in front of the looming castle. It looks like we've gone back in time. Other than a few vines growing higher on the side of the castle, it's just as it was when I was last here.

"Ready?" Langston asks me.

I nod.

"You know that you don't have to come. I can meet with your brother on my own," he says.

"I know, but if he's going to listen to anyone, it will be me."

We both walk with our guns up to the castle. Langston won't let me get too close to the door, as he knocks, in case it's booby-trapped.

There is no answer, so Langston picks the lock and opens the door. He points his gun in as he enters the house, motioning for me to wait.

A moment later, he returns to the door and waves me inside. I step in and a cold chill courses through me. If anyone is living here, they live a very cold, empty life.

"Easton, it's Aria, your sister. We just want to talk," I say, hoping that if my brother is somewhere in the house, he'd respond to me.

We creep around the large, seemingly abandoned castle, until a voice stops us in our tracks.

"You should leave."

We turn around, trying to find where the voice is coming from, but I can't tell.

"Do you see where he is?" I whisper to Langston.

"No," he replies, his eyes peering around, trying to find him.

"We want to destroy the box. I should have never left it here. I should have destroyed it," I say.

Suddenly, a man steps forward from the shadows—my brother.

"Easton?" I say.

"Yes," he responds.

I lower my gun, then push Langston's down, although Langston doesn't seem happy with it. He keeps his gun aimed at Easton's feet.

"You don't have to give us the box. Just destroy it in front of us. Or go destroy it and bring back the box if you wish. But there are evil men coming for it. They could be hours or minutes away. We have to destroy it—now," I say.

"I can't," Easton says.

I frown. "Why not? I know I thought it was best to keep it around in case someone figured out a way to use the cure without unleashing the virus, but that opportunity has passed. We have to destroy it."

Easton steps forward, ignoring Langston until he's right in front of me. "It's good to see you again, little sis. I wish I could help you, I really do, but I swore to you a long time ago that I wouldn't. I said I would protect the box, and that's what I'm doing. Only someone who truly wants the box can get it. Only someone who is willing to give up everything, sacrifice the love of their life, and their own life will be able to send the box to someone."

"What did you do with the box?"

Easton doesn't speak, but his eyes tell me. They shoot across the ocean to an island through the window. He hid it there, not here.

"Don't go after it. It's perfectly safe, Aria. There is no reason to go," Easton says.

I bite my lip and close my eyes. It's not his fault. He did what I asked and protected it with everything he has. "The box may be safe, but the men coming for it won't stop coming after my family until they have the box or it's destroyed. The only way you can help save me from these terrible men and the world from the virus is to tell me how to get the box."

Easton looks at me and then Langston.

I turn to Langston. "Leave us alone, please."

"Siren, I can't. I—"

"It's okay, Easton won't hurt me. We just need to talk, sibling to sibling."

"I'll be right outside the door," Langston says, giving Easton a stern look and then walking outside.

"Tell me, Easton. Please, we are on the same side. Tell me what I need to do to destroy the box."

Easton steps forward and whispers in my ear, afraid Langston will hear. I listen carefully, my heart thudding wildly with fear and pain at what must happen, and who must do it.

Once Easton finishes talking, he walks to the front door to let Langston back in. When he opens the door, a bullet flies at his chest.

Easton falls down dead in front of me.

"No!" I scream at the sight.

I turn to look at the door, afraid to see what I'll see when I look. But I look anyway.

"Daddy?"

CHAPTER 31
ZEKE

Julian and I stare up at the hill with Julian's men surrounding us.

"Siren's here, good work. We will ensure she stays safe as long as you help me get the box," Julian says.

I don't say anything. He's crazy if he thinks I'm handing him over the keys to the virus that could kill millions of people—not going to happen.

But I need Siren alive. And for the moment, I'll do anything to keep her alive, so I keep my mouth shut.

I tracked the plane Siren and Langston got on, then had Enzo and Kai track the car they rented here. Enzo and Kai tracked them here.

We start up the hill as bombs start going off all around us. It's a minefield heading up the hill. If I'm lucky, one of them will kill Julian, and I'll have one less person to worry about. But if he's dead, Siren's father could just hire another man to come after us. As good as I am with security and tracking people down, I know it can take a lifetime to find someone who doesn't want to be found. That's not the life I want for Siren and me, so I'll let Julian live until he's no longer useful, then I'll kill him.

Julian and I make it up the hill. By my estimate, less than half the men we started with join us. We both gasp for air, but we don't get a chance to catch our breath. I spot Langston standing outside the giant castle at the top of the hill.

We both raise our guns in his direction.

"Where is Siren?" I shout at him.

Langston looks at me, then Julian. He realizes neither of us is on his side, not anymore. He betrayed us both, and now he'll pay for what he did.

"Where the fuck is she?" Julian yells, growing impatient.

Julian won't be the one who kills Langston. What Langston did is personal. If anyone kills him, it will be me.

I fire my gun in Langston's direction, purposefully missing just enough to scare him into answering my question. Instead of answering or fighting me, Langston starts running.

Without thinking, I chase after. I fire another warning shot at him as he runs around the back of the castle. Hopefully, he's leading me to Siren. A moment later, a firefight breaks out behind me.

I glance behind me in time to see Enzo and Kai leading a cavalry of men and women toward the house. Julian's small army won't stand a chance. But then droves of men are suddenly coming to join Julian's men—Siren's father's army, no doubt.

Fuck.

Langston keeps running, and I continue chasing him around the back of the castle, needing to know where he hid Siren. I want answers. I want to torture him for what he did, although there isn't time for that.

We make it to the other side of the castle, away from the fight.

"Where is Siren?" I yell at him.

Langston ignores me and turns his back to me, as he stands on the edge of the hill, looking me straight in the eyes. I aim my gun at his heart.

"Where is she?"

He jumps.

I run over to the edge where he jumped and see him sliding down the side of the hill, the slick wet grass making it easy to slide down.

I get a running start then start sliding down the hill, hoping my added speed and weight help me to catch up to him.

We reach the bottom of the hill almost at the same time, but Langston has a slight head start on me. He's faster than me, and I'll never catch him on foot.

Where is he going?

He runs faster down to the beach.

"Why did you do it?" I yell.

He keeps running, while my heartbreak continues to drive me. I suspect it is a feeling that I will have to live with for the rest of my life. Here on out will be either great heartache or times of anger; I don't think I will ever be at peace. I will never experience anything between heartache and explosive anger again.

I fire again, and this time I hit Langston in the back. He falls, and now I have a chance to run up to him.

He rolls onto his back, breathing hard. He doesn't try to get up, even though I can see from where his shirt rode up that he's wearing protective gear under his clothes. The shot just knocked the wind out of him; it didn't penetrate his skin. So I don't know why he stopped running.

"Why?" I say again, through my anger.

Langston looks at me. "I can't. Not yet."

"You can't what?"

Langston shakes my head. "Shoot me if you have to. Do it, but it won't save Siren."

"Where is she?"

"The question you should be asking is how to save her."

I frown. "What the hell is that supposed to mean?"

"The box isn't here."

"Where?"

Langston glances behind him, and I spot the island out in the distance. The box is there. *Why is Langston telling me this?*

I hold the gun to Langston's head. He either tells me the truth now, or I'll kill him, just like he killed my child.

"Zeke!" Siren's voice rings behind me. I turn just in time to see her with fear in her eyes. When I turn back, Langston is gone.

But Siren is alive. I can see her. That's all that matters.

CHAPTER 32
SIREN

"Daddy?" I stare at the man standing in the doorway of the castle. My brother lies on the floor.

"Yes, it's me."

Jesus.

I lean down and put my finger to Easton's pulse. I feel nothing. He's dead from a single shot.

A tear forms in my eye for the brother I never got to know. A brother who became a hermit so my parents wouldn't use him for their own means—a brother who committed his life to protecting me and the box.

Gone, just like that.

I stand back up and look at my father. There are more wrinkles around his eyes since the last time I saw him, and his head is almost completely covered by gray hair.

"You didn't have to kill him, you know," I say, my anger on full display.

He ignores me and steps into the castle over Easton's body.

I could run, but I don't. I need to understand my father's role in this, and how he's alive when I thought I killed him along with my mother.

"Is Mom—?" I ask.

"Dead. You managed to get that part right."

"How are you alive?"

"The same way your boy toy is alive. You threw me in the water with a bullet in the chest and expected me to die. But an angel came along and saved me."

"You've been behind everything. You're financing Julian's ventures."

"I am, not that the money has been very well spent so far."

"Why?"

"My mission never stopped. I've always wanted the virus. I've wanted to control its cure, to decide who is worthy of living and who isn't. It's the only way to ensure the world survives. There are too many dangerous, evil people in this world."

"Yes," I hiss. "People like you."

"Oh, my dear Aria. Or should I call you Siren? That's what you call yourself now, right? A siren. Doesn't sound like you've turned to the good side, my dear."

I ignore him, which only pisses him off.

"Where is the box?"

"Maybe you shouldn't have killed Easton, and he would have told you."

He grabs my arm. "Where is it, Aria?"

He moves to strike me, but I stop him, shoving his arm back. "I'm not a child anymore, Father. I know how to protect myself. I know how to fight back."

"And I have an army of men just outside that will kill you if you so much as step foot outside the castle. You're stuck with me inside. Where is the box?"

I shove him back. "I'm not afraid of your army."

He lands a punch before grabbing my neck and shoving me hard into the stone wall behind me. "You should be. You should be very afraid, my dear daughter."

"You're a monster. You killed your own son. And now you want to kill your daughter."

"If I have to, yes. I don't enjoy killing like your lot do, but I will do whatever it takes in order to reach my goal."

"Well, we have that in common then, Father."

I head-butt him, and he releases me. I have my gun in the back of my pants. I could shoot and kill him dead and be done with this mess, but I don't. This is personal between us. I want him to know how strong I am before he dies. I want him to know what he missed by going after this ridiculous mission instead of being a good father to me.

My father steps back, surprise in his eyes. He pulls out his phone, I'm sure to call for help.

"Really? I'm just a girl. Don't think you can fight me one on one?"

He frowns and puts his phone away. "I just didn't want you to get hurt." He rolls up his sleeves, and I roll my eyes. He seriously thinks he's going to win this fight. He doesn't know me at all; he never did.

He swings at me, and I dodge it easily. His swings are slow and lazy. The mark of a man who never has to fight. His men do that for him.

He swings again, and this time I let his fist brush the side of my ear.

He smirks like he's won. I haven't fought back yet. I'm buying my time, letting him think he's powerful before I make my move.

But I won't let him hurt me.

When he reaches into his pocket, pulls out a flask to drink, and then throws whiskey into my eyes, I lose it.

I can't see, my eyes burn from the liquor, but that won't be a problem to take down my father.

I punch him in the gut, knocking the wind out of him. Then I kick his legs, knocking them out from beneath him. I twist his arm behind his back as I drag him to the staircase in the center of the foyer.

I blink rapidly, trying to get the alcohol out of my eyes, and then wipe it on my sleeve.

"You bitch," my father growls.

"No, I'm not a bitch."

I leave him for a second as I grab one of the frayed curtains and then use it to restrain his arms behind his back and tie him to the staircase.

"You're no father of mine. You never were." I spit on him. "I hope you burn in hell."

I start to walk away when he says, "Still not strong enough to finish the job, I see. You just leave me here tied up. I could escape death once again."

I turn with an evil grin. "You could, but I'm much stronger than I was before. And trust me, before the day is over, you'll be burning down with this castle."

I walk away, headed toward the front door, stopping at Easton's body.

"I'm so sorry, brother. Rest in peace."

And then I walk out the door.

There is a battle ensuing, but I don't see anyone I recognize. I need to get to the box. Easton told me where it is—on the small island across the channel.

I sneak around the edge of the castle with my gun drawn. I spot the island through the fog and head in that direction, when two men at the edge of the water draw my attention.

Langston is on the ground, and Zeke stands above him with a gun to Langston's head. Zeke doesn't understand the truth. He doesn't know what Langston has done, so I can't let Zeke shoot him.

"Zeke!" I yell, giving Langston a moment to get away. But when Zeke looks at me, all I see is Zeke, and my heart leaps to him, trying to comfort the pain I know he's in.

I start running toward him.

CHAPTER 33
ZEKE

Siren starts running down the hillside while I run up the beach. I catch her as she jumps from the bottom of the hill into my open arms.

"I was so scared that Langston hurt you," I say, holding her close.

"Just as I was worried that Julian hurt you."

I hug her tighter. I wish we could stay like this forever, but there is a battle happening just up the hill. Langston is gone. Julian is loose and possibly has already found the box. And her father is who knows where.

"We have to get to the island," Siren says.

I nod, already knowing this from Langston. "Let's go."

I grab her hand and pull her down the beach to the small wooden boat stuck in the sand. "Get in."

"Won't you need help to get it in the water?"

"No, get in."

Siren jumps into the small sailboat just as a crack of lighting bursts overhead. A storm has moved in right over us, and its dark, heavy rain clouds are about to drown us with rain. Of course, the world couldn't make this easy for us.

I push with all my might, my feet digging into the sand as I push the sailboat into the water. Siren, of course, already has the sail up as I hop into the boat.

I come up behind her, helping her to guide the sail and giving me an excuse to hold her.

"I love you so much, Siren. So much." I kiss her neck.

"I love you, too. But we aren't going to say goodbye again. We are going to battle this together. Even if we are separated, it's not the end; it's not goodbye."

I turn her head and kiss her on the lips. "I agree, no more goodbyes."

I kiss her again, knowing that even though we won't say goodbye, this could still be our last kiss, so I make it worth it.

As we kiss, the rain falls around us. The winds pick up and thunder rolls through.

Together we grab the sail and hold on, trying to get the wind to push us toward the island. But the wind is hitting us from the side, pushing us further out to sea instead of toward the island. It's going to be a battle in this weather to get us to the island, or even near enough to jump and swim.

I have to let Siren go so we can both go yank on the sails. The rain pours down in sheets, until we are both soaked.

"Steady the boom," Siren shouts through the wind.

"Get in front of the tiller," Zeke says.

The boat rocks hard and back forth. This tiny boat wasn't meant to withstand this level of storm. We shouldn't have taken this boat out, but it's too late for that now.

That's when I see the other boat coming—yacht, to be exact.

"Siren," I shout through the rain. She looks at me, and I point in the distance. She sees the yacht as well.

We don't know who is driving the yacht—Julian, Enzo, or Kai.

We don't know if help or danger is coming toward us.

"We have to get to the island," Siren says, not wanting to wait to find out the intentions of the yacht.

I know what she's about to suggest, and I hate it.

"No," I say.

She lets go of the rope she's holding. The boat rocks hard as she walks to me. "Get me to the island. I'll get the box. It's the safer job," she says.

I rub my arms up and down her arms, knowing none of this is safe.

"Kill Julian," she continues.

"I can't until—"

"My father is tied up in the castle. Tell Enzo or Kai to blow it up."

I blow out a breath. I can barely see her through the rain. It's impossible to see or feel anything but the heavy rain.

"Just get me close to the island," she says.

"I'm not dumping you in the ocean in the middle of a storm."

"Yes, you are. I'm a big girl. I can swim."

She kisses me again.

"And don't kill Langston, promise me. Not until I return with the box."

"Why? I have to kill him after what he did to you and..." I can't bring myself to finish without turning into a blubbering mess.

"I know, and he'll pay for what he did. But I need to be there when it happens. Promise me," she says.

"I promise," I say, although I don't understand it.

"Kill Julian; I'll destroy the box," Siren says.

"And then we will live happily ever after in our forever."

She kisses me hard, yanking on the rope to turn us hard toward the island.

It takes all my strength to let her go, but I have to. If Julian is on that yacht, I don't trust that she will be safe.

I watch her dive into the ocean; she's close enough to the island now to make it. I watch nonetheless as she swims through the waves. Siren is an excellent swimmer, and for once, the waves seem to be working in our favor, pushing her quickly toward the island.

I wait until I see her standing on the beach, and then I turn toward the yacht that is still headed toward me, and I make a stand. Julian will not get to the island. He will have to go through me first. And finally, I have the power to kill him.

CHAPTER 34
SIREN

I stand on the island as I look back at Zeke. I'm terrified that we are going to lose, and that I just lost my chance to explain to Zeke what truly happened. But now wasn't the time to explain to him the truth, the sin I committed.

He has a battle to fight against Julian, and I have a battle to fight inside this castle against the obstacles that Easton setup. He told me the main keys to getting through the castle and obtaining the box, but it doesn't guarantee that I'll survive, especially given the final obstacle.

I stare up at the ruined castle. While the castle on the mainland was complete, this one is in pieces, although twice the size.

I grip my stomach, knowing the cost of failing. Zeke would never forgive me. I would never forgive me.

I won't fail. I can't.

Just like Zeke won't.

Or Enzo and Kai.

I walk carefully to the edge of the castle. There are three main security obstacles in place before getting to the final room, where the box and one final obstacle wait. The three main obstacles don't seem too hard. The hard part is figuring out which room the box is hidden in and then claiming it.

The first room is the easiest—lasers.

I open the door to the old castle. It feels the opposite of modern. It shouldn't have a security system like this in it. I don't know how Easton managed to build such a feat, but I'm guessing it took him years to build this.

I take one step, and the lasers turn on. I take a deep breath as the lasers come near but never touch me.

I've got this.

Two steps forward.

Three to the left.

One forward.

Two to the right.

I repeat the steps Easton gave me, with the memory of him saying he would never help me playing in the back of my head. I hope his instructions are the truth and not a trap.

I take my final step out of the room and exhale a breath. *First obstacle down.*

The next is deciding which of the three doorways to head through.

When in doubt, follow your heart, Easton's voice rings through.

I step forward into the center room. That's what my heart tells me, so that's where I go.

This is one of the rooms I'm dreading. The smoke that starts billowing confirms that I chose the correct room. The door behind me slams shut, locking me in here.

You have sixty seconds once the door closes to pick the lock at the other end before the smoke kills you, Easton's voice reminds me.

I run to the other end of the room, coughing as the smoke begins to enter my lungs. I pull out a hairpin and go to work on the door. There are three separate locks—two deadbolts and one on the doorknob.

I start on the two deadbolts first.

The first unlocks.

Then the second.

I have plenty of time left to unlock the third and easiest one, but the pin breaks off in the lock.

"Fuck," I cough.

I try to use my nails to dig it out, but it's stuck. I rattle the door handle, but it doesn't budge.

I feel my lungs fill up with toxic smoke. It burns worse than the last time I breathed in smoke like this. This smoke is ten times as toxic.

My body wants to crumble to the ground.

You promised me, don't give up, Zeke's voice echoes in my head.

I keep myself standing, and I study the door as best as I can through the smoke. I can't find any weaknesses in the door. The door isn't too thick. *Maybe I can break it down?*

I kick the door as hard as I can. It only makes a small dent, but it gives me enough motivation to keep trying. I kick over and over, hoping it's enough to make a crack that will give me a means to escape.

I cough harder, my head growing dizzy and light. It won't be long until I pass out, and I won't be able to make it out of here alive.

Suddenly, the door is thrown open, and a man's hands grab me and pull me out of the room.

We both cough loudly several times as we grip the floor.

"Can we agree that you won't walk into a room filled with smoke anymore?" Langston says between coughs.

"Thanks for saving me again."

"You don't need to thank me for saving you."

I smile at him until I see the blood and sweat covering him. "Langston! You're hurt. What happened?"

He rests on his back as he slumps against the hallway. I lean against the wall next to him.

"The next room got the better of me."

I frown and remember what Easton said. *Bullets capable of penetrating any armor.*

He nods.

I pull his shirt open, until I find a bullet lodged in his chest. "Oh, God."

"It looks worse than it is. It missed my heart. But I failed, I couldn't get the box."

"If you hadn't had failed, you wouldn't have been here to rescue me."

He smiles at that.

I rip the bottom of my shirt off and use it as a bandage to wrap around his shoulder. "Do you have a way to contact Enzo and Kai and let them know where you are?"

"Yes."

"Good." I stand up, my head no longer pounding, and I'm able to stifle a cough.

"Don't go, Siren."

"I have to."

"No, you don't. You could die. The next room is no joke. I won't be able to come in and save you. You'd be on your own."

"Call Enzo and Kai. Tell them to be ready to pick you up soon."

"Pick *us* up," Langston says.

I turn and walk to the next room.

"Siren! Don't!" Langston tries to get off the floor, but he's too weak from blood loss.

I can't think about Langston. All I can think about is Zeke and our future. I have to do this, so that we will have a future instead of living in constant fear. I have to protect Zeke.

CHAPTER 35
ZEKE

The yacht continues straight at me. And if I didn't know before, I know now who is driving the yacht—Julian.

If it were Enzo or Kai, they would have turned by now instead of ramming the side of my tiny sailboat.

I brace for impact. I could jump into the water, but I'm tired of being in the ocean. I'd rather stay standing for as long as possible, even if I'm just as soaked on this boat as I would be in the water.

I hold on tightly as the yacht hits my small boat—the sound of the wood breaking cracks as loud as the lightning. The yacht drives through the heart of my boat. And just before it pierces me, I jump, grabbing onto one of the ropes hanging from the side of the yacht. I quickly begin climbing up the side of the yacht as more thunder cracks over and over, the weather warning me of the danger ahead.

I reach the top of the yacht and am immediately punched in the head. I take the hit but stumble backward.

"I thought we were on the same side," I say.

Julian laughs. "We were never on the same side. We were always just using each other to get what we wanted."

I pull out my gun and start shooting at him. He ducks, avoiding the spray.

"Where is the box?" Julian pulls out a grenade launcher and aims it my way.

"Go to hell," he says.

I dive just as he shoots it, blowing a large hole into the ship.

"Really? Going to hide behind a gun instead of fighting me face to face?"

"I really don't care how I kill you, just that I do." He fires again, blowing another huge hole.

Kill him, Siren's words play through my head on repeat. *Blow up the castle.*

Julian's gun is out of rounds, and he fumbles with finding ammunition. I pull out my phone and type a quick message to Kai and Enzo to blow up the castle and then pick Siren up on the small island.

Julian has changed to using a machine gun to fire at me as I hide behind a wall. *Thank goodness the entire ship is bulletproof.*

I look up at the sky, trying to come up with a way to kill this psycho.

The storm picks up the wind, until I have to grip the door handle behind me to keep from blowing overboard. The ship moves far out, away from the land.

I hear an explosion and see smoke in the distance.

Enzo and Kai succeeded in their first mission. Hopefully, Siren did too. Now it's just up to me.

I don't hear any more bullets. Julian must have moved inside where it's safer.

I yank open the door and throw myself inside, out of the wind and rain—the boat rocks in the huge swells. I know how strong these boats are, and I know how much force it will take to bring one down. But the sounds the boat is making, the creaking, and the screeching have me worried.

A bullet whizzes past me. I've found Julian.

I run after him, shooting whenever I spot him. I catch his shoulder. He fires back as the yacht lurches sideways. I take an incorrect step, and the bullet hits my chest, knocking the wind out of me.

Don't stop. Kill him. And then come back to me.

I march forward, chasing Julian through the ship, us both exchanging shots at each other.

We reach the bridge just in time to see lightning strike the yacht igniting a fire. We both realize the yacht is sinking.

Julian tries to fire his gun at me, but he's out of bullets.

I fire my last shot back, hitting him in the leg. There is nowhere for him to run. I toss my gun down, and then I run at him with all the rage he's caused me, for all the pain and heartbreak. I put everything into it. I do it for Enzo, for Kai, for Siren, for myself, and for the baby we lost.

I should think of a way to save myself. The yacht is going down, sinking to the depths of the sea. I have no way to know where we are or how far we've been swept out to sea, but I know that we have been pushed far out with the storm.

Instead, I'm focused on my mission—killing Julian.

My body collides with his. I run into him so hard that we break through a glass window and fall hard into the ocean, my body slamming down hard on top of his. The water engulfs us; the waves crash down one on top of the other. If I don't kill Julian, the storm will, and I'll end up dead in the process.

We both kick for the surface, while fighting to push the other down, as we are desperate for oxygen.

We both crack the surface at the same time. The water continues to hit us over and over, and it becomes more of a battle of survival than a battle with each other.

This has to change. The only way I have a chance at surviving is to kill Julian. Then I can find a way to save myself.

So when the waves hit us next, I grab onto Julian and hope that my large body can hold more oxygen than his. I pull him down into the ocean with me and hold onto his legs, hoping he didn't get a good breath.

He kicks against me, but I hold my grip tighter, knowing that I'd rather him die along with me than let him get another ounce of air.

He kicks hard, but I pull him deeper into the ocean as my lungs start to tell me they need oxygen. Fear and anxiety start racing through me, but I let it fuel me to sink further down instead of going up.

Julian is getting desperate above me. Desperate for oxygen, for last words before he dies, but he'll get neither.

He digs into his pocket, and I see the shininess of the knife that he holds. But if I let go, he'll get away. He stabs my hand. I grip my teeth tighter together to ensure I don't let any spare oxygen out. He drives the knife again and again into my hand, but I hold on. We are close. He's using too much energy. He will run out of oxygen soon.

Julian looks at me with desperation and a wildness in his eyes. If he's going to die, he wants me to die with him.

I know what's coming, and I brace myself.

His knife slices through my neck, a wound that unleashes plenty of blood. I need oxygen. Now, if I'm going to survive.

Instead, I hold on, praying that my oxygen supply doesn't run out. When I can't hold on any longer, I let go and kick to the surface. I hit the air, still filled with pouring down rain, expecting Julian to hit the surface a second later. But he doesn't.

I look down into the water and watch as his body drifts down—Julian's dead.

I take a deep, calming breath—*Julian Reed is dead.*

Finally, I succeeded.

I hold my hand to my neck, hoping to stop the blood as I look around, trying to find out where I am. The storm is still beating down on me, and I can't see very far, but I don't see land. I don't see any boats. It's just me, once again in the middle of the ocean all alone while I bleed to death.

The truth broke us.

Love destroyed us.

Sin saved us.

How far will I go for love?

As far as it takes...and in my case, saving Siren means I'm to once again die in the ocean. But I have no regrets.

I died for the love of my life.

CHAPTER 36
SIREN

Trust your heart, Easton's voice rings in my head.

I step into the room and look at all the guns lining the walls. Guns capable of penetrating the armor I'm wearing. I could end up shot just like Langston.

Trust your heart.

My eyes say to stick to the right and move as quickly through the room as possible. But my heart says to take it slow, one step at a time, and to stay by the walls.

I move to one side of the wall and take a careful step. The guns start, but I'm able to jump and avoid getting hit. The guns reload before firing higher this time, and I duck.

I take a deep breath. *I can do this.*

Step by step, I do the same. One step forward and dodge the bullet spray before moving on to the next. Everything in my body is telling me to run, but then I can't watch the guns change direction a second before firing. I won't know to duck or jump to avoid being shot.

Finally, I take my last step out of the room. I've survived in one piece.

Now I just have to find which of the many ruined rooms left that the box is in, and survive the final test.

"Okay, Easton, where did you hide it?"

There are five rooms left. Two are open to the sky, and the rain continues to pour down. The other three have roofs.

The smart thing would be to hide the box in one of the more complete rooms, but something hidden shouldn't be obvious.

I step into the room on the far left. It's the most incomplete, the least obvious room. I shield my eyes from the rain as I look around for where he hid it. *Surely, he didn't just bury it in the ground.*

My hands go against the walls, and I find a crevice that my hand fits in perfectly. I slip my hand in and all of a sudden, the room is moving. New walls are going up, the floor shifts, and a roof starts covering overhead. And just like that, I'm in a high tech room.

Easton went all out to protect the box, as he should have.

I just don't know if I'm worthy of getting the box. I asked him to protect it, even from me, so the last test will test me as well as anyone else.

A computer comes up from the ground with the highest tech safe I've ever seen. I don't see a door on it or any mechanism that could be cracked.

I walk over to it and try to lift it, but I can't move the safe as I expected. The only way to get the box is to complete the last test. I look around the room—no doors, no windows, no escape. I won't be getting out of here until I complete the test either.

I look at the computer screen on the safe, my new enemy. I know what is about to happen—Easton told me. But I still haven't figured out how to solve his puzzle. All he told me was that wanting to destroy the box wasn't enough to open it.

Suddenly, the screen comes alive, and the computer voice speaks. "Are you here for the box?"

I walk to the screen and press the button that says, "Yes."

"How far are you willing to go?"

I stare at the screen, my mind whirling. Easton told me that I would have to give up everything if I wanted to get the box.

I rest my hand against my stomach, feeling my baby kick. I think about Zeke on the yacht, who has hopefully killed Julian by now.

I don't want to lose either of them. I'm not willing to lose either of them.

I will do what it takes to protect them, yes. But I won't give them up to get this box. I won't give them up to save the world.

A symbol pops up on the screen, telling me that it's listening to my voice. Now is the time to speak. I see the guns come out; all pointed at me. I see the timer on the wall with a countdown.

If I answer incorrectly, the guns will go off, the room will be destroyed, and the box will be gone forever. It's what I want, the box gone. But I don't want to sacrifice my child to save the world.

My child is more important.

My love is more important.

Follow your heart.

"I'm not willing to go far at all for a stupid box. I'm not willing to give up my family, my husband, my child, my love. I won't give up the love of my life to protect the world. All I'm willing to do is give up myself, lose my own life to get the box. But I can't even do that since my life is tied to another. How far will I go for a stupid box? Not far at all. How far will I go for those I love? As far as it takes."

I close my eyes, not having a clue if I said the right words or not. I wait for the bullets. I wait for the guns, the bombs. I wait for death.

But it doesn't come.

I open my eyes, thinking maybe I've already died, when I see the screen swirling. The safe unlocks, the room opens. I did it. I'm free.

I grab the box from the safe and then run out of the room before the guns accidentally go off.

As I step foot outside of the castle, I hear the whirl of a helicopter. I look up and find Enzo, Kai, and Langston peering down at me. *Thank God.*

I wave at them, and the helicopter lands next to me. I climb in.

"Where's Zeke?" I ask Langston, sitting in the back next to me and his arm bandaged up properly now.

"We are going to search for him now. The yacht got pushed out to sea in the storm. We'll find him," Langston says.

Kai and Enzo give me a look, and then we are flying over the ocean. I hand Langston the box to keep safe, while I look out the window in search of Zeke.

Three hours later and we still haven't found him.

All eyes are on me.

"We aren't giving up," I say, firmly.

"We aren't asking you to," Kai says gently.

"Then what are you asking?"

"I'm telling you that we are almost out of fuel. We are going to have to head toward land to refuel and make a better plan to find him."

My tears come back, but I choke them back. I have to be strong for Zeke. I have to.

"We won't give up. We've given up on Zeke before, we won't again," Enzo says.

I look around at the three people outside of me who care about Zeke the most. We will find him. We have to.

CHAPTER 37
ZEKE

It's been three days.

Somehow I'm still alive, still floating in the water.

I'm delusional. I won't last much longer. My body is too weak. If it was up to my heart, I'd fight forever, but my heart isn't in control anymore. My lungs are, and they are about to give out.

And then I hear a new sound out of nowhere. All I've heard for days are waves, wind, and the occasional bird. But this, this is heavenly.

It's not real, I know it. I'm dying; the beautiful sound is my brain easing my pain as I take my last breaths. I'm thankful.

I hear a splash and look over, assuming I'll find a dolphin or, with my luck, a shark.

Something is swimming toward me—my angel.

"Zeke!" I hear her scream as she grabs onto me. "Oh my god!"

Her hand goes to my neck immediately, but the wound stopped bleeding long ago.

"You're alive," she cries.

"My angel, my beautiful angel."

She laughs through her tears. "No, your Siren. I've been calling out to you for days. I finally found you, time to go home."

"This is the best dream ever," I say.

She shakes her head and then pulls me hard. Next thing I know, I'm being lifted onto something hard that rocks. It doesn't make sense to me, but it doesn't matter, I won't be conscious much longer.

"We need to get him to a hospital, now," a voice says.

"Hold on, baby. Just hold on. Keep your promise to love me forever," Siren says, and then she presses the sweetest kiss to my lips before the world goes dark.

I open my eyes, and all I see is light. *Am I dead? Is this heaven?*

"Zeke," I hear a voice so tentative and scared.

I turn my head, and Siren jumps on me before kissing me all over.

"You're alive. You're awake. Thank God," Siren screeches as she kisses me everywhere.

"I am, it seems. Thanks to you."

She kisses me once more before curling up next to me in what I realize is a giant bedroom on a beach that looks an awful lot like Miami.

"You're home in Miami," Siren says, answering my unspoken question.

"And everyone?"

Siren whistles, and the door opens. Enzo and Kai walk in. Kai has tears flowing from her eyes, while Enzo tries and fails to hold his back.

"You're alive! We were so worried," Kai says.

"Come here, Stingray." I hold out my arm to her and pull her into a hug, while Siren lies on the bed next to me, still holding onto me.

"So glad you made it through," Enzo says, avoiding eye contact so he doesn't start crying.

"When you heal, you'll come back to work for us, won't you?" Kai asks.

"I need to discuss it with Siren first, but I know that I won't want to be stepping foot on a yacht or on the ocean anytime soon."

Everyone laughs at that.

"Come on, Stingray, we should give them some time alone," Enzo says, pulling Kai off me. Together they walk out of the room.

"Julian? Your father?" I ask Siren.

"Both dead."

"Your brother?"

"Dead."

"I'm so sorry."

"I'm sorry my brother's gone, but I know this is what he wanted, to die protecting what he knew he should and saving the world."

"You saved the world," I say, kissing her hand.

"With some help."

I smile at that.

"And Langston?" I feel the anger and pain returning at his name.

"He'll be in to visit soon."

I frown. "I'm going to kill him."

"Wait, listen first."

I narrow my eyes as she takes my hand and puts it under her shirt to her stomach.

"What are you doing?"

"Just wait."

A second later, I feel a kick.

"Oh my god! The baby?"

"Is alive."

I pull her tighter to me. "How? I thought Langston hurt you and the baby. I thought—"

"No, he realized when we got back to the room that night that Julian was watching. He needed to make my reaction as real as possible, so he did the minimum to physically hurt me to make me fear him. To put on a show for Julian."

"What are you saying?"

"I'm saying Langston saved me. He didn't actually rape me, just pretended."

"But the blood?"

"I caused it. I found a knife and used it to cut both Langston and my thigh to cause all the blood, so you'd think I'd lost the baby."

"But why?"

"I needed to see you broken to trigger my memories, and that was the most traumatic thing I could think of. I'm so sorry."

"Shh, you have nothing to be sorry for." I rub her stomach. "In fact, you just made me the happiest man to know that you're still pregnant. We are going to get our happily ever after finally."

And then I kiss her, and kiss her, and kiss her, long into the night.

Until a knock at the door draws our attention away from each other.

Langston pokes his head in. "Sorry to interrupt, but I think it's time we destroyed this since we all risked our lives to get it."

Siren stands and helps me out of the bed, although I don't really need the help. I do enjoy being so close to Siren, though.

Langston looks at me, and I look at him with a nod. All the lies and sins we've committed will take a while to heal, but I know that he cares about Siren and that he will protect her with his life. That makes him one of the best men I know.

Langston motions for us to follow, and so we do until we are all outside on the sand—Enzo, Kai, Langston, Siren, and me.

Langston puts the box in the center of our circle along with driftwood. He douses the wood gasoline, and then he hands a box of matches to Siren.

Siren strikes one of the matches. "I should have done this long ago, then maybe we wouldn't have gone through hell."

"We got rid of two more evil men who would have continued to terrorize the world without us. It was worth it," Kai says.

Siren nods. "Still, it feels silly that I kept it around because of a feeling that it needed to exist. That time never came. Now it's time to destroy it."

And then with that, Siren tosses the match onto the wood. We all stand around the fire, watching the box and contents slowly burn.

Kai and Enzo walk back to the house. Followed by Langston. And then it's just me and Siren on the beach.

"Truth or sin, what did you do to get the box?" I ask. She's told me the story of what her and Langston did to save the baby, but not what she did to get the box, what danger she put herself in.

"Truth or sin, what did you do to kill Julian?" she asks back with raised eyebrows.

We've both done incredible things for love. We burned a castle down, lied, and hurt and killed so many people. But in the end, our love prevailed, and it will continue to prevail forever.

"Sin," we both say at the same time. The truth doesn't matter now, and sinning together is much more fun.

"Fuck me, Zeke."

I grin. "Oh, I plan to, over and over and over. Just like I plan on loving you, forever."

EPILOGUE
SIREN

"Cayden is so sweet," Kai says as we stare over my six-week-old son. Zeke got his way in the end and got to name him, the perfect name for our little warrior.

"He is sweet when he's not crying. I don't think we've slept more than an hour these last few weeks," I say, staring down at my sleeping boy in his crib.

"It gets better, trust me. Soon you'll want these days back."

I sigh, my life couldn't get any better. Kai hugs me, holding me close to her.

"You need to take your time and enjoy your son, so this isn't the time to talk about it, but I can't wait until you get back to work. It's such a boys-fest without you."

I laugh. "We definitely need to hire more women."

"I agree."

Zeke and I have been working for Kai and Enzo these last few months. I've mainly worked from the office with Kai, while the boys have done the more hands-on work. Although, Zeke has yet to step foot back on a yacht or in the ocean. I'm sure he will as soon as our son is old enough to ask him to take him out on a boat, as we do live in Miami on the beach.

I yawn.

"Go take a nap, I'll watch this little guy for you," Kai says.

"You're a good friend."

I leave the nursery, guessing I won't get more than a twenty-minute nap in before Cayden wakes up, but I'll take what I can get.

I walk to my bedroom and close the door, when Zeke grabs me from behind, holding me in his arms.

"We're alone," he says.

"It seems we are," I respond. "Although, Kai is in the nursery. And Enzo is watching football in the living room."

"They can wait."

"Oh, yea? What do you have in mind?"

"Your doctor cleared you, right?" He kisses down my neck, and I moan.

"Yes," I breathe, forgetting how wonderful it is for him to be kissing me like this. To make me come alive with one touch. I've been so busy focusing on Cayden's every need that I forgot for a moment that I have needs.

"Can I fuck you, Mrs. Kane?"

I smile. "You sure can, Mr. Kane." Our fingers intertwine, as he lifts me and carries me to our giant bed. We got married officially, just the two of us in the courthouse a month before Cayden was born. We didn't want anyone there. In our eyes, we got married in the ocean. Something positive that I can remind Zeke of soon to coax him back into the ocean.

I look like a mess in my leggings and an oversized shirt. I haven't showered in two days, and my hair is in a messy bun on top of my head, but Zeke doesn't care. His eyes heat all the same when he removes my shirt and leggings.

"God, I've missed you, baby," he says when he has me naked beneath me.

I grab his long hair and yank him toward me. "Shut up and fuck me."

He chuckles against my lips as he kisses me. He's trying to take his time, but now that he's reminded me what this feels like, I'm desperate for him to be inside me.

I grab his shirt, yanking it off to reveal his sexy six-pack. I'm one of the luckiest girls in the world to get to have this man any night I want. He helps me remove his pants, and then he's at my entrance in record time. His fingers tease my clit.

I grab his hips, trying to pull him inside me. "Slow, baby. I don't want to hurt you."

"You can't hurt me. It's not possible." I roll my hips, pushing his tip inside me.

He gasps, and I think he might explode from this moment alone. He bites his lip, pushing his orgasm down.

"You make me crazy, Siren."

"Then fuck me already."

With that, he eases into me. It's perfect and wonderful, and the missing piece that I didn't realize I had been forgetting.

"I love you, Siren."

He thrusts into me, and I can't speak. He starts off slow and then moves faster and faster. I can't speak; all I can do is moan, cry, and scream. *Thank God for soundproof walls.*

Then we are both coming so hard that I feel like I'm going to explode.

"I love you, too," I say when I can finally catch my breath again.

We lie in the bed until I hear Cayden crying through the baby monitor, and there is a gentle knock at the door.

We both jump up and get dressed. I assume it's Kai at the door telling me Cayden is hungry, but when I throw the door open, it's Langston.

"Lang! You made it." I throw my arms around him. We haven't seen him since the birth of Cayden.

"I was tired of your phone calls telling me to get my ass over here more."

I smile at that.

"But next time you invite guests over and decide to fuck, make sure you turn the baby monitor off," Langston says.

I blush.

Zeke dies laughing.

"It's good to see you, man." Zeke pats Langston on the shoulder. "I'll grab you a beer, and we can watch the game together."

"Be right there," Langston says as Zeke leaves us alone.

"What are you running from, Lang?"

He steps into my bedroom and shuts the door. "I'm not a good man, Ren. I don't belong in this world. I'll just bring more danger into your life."

I shake my head. "Not possible, you've saved my life so many times. And everyone else's. You're a good man."

"You don't know me that well, Ren."

"I know you better than anyone. I've seen your darkness. I know you are running from pain. From Liesel? I invited her, I want to meet her, but she never answered."

"Liesel won't answer. She's out of this life for good," Langston says, walking to the window and staring out of it.

"Maybe you should go talk to her."

"She doesn't want to talk to me."

I sigh. "I just want you to be happy. And if that isn't with the woman you love, then it should be with your family. We are your family."

He shakes his head. "I can't stay, Ren. I'm sorry. I wish I could, but I can't."

"Why?"

There is another knock. I open it, and Kai is holding a crying Cayden out to me.

"I tried to hold him off as long as I could, but he's hungry," Kai says.

I take Cayden from her. "Come on, let's go watch the game together and relax. We can talk later, Lang."

He nods, and then we all walk to the living room. I sit with Zeke and start feeding Cayden. Kai and Enzo sit, their twins climbing all over them. Langston sits off in a chair by himself.

Seeing Langston by himself shows me how hard this must be for him. He has to watch Zeke and me, Kai and Enzo live our happily ever afters, while he's alone.

Langston still hasn't told me what happened between him and

Liesel, but I do know that without him facing his past, he won't be able to move on and find love again.

Kai must notice the awkwardness too. "Hey, Langston."

He turns and looks at her. "Stop moping; you'll find love soon."

"I'm not looking for love. I'm a forever bachelor. I don't need a wife or family," he says.

"Yea, yea, whatever you say. Just promise me that when you do find the love of your life, that you don't drag us into your love story and make us risk our lives, okay?" Kai says with a smile trying to lighten the mood.

Everyone laughs. Everyone but Langston. He's lost in thought.

I'm going to have to have another talk with him and get him to spill the truth to me. He owes me that.

"Look, he's smiling at us," Zeke says.

I look down at our son, who has stopped feeding. He's smiling up at us. He's perfect and has Zeke's eyes and large frame. He was over ten pounds at birth. I have no doubt at all that he's Zeke's child.

"He's going to keep us on our toes, isn't he?" I ask.

"Definitely. Any child of ours is going to be trouble."

I lean my head against Zeke's chest, my son in my arms, and my family all around. I look over at Langston, and even he is smiling at me.

"I can't wait to live our happily ever after, forever with you," Zeke whispers into my ear.

"It's here, baby. It's here. This is the first part of our forever, and I can't imagine anything better."

THANK YOU SO MUCH FOR READING ZEKE AND SIREN'S STORY! READ Langston & Liesel's story VICIOUS: A Truth or Lies World Collection.

She hates me. I loathe her. The only thing we still share are the lies...
One-click VICIOUS now >

"All I can say is WOWSAAAA!!!!"

ALSO BY ELLA MILES

LIES SERIES:

Lies We Share: A Prologue

Vicious Lies

Desperate Lies

Fated Lies

Cruel Lies

Dangerous Lies

Endless Lies

SINFUL TRUTHS:

Sinful Truth #1

Twisted Vow #2

Reckless Fall #3

Tangled Promise #4

Fallen Love #5

Broken Anchor #6

TRUTH OR LIES:

Taken by Lies #1

Betrayed by Truths #2

Trapped by Lies #3

Stolen by Truths #4

Possessed by Lies #5

Consumed by Truths #6

DIRTY SERIES:

Dirty Beginning

Dirty Obsession

Dirty Addiction

Dirty Revenge

Dirty: The Complete Series

ALIGNED SERIES:

Aligned: Volume 1 (Free Series Starter)

Aligned: Volume 2

Aligned: Volume 3

Aligned: Volume 4

Aligned: The Complete Series Boxset

UNFORGIVABLE SERIES:

Heart of a Thief

Heart of a Liar

Heart of a Prick

Unforgivable: The Complete Series Boxset

MAYBE, DEFINITELY SERIES:

Maybe Yes

Maybe Never

Maybe Always

Definitely Yes

Definitely No

Definitely Forever

STANDALONES:

Pretend I'm Yours

Finding Perfect

Savage Love

Too Much

Not Sorry

ABOUT THE AUTHOR

Ella Miles writes steamy romance, including everything from dark suspense romance that will leave you on the edge of your seat to contemporary romance that will leave you laughing out loud or crying. Most importantly, she wants you to feel everything her characters feel as you read.

Ella is currently living her own happily ever after near the Rocky Mountains with her high school sweetheart husband. Her heart is also taken by her goofy five year old black lab who is scared of everything, including her own shadow.

Ella is a USA Today Bestselling Author & Top 50 Bestselling Author.

Stalk Ella at:
www.ellamiles.com
ella@ellamiles.com